Resorts, Regrets, and Returning to Love

by

J L Wilson

Resorts, Regrets, and Returning to Love

Contact Information: info@thewildrosepress.com

Cover Art by *Kim Mendoza*

The Wild Rose Press, Inc.
PO Box 708
Adams Basin, NY 14410-0708
Visit us at www.thewildrosepress.com

Publishing History
First Crimson Rose Edition, 2014
Print ISBN 978-1-62830-291-2
Digital ISBN 978-1-62830-292-9

Published in the United States of America

"It's your home, Nate."

She looked around the old resort. "I had a great summer here. Because of you. Despite everything that happened—and almost happened to me—it was a summer of love and happiness. I've never felt anything like it, before or since."

I knew what she meant. "I know. It was almost magic, wasn't it?"

Our eyes met and held. I knew what she was thinking. It *had* been magic, a very special kind. The magic of love. Then she took my arm. "Let's go to town and give the gossips something to talk about."

I left my truck at the station and we walked to Cora's Cove, the one restaurant in town. Cora made sure we were seated front and center. I spent most of lunch fielding greetings, nods, and raised eyebrows. Emily finally leaned over to whisper, "I think everyone is watching us, Chief."

I frowned. "Yeah. This might not have been such a good idea."

"I think it was an excellent idea."

"You do?"

"Sure. It adds to the whole 'love lost' image. You'll have girls falling out of the woodwork after I'm gone, anxious to mend your broken heart."

I touched her hand. "I'd rather you stay in town and mend my broken heart."

She looked into my eyes. "I think I might like that. We'll have to see."

Dedication

This one's for you, Sooz. Finally!
And remember...nobody puts Baby in a corner.

Chapter 1

Present Day

I expected a walk down memory lane on that warm October day.

I didn't expect a skeleton.

As I wandered the grounds at Pine Place Inn, it felt like my heart was breaking all over again. Bobby Goldman was remodeling the old resort and they were tearing down the cottages where the summer staff used to live. Bobby asked me to look over the plans because I knew the place from the old days and my summers as a Maintenance Guy for the resort. I made a note about the day they started demolition at the cottages. I needed a last look at the place where Emily and I spent the summer.

I walked through the rooms, but nothing remained, nothing to show the only woman I ever loved had lived there. I went into the bathroom of the old cottage. Some fit of nostalgia made me unscrew the hot and cold knobs from the bathtub and stick them in my jacket pocket. I jiggled the old-fashioned porcelain handles, making them rattle. I needed something from those days, something besides the faded pictures.

I knew she had a business in Minneapolis. She exchanged Christmas cards with Dorothy, the police department secretary, so I occasionally had updates on what Emily was doing. I tried to write to her a dozen times in the past thirty years, but I tore up the letters. I told myself she wouldn't be interested in an ex-football player who was now a cop in Little Bay, Michigan, population 4,500. True, I had stayed in shape but I wasn't the six-five, two-hundred-twenty-pound, twenty-one-year-old guy who made love to her day and night.

Now I was in my fifties and I wasn't as muscled as I used to be. I had gray in my black hair, lines around my eyes, and my days of twenty-four-hour stud love were behind me. So I never mailed the letters, figuring she had her life to live and I had mine and she wouldn't be interested in rekindling an old flame.

I think maybe I was afraid to find out if I was right.

I left the cottage to watch the backhoes digging a hundred feet away then I headed for my squad car. As I opened the door, I heard a commotion above the noise of the construction equipment.

"Hey, Chief Boltz! Nate!"

The construction foreman was waving to me. I walked over to the group of men standing around a large hole. The backhoe operator had shut off his machine and his face was ashen. I looked down in the hole and that's when I saw the skeleton.

****

Four hours later I watched Dr. Stewart, the county coroner, pick at the bones with a special trowel. The area was roped off and the construction crew gone for the day. All that remained were me, the medical team, Bobby Goldman, and Mike Sawyer, the county D.A.

"I'm done, Chief," Doc said, setting aside his tools. He mopped at his red face with a hanky and leaned back against the wall of the makeshift grave.

I jumped into the hole and squatted next to the bones which were preserved in four feet of Michigan clay.

"What part of the resort was this, Nate?" Mike asked from above. He had never worked at the resort like I did. Mike worked with his dad at the hardware store in town.

I looked north, over my shoulder. "Old access road that way." I gestured east. "Cottages that way. The main resort was back the way we came. This spot was used as a storage area for grounds equipment."

Bobby Goldman, the resort owner, nodded. He was a small, hunch-shouldered man with bland features and wispy, faded brown hair, a bit older than Mike and me. Bobby's face was pale in the morning light and he looked ill. Finding dead bodies does that, I guess.

He looked down at the frail collection of bones then looked at Dr. Stewart. "Any idea on how long it's been here?"

Doc was overweight, sweating, and wilting in the hot October sun. "At least twenty years, probably more. She was pregnant." He pointed to some little gray sticks underneath bigger bones. "That's the fetus."

"Aw, damn," I muttered.

Doc nodded. "Anybody go missing around here in the last twenty years?"

Mike and I exchanged a glance. "Thirty-some years ago, yeah," I said. "Maybe."

Stewart heaved himself out of the hole with an assist from Bobby Goldman. "I'll do the dental charts and call you." He started to waddle off. "If she's local, I'll know by this afternoon. She had some pretty distinctive dental work."

"Thanks." I looked down at the pathetic remains.

"What are you thinking, Nate?" Bobby asked quietly.

"Peggy McBride. Remember her?" I scrambled out of the hole.

Bobby thought about it, his forehead wrinkling. "Waitress? Maid?"

"Maid. Worked here back when I worked here. She told me she was running away to get married. No one's ever seen her since. Her parents never heard from her."

Bobby looked down at the bones. "Poor kid," he said softly. "Whoever she is."

Mike and I drove back to town in the squad car. He and I grew up together and he knew what I was thinking. "So that's where you and her lived?" he asked.

I nodded. "Yeah. For three months."

"Hmm." Mike glanced at me. "Why didn't you ever call her?"

"I told you. She's got a business to run and a life in the city."

"And no husband and no love life. At least, none you know about."

I shrugged. "So? I have no love life. Doesn't mean I want to change things."

Mike snorted. "Yeah, right. If she came back into your life, you'd drop everything. Don't tell me you wouldn't."

I didn't answer for a mile or so. "Maybe," I finally admitted.

"If it's Peggy McBride back there"—and Mike jerked a finger back the way we came—"you'd better see Emily again. Because somebody you two worked with was maybe a murderer."

"Yeah. I'm thinking the same thing."

I dropped Mike at his office in the courthouse then went on to the jail, three blocks away. Dorothy, our resident busybody, and Sada, a police widow who helped in the office three days a week, were waiting for an update.

"Who was it, Nate?" Dorothy asked, propping one generous hip on her desk. Her short black Afro was liberally sprinkled with gray but her brown eyes were sharp as tacks.

"Won't know until autopsy and dental comes in. If then." I started toward my office, in the back of the building.

"Peggy McBride," Sada said with certainty. "I always knew that poor child would come to a bad end. Her mother was wild."

I sighed. "Sada, my mother was wild and I grew up to be Chief of Police."

Both Dorothy and Sada laughed. "Your momma was a hippy. She wasn't wild the way Polly Saunders was wild." Sada nodded. "You mark my words. It's poor little Peggy out there. Some Summer Boy knocked her up then got rid of her."

I immediately thought of some of the Summer Boys I'd known. "Maybe."

"You gonna call Emily Sutherland?" Dorothy asked.

"Why would I do that?" I said as I walked down the hall, glad my red face was hidden.

"She worked at the resort the summer Peggy ran off. Emily was one smart girl, as I recall. She might be able to help you figure out what happened."

"I don't need to call in civilians to help with this. Besides, Emily Sutherland has a business to run. She can't drop everything and come out here."

There was a brief pause. "Uh-huh," Dorothy said then I heard her say, "I'd better get her phone number ready, just in case."

"Yep," Sada said. "Makes sense. You never know."

I slammed my door a bit harder than necessary. I knew that wasn't the end of it. In the thirty-some years I've known her, Dorothy never could leave well enough alone. About an hour later, she poked her head around the door.

"What?" I asked.

"Don't take my head off just because your woman isn't here yet," Dorothy said with the cool dignity she wore like a shield. She edged into the room, tugging her bright red cardigan around her black-and-white blouse. Dorothy always wore red, black, and white, calling it her *signature look.*

I figured she just watched too much fashion TV. "She's not my woman. And she's not coming here." My voice came out a bit snappier than I meant.

Dorothy waggled her eyebrows. "That might change if you exerted yourself."

I struggled with that for a minute then curiosity won out. "How do you know?"

Dorothy regarded her red fingernails. "I have my sources."

I fought again with curiosity and, as usual, lost. "What?"

"My cousin Mabel, out in Minnesota? She's got a girl, Patrice. She went to Emily's employment agency in Minneapolis to find summer work. Patrice being just nineteen, Mabel wanted somebody she could trust, so I said she could trust Emily and Patrice should go there. It turns out Emily is going to be selling her business to some hot-shot businessman from Chicago. That man has been wining and dining her to no end."

"You got all this from your cousin?"

"Not just my cousin. You see, Emily's secretary, a girl named Carol—she took a liking to Patrice because they shop at the same vegetarian market." Dorothy waved a hand. "I don't know why that child is vegetarian, but who knows with teenagers? Although a grown woman like that secretary should know better. Anyway, Carol told Patrice this man was making the moves on Emily, but Emily didn't seem too convinced. So it stands to reason she is waiting for the right man to come along and sweep her off her feet. Because, according to Carol *and* Patrice, who saw him, this man is a stud businessman and not just some Joe off the street." Dorothy waggled a finger. "No, no, no, he is red hot. Emily is putting him off *but* you'd better make your intentions known or you may lose her all over again."

I stared at Dorothy in astonishment. "How do you do it?"

"It's all about family," she said with confidence. "You mark my words. Treat her and you'll be sleeping warm and toasty for the rest of your days." She smiled at Doc Stewart as he appeared next to her in the doorway and gestured him into the room. Then she left, throwing me a sharp glance over her shoulder.

"Hey, Doc. What did you find out?"

"I didn't have to look far," Doc said, settling into

the worn wooden guest chair across from me. "I checked locally first. We were right. It's Peggy."

"Damn." I pulled over a notepad. "Cause of death?"

"This isn't official, you understand," the old man said. "I haven't done a complete exam. Her skull was fractured."

"Murder?" Then I shook my head at my own stupidity. "Hell, yeah, it was murder. She was buried."

"It takes some effort to bury a body so deep. Wasn't it busy there?"

"No, it was used mainly for tool storage and to park equipment trucks. I used to park my motorcycle back there."

"That's right. You worked out at the resort, didn't you?" Before I could confirm or deny he said, "You dated a pretty little girl, what was her name?"

"Emily Sutherland," Dorothy called out. "I got her phone number right here, Chief."

"Thank you, Dorothy," I called back. "But I don't think—"

"Call her right now if you'd like," Dorothy offered in a singsong voice.

I smiled at the doctor. It was that or I'd have to go strangle Dorothy. "Get me a full report as soon as you can, okay? This is going to be a tough one to solve. It's one heck of a cold case."

Doc stood up as Dorothy came into the room, waving a scrap of paper. "It shouldn't be hard no matter how long ago it was." His rheumy green eyes twinkled as he looked from Dorothy to me. "Seems to me you might want to talk to folks who worked with you back then. I doubt a guest would know to bury a body back there. Not to mention why—why would anybody want to do in Peggy McBride?"

I fiddled with a pencil cn my desk. "After all this time, it's going to be hard to figure out."

"It had to be one of the Summer Kids," Doc said. "You know and I know there was always trouble with Summer Kids."

"Not always," I said half-heartedly. He was right, of course. My father had been sheriff for years and I was well aware of the skirmishes between the Townies and the Summer Kids who worked the resorts on Lake Michigan.

Dorothy nodded. "Seems to me the doc is right," she declared.

I sighed. If nothing else, I had to try to touch base with the people who had worked there and see if they had any memories of a long-ago night. I know I sure as hell had a lot of memories.

Doc headed toward the door. "That poor girl deserves some kind of justice." He nodded to Dorothy as he left. "She deserves better than a cold grave at the back end of an old resort."

I took a long, deep breath. Doc was right. I couldn't let my personal feelings interfere with justice for Peggy.

"Okay," I said. "Call Emily."

Chapter 2

Thirty-Four Years Earlier

Nate meandered toward a pile of driftwood, thinking he might make a bonfire on the beach. It was cool for early June, with a damp snap to the air. He settled on a log to stare broodingly at Lake Michigan in the dying twilight.

"Hey!"

He looked around.

"Hey, you—big guy!"

Nate stood up. There was no one else on the beach he could see.

"Yeah, you, the guy sitting on my clothes."

Nate looked down. He had, indeed, been sitting on a pair of shorts draped over the log. He whirled to look at the water. A girl was standing in the shallows. The water lapped up to her waist and she held her arms crossed over her chest, barely hiding her large breasts. She was naked. And she was absolutely beautiful.

Nate thought at first he must be dreaming. This was like one of those erotic stories out of *Penthouse* or *Playboy*, where a mermaid comes out of the waves and acted out a man's fantasies. Except this mermaid looked like a teenaged girl. A really cold teenaged girl. In fact, she looked like the girl he'd seen working at the front desk. The resort management hired pretty girls for the front desk and this girl wasn't an exception. If this was the one he was thinking of, she had an hourglass figure, perfect ivory skin, silky brown hair and big green eyes.

"Yeah?" he called out.

"Would you quit sitting on my clothes so I can get out and get dressed?" she asked as the waves lapped around her lower half. Nate's eyes were drawn to her flat stomach and the confident, easy way she stood in the water, staring at him.

"Okay," he said. "You got a towel?"

She jerked her head to the left. "Other side of the logs."

Nate went behind the log pile, finding two towels, neatly folded. He picked them up and walked to the edge of the shale. "I'll leave 'em here."

"No, they'll get wet." She hesitated.

Nate closed his eyes, turned and held the towels behind him. After a long moment, he felt her snatch them out of his hands.

"Thanks," she said.

Nate opened his eyes. She was securing a towel around her body as she walked past him up the beach to the logs. She paused and wrapped the other towel around her head then she kept walking, seemingly indifferent to the fact she was naked and a six-feet-two-inch, two-hundred-ten-pound man was walking behind her. Then she looked over her shoulder, giving him such a quelling look that Nate faltered and stayed where he was.

"Sorry," he said as she strode up to the log to grab up her clothes. "I didn't know it was a private swimming place."

She walked to the far side of the logs. They were piled just tall enough so he didn't see what was happening. She soon came around the logs to face him dressed in shorts and a blouse, pulling a comb out of a pocket. Her hair fell to her shoulders in a thick, straight line of dark honey-brown, almost black now that it was wet. "I'm Emily Sutherland," she said, sticking out a hand.

He shook it. "Nate Boltz."

She continued combing out her tangles. "You're the Townie who handles the interior maintenance, right?"

"Yep. Who are you?"

"Front desk clerk, eleven to six. Minnesota."

He looked around the now darkening beach. "Dangerous to be out here alone."

"Maybe." Then she smiled. "Good thing I found you to protect me."

Nate decided to ignore that comment. "How come you're out here and not with your boyfriend?" He'd seen her and a tall, blond guy, one of the Summer Boys.

She wrinkled her nose and made an ugly face. "He's not my boyfriend anymore."

"Really?" Nate was surprised. It seemed to him that Blond Summer Boy and Brunette Summer Girl was a match made in heaven. Blond Summer Boy had a waiter's job, another slot where management hired the cute kids. Some of the Summer Boys picked up more than dinner tips or so Nate heard. Some of the lady guests sometimes slyly suggested some room service. Summer Boys made good money if they wanted to. Even Nate had even been propositioned a few times and he wasn't one of the pretty guys. He was rough around the edges with his broken-and-not-set-right nose and long, dark curly hair.

"I broke up with him last night."

"Oh." There didn't seem to be any good response.

She sat on a log, looking at him as she slowly combed her hair. "I caught him with his dick in Mary Jo Martin's mouth," she said.

Nate stumbled as he sat on the log. "What?"

She nodded and squinted at him. "Does it really feel so good?"

Nate stared at her, open-mouthed

"Does it?" she insisted.

"Do you always go around asking strange guys questions like that?" She flushed a painful red and looked defiant. "How old are you?" he asked suspiciously.

"Eighteen." She said it so promptly Nate was certain she was a brand-new eighteen. "How about you?"

"Twenty-one. Almost twenty-two."

"Wow. You're like, a grown-up." Her eyes had little shafts of gold mixed in with the green. Now they were mischievous, with a hint of laughter.

"You making fun of me?" he asked, semi-seriously.

"Oh no." She tilted her head to one side, turning to swing one leg up and over the log, straddling it. Her crotch was pointed right at him. She wasn't flirting, Nate realized, glancing at her guileless face. She had no idea how short those shorts were or how sexy she looked. "What do you do besides work summers at the resort? Are you going to school?"

He nodded and sat down at the other end of the log.

"I'm on scholarship at Western Michigan."

"What kind of scholarship?"

"Football."

She eyed him. "What's your major?"

"Criminal Justice. I want to play pro after school, but odds are I won't get drafted."

She looked him over again, more completely this time. "What do you play? Tight end? Running back?"

Nate nodded, surprised she guessed his position. Most girls didn't know much about football. "It was me, four brothers, and my dad," she explained, seeing his look. "My mom died when I was little. I'm just one of the guys."

"Yeah, right," he muttered.

"Why are you out here walking along the beach and being melancholy?"

"Melancholy? Do I look melancholy?"

"Kinda. Did your girl break up with you?"

"She wasn't really my girl. Just somebody I hung out with."

Emily pushed her hair over her shoulders. "You can hang out with me."

Nate shrugged, trying not to laugh. "Sorry. That's not exactly what I meant."

"Oh." Emily's eyes opened wide. "Oh. You mean—*that* way?"

Nate didn't say anything. *None of her damn business*, he thought, tossing a rock toward the surf.

"Well, sorry, I don't hang out like that."

He glanced sidelong at her and nodded. "I didn't figure you did."

"What's that mean?" she asked quickly.

"I'm saying you're a nice girl," Nate said quickly.

Emily kicked up a small rock with the toe of her sneaker and glanced at him. "I drink beer," she said.

Nate ducked his head to hide a smile. "Does your dad know about it?"

"Oh, hell, it was only once." She wrinkled her nose again and sighed. "I didn't like the taste. I like wine. But it seems like boys like to drink beer. I don't understand boys." She glanced at him. "Or men, I guess."

"What's to understand?" Nate leaned back to stare at the lake.

"Can I ask you a guy question?"

"What kind of guy question?"

"Do guys—" She wiggled a bit on the log and tried again. "Does your, you know, your—" She chewed on a nail and continued doggedly on. "Do guys get, you know, excited, just by looking at a girl?" she finally said in a rush.

"Huh?" Nate pulled his eyes away from the sight of her taut nipples, clearly outlined by her blouse, and back to her face. "Excited?"

"You know," she said meaningfully, glancing swiftly at his crotch.

Nate stared at her then he covered his face with one hand and shook his head. "I don't believe I'm having this conversation," he muttered, acutely aware of his own hard-on which had occurred, yes, just by looking at Emily Sutherland.

"I need to talk to a guy about this stuff. I can talk to David but he's gay and it's not the same. My brothers won't tell me anything. They act like I'm a nun. And their friends—" She made an exasperated noise. "They act like I've got cooties, they avoid me so bad."

It's because they're afraid your brothers will pound them to a pulp because they have a hard-on for their little sister, Nate thought. *Can somebody this innocent still be alive in the world?*

He cleared his throat. "Emily, you shouldn't ask a stranger on the beach if he gets a hard-on when a pretty girl goes by." He realized she had somehow gotten so close their knees were almost touching.

When did that happen?

"Do you?" she coaxed. "Come on, tell me."

"Do you get excited when you see a good-looking guy?" Nate saw her eyes open wide with startled realization. *Bingo.*

"Not really." She started to edge backwards.

Nate put a hand on her knee and held her in place. "My turn to ask a girl question."

Her lips parted in surprise. "Don't you have a girlfriend? Or a sister?"

He shook his head. "No girlfriend, no sister."

"Okay." She tilted her chin up. "You can ask me a question if you'll answer mine."

"Fair enough." Nate slowly moved his hand off her knee. Her skin was smooth and silky. "I can get, well, interested if I see a pretty girl. But usually I have to be talking to her or, you know, be *with* her to get excited. Just seeing somebody pretty doesn't usually turn me on." *Except you*, he thought. "Now you have to answer my question."

She nodded, her eyes as big as saucers.

Nate leaned forward. "How do girls get their legs so smooth?" He moved one callused palm slowly down her leg.

She shivered and her eyes got even bigger. "Oh."

This time it wasn't an "oh" of surprise. There was a definite erotic edge to it that sent shivers down Nate's spine. "Well?" he asked.

"What?" Her eyes looked far-away and dreamy.

"How do you get your legs so smooth, Emily Sutherland?"

She looked down at his hand, resting on her thigh then up at him. "It depends on the girl, I guess. Some use that Nair stuff. Some use hot wax. I use a razor."

He ran his hand along her thigh. "This is so smooth, though."

"I do it every day." Her voice was so low he leaned near her to hear. "In the shower. When I get up."

Nate closed his eyes and surrendered to the mental image of Emily Sutherland in the shower, looking down at her leg, examining it to make sure it was smooth enough. When he opened his eyes, he surrendered to her green gaze for one long second. Then she pulled back and the moment was gone.

"Come on." He swung his leg over the log. "I'll walk you back."

"Why?"

"Why what?"

"Why go back now?"

He stood up. "Because if we don't I'm liable to do something I'll regret."

"Like what?" She leaned back on her hands to regard him.

He stared out at the lake, avoiding her eyes. "Like kiss you, Emily Sutherland. You're a Summer Girl and I'm a Townie. The two don't mix."

She sighed. "I suppose you're right. After all, you're an older man and of course you know best." He looked quickly at her but she was staring at the ground. It was impossible to read her expression. “Would you regret it, though?”

“Regret what?”

“Regret kissing me?”

“I guess we won’t know, will we?”

Emily sprang to her feet and waved to a bunch of Summer Kids on the beach who were hauling coolers, chairs and blankets to a spot not far away. “We’re going to have a bonfire. Stay around?”

“Nah.”

“Why not?”

“I told you. I’m a Townie.”

“So? Is there a law you can’t be seen with me? You got cooties or something?”

Nate turned away. “The way the Summer Girls act, well, yeah, maybe I do.”

Emily put her hands on her hips. “I don’t think that way, so quit acting like a pissy sissy.”

“A what?” Nate regarded her over his shoulder, not sure he heard right.

“A pissy sissy.” She sounded less confident. “My brother says that sometimes.”

“I’ll bet he’d rather you didn’t say it.”

“Probably.” She walked with him to the steps leading to the resort on the bluff overhead. “Thanks for answering my question.” Nate paused at the steps and she hopped up. With her on the step, she was just even with his eyes. “I don’t know much about guys. It’s nice of you to talk to me like that.” Then she leaned down and put her lips on his.

Her lips were soft and sweet, at least until she opened them. Then their tongues started to tangle and

Nate was stabbed by a surge of lust so strong he went dizzy. He put an arm around her and pulled her to him. She slipped off the step so Nate held her off the ground. Her taut, hard nipples pressed against his chest and her hands slipped around his neck to tug at his curly hair.

Then she was gone, pushing away from him and looking back over one shoulder as she joined the Summer Kids hurrying down the beach. “I don’t regret it, Nate. I hope you don’t, either.”

Chapter 3

Present Day

It took about five minutes then Dorothy reappeared, her short and substantial bulk filling the doorway as she idly swiped at her nails with a nail file. "I've got her secretary on the line."

I picked up the phone, my finger hovering over the blinking *Line 1* button. Dorothy didn't budge from her spot. I looked at her curiously.

"According to her—Carol"—and she pointed to my phone with her file—"Emily is an inch away from signing the contract to sell Winter Dreams/Summer Schemes, her employment agency." Dorothy filed a miniscule portion of red fingernail. "She inherited it in her divorce, you know. Jonas Hawthorne guy is on his way to the office as we speak."

"Her secretary told you all that?" I asked in disbelief.

Dorothy shrugged. "When I told her I was with the police department and you and Emily were old friends, she confided in me."

"Confided?" I imagined two gossipy secretaries, sharing company secrets.

Dorothy ignored my skepticism. "Besides, us secretaries stick together. According to Carol, Emily might get a tidy severance package or she can continue working there as an executive." She looked up from her manicure, dark eyes guileless. "Carol suspects Mr. Hawthorne wouldn't mind if Emily stayed around in another more personal capacity, too."

I took a deep breath. It was stupid to worry. After all, Emily had been out of my reach for years. Why panic now?

"But Emily's not leaping at the chance, if you get my drift."

I let out the breath. "You got all of this out of a two minute phone conversation with a total stranger?"

"Oh, she's not a stranger. Remember I told you about Patrice, my cousin's girl? Well, Patrice and Carol's daughter are best friends and roommates in college. I drove out there last summer to visit Mabel and I met Carol." Dorothy shot me a triumphant smile. "We had dinner together at the girls' apartment."

I counted to five slowly. "Thank you, Dorothy."

"You're welcome, Chief."

I tapped the button and picked up the phone. "Emily?"

"Just a minute, please." I heard voices in the background and a voice say, "Nate Boltz? Are you kidding? Oh my God, of course I'll talk to him!" A second later, a familiar voice said, "Nate Boltz? Lightning Boltz?"

I felt a jolt right down to my toes. Emily had one of those sexy, whisky-soaked voices. I laughed. "It's been a long time since anybody called me that."

"Is it really you, Nate?"

I leaned back in my chair and swiveled, looking out my window at the sun-soaked parking lot behind the station house. "Yep."

"Where are you calling from?" she asked.

I closed my eyes, imagining her on the beach, the firelight dancing on her tanned, naked body. Damn. I needed to keep those thoughts at bay if I was going to get through this conversation without breaking into a sweat. "It's about the Pine Place Inn." I heard a sudden loud noise from the other end of the phone. "Are you okay, Emily?"

"Sorry. I almost tipped my chair over backwards. Say what?"

I chuckled. "Pine Place. I'm Police Chief in Little Bay now."

"I thought you were going to play professional football?"

"I did for ten years. Then I went back to school, got some degrees, worked in Miami as a cop then settled down here. I've been here for the last ten years or so."

"Wow. You went home. So did you marry your high school sweetheart?" Her voice was teasing and light, but I heard a hint of true curiosity in it.

I decided to test the waters. I wasn't quite ready to take a plunge. "No. She left and went back to college, remember?"

There was a long pause then Emily said softly, "Yeah. I do remember."

The memories suddenly were in the room with me. Memories of a soft, voluptuous body with me as we lay on the beach, entwined in lovemaking. Memories of hot summer days in a small cottage. Memories of showers at dawn and passionate kisses in the back seat of an old Chevy. Thirty-four years ago I loved Emily with every molecule of my being. For an instant, my remembered love overwhelmed me.

A patrol car pulling into the parking lot woke me up. "Emily, I'm calling for a reason."

I think she put her hand over the phone because her voice got muffled. "Come in," she said.

"I'm sorry, am I interrupting something?"

"No, it's fine, go on."

"Do you remember Peggy McBride?"

Emily was quiet for a minute. "Of course I remember her. I have mixed feelings about Peggy." She gave a sharp laugh. "A mix of pity and rage. Peggy left town the last night of the season, didn't she?"

"We found her body, buried out on the resort." I hesitated. "She was murdered. And she was pregnant."

Emily sucked in a breath. "Oh, no."

"And Emily?"

"Hmm?"

"I know of two people who didn't have anything to do with her death." I patiently waited for Emily to analyze my implications. "You know what I mean?"

Her voice was soft with memory. "I know what you mean."

Emily and I spent our last night together, making love and crying in each other's arms as we prepared to be separated after our Summer of Love. I suddenly realized that while we were making love, Peggy was being murdered and buried not too far from where Emily and I lay.

"Is there any chance you can come here for a vacation? I want to get some of the old group together, try to reconstruct what happened that night."

Her voice was hesitant. "It's been such a long time."

"I know. But I'd like to do it for her." And do it for

myself, but I didn't say it.

Emily knew what I was thinking. "You sound just like your father. He always had such a sense of responsibility to the people in town."

I looked at the framed picture of my father and mother on the low brown file cabinet near my desk. "I suppose you're right. Now I know how he felt when he was sheriff."

"Hold on while I check my calendar." There was a pause then she said, "I'm getting ready to sell my company, Nate. I want to take some time off to read over everything and think about it. This would be perfect. I'll come as soon as I can."

This time I heard the voice in her office say, "Excellent. Does this mean I've bought your company, Emily?" Then I heard a man laugh.

I wondered if it was the Hawthorne guy Dorothy mentioned. "Thanks, but if it's going to get in the way of your business, you don't have to." I bounced a pencil off the blotter on my desk and glared at the pristine October day, Lake Michigan in the distance reflecting the blue of the sky in its gray-blue waves.

"No problem. Can you give me your phone number? I'll call you back as soon as I know when I can get there." Again her voice became slightly muffled and she said, "I realize that, Jonas. But I still want to read the contracts." Her tone was sharp and a bit angry. For some reason, that cheered me up.

I gave her my phone number at the office and home. "Emily?"

"Yeah, Nate?"

I decided to dabble a bit and see how the water felt. "Are you remarried?"

"No."

"Are you dating anybody?"

"No."

"Good. I'll see you in a few days." I hung up before I put my foot in it any further.

Emily Sutherland. The first woman I ever truly loved. She was an eighteen-year-old virgin when I met her. I was the first man she ever made love with.

There are some women a man doesn't forget.

Emily.

Dorothy sauntered through my open door. "I wonder where she'll stay when she's in town. The only place other than the resort is the No-Tell Motel out on Highway 8. The resort is closed for the season."

"She'll probably stay in Kalamazoo or Holland," I said. Those were the two cities of any size close to Little Bay and each had good motels.

"Maybe she can stay in the apartment over your parents' garage," Dorothy suggested. "They're between renters, aren't they?"

The phone rang, mercifully saving me from answering. I heard Sada pick up the line in the outer office. "Dorothy, it's for you. Carol somebody from Minnesota."

Dorothy ambled back to the front.

I considered her words. I had fond memories of the apartment over the detached garage at my parents' house, on the northeast side of town. I remembered how Emily and I would have Wednesday night supper with the folks then "*go out to the garage to listen to records*." I was pretty sure Mom and Dad knew exactly what we were doing out there in the apartment but they never commented, nor did they comment on my frequent overnight absences that summer.

I made a note to check with Mom about the apartment.

The next evening I got an e-mail at home from Emily, forwarded to me from the Little Bay Police Department's web site.

Nate: Is there a B&B in town now? The resort is closed and I need a place to stay.

I fired off a reply, telling her the old apartment was available. I got a fast reply. She must have been sitting near the terminal, even though it was almost nine at night.

Great. Are your parents still alive? I'd love to see them.

That set off a chain of e-mails over the next few days. I updated her about my parents, who were alive and kicking and told her about the Apple Festival coming up in conjunction with high school Homecoming. I casually suggested maybe she might stay for the Apple Harvest Dance. When Emily asked if she needed formal wear for the party, I was stumped and told her I'd get back to her.

I mentioned it to Dorothy, who said, "Just tell her to pack a little black dress."

"Every woman has a little black dress, Chief," Sada chimed in from her spot at the main reception desk. "It would be perfect." Both women gave me polite nods before going back to their work.

I decided they were probably right. After all, how important was a dress at a local dance?

That night I sent Emily back a *Nah, we're casual, a little black dress should do it* reply. When she answered with, *I have just the thing,* I relaxed. Apparently the little black dress was a code between women and Emily had deciphered it correctly.

I turned my attention to the list of Summer Kids Emily had forwarded to me. When we found Peggy, I asked Bobby Goldman for employment records from that summer, but much of the resort's papers were lost in a fire a decade or so earlier.

I started making notes, pulling over my computer keyboard and accessing a few databases to do some searching. Then I realized this was a great opportunity to get my junior officers involved. I typed up some instructions, printed it, and left it for Cynthia Bartlett, asking her to do an address search for everyone on the list.

Then I replied to Emily: *Thanks for the information. I didn't know you stayed in touch with folks. What about Greg the Monster? Do you know what happened to him and those guys?*

Again, she replied immediately. *I know somebody who did stay in touch with Greg. I'll give Howard a call and see if he has any news on the Ugly Bunch.*

I answered with, *Thanks, Emily. It's late, you need to go home and catch up on your sleep. You're working awfully hard.*

After a few minutes, she replied. *I'm selling my business and there are lots of details to wrap up. And the only creature waiting for me at home is my cat and he sleeps just fine without me. What about you, Nate? You've sent me some late e-mails. Surely you have someone waiting for you at home?*

I read and re-read her e-mail about a dozen times, wondering how to answer it. That's the good thing about e-mail, you've got a chance to sit and think about how to phrase something.

Nope, nobody waiting for this old cop. I guess I'm just a confirmed bachelor. I hit send before I realized how it might sound and experienced one of those oh-no moments.

Yep, that's the good thing about e-mail. You can make a fool of yourself without seeing the face of the person laughing at you.

Chapter 4

Thirty-Four Years Earlier

The day after meeting Emily, Nate went to the main building to work on a broken fan in the lobby. The two hundred rooms in that building plus the twenty housekeeping cottages meant Nate and ten other "interior" guys were kept busy.

When he got to the lobby Nate saw Emily behind the front desk. It was two in the afternoon and the post-lunch rush was starting. She was in her uniform of dark green golf shirt with the resort logo strained across one breast and a short denim skirt. Old Man Goldman, the owner, kept his eye on her and took a lot of opportunities to brush against her while Emily and he were behind the tight space of the desk counter.

At one point Emily glanced up and waved. "Hi, Nate," she called out over the shoulder of one of the guests checking in.

Old Man Goldman scowled at him. Nate waved to Emily, returning quickly to his work. He saw Goldman try to cop a feel of Emily's boob and saw her stiffen in outrage. She said something in a low voice to the old man. He glared at her but moved away and stayed away the entire time Nate worked in the lobby.

Nate took his time so it was pushing four o'clock before he left. Emily Sutherland could take care of herself, he decided. She wasn't his responsibility. Then he remembered Old Man Goldman and Nate got pissed, just thinking about it.

He went back to the maintenance shop and checked the assignment list for the next day. If he hustled, he might get some work done ahead. Nate went to the cottages on southeast side of the resort and fixed the plumbing leak in 7B then checked the electrical in 10A. By then it was almost five-forty-five. He put his tools away then walked across the resort grounds to the kitchen building, a separate structure that kept the worst of the heat out of the un-air-conditioned dining room in the main building.

When Nate walked in, Emily was getting a plate and heading for the line cooks. She grinned at one of them and said something in Spanish and the guy chattered back at her. Nate watched as the guy loaded her plate with a pork chop, potatoes, and green beans.

When Nate approached with his own plate, the guy gave him a surly glance. Emily looked around and saw Nate standing behind her. "Hey, I thought you were done working by now." She said something in Spanish to the cook. He looked at Nate with more interest. She said something else and the man ladled some food onto Nate's plate.

"I had to work late," Nate lied. He looked down at his plate. "You got an in with the cooks or something?"

She said a farewell to the cook, who grinned and said something back. "I told him you're the man who keeps the fans running. They'd better keep you healthy."

"Thanks." He jerked his head toward a small four-person table at the side of the room and they sat.

"Where'd you learn Spanish?"

"In high school. Daddy insisted I have a foreign language." She dug into her potatoes. "It comes in handy."

Nate thought frantically of some topic to keep the conversational ball rolling. "What college are you going to?"

"I'm a sophomore. University of Minnesota."

"Sophomore? You're only eighteen. Brainiac," he teased, waving his fork at her.

She shrugged. "Not really. I just work hard."

"I thought you'd go to a private school. Most Summer Kids go to private schools."

"Not me. My dad has five kids and he's just a research chemist at 3M. My brothers, Silas and Dan, are graduated and they're paying Daddy back for their tuition. I hope I can earn enough to pay him. And besides, I'm not smart enough for a private school."

Nate snorted. "You don't have to be smart for private school. Just rich." He glanced up at a flurry of activity at the front of the kitchen. "Dinner rush must be starting." Guests were assigned to eat at certain times, just like on a cruise ship. The first seating was from 5:30 to 7:00 and the second from 7:30 to 9:00.

Emily glanced up disinterestedly. "Yeah, I guess so."

"Hey, Emily!"

Nate saw Emily's ex-boyfriend, the blond guy, making his way toward them. "Emily, honey, where've you been?" the guy asked, looming over her. "I tried to find you last night. We need to talk."

He was dressed in the waiter's uniform of dark blue golf shirt and white denims. He was tall and lean with big shoulders and straight blond hair. His killer tan contrasted nicely with his bright blue eyes. *The guy probably rakes in the tips,* Nate thought. In the dining room and out.

"Nothing to talk about, Greg," Emily said breezily. She glanced at Nate. "I'm sorry. Nate Boltz, this is Greg Hoffman. Greg, this is Nate. Nate's a mechanic here at the resort."

"Hey." The guy glanced at Nate, dismissed him, then sat down next to Emily and leaned on the table. "Honey, come on, you know how I feel about you." Nate saw one of Greg's hands disappear under the table.

Emily squirmed. "Get your hand off of me, Greg."

"Oh, baby, come on," he coaxed. "You know how I feel about you."

Nate saw fear and embarrassment in Emily's eyes. "You about ready to go, Emily?" He shoved his plate aside. "We don't want to be late." He stood.

Emily looked up, her eyes big then she stood, too, almost upsetting Greg. "Wow. You're right. It's late."

Nate saw Greg disentangle his hand from the hem of Emily's skirt. Emily's flushed face told Nate how welcome it had been. "Come on, let's go," Emily babbled. "See you, Greg."

Greg remained at the table, giving Nate a cold, calculating look. One of the Mexican workers called out something and Emily answered. They looked at Greg and laughed.

"Wow. Thanks," she said as they emerged from the kitchen. "He's such a jerk." She tugged at her skirt and for some reason the action irritated Nate.

"It *is* a short skirt."

She glared at him. "It's the style nowadays. Mini-skirts, remember?"

"Well, maybe. But it's hard for a guy when a cute girl wears clothes like that."

She put her hands on her hips. "So you think you can maul me, just because I wore a short skirt? What's a girl supposed to do, go around dressed like a nun? Of course, there're guys out there who would just love to jump a nun, too. Maybe I'm supposed to cut off all my hair and draw scars on my face and—"

"Whoa." Nate held up his hand. "You're right." He looked around. "Look, you want to go for a walk?"

"I'm sorry." Emily put a hand on his arm. "I don't mean to flirt. I think I do, though. And it gives guys the wrong ideas. But I don't even know when I'm doing it. I don't think so, at least."

She looked so worried Nate couldn't resist. He leaned over and kissed her lightly. She looked startled and he laughed. "Yes, you do flirt. Don't apologize for it. Just don't be so surprised when a guy takes you up on it."

"Oh." She looked down at the ground thoughtfully, then up at him, eyes dancing with mischief again. "Really?"

He laughed again. "Yes, really." He tucked her arm under his. As they walked toward the beach, he glanced back over his shoulder. Greg Hoffman leaned in the back door of the kitchen, watching. *This is going to be trouble.*

Nate and Emily walked around the grounds then settled on the beach. She snuggled against him and they talked. At nine he told her he had to leave even though there was nothing he really had to do. Nate knew he was dangerously close to really liking Emily Sutherland and that wouldn't do at all. It was best to nip it in the bud, Nate assured himself as he walked her to her dorm near the mechanic's shed where he parked his cycle each night.

"Thanks for rescuing me tonight, Nate." She leaned against the doorway as he looked down at her. "And for rescuing me last night, too. From the big old dangerous beach." She looked up at him through her eyelashes.

He laughed softly. "You're flirting again, Emily."

"Oh." She stared down at the ground between them. "Remember last night, when you asked me if I get excited when I see a good-looking guy?"

Nate nodded but she didn't see it. "I do, sometimes," she said in a breathless little voice. "But only if he's, well, if he's nice and good to talk to and if he's, well—" She looked up at him. "If he's nice."

"We know what happens to guys when they get excited." Nate moved closer. Inches separated them. He wondered if she could tell how excited he was. Then she looked down and her eyes landed on his belt buckle and the territory south of it. *If she has any eyes at all she can tell.* "What happens to girls when they get excited?"

She twined her fingers in his belt loops and tugged him until they were touching. Nate put his arms around her. "I get sort of, um, warm." She did an interesting little wiggle in his arms.

Warm?" Nate asked softly, his lips nearing hers.

"Yeah," she said dreamily. "Awfully warm."

"Hmm?" His lips moved close to her ear. "What else, Emily?"

She stood up on tiptoe and whispered, "I get all

throbby and damp. *There*."

He closed his eyes. "You're too damn sexy to exist."

"So are you," she said before their lips met.

Nate was trembling when they broke apart. He leaned his forehead against hers. "You're too much," he said in a low, raspy voice. "I mean it."

She looked flushed and embarrassed. "I'm not real experienced. I mean, I don't know much about what guys like and all."

He put two fingers against her lips. "You're doing just fine. We'll take this nice and slow and see where it goes, okay? No pressure."

She leaned against him. "I'm kinda nervous."

"Don't be." He hugged her. "Just relax. It's all up to you."

She nodded. "Thanks."

"And Emily?"

"Hmm?"

"If you want to back out because I'm a Townie, I won't bitch about it."

She went still in his arms then she pulled away, her expression cold. "I'm not some shallow, class-conscious, mercenary bitch."

"All I meant was—"

"No, you listen to me, Nate Boltz," she spat, riding over his words. "I don't care if you're a Townie. I don't care if you're rich or if you're uneducated or—or—I like *you*. So there." She whirled on her heel and headed into the dorm. Then she poked her head back out and glared at him. "And you had damn well better get used to it."

Nate stared at the door then he shook his head and

continued down the walk to the mechanic's shed where he parked his cycle. He kicked it into life and drove back to town, trying to figure out what the hell was happening to him.

Oh, shit, he thought as he drove the four miles into town. *I know what's happening. I'm falling for Emily Sutherland. I don't want to love a Summer Girl. I don't want to have my heart broken when she goes away.*

He groaned. *Oh, hell, who am I kidding?*

It was already too late.

Chapter 5

Present Day

A week after we found her body, I looked down at the coroner's report about Peggy McBride. When you cut through all the medical mumbo-jumbo, some big, heavy object smashed Peggy's skull, probably killing her on the spot. I remembered the machine shed and the area around it. There was a large number of possible weapons right there, like wrenches, tire irons, and crowbars.

Who would want to kill Peggy? She was a Townie girl who worked at the resort just like I was a Townie boy who worked there. She had been loose and a bit wild but that wasn't a cause for murder. I remembered the degrading sexual games Peggy got into with Greg Hoffman and his friends. Greg liked to share his girlfriends. Greg was probably a suspect. Hell, Greg and any of his friends from that summer would be suspects.

I looked at the clock again. It was ten minutes later than the last time I looked. Three o'clock. Emily would be here any time. If I had a bigger office, I'd pace. But there was barely room for my desk and chair, a file cabinet, two guest chairs and me and at six-five and two-hundred-twenty pounds, I took up some space.

I shuffled papers around then gave up, pushing

away from the desk and standing. I jammed my fists into my jeans pockets and stared unseeing through the window at the parking lot behind the station. I was fifty-five years old and fidgeting like a boy on his first date. *It's just Emily*, I told myself. *She's an old friend. It's all we have left from our summer. We're just friends.*

Yeah? Then why did my stomach clench when I thought her name? Why was I jumpy? I sat back down. It was always about Emily. No matter who I was with, no matter what I did. She was always in the back of my mind, a little memory I pulled out occasionally, like I pulled out the photo of us sitting on Mike's car, our arms around each other. Both of us so young, so tanned, and so carefree.

There had been other women in my life. I lived with Sylvie for almost three years before we gave it up. And Janet and I tried, off and on, for almost six years. There were others, too, when I played pro ball. But it always came back to Emily.

And now she was coming here because of poor Peggy. I shook my head, my fingers buried in my hair. I didn't know if I could stand to see Emily again. I had thought I'd go to my grave and never see her again. "Damn it, Emily," I muttered.

"Now what did I do?"

The husky, teasing voice made me jerk upright. I stared at the doorway. Emily was standing there, smiling at me.

She was still beautiful. Her faded jeans were just tight enough to show me her hourglass figure and her brightly patterned blouse under the denim jacket was tucked in, showing off her breasts. I swallowed hard. I remembered those breasts with an awful lot of fondness. Her dark brown hair was tousled and windblown and she was smiling, her green eyes snapping with merriment. It was then I realized I was lying to myself for more than thirty years.

I *was* still in love.

"Emily." My voice came out really low, probably because I almost had heart failure and was still recovering. I shot to my feet and came around the desk in a couple of seconds, flat.

"Nate." She raised her face to mine and it was the most natural thing in the world to put my arms around her and kiss her gently.

"Emily." I lifted her off her feet and she laughed, her giggly, low laugh that always made me grin. I released her but kept a hand on her shoulder to steady her. Then I jerked my hand away when I realized I was trembling.

"You look good, Nate. You still look just like Bruce Springsteen—a very tall Bruce Springsteen." She touched my hair, which was a tangle of black-and-gray curls. I wore my black T-shirt with *Little Bay Police Department* in a small logo on the left pocket and my gray jeans. She raised an eyebrow then looked around the office. "Are you taking a day off? Your dad always wore a uniform. I didn't recognize the place. It's been remodeled."

"About twenty years ago." We were still in the original one-story brick structure built decades ago, but it had been added on to until the building looked like it was sprouting wings. "I'm going to retire in a year or two and let my successor take on the job of getting a new station built." I gestured to one of the chairs. "And yep, I'm off-duty now you're here. You look good, too. Cut your hair, I see."

She sat down and I took the other chair next to her. "The older I got, the clumsier I got with the curlers."

"Thanks for coming. I'm glad you could make it, Homecoming week is a big deal here." I was babbling but I was nervous, so I guess babbling was allowed. "It's a whole week event. We have the Sunday Scrub. It's when everybody cleans up the beach. Then there's Merchant Madness on Monday, it's the big sidewalk sale. And Tuesday are the treats, there's the bake sale to raise money, and—"

She nodded, her green eyes laughing. "I saw the sign out in the lobby. It sounds like a lot of fun. I'm looking forward to it."

I took the hint and got off the subject of Homecoming. "I hope this isn't an inconvenience. How was your trip? You said you had business in Chicago this morning?"

She set her purse on the floor underneath her. When she straightened, her face was flushed. "I flew in to Chicago and Jonas met me. Jonas Hawthorne," she explained. "He's purchasing my employment agency. He wanted to go over some...details about the contract."

Her little hesitation got me curious. "Is it a good deal for you?"

She touched her dark hair, a gesture I remembered. Emily fidgeted when she was trying to think what to say. "It's very good. I can stay on in an executive capacity or retire with a nice buyout package. But I'm not sure how Jonas will handle the transition for my employees and it concerns me." She frowned, her eyes narrowing as she remembered something. "Jonas is a bit dominant when it comes to people." Then she seemed to push the thought aside. "Well, I'll deal with him later. He and I met this morning then I drove up here. It's still such a beautiful drive along the lake. The area hasn't changed much at all."

"Yeah, we're sort of in a time warp here."

"Can you tell me what happened?" She leaned toward me. "I was so surprised to hear from you."

I locked my hands on my thighs to still their trembling. "They tore down some of the old buildings out at the resort. Getting ready to put up a new building, out on the north side of the property, near the access road."

"Oh." She frowned. "Is our cottage being torn down?"

"It is. But I went out and got us a souvenir." I got up and leaned over my desk, pulling the small porcelain shower fixtures from the top drawer. "Remember?"

She turned them over in her hands. "Yeah. You were so mad."

"No kidding." Some asshole had reversed the hot and cold knobs. The first time we showered together, Emily almost leapt out of her skin at the cold temperatures. I cursed a blue streak and got out my plumbing tools to fix it. Emily had teased me as I worked, buck-naked in the shower.

She started to hand the *H* knob back but I put out a stopping hand. "You keep one. I kept the other one."

"Thanks, Nate." She fumbled the little fixture into her purse.

"Anyway, they were tearing down the cottages and the old equipment shed."

She looked thoughtful. "There were four cottages

back there plus the shed and some kind of machine shed, wasn't there?"

"Yep. They were tearing down the cottages and just starting on digging to get the old pipes out. That's when they found the body."

Her eyes were still an odd mixed color, the clear, dark green highlighted with little gold arrows of light. Her skin was still flawless, too. A lot of women showed the effects of sun and time but Emily looked like she was thirty-two, not fifty-two. I looked down at my banged-up hands, scarred from years in football and outdoor work. I was probably showing every one of my fifty-five years.

"Where was she?" Emily asked.

"She was between the last cottage and the back mechanic's shed. She wasn't buried real deep, but deep enough. You remember how the ground was all scuffed up back there? It's where we stored the heavier equipment so it was always torn up."

"It was always messy there. The tractors and the golf carts carried in sand by the bucketful. Everybody tracked it in from the beach and it got picked up on the tires."

I relaxed. It was good to talk to somebody who remembered the old place. I forgot about the sand but she was right. That equipment always tracked sand around.

"How did they know it was her?" Emily was picking at her cuticles, a nervous habit she apparently still had. She wore a heavy gold ring with a ruby and four small inset diamonds on the middle finger of her right hand. Her hands were tiny, like I remembered and they were still pale and prettily shaped, with long, tapering fingers. I remembered how she used to caress me with those hands, how those fingers used to walk up and down my body.

I blew out a shaky breath. "A necklace she wore. Her parents are still alive. They recognized the necklace. They said her boyfriend gave it to her. There're the dental records, too. It pretty much sealed the case. I remember how proud Peggy was of her teeth. She had braces to get 'em straightened and a couple of crowns. She thought it was just so cool."

"I remember." Emily's eyes had that dreamy quality she got when she was thinking of something a million miles away. Or when she was getting ready to orgasm, I remembered suddenly. Her eyes would take on a sultry, dreamy look as her body started to...

"Anyway," I said, leaning away from her. "They found her buried about four feet deep. I was out at the resort when they found her. Bobby was there, too." I probably sounded like a babbling idiot, but memories were starting to crowd in on me.

"Bobby took over the resort from his father? He always hated working there. I'm surprised he didn't just sell the place and move on with his life."

"The old man put something in his will." I suppose my disgust sounded in my voice. "If Bobby sold within ten years of the old man's death, he'd lose everything." I shrugged. "I wasn't around then, my dad told me about it."

"Your dad? He's still around? And your mom?"

I heard the happiness in her voice. Emily always had a close relationship with my folks. "Yep. That's why I was so sure you could use my old apartment. They rent it out and they're between renters now. They still argue about politics and Mom still tries to grow marijuana in a pot when Dad isn't looking. When I told 'em you were coming to town, they insisted you stay at the apartment. 'Just like old times,' my mom said. How's your family?" I remembered to ask, trying desperately to make small talk and not just gawk at her.

She touched the ring on her finger. "Daddy died about five years ago. This was his ring." She held out her hand and I took it.

I looked at the four diamonds and one ruby. "I know who was the ruby in his life."

"Yes." If she noticed I continued to hold her hand, she didn't say anything. "He had a heart attack and passed quickly, thank God. Silas, Dan, and Jason are all married and have popped out a bunch of kids so I'm an aunt many times over. Ben refuses to settle down and is still bouncing around the world." She smiled indulgently. "He always was the adventurer among us."

I gently rubbed my thumb along her hand. "What about you? You were married, right?"

"John and I were married for about five years. It didn't quite work out." She made a face. "I caught him with a younger woman."

I made a face right back at her. "Stupid man. But I'm glad you're single."

"That's me, still single after all these years." She looked around the office and I knew she was flustered. "Have you had any luck contacting the Summer Kids?"

Her question jerked me back to the present. I went to the desk and pulled papers out of the top desk drawer. "I got hold of fifteen people from around here, in Chicago or Lansing, who said they could come this weekend. I thought we would go to the resort on

Sunday then meet someplace afterwards and try to put together a timeline." I came back to the chair, bringing the papers with me. "I made a list of guys who might have been with Peggy that night." I handed her the paper.

Emily scanned the names. "No, it's not quite right." She looked up. "Pencil?" I handed her one and she put a mark through three names. "The tennis pro would have been with a guest." She made a small face. "He did guests. And I think Bobby Mack was with a guest. Donny Beason was in town. He had a girl there and he was faithful to her." Emily set the list down. "Those were pretty promiscuous times. There was an awful lot of bed hopping."

"Not for us," I said before I thought it through.

She took my hand. "Not for us. You were my guy, Nate. My only guy."

I stared at her. "You were my girl, Emily. My only girl."

Our eyes met. I wondered if she saw the wanting in mine. For just a minute I felt like twenty-two again, staring at her for the first time.

"Uh-huh."

I looked up to see Dorothy lounging in my doorway, eyeing us. Emily dropped my hand and twisted in her chair. "Dorothy? You're still working here?"

"Uh-huh. I was gone from the desk a few minutes ago. You must have met Sada."

"I certainly did." Emily jumped up and crossed the room to hug the resident busybody. I watched, my heart still pounding furiously from our eye-to-eye contact.

"It's good to see you," Emily said. "I swear it

seems like nothing's changed around here." She looked from Dorothy to me.

Dorothy looked at me. "Uh-huh," she agreed.

My face got hot. "We should move along, Emily."

"You staying with the sheriff?" Dorothy asked politely.

"In the old apartment," Emily said, reaching for her purse and missing the look Dorothy shot me. "I'm lucky it's available. There aren't a lot of hotel options in Little Bay." She smiled at me. "Your parents are sweet to volunteer to put me up for the week."

"Sweet," Dorothy murmured. "That's the sheriff all right."

I rolled my eyes and steered Emily out of the office, grabbing my jacket from the rack near the door. "Did you park in back?"

She nodded. "I rented a car in Chicago. It's a Bug. I've always wanted to try one of those and this was the perfect excuse."

"You can follow me. I'm parked out back, too." I shot Dorothy a look. "I have my pager so if you need me, just call."

"You bet, Chief," Dorothy said with a nod.

I led Emily down the short corridor past our small kitchen and dining area. As we reached the door, Rob Sloan came in the back door. "This is Officer Sloan, Emily," I said, pausing. "He joined the force a couple of years ago. This is Emily Sutherland, Rob."

Emily held out her hand to Rob, a small man in his thirties with thinning brown hair and pale brown eyes. "I used to work at the resort," she explained.

Rob nodded. "I heard some folks were coming back."

Emily looked at me and I saw the sympathy in her eyes. “It’s too bad about Peggy. She didn’t have many chances in life then to die like she did.”

“Did you know her?” Rob asked.

Emily shrugged. “A little bit, I guess. She didn’t have many friends.”

“Just boyfriends,” I said, exasperated. “That’s the problem, figuring out who she might have been with.” I nodded to Rob. “See you tomorrow, Rob.”

“ ’Night, Chief.”

“He seems competent,” Emily said as I opened the back door for her.

“We’re lucky to get him. He worked in Detroit and wanted to get out of the city.”

“Smart boy,” Emily murmured.

I saw Cynthia coming toward us across the parking lot, sunlight glinting off the badge on her uniform. “Chief,” she said with a big smile.

Once again we paused. “Emily, this is Cynthia Bartlett, one of our officers. Cynthia, this is Emily Sutherland. She used to work at the resort.”

Emily held out a hand. After a moment’s hesitation, Cynthia gave it a brisk shake. “Miss Sutherland.” Cynthia turned her attention to me. “Are you out for the night, Chief?”

“Yep. See you tomorrow.”

Cynthia looked disappointed. “I was hoping to look at the coroner’s report. I haven’t had much chance to work a murder.”

She was right. It would be a good learning experience for her. I knew Rob had worked some homicides in Detroit, but Cynthia came to us fresh out of the academy. I hesitated but I didn’t want to hang around. “We can go over it tomorrow.”

“Okay.” Cynthia Bartlett nodded to Emily. “Nice to meet you, ma’am.”

“Nice to meet you, Cynthia.” Emily turned to look at Cynthia as we walked into the parking lot. “Ma’am,” she muttered. “Well, I’ll bet she gives you a run for your money.”

“What? Run for my money?”

Emily laughed, putting a hand on my arm. “That girl has the hots for you.”

“What?” I was floored. I mean, I knew Cynthia acted a bit, well, girly when she was with me, but I just figured that was how she was. I considered it. Nah. She was thirty years younger than me. Nah. Emily was wrong.

Emily gestured and I leaned down. She said in a low voice, “She wants your body.”

I must have looked shocked because she laughed again. “Oh, Nate. Don’t you realize how handsome you are?”

She started to walk to a red VW Bug but stopped when I put a hand on her arm. “I am?”

“Honestly.” Emily shook her head. “Why you’ve never married is beyond me.”

I stared at her. I felt as though my life was balanced on a pivot, teetering between the known and the unknown. I could let this chance pass or I could grab it. “You know why, Emily,” I said softly, making a sudden decision.

She paused with her hand on the door handle of the Bug. “Oh, Nate.”

I saw the memories in her eyes. I moved closer. It felt as though time was standing still. What was she thinking? Was she surprised by me? Surprised by how I looked or acted? It felt like those intervening years had vanished and all that was left was this moment, now. I held my breath.

Then, as though shaking herself out of a trance, she moved slightly. “Shall I follow you?”

I stepped away. “Sure.”

Emily looked beyond me. I followed her gaze and saw Cynthia Bartlett watching us as Emily got into her car.

Chapter 6

Thirty-Four Years Earlier

About ten days after they first started dating, Nate walked her back to the dorm after they went to town for a movie. They leaned in the shadows of the building and kissed. Emily rubbed against him, feeling the hard bulge in his jeans. Every time she felt it, she wanted to feel him closer, wanted to touch him. This time she threw caution to the winds and hesitantly touched his hardness, running her hand over it.

Nate pulled away from her and she blushed furiously. "Does it hurt?" she asked. "I just wanted—" She stopped and stammered, "T-t-touch it. Touch you."

"Emily." Nate's voice had a whispered, stunned sound. He leaned against the wall as though his legs wouldn't support him.

She pulled away from him. *Oh, God*, she thought. *I'm not normal. He thinks I'm a pervert. I just wanted to feel it. It feels so big. It can't really be so big, can it?* Emily was so red she was afraid her face would burst into flames. "Is it normal to...to feel like this?"

"Like what?" he asked.

Emily looked anywhere but at him. "I get so..." *Wet*, she wanted to say. She got wet and hot and her insides throbbed whenever he touched her. Her nipples ached. She wanted something but she wasn't sure what it was. Some part of her brain was telling her she wanted that bulge of his, but she wasn't sure how the mechanics of it all worked.

"How do you get?" His voice was softer and more insistent.

Emily turned away but Nate wouldn't let her go. He put a gentle hand on her shoulder. She leaned against the wall so she faced him. He put a thumb under her chin to lift her head up. "Emily?" he prompted.

"I get so wet," she admitted. "Down there. Am I supposed to? I get so—"

"So what?"

"So anxious or something." Emily wasn't sure how to explain it. Her hand reached out of its own volition and she stroked his jeans gently. He flinched but didn't pull away this time. Emily decided maybe she'd just startled him. Maybe it didn't hurt after all. She pressed her hand against his fascinating bulge and looked up at him. "Is it all you? It's so big."

Nate leaned his head against the wall. "Emily," he said, leaning over to kiss her. "You're not normal."

"Oh!" She withdrew her hand and started to pull away from him.

"You're better than normal. You're sexy and you're sweet."

She moved closer to him, fitting her hips to his. "I am?"

"In fact, you're so sexy I may die of wanting you. You're like a firecracker."

"I'm a cherry bomb." Emily put her arms around his neck. "Please, Nate. Help me. Teach me. Set me off." Her hand crept between them and firmly massaged him through his jeans.

"Emily," he croaked.

She took one of his hands and moved it to her crotch. "I'm sure."

"A girl's first time is really important," he murmured.

"And I want you to be the guy." She pressed herself into his hand. He started to massage her and she made a small moaning noise. "Please. I want it."

"Want what?" he asked as his finger crept up under the hem of her shorts.

She gasped and raised herself on her tiptoes, pressing herself against his chest and simultaneously shifting position so his finger slipped up under her panties. "I don't know," she gasped against his neck. "But I think it's there in your jeans. What are you doing?" she murmured, feeling liquid and soft against him.

"Just playing."

Emily leaned against him. Should she? Shouldn't she? Before he could stop her, she tugged his jeans zipper open and slipped a hand down the flat of his stomach.

"What are you doing?" He looked so shocked she was surprised his voice worked.

"Just playing," she murmured. Her hand slid lower. "I just want to feel it, Nate. Oh, it's so hard," she said in a whisper. "And it's so smooth." Her hand moved on him. "It's so big. Will it fit? I mean, isn't it supposed to go inside me? It's so big."

Her hand closed around his erection. "It's damp here at the top. Just like me."

Nate laughed shakily. "Not quite as damp as you." He pulled back. "We have to stop."

"Oh, why?" Emily felt like she was in a dream, a dream she never wanted to end.

"Because if we don't, I'll embarrass myself." Nate moved away from her and when Emily's hand slid out of his jeans, he made a little groaning noise.

"Soon, Nate?" She leaned against the wall, not sure her legs would support her. "Please?"

"I want it to be right for you."

She gently touched his face. "If it's with you, it will be."

****

"You've got it bad," Mike Sawyer said then he tipped his bottle of beer up for a long swallow. Mike and Nate had been friends since childhood. Nate had just mentioned he was dating a Summer Girl.

"She's a nice kid." Nate slumped in his chair at the Bare Knuckle Bar and Grill, a local hangout.

"What's she look like?" Mike asked.

Nate took a deep breath and tried to figure out how to describe honey-brown hair, green eyes, freckles, big breasts, a tiny waist and a devastating sense of humor. Mike shook his head before Nate could speak. "She can't be that good."

"Oh, she is."

Mike and Nate turned. Greg Hoffman stood—or rather swayed—behind them. The Knuckle was thinly populated on a Tuesday night, with just a few town regulars sitting at the bar. Mike and Nate were the only ones sitting at the small tables.

Mike looked from Nate to the newcomer. Then he glanced at Clancy, the bartender, who nodded abruptly and reached for the telephone.

"Let me describe her for you," Greg slurred. "She's

about five-two and a hundred-twenty pounds. She's got brown hair down to her shoulders, she's got cute little freckles, she's got a sweet little ass, she's got pretty tits, and she's a virgin." He glowered at Nate then leaned on the table to peer at Nate. "And I'm going to get her cherry."

Nate leaned back, away from Greg's beery breath. "What Emily does and who she does it with, it's up to Emily." He swallowed, hard. "If she wants to stay a virgin for the rest of her life, it's her decision."

Greg made a rude noise, splattering spit on Mike in the process. "Bullshit. You're just a fucking Townie. You're not good enough to lick her shoes and shine them. Do you know what her dad does? He's a research scientist. He's, like, brilliant. Two of her brothers graduated from M.I.T. in robotics research. Hell, she's got a scholarship in business administration. You think she's going to hang out with some fucking mechanic?"

Nate had discovered a long time ago it didn't pay to get pissed off at the Summer Kids. They were mostly inoffensive and somewhat stupid. It was like getting mad at a dog. "That's up to Emily. Like I said, she's an adult. She can make her own decisions."

"Not where this is concerned." Greg enunciated each word carefully. "She's mine, asshole. I'm going to have her cherry. I'm going to fuck her brains out before the end of this summer, whether she wants it or not."

Both Mike and Nate sprang to their feet. "What the hell did you say?" Nate demanded, grabbing Greg's shirt collar.

"I heard him," Mike said. "He was talking about raping this girl."

An ugly murmur started in the bar. Several of the

other men had apparently heard it, too.

Greg glared back in defiance. "She's mine," he spat. "Nobody gets her but me."

Nate's hand tightened on Greg's shirt. "If anything happens to Emily this summer, I'll kill you," he said evenly.

"Nate."

The quiet voice cut through the red haze in Nate's brain. He slowly swung his gaze and saw the sheriff's badge swim into view. Then he saw the shirt and the body and the man the badge belonged to. He released Greg.

"Hey, Dad," Nate said softly.

Chapter 7

Present Day

I used the drive to my parents' house on Piney Ridge Road to compose myself. I hadn't expected she'd be so, well, so *Emily.* Her oval face, dark auburn hair, and those big green eyes—nothing had changed. When I picked her up for that hug in the office, I swear I felt like a kid again.

I chose not to dwell on the fact she evaded my comment in the parking lot. I was pushing her, probably. After all, she just arrived. How would she know how I felt? I should play it cool for a while and not expect too much from her.

How did I feel? Hell, I wasn't sure. Stunned, surprised, overwhelmed, horny. I shook my head in exasperation. Damn. Emily always did get me hot and bothered. And what was the deal with Cynthia? I drove my truck on autopilot, wondering why Emily was so peeved Cynthia had called her "ma'am." It was standard police procedure to be polite to everyone, using "ma'am" and "sir." I needed to explain it to Emily the first chance I got. It wasn't anything personal with Cynthia.

I pulled into the driveway behind her and was out of the truck in a flash, opening Emily's door as she gathered up her purse. "Come on," I said with a grand gesture. "Meet the folks."

She hopped out of the Bug. "I know the folks, remember?"

"Emily?" I heard Mom call from the house.

"Be prepared," I warned.

We both turned as Mom came out onto the back stoop, peering at the driveway shaded by the tall oak tree. "Emily Sutherland, is that you?"

"Natalie?" Emily raced across the yard and took Mom in her arms. I smiled at the sight. Mom's hair was curly, but it was white now and she was shorter than Emily, but not by much. "Natalie," Emily said, her voice thick with emotion. "I've come back."

"Oh, baby, it's so good to see you. Sam, get out here!" Mom commanded over her shoulder. "Oh, sugar, it's so nice to have you home again."

"Is that our girl?" Dad demanded, coming out onto the stoop.

Dad's thick, curly hair was completely white now and he was wearing glasses, but I'll bet Emily still saw Sheriff Boltz from her youth. "Oh, Sheriff, it's so good to see you," she said, moving from Mom to Dad's embrace. "How are you?"

"I'm good, child. How are you?" Dad hugged her tightly, lifting her slightly off the ground, just like I did.

"I'm fine." Emily swiped at tears. "It's so good to see you two." She looked at me where I stood on the bottom step, watching them. "I didn't know I missed you until I saw you again."

"That's how it goes sometimes," Dad said. "Come inside here and let's talk. We've got catching up to do." He put a heavy hand on Emily's shoulder.

I realized with a pang that he needed her support.

Emily covered his gnarled hand with hers. I felt a rush of affection that made my eyes teary as I watched them all together.

The feeling of homecoming was reinforced over supper. It was, indeed, like old times as we talked and laughed over the meal, getting caught up on all that had happened in our lives. When it finished, Dad said, "I'll bet you're beat with all your traveling. Nate, why don't you take Emily over and help her get settled? We'll see you both for coffee in the morning, okay?"

"Sure." I got up from the table.

Emily started to protest. "Let me help clean up."

Natalie shooed us away. "I've got a dishwasher now. Nothing to it. You kids go on. I put a few things in the fridge so you wouldn't starve. We'll see you tomorrow."

Emily and I went out the back door. "Kids," she said.

I grinned. "Yeah, we're still just the kids to them." We went to the rental Bug and I pulled out Emily's small suitcase, garment bag, and briefcase. "Lead the way." I nodded toward the garage.

Emily darted up the exterior stairs covered by the dark green awning which matched the shutters. When she got to the door at the top, she paused. "It's unlocked," I said. "Mom said she'd leave the key inside."

Emily opened the door and turned on the overhead light. "Oh, Nate. It's so much the same." The furniture was different, of course. Now there were overstuffed chairs and a big couch. But it was still just one big space for the kitchen and living room with a small hall leading to the bathroom and the bedroom. The kitchen was a series of cabinets and appliances against one wall and a kitchen island that could be used for prep work or for eating.

I walked past her to the bedroom and set the bags on the double bed. Emily followed. “It’s still the same, Nate,” she said, looking around at the high-ceilinged room.

“Sort of,” I agreed.

“Where do you live now?”

“I have a place outside of town. It’s small, but it suits me.” I felt awkward in the bedroom with her, so I started to amble toward the kitchen. Emily followed, looking around. I saw her memories of the place reflected in her face.

“It’s like coming home.” She pulled open the fridge door then held it wider, showing me the stuffed interior. “A few things. You want a beer? Can you stay? Talk for a bit?”

“Sure.” I grinned like an idiot, glad she wanted me to hang around. Emily got me a beer then poured herself a glass of wine from the bottle in the fridge. “I told Mom what kind of wine you liked.”

She smiled gratefully. “Thanks. Beer always makes me belch.”

“I remember.” I led the way to the lumpy flowered couch.

“I don’t know if it’s okay that I don’t have secrets from the law.”

I sat at the other end of the couch from her, my arm across the back. “No secrets,” I agreed.

Emily sipped her wine. “She’s got a huge crush on you, you know.”

It took me a second to process her words. I was so

happy to be sitting there, relaxing with Emily that they didn't make sense. "Huh?"

"The policewoman."

My face got hot. "I knew she acts a bit odd around me but I try to ignore it. She'll get over it."

"Nothing says you and she can't—" Emily wiggled her eyebrows.

I shook my head and picked at the label of my beer. "Nah. I don't think so."

"How come?"

I took a swallow of beer. "Well, besides the whole professional problem and sexual harassment, I just don't have much interest anymore. I guess I'm getting old." I checked out her reaction covertly, darting a quick glance her way.

She waved a hand. "Oh, it's just hormones. I'm the queen of hormones. I'm back on the pill because of hormones. Once you get close to her, it might change."

"Nah. She's not my type."

"Your type?" She was teasing me now. "What's your type?"

I opened my mouth to speak when a cell phone rang. "Sorry." Emily grabbed her purse and found the phone, staring at the tiny screen. "I don't usually have it set to ring, but I'm trying to close my deal." She pressed a few buttons and the phone shut off.

"If you need to take the call, it's okay." It seemed like the polite thing to say.

"No, it's just Jonas." She put the phone on the coffee table and sat down, tucking her feet under her and turning to face me. "I can call him back later."

"Is he your type?" I blurted. Whoa. Where did that come from? I ducked my head, not wanting her to see my flustered look.

Emily regarded the question seriously. “He wants to be,” she finally admitted. “And he’s a lot of things I like in a man: he’s handsome, well-educated, cultured.” She took a sip of wine. “But I don’t think he’s my type. We spent the morning together today, Nate, and it was the oddest thing.”

I took a shaky swallow of beer. “What was?”

“I flew to Chicago and rented a car for the drive up here. He met me at the airport. I thought maybe we’d have breakfast and do some sightseeing. But we went to his company and spent the morning going over his books.” She made a face. “I wanted to see the cows. You know the ones I mean? Those painted cows all over downtown Chicago? He looked at me like I was crazy when I suggested it. I wanted to go on a cow hunt and he reminded me he’s not a frivolous person.”

“Reminded you?” The guy sounded like a jerk. A rich jerk, maybe, but a jerk.

Emily sipped some more wine. “He already informed me he doesn’t like to spend time on frivolous things.” She shook her head, looking confused. Then she shot me a wicked smile. “Enough about me. We were talking about you and the policewoman who’s got her eye on you. So what’s holding you back?”

I shrugged. “Like I said. Not my type.” I glanced at her sort of sideways.

She grinned. “I remember that look. You’re trying to figure out how to say something tricky.”

Damn. Emily always could read me like a book. I decided to take the dive into the deep end. “She’s not short and she doesn’t have green eyes and her name isn’t Emily.”

She paused while lifting her wine glass. “Nate?”

“I guess that’s my type.”

Emily stood abruptly and went to the fridge. I followed her and when she tried to turn away, I blocked the only way out of the small space. “Emily. I don’t want to scare you or anything. But I want to talk to you about this. This is something I think we need to consider.” I took the wine glass out of her hand and set it on the counter. Then I put my hands on her waist and lifted her to the counter to sit. “Don’t we?”

“I’m not sure.”

“Don’t we need to at least consider it?” I leaned toward her.

She looked up, her eyes like dark green pools of mystery. I saw when it changed for her. Her pupils got bigger and she relaxed slightly. “Maybe,” she murmured, opening her legs slightly. “I guess I didn’t think you’d—I guess I didn’t think I—”

I suddenly remembered another time in the same kitchen, thirty-some years earlier. I had Emily on the counter and we did it right there. Lord, we had sex just about everywhere in the apartment. My heart hammered in my chest so hard it felt like it would bounce out.

I snuggled in close to her, putting my arms around her waist and pulling her closer. “Emily, you’re my type.” I bent my head and our lips met.

I wasn’t sure what I expected, but I hadn’t expected this feeling of *rightness*. Her arms tightened around me. I was suddenly spiraling into passion with a speed that made me dizzy. My entire body ignited and I felt Emily’s warmth, too, as she pulled me closer. When I moaned, Emily pulled away from the kiss and looked at me.

I smoothed her hair back. “You’re so sweet, Emily. You’re so sexy and—” I bent to her again.

She pulled me close, her breasts pressed against my chest. I’m sure she felt my erection, pressing into her warm center. After a long, breathless, hot moment, she started to pull away. “Nate, we can’t,” she murmured.

“Why not?” I kissed her throat. “We’re adults. We’re both single. Why not?”

“I need to think.” She pushed at me. “I didn’t plan on a passionate interlude with the man who took my virginity lo, those many years ago.” She laughed shakily and for a split second I saw fear in her eyes.

I released her but leaned forward, my hands on the counter so I was staring into her face. I figured it was time to come clean about my feelings. “I care for you. I always have. I want you. But I won’t do anything you don’t want to do.” Unspoken but lying between us was the memory of the near-rape she endured so many years before.

Emily ran a hand down my arm and I shuddered at the contact. “I need to think about all this, Nate. I don’t know what I’m feeling.”

I pulled her to me in a gentle hug. “Surprise?” I asked.

She laughed. “Yes. And flattered.”

I ran a hand down her denim-clad leg and felt a sense of homecoming again. Her face, her voice, her eyes, her touch—they were all so familiar and so erotic but they were new after all this time. I pushed away from the counter and I saw her eyes drift to my jeans. I grinned. “Yeah, you still have that effect on me.”

She slid off the counter. “I guess you don’t have to worry about any hormone problems.”

"No, as long as you're in the vicinity, I don't."

We both heard the cell phone ringing. Emily smiled apologetically. "I'd better get it. I'm close to closing the deal." She grabbed the phone from the coffee table and put it to her ear, walking toward the bedroom. I knew she was happy for the interruption.

I was half-glad myself. I wandered away, my trembling hands jammed into my pockets. If she ever did go to bed with me I'd probably go off like a Roman candle before we even got undressed. It was a long time since I was so aroused. She always had that effect on me, though. My mind shot back to the time we first slept together. Then there was the time when we did it against the door. And the time—

I jerked my thoughts away from those memories as Emily walked back into the room, phone pressed to her ear. "Of course I have you on speed dial, Jonas," she said with a small laugh. "No, I'm not alone, a friend is here."

Friend? I raised an eyebrow and Emily shook her head at me. "An old, very special friend." I perked up at that description. "No, you can't." She listened intently. "Of course. Okay, thanks. Good night, Jonas."

Did her voice linger on his name? It sounded sort of caressing. She folded up the phone. "He just wanted to chat." Emily set the phone on the end table and walked back to the kitchen to pick up her wine glass.

"So, what's a guy got to do to get in your speed dial?" I asked casually.

"I have everything in speed dial. I can't remember a phone number to save my life."

I was relieved. Maybe the guy wasn't special after all. "So you're selling your business?"

"Yep. I figured it was time. I don't seem to enjoy it as much as I used to." She frowned. "Nate, about us."

I didn't want to talk about it. I didn't want to see the confusion and uncertainty on her face. "Don't. I didn't mean to upset you."

"I'm only here for a week." Emily looked around the apartment. "It must just be the memories." She laughed but it sounded fake. "Surely you can't be still thinking about me after all these years."

"Don't worry about it. Please. I didn't mean to upset you." I crossed the room to the chair where I tossed my jacket.

"I'm sorry. I'm just a bit confused."

"That's okay. I want to go out to the resort with you tomorrow morning before the others get here, okay?" I tried to hide the anger I was feeling, but I'm not sure I succeeded. What did I expect? Hearts and flowers? Love and kisses? Geez, I was such a sap.

"Sure. But I need to go for a walk in the morning. I try to get a walk in when I travel if I can't get to the gym. Would you mind waiting?" She was looking anxiously at me.

"Okay. I'll come at seven-thirty or so. We can walk then go out to the resort."

That seemed to ease her mind. "A walk would be good. Thanks. You don't have to go with me unless you want to."

I shrugged. "It's okay."

"Okay." She crossed the room as I opened the outside door. "Nate?"

I turned back to look at her. She came forward and put her arms around my waist. I automatically enfolded her in a hug, resting my chin on her head. "It's good to be back."

I savored the feel of her in my arms before releasing her. "It's good to have you here." I rubbed my thumb against her check then I dashed down the stairs. "See you tomorrow."

I left before I screwed it up even more.

Chapter 8

Thirty-Four Years Earlier

Sam Boltz handled it with his usual calm efficiency. As soon as Nate unhanded Greg Hoffman, Charlie Madison, Sam's deputy, hustled Greg into a corner and pushed him into a chair. Sheriff Boltz chatted with the other patrons of the bar and got their version. "I heard him, Sheriff," old Mark Taft babbled. "He was talking about forcing a girl. You should lock him up. There ain't no morals anymore in this country."

Sam nodded sympathetically, took notes in the little pad he always carried, and walked over to the corner where Greg Hoffman glowered at him. "You haven't done anything wrong. But I'm putting you on notice. The men in this bar heard you make threats against a girl." Sam pulled out his notepad. "Miss Sutherland. If anything unpleasant happens to Miss Sutherland this summer, I'll know who to talk to.

"Who, your son?" Greg's gaze shifted to Nate, who sat at the bar, ostentatiously turned away from Greg's corner. "He's after her too, you know."

Sam raised one eyebrow. "I like to think I raised Nate right. I'm pretty sure he wouldn't bother a girl who didn't welcome his attentions. But just to be on the safe side, maybe I'll talk to this girl and make sure."

Greg's jaw sagged and across the room Nate

stiffened. Mike patted his shoulder sympathetically. "This has nothing to do with her," Greg sputtered.

Sam cleared his throat. "This has everything to do with her. Why don't you go back to the resort and get some sleep? Did you drive into town?"

"My car's outside. I can drive."

"No, you can't." Sam gestured to Charlie. "Have Desmond meet you out at the resort. You drive Mr. Hoffman back in his car." Sam Boltz turned away from the Summer Boy and walked over to his son.

"If he hurts her, Dad, I don't know what I'll do," Nate said as soon as Sam got close.

"If he hurts her, I wouldn't blame you." Sam nodded to Clancy, the bartender, who moved down to the other end of the bar to give Sam and his son some privacy. Mike took the hint and drifted away. "But I do need to talk to her, Nate. I'm sorry, but I want her to be on her guard against this guy."

Nate nodded miserably. "I know, Dad." He ran a hand through his hair. "Dad, Emily's special. Really special. She's a nice kid. An innocent kid."

"Was he right?" Sam asked, glancing over his shoulder as Greg was escorted out of the bar. "A virgin?"

Nate flushed red to the roots of his hair. "I think so. Hell, yeah, I'm pretty sure of it," he said in a low voice.

"For some men, it's a powerful aphrodisiac." He met Nate's eyes in the mirror over the bar. "It's a big responsibility for a man, to show a woman how to make love."

Nate nodded dumbly, his face red with embarrassment.

"Seems to me that guy's just looking to collect a

trophy. Doesn't seem like he cares much about her." Sam looked at the mirror over the bar and marveled at the young man his son had become. Once again the responsibility he always felt for raising another person awed him. "A man shouldn't do that with a girl unless he cares for her." Sam cleared his throat. "That's how it was with your mom and me."

Nate blushed even redder than before. Sam struggled not to smile at his son's consternation. "All I'm saying is for you to keep an eye on the girl. She could be in trouble by the time the summer's over."

Nate nodded. "I will."

"And I will chat with her tomorrow," Sam said. "As discreetly as I can so as not to embarrass her." *Or you*, he thought.

"Okay, Dad. Thanks." Nate stood up and held out a hand and Sam shook it, as always bemused his son had grown so much they couldn't hug anymore. Sam nodded to the other men in the bar and went out the back door to the Impala parked there. He made a mental note to talk to Natalie about tonight's little episode.

Their son had found himself a serious girlfriend. At least, that's how it looked to Sam Boltz. He grinned at the dark Michigan night.

It was about damn time.

****

Emily looked down at the scrawled note and tried to swallow around the panicked lump in her throat. "Why does the sheriff want to talk to me?"

Esther, her roommate who took the message, shrugged indifferently. "Don't know. Some woman called and said the sheriff wanted to talk to you. He knew you worked the eleven to six so you're to come in this morning before going to work." Esther was a tall, cool, black girl with corn-rowed hair. She was on the desk for the six p.m. to midnight and had a boyfriend in town. Emily didn't usually see much of her.

"Always good to deal with the man upfront, honey," Esther said from the vast depths of her twenty-year-old, Detroit-laden knowledge base. "Go see him, confess, and get it over with."

"I didn't do anything," Emily said.

Esther shrugged, a knowing gleam in her dark brown eyes. In contrast, Emily felt like a hick farm girl with freckles and pigtails. *Probably because I am a hick farm girl with freckles and pigtails*, Emily thought with despair as she went to the bike rack and grabbed the battered three-speed she was assigned for the summer.

She pedaled slowly through the grounds then along the tree-lined road to town. The sheriff's office was in the Law Enforcement Center near the courthouse. Emily locked her bike on the rack outside and meandered up the steps to the heavy oak door. She pushed it open and peeked inside. No one was behind the reception desk/counter. She considered turning around and fleeing but a head poked up from behind the counter. "Can I help you?"

It was a black woman in her mid-twenties with a short Afro cut. She was plump and pretty, in a homey, earthy sort of way. "I guess so," Emily said. "Somebody called and said I was supposed to come down here."

"That was me," the woman said. "You must be Emily Sutherland." Her dark eyes swept Emily from the tip of her pigtailed head, past the golf shirt with resort logo, to the shorts then to the point of her Keds sneakers. "Uh-huh," she said with satisfaction. "You must be Emily. You just have a seat, girl, I'll see if Sheriff Boltz can see you."

Emily felt punched in the gut. "Boltz?" she gulped. "Boltz?"

The black woman nodded. "Uh-huh. Nate's daddy." She bustled through a door behind her and Emily heard voices rumbling from an office there.

Emily looked around wildly. Was there a law or something about kissing a sheriff's son? Where was the harm in it? Although she privately admitted in her secret heart of hearts, if it led to more than kisses she for one wouldn't mind because she thought Nate Boltz was the sexiest boy she'd ever known and she was willing for him to do *whatever* It was that girls did with boys.

She thought sometimes she was ready to bust with wanting to know about It. She picked Nate as the boy who was going to show her. But now here she was and his father was probably going to arrest her.

"You can come in, Miss Sutherland." The black lady ushered Emily behind the counter, down a hall, and through a door before Emily could draw a breath to protest.

Emily stopped in the doorway and stared at the big man behind the big desk. The lady put a hand in the small of Emily's back and gave her a gentle push. "Miss Sutherland, Sheriff."

The man looked up and Emily saw Nate's eyes in an otherwise strange face. Then the man smiled and a rush of relief went through her. *This is Nate's dad*, she thought. *He's not going to arrest me.* Like Nate, the sheriff was husky with black hair cut in short waves on his head and intense gray eyes. Emily, accustomed to big men in her family, felt comforted by the sight of him. She stepped forward and held out her hand. "Hi, I'm Emily."

The black woman raised an eyebrow at the sheriff, who nodded. "Thanks, Dorothy. You can close the door now." He engulfed Emily's hand in his and gestured to a chair.

"Uh-huh," the black woman said with a last look over her shoulder. She closed the door as Emily sat on edge of the chair, her knees together and her spine straight the way her father had taught her.

"Is there something wrong?" she asked, glad her voice didn't reflect her anxiety.

The sheriff regarded her, his craggy face serious. "Miss Sutherland, I've asked you to come here because a threat was made against you."

Emily leaned back, her jaw sagging open in disbelief. "A threat? What kind?"

"I'd rather not go into the details." The sheriff seemed to be considering what to say. "But your ex-boyfriend, Greg Hoffman, was heard talking about you in a bar last night."

Emily sat up straight. "Oh, Greg. He's such a bunch of hot air. I broke up with him and he's just pissed off." She covered her mouth. "I mean, mad." Her ears flared red with embarrassment.

The sheriff looked like he was trying not to smile. "Miss Sutherland, please be aware Mr. Hoffman is indeed 'pissed off.' Several men, including my son, heard him make nasty comments about you."

"Nate was there? Did he, like, yell at Greg?" Emily chewed on a fingernail. "Nate's already rescued me from Greg and Greg was so mad. Oh, that's bad."

"What do you mean Nate's already rescued you from Greg?"

"In the dining room. Greg grabbed my—" Emily blushed so red it hurt. "Under my skirt," she whispered, leaning forward. "And Nate managed to get him away from me. Greg will be so mad at Nate because Greg hates Townies." She flushed again. "I mean, kids who live in town."

"I know who Townies are, Miss Sutherland," Nate's father said.

"Call me Emily, please. I'm dating your son. You may as well call me by my first name."

The sheriff sat back in his chair and looked at her. "Really?"

Emily scooted back in the chair and relaxed, her feet barely touching the floor. "He's all hung up on this Townie/summer kid thing. But I think it's silly. I want to date him. So I'm going to."

The sheriff regarded her with wary amusement. "You are?"

"Is that okay?" *Oh, damn*, she thought. *What if he thinks I'm wrong for Nate?*

"It doesn't matter what I think. It's just that Nate has always avoided the Summer Kids. And I can see why. At the end of the summer, there's often heartbreak."

"Well, maybe we'd defy the odds." Emily swung her feet, looking around the office with unabashed curiosity. "I mean, heck, Michigan isn't so far from Minnesota. We can visit and write letters and call each other. I'm not going to be cheated out of a love affair just because of worries about the future." Her eyes opened wide. “I mean, a relationship,” she amended. “Cheated out of a relationship, I meant.”

He looked down at the papers on his desk. It looked like he might be smiling, but she wasn’t sure. “I just want you to know you should avoid Greg Hoffman as much as possible,” he said.

“I’ll be careful.” Emily bounded to her feet and offered her hand.

“Good.” He stood and smiled at her, suddenly looking so much like Nate that Emily blinked in surprise. “I’ll look forward to seeing more of you this summer.” Then he winked.

The bike ride back to the resort flew by. Compared to the dread she felt riding in, this was euphoria. When she pulled into the resort, the first person she saw was Nate, on his way to one of the cottages. “Nate!”

He paused and glowered at her. She faltered as she brought the bike to a halt near him. “I’m sorry, are you mad at me for talking with your dad?”

“What?” He looked down at her and shifted his plumbing tools from one hand to another. “Yes,” he said sullenly. “No,” he finally admitted. “Sort of.”

“I’m sorry,” she said. “He said he wanted to talk to me.”

“Look,” Nate said, staring at the ground. “I’m a Townie. You shouldn’t hang out with me.”

Emily raised her chin. “I’ll hang out with who I want to.” She jerked her bike around and started to stomp off toward the back of the main building to store her bike. She wasn’t aware Nate was following her until he jumped in front of her and she almost ran him down. “Get out of my way.” She felt the first quiver of her lip and she clamped down on her emotions savagely.

"Emily, please." Nate put a hand on her bike handle to prevent her from moving.

"What?" She jerked the handlebar as a tear wound its way down her cheek.

"Aw, geez, don't cry. I can't stand it when girls cry."

"I'm not crying. I got something in my eyes."

"If you say so," Nate said doubtfully. "Did my dad talk to you about Greg?"

She nodded. "We had a long conversation."

"Well, you need to be careful."

"Thanks for that little piece of advice." She swiped at the tear trickling slowly down her cheek. "Now let me by."

"You're just so—" Nate stopped. "You're so cute and Greg is liable to—"

Emily rolled her eyes heavenward. "I can't help it if I have big boobs and a small waist and pretty hair and nice teeth. And I refuse to apologize. Now let me go." She stomped past him, almost tangling with the bike but managing to right it before she humiliated herself completely.

She was still upset when she went on duty. Luckily Mr. Goldman wasn't at the front desk. He was fat and old and he loved schmoozing with the guests. He always smelled like sauerkraut and cigars and he leered at her or tried to cop a feel. Emily had become adept at dodging his pudgy little hands.

Today, though, he was gone to Chicago. His son, Bobby, was at the desk when Emily came on duty. She liked Bobby. He was in his late twenties, a plain, studious looking man with a sweet smile marred by a weak chin. He was only a few inches taller than Emily, which she secretly liked. Almost *everybody* was taller than Emily.

"Keeping an eye on things, Bobby?" Emily asked as she pulled over her bar stool and accepted the cash register from Pauline, the morning desk clerk. Emily always either sat on a bar stool behind the desk or used a stepstool so she could see over the high counter.

"With you, I know we're in good hands," Bobby said. "You girls are the best."

Pauline glowed with the compliment. She was a big girl with straight blonde hair and a voluptuous figure. Her boyfriend was a beach lifeguard and he usually took the morning shift so he and Pauline could spend the afternoons and evenings together. Emily sighed. *There would be hot times in the old dorm tonight*, she thought resentfully. *Hot times for everybody but me*.

"Trouble, honey?" Bobby asked sympathetically.

"Oh, just boy trouble." Emily shrugged.

Bobby laughed. "Your biggest problem must be choosing which boy to date."

Emily looked at him gratefully. "That's sweet, Bobby. Thanks."

He nodded. "I mean it, Emily. You're the prettiest girl here." She made a disparaging noise. "I mean it. There may be others who are more, well, more striking? But you're sweet, honey." He patted her on the shoulder in a brotherly way and Emily suddenly missed the roughhouse antics of her own brothers. "Sweet counts a lot when it comes to beauty." His face changed slightly and Emily thought she saw the shadow of something in his pale brown eyes, as though an old pain had flared up. Then it was gone and he was his old self again. “You’re a real asset for the hotel. Give us one of those smiles, okay?” he coaxed.

Emily looked up as two guests walked into the lobby and she gave them one of “those” smiles as they approached the desk to buy postcards. “Thanks, Bobby.”

He patted her shoulder again and Emily settled down to the business of dealing with guests and trying to figure out how to seduce Nate Boltz.

Chapter 9

Present Day

I drove to my house four miles away on the north side of town. Hell, the town was so small everything was only few miles away. J. Edgar, the tabby cat who sauntered into my back yard and adopted me five years earlier, greeted me at the door between my kitchen and the attached garage. I got him settled with his cat food before I opened a beer then dropped onto the sofa to stare at the dark television set.

What did you think would happen, you idiot? Did you think Emily would fall into your arms and tell you how she's missed you?

She looked so surprised and confused. How could she still be so sexy and sweet? It didn't make sense. It had been thirty-four years. How could she still be somebody I wanted? For a minute there I thought she wanted me. She put her arms around me and drew me closer. Maybe there was a chance.

Then I remembered her puzzled look.

Shit.

J. Edgar wandered in and plopped down on the couch next to me, cleaning his face with his paw and breathing tuna fumes into my face. "What do you think, cat?" I mumbled. "Did I blow it?"

He peered up at me, considered the question then

got into a yoga pose to clean his privates. It was answer enough for me. I finished the beer and tossed the can on the battered old coffee table. Emily had Mr. Jonas Hawthorne in Chicago waiting for her. She had her condo in the city and her business she was selling for a tidy little profit. A hick small-town cop wasn't needed in her life.

I opened another beer.

****

On Saturday morning I dragged on a pair of worn jeans and a blue shirt then zipped on a gray hoodie with *Little Bay Police Department* stenciled on the front. I knocked on the apartment door at seven-thirty sharp.

Emily opened the door, gesturing me inside. "Hey," she said, yawning.

I stepped inside and almost passed out when I saw her shuffle to the kitchen, wearing a long flannel shirt and apparently nothing else.

"I didn't sleep so good. I'm moving a bit slow." She yawned again.

"That's okay." I stood rooted to the spot. "No rush."

"Good." Emily glanced at me and must have seen my look. She twitched her shirt to show me boxer shorts hidden by the tails. "Pretty sexy, huh?"

"You bet." She was showing a lot of smooth leg. I swallowed hard. "Could I have some coffee?"

"Oh, I'm sorry." She got a mug and poured me coffee then added a dollop of milk and swirled it around then handed it to me. "I'll get dressed. How cold is it outside?"

I looked at the mug. She remembered how I liked my coffee. "Crisp. Light jacket."

"Okay. Be right back."

She started singing as she walked to the bedroom. It took a second, but I finally recognized "Cry Baby." I grinned. Emily always did like Janis in the morning. I made a mental note to bring over a boom box. We always had music playing in the old days.

I sipped coffee and looked around. We used to spend most Wednesday evenings in this apartment. It had a lot of memories, most of them good. Then I suddenly remembered the incident with the slashed bed. It was never solved. Dad investigated but never found out who did it.

After Emily left the resort that summer, I went back to college then on to pro football. I didn't come back to the apartment because the folks were renting it out. Maybe that explained why the memories were so strong. I hadn't been here for so long and now she was here, too.

Emily's cell phone, sitting on the end table, rang. "Your phone's ringing," I called.

"Answer it, would you?"

I picked it up warily. "Emily's phone."

There was a long silence on the other end. "Emily Sutherland?" It was a man's voice, deep and strong.

"She's busy at the moment. Can I tell her who called?"

"This is Jonas Hawthorne. Can you get her to the phone? I think she'll want to talk with me." The voice was arrogant and self-assured. I immediately disliked the guy.

"She's busy." I heard Emily in the bedroom, blasting out "After the Gold Rush" in a wavering falsetto.

"Who is this?" Hawthorne demanded.

None of your damn business, I thought. "Nate Boltz. I'm Chief of Police in Little Bay."

"My God, is something wrong? Is Emily all right?"

The guy sounded genuinely worried. It was a point in his favor, but I still didn't like him. "Emily and I are old friends."

"Oh." There was another long pause. "You're the person she went to see."

I smiled. Hawthorne sounded concerned. "Yes. I am."

"Who is it?" Emily stood in the bedroom doorway, pulling on a "Rust Never Sleeps" sweatshirt over a plain white T-shirt. I watched regretfully as her full breasts were hidden behind a Neil Young guitar logo. She wore pale blue jeans and red Keds sneakers and her hair was still tousled and fluffy looking.

"Hawthorne." I held out the phone.

Emily took it. "Jonas?" I wasn't sure if her voice was happy or wary. "Is there a problem?" She meandered to the coffeepot. I followed, trying not to look interested. "Not at all." She glanced at me. "We're going for a walk. It's so pretty here in the morning. I'm on vacation, remember, Jonas?"

There was a long pause as she listened. Emily raised an eyebrow. "Had I known," she said lightly. "Maybe tomorrow." She listened some more. "Thanks, Jonas." She closed the phone then put it in its charger on the kitchen counter before joining me at the coffeepot. "Early morning business."

"Sure." I put my mug on the counter. "Ready to enjoy our pretty little town in the morning?"

"Are you making fun of me, boy?"

"Never." I led the way out of the apartment and said, "Don't forget to lock up."

Emily shrugged. "Is it necessary?"

I sighed. "This may be a small town but we do have crime. And since I'm the Chief of Police, I try to set a good example."

Emily went back into the apartment and came back with the key Mom had left on the kitchen counter. She locked the apartment door and followed me down the steps. "Is your mom expecting us for breakfast?"

"No. I told her we were going out. I'll call her later."

"Okay." We moved out to the sidewalk and I let Emily set the pace with her shorter legs. We had gone a block when another walking couple approached us from the opposite direction. "That's Pastor and Mrs. Roberts," I commented. I looked down at Emily. Her cheeks were pink and she was looking around the tree-lined street at the houses, most of them with Halloween decorations.

As we neared the other couple, Pastor beamed at me. "Chief," he said in acknowledgement.

I nodded. "Reverend. Mrs. Roberts."

"Emily." The minister nodded to her.

Emily's head snapped around and she nodded back. "Hello." After they moved past, she asked me, "Do I know them?"

"Probably not."

"How do they know me?"

I picked up the pace and she had to work to keep up. "Oh, not many secrets in a small town." I nodded to Mrs. Patterson, who was outside watering her azaleas. She watched us with interest, her gaze zeroing in on

Emily.

We proceeded on. “This really is a nice place,” Emily said, starting to puff slightly. I was clipping along. She scowled at my long legs eating up sidewalk while her shorter legs scurried to keep up. “I guess I never noticed much when I was a kid.”

“I don’t think we notice stuff like that until we’re older. What about where you live?” I smiled at Mrs. Johnson, who stood in her yard, watching us. She appeared to be bringing in the morning paper, but obviously Emily and I were far more intriguing.

Emily hurried to catch up with me. “I really don’t like it in the city. I guess there aren’t any small towns anymore within driving distance of a metropolitan area. They’ve all become part of cookie-cutter suburbs.”

“I can imagine. You’ve got to come to a place like this to find a small town.”

“Hmm.” We moved on to Main Street, where only the café, hardware store, and coffee shop were open so early in the morning. As we walked down the wide sidewalk I nodded a greeting to several people.

“I guess you’re pretty well known in town,” Emily puffed as yet another person greeted the “Chief.”

“I grew up here. And I’ve lived here except for stints in New York and Miami.”

“Miss Sutherland?”

Emily paused and looked at the woman standing in the door of the coffee shop. “Yes?”

“You’re Nate’s friend? Staying at the sheriff’s apartment?”

“Yes, ma’am.”

“Nice to meet you. Natalie and I are such friends.” The lady stuck out a hand. “Christie Beamer.”

"Nice to meet you."

The old lady regarded me. "Nathaniel."

"Mrs. Beamer. If you'll excuse us, we're taking a morning walk."

"So I see. Say hello to your mom for me."

"Will do." I nudged Emily and we proceeded down the sidewalk.

"Am I to assume many people know I'm back in town?" she asked as we walked through the remaining two blocks of downtown and turned south toward the pier in the distance.

"Oh, probably. Between Mom and Dorothy, I suspect quite a few folks know. Any problem with that?"

"Nope. I don't believe it, but I'm hot." She started to pull off her sweatshirt but her T-shirt got tangled. I obligingly put my hands on her waist to hold down the T-shirt while Emily tugged at the sweatshirt. She looked a lot pinker in the face when she got done. "Thanks." She tied the arms of the sweatshirt around her waist and let it flap over her butt.

"My pleasure." Her nipples were pressed against the T-shirt. My word, she did bounce. She had them reined in but they still flowed. I enjoyed the sight of her bounce. "Enjoying your walk?"

"We're setting a quick pace," she said grumpily.

"I can go slower."

"No, it's okay." We walked past a couple of bars and the video store and soon were on the boardwalk that traced a path along the lake. "I need to work out," she said as we went up the stairs to the boardwalk. "I can't afford to gain any more weight."

"You look good, Emily." I watched her ass twitch

in her tight jeans as she mounted the steps ahead of me. “Really good.”

She made a dismissive noise. “For my age.”

“For any age.”

She slanted me a suspicious look. “Really?” She started walking down the boardwalk without waiting for an answer.

“Really.”

“What about little Miss Perky?”

“Who?”

“Your policewoman.”

Miss Perky? I grinned at the description of Cynthia. It was apt. She did have a perky look about her with her dark blonde hair and cheerful disposition. “She’s not *my* policewoman.”

“She’d like to be,” Emily shot back. Her T-shirt was sticking to her shoulders and upper back. There was a stiff, cool breeze blowing off the lake, though, which had an effect on her nipples. My fingers twitched to touch her.

“Wish I could,” I muttered.

“Could what?” Emily demanded, turning. I bumped into her and felt the brush of those soft breasts against my arm. I jumped back. “Could have little Miss Perky?”

“What?” The feeling of Emily’s body had successfully fogged my brain.

“I asked you if you’d like to have Miss Perky for your own and you said ‘wish I could.’” She continued down the boardwalk, stomping loudly.

“That’s not what I meant. I was thinking about something else.”

“Oh, sure.”

"Emily, come on. I told you last night, I'm not interested in Cynthia Bartlett."

"She looks fit. I suppose you and she work out in the police training room." She shot me a glance. I tried to look innocent. "You do," she accused.

"Yeah, she's been there when I'm working out."

"I'll bet she'd like to work you out," she fumed.

Emily was working herself into a snit, which I found interesting. *Thank you, Cynthia. You may not realize it, but you might have given me the lever I need.* "She's not my type, I told you." I paced Emily easily, my long legs eating up the distance. "Besides, it wouldn't be professional."

"Ha!" She pounced on it like a duck on a June bug. "That's a lame excuse. You would like to jump her."

"Emily?"

"What?" She was glowing with anger. Her breasts were bouncing and her ass was twitching and her green eyes were spitting fire.

I never saw a more beautiful woman in my life. "Your headlights are on," I said bluntly. "They're on bright."

"What?" she demanded.

"Your headlights."

"My..." Emily looked down at her chest and blushed so red it looked painful. "Oh, for heaven's sake. They're just tits, Nate." She put on a slight burst of speed.

I hurried to keep pace with her. "Those aren't 'just tits,' Emily. Believe me."

She scowled. "I don't think it's very appropriate that we be talking about my tits."

The scruffy looking guy ahead of us turned and I

saw who it was. “Hey there, Chief,” he said, grinning broadly.

“Porter, how are you today?” I asked as we came abreast of him.

Emily slowed, watching Porter scatter popcorn to birds on the sand below him. He watched us with his usual toothless grin. Emily smiled tentatively at him.

“I’m fine, Chief. Is this your girlfriend, Miss Emily Sutherland?”

“For Heaven’s sake, does everybody know my name?” Emily muttered.

Porter bobbed his head and grinned. The scar still shone whitely on his tanned dome after all these years, barely covered by his thinning blond hair. “Oh, yeah. We know how you and the Chief was in love years ago and how you’ve come back to town to visit him.” Porter’s watery blue eyes regarded Emily with approval. “It’s so romantic. So good to see love conquer all.”

She opened her mouth, closed it then opened it again, obviously to correct him.

“You’re right, Porter,” I said gently. Emily, alerted to something in my voice, closed her mouth. “It’s very nice, isn’t it? I’m sorry. I forgot to introduce you. Emily, this is Porter Graves. Porter, this is Emily Sutherland.”

“Pleased to know you.” He nodded his head vigorously. “She’s real pretty, Chief.”

“She is.” I nudged Emily. “We’ve got to go, Porter. You have a good day.”

“It was nice to meet you, Miss Emily,” he said, holding out a grimy hand. “Mrs. Sheriff told me about you. She’s such a nice lady. Even though she does dress funny," he added.

Emily gamely shook the hand. "And a pleasure for me, too. Have a good day."

We continued down the boardwalk. As soon as we were out of earshot, she hissed, "What the hell was that all about?"

"He's harmless. He's been bugging me for a week about your visit. He's got it in his head you came back here to, um, pick up our relationship."

"And who gave him that idea?"

I glanced down at her. Her headlights were still on. Damn. "Porter's not quite right in the head, in case you didn't notice. He and I went to school together. He caddied at the golf course in the summer. One day he got hit in the head with a golf club and almost died. He hasn't been the same since."

"That's awful. Couldn't they do anything?"

"It happened the summer you and I were together. There wasn't much they to do. I guess he saw us then and he's fixated on it. He doesn't have much short-term memory anymore but his long-term memory is hell on earth."

"So who gave him the idea I've come back here to renew our relationship?" she asked as we descended to the beach again.

"I had my hopes." I spied Max's Donut Cart in the distance with the small beach nearby. It was just the spot for us to sit down and hash out our future.

I hoped.

Chapter 10

Thirty-Four Years Earlier

It took a picnic on the beach, flowers, and a lot of cajoling, but Nate convinced Emily to forgive him, even though he wasn't sure what he needed forgiveness for. Their days took on a cream-like quality, full of work, a movie or a walk, then an hour or two of heavy petting and half-naked bodies entwined in passion.

One night, as usual, Nate waited for Emily on the front porch at the resort but she didn't come out. He poked his head inside and didn't see her at the desk in the main lobby. They'd been dating for almost three weeks and she was always prompt, finishing her work by six if not earlier so he didn't have to wait long. He came in to the front desk in the resort lobby and asked Esther, the night girl, "Where's Emily?"

"She got a note and said she had to leave early, so I started a few minutes earlier than usual." Esther was a big black girl, tall and statuesque. Rumor had it she and Tom Judson were dating. Tom had a reputation in town for fast cars, booze, and gambling. Esther looked like she could handle him just fine.

Nate's stomach clenched so hard it hurt. "Who sent the note?"

Esther looked into the wastebasket. "I saw Emily throw it way. Here," she said, unfolding a scrap of pink

While You Were Out paper. She shoved the paper across the desk to Nate. "Is everything okay? Farm Girl isn't in trouble, is she?"

Nate scanned the message. *Sheriff Boltz needs to see you immediately. Nate is hurt.*

"I don't know." Nate crumpled the paper, tossing it back on the desk. He raced out of the lobby, going to the kitchen where he hoped Emily was waiting for him. The cooks all shrugged when Nate said her name. Then he grabbed one of the waitresses and asked about Greg.

"He's sick tonight," she said. "Some kind of stomach flu. Can't wait tables."

Nate raced past the girl's dorms but Emily wasn't there. He stopped, struggling to think. The beach was too exposed and far away, so Greg wouldn't take her there. Nate whirled and raced toward the far side of the property and the abandoned old cottages that were no longer rented. Four of them stood behind a row of trees, two used for storage and the others empty. As Nate neared the side of the last cottage, he heard voices. He walked around to the back, which faced heavy shrubs and the access road. He stopped so suddenly he almost tipped over.

Greg had Emily pushed against the wall, his hand covering her mouth. Her blouse was pulled up and her bra was torn with her breasts exposed. Her panties dangled on one leg and as Nate watched, he saw Greg's hand clamp onto her pubis then go back to his shorts.

Emily struggled but she looked as if she was moving in slow motion, her arms weakly trying to push him away although her eyes wide and terror-filled. Two of Greg's friends sat on the ground nearby, watching. One had his arm around Peggy McBride, his hand down her shirt and fondling her breast. The other had Peggy's skirt pulled up and his hand down her panties. They were all watching Emily struggle with the detached appearance of onlookers at a play.

Nate took just a minute to fix the scene in his head. Then he waded in, fists flying. Greg stumbled, releasing Emily. She screamed so loudly Nate thought she might rupture something. One of the guys leveled a kick at Nate he barely dodged. Greg was teetering, his shorts tangled around his legs. The other guy landed a punch on the side of Nate's shoulder that sent him spinning. In the melee Peggy vanished then Greg got organized and grabbed Nate by the shoulder, jerking him around and taking aim.

Nate took the shot on his face and for a minute he saw stars. When his vision cleared, he saw Emily beating at one guy on the ground, landing a few blows but mostly missing. The other guy lunged for Nate just as Greg took aim again.

"I don't think so," a deep male voice said.

Greg's arm jerked back suddenly. An enormous black man with a huge Afro had materialized out of the heavy shrubbery behind the cottage. Nate fended off the other guy easily, decking him with a right to the jaw. Greg was kneeling on the ground, his arm pulled up behind him by the black man, who looked at Nate.

"Tom Judson," he said in a low, rumbling voice. "I'm a friend of Esther's. I just dropped her off for work. She came running out and said you might be needing help." He glanced at Emily. "You can let him be, now, honey."

Emily let up in her pummeling and stared, her eyes huge in her face. Then she flushed a painful red and dragged her shirt down. She got shakily to her feet. "You son of a bitch!" She aimed a kick at Greg but got tangled with her panties. With a muttered curse, she pulled them off, her face red as a beet.

Tom glanced at Nate. "You're the sheriff's boy, right?"

Nate nodded and felt gingerly at the bruise on the side of his face.

"Nate!" Emily flew to him, putting her arms around him and burying her face in his chest. He hugged her fiercely.

Judson looked down at Greg. "We can turn him over to the law." He twisted Greg's arm slightly. Greg winced and knelt even further, head bowed low, trying to get away from the pain. "Or I can handle them." His dark brown eyes met Nate's in a long, assessing stare. "She's a friend of Esther's. I take care of friends."

"Yeah," Nate said slowly. "I see you do." He looked down at Emily, sobbing on his shirt. Then he looked at Greg. A Summer Kid. "I'll check with Dad and let you know."

Emily straightened. "Shouldn't we just call the police?"

He looked again at Tom Judson, who jerked Greg upright. "It'll be fine. Let's you and me go to town." He nodded once to Judson, who nodded gravely in return. "We'll talk to Dad."

****

Natalie Boltz and Busby the basset hound greeted them at the door at Nate's parents' house. Natalie took one look at Emily's bedraggled state and bustled the girl into the kitchen for tea (*with just touch of brandy, but don't tell my husband*), and cookies. Busby snuffled at Emily's legs then flopped onto her feet with a big sigh.

Emily was astonished at this first sight of Nate's mom, who was a full-fledged, honest to God, hippie from the top of her frizzy, curling hair to the tie-dyed linen dress and love beads, to the handmade sandals. This was the first hippie Emily had ever met *and* she was the mother of the guy Emily wanted to sleep with. Wow. What a summer.

Nate disappeared to make phone calls and a short time later his father walked in the back door. "I was so stupid," Emily said, nibbling on a cookie. "Greg grabbed me outside of the dorms when I went to get my purse." She wiped her face with the napkin. "He put something on my face that smelled bad. When I came to, he had me at the cottage."

The sheriff picked up her napkin and sniffed. "Chloroform, maybe. Or some kind of glue. A light dose. Lucky for you Tom Judson was there." He glanced at Nate. "You should have called me right away, though."

Nate shrugged. "Probably. But it seemed best to get Emily out of there."

"No offense, Sheriff, but I bet Greg gets more justice from Tom Judson than from a legal system that favors rich white kids, especially those who work for Old Man Goldman and the resort that brings in so much summer money." Emily smiled at the sheriff and Nate's mom to take the sting out of her words. "And if I tried to take him to court it would be my word against his and since I was wearing a mini-skirt, people would say I deserve it." She glanced at Nate as she said it and was gratified to see him look ashamed. "Women's lib hasn't come *that* far, Sheriff."

"I can't believe it," Natalie said, wooden bracelets jangling on her wrists as she sat at the table, holding Emily's hand. "I can't believe it. Evil boy. His karmic debt must be huge."

Karmic debt? Emily looked at Nate. He just shrugged. "My brothers are going to kick the piss out of him," Emily said sleepily, the brandy and excitement catching up to her. "I'm going to call Silas *and* Dan. I don't dare call Ben. He's working in Maine this summer and knowing him, he'd hitchhike across the country if he found out about."

"What's he doing in Maine, dear?" Natalie asked, her voice so soothing and calm.

"He's working on a fishing boat. It's his Summer of Real Life."

"His what?" the sheriff asked, leaning against the counter and watching.

"Daddy wants all of us to have a well-rounded education. So he insists we do at least one summer job with some kind of meaning." Emily yawned and settled her head against Nate's shoulder. "One year I worked with welfare mothers helping them to learn to read and write better. And one year I worked in a canning factory." She made a face. "That sucked big hose, I can tell you."

There was a startled silence in the room. "That was my Summer of Real Life." Emily yawned. "When Silas did his Summer of Real Life he worked in a coal mine. Which is why he's in robotics now." She saw the blank looks on the faces around her. "If there were robots to help the miners, maybe they wouldn't have accidents. Silas was in a cave-in." She shuddered. "He's okay, but man, he said it sucked big hose."

"I wondered where you heard the expression," Nate murmured.

"I'm going to write to my brothers. I don't want Daddy to know about this, he worries so much. But Silas will know what to do. I'll write to him."

"Why don't you let me do it?" Sam suggested. "Give me his address and I'll send him a letter. It might be good for him to hear the facts from me."

"I'll write to him, too. But I'll wait until after you write him. Otherwise he'll just come out here loaded for bear. Silas is tough."

Sam nodded. "You give me his address and we'll keep your family informed about this. We'll see you're kept safe."

Emily smiled at Nate. "I know I will be." She yawned.

"Honey, you're sleeping on your feet. Let's get you upstairs," Natalie said.

"Oh, ma'am, I shouldn't impose. I can sleep at the resort. I won't have nightmares." Emily wondered if they heard the doubt in her voice.

Natalie made a shushing noise. "Since Nate moved out we've got lots of room. I'll put you in his old room." Natalie helped Emily to her feet and put an arm around the girl's shoulders, leading her from the room. Busby padded after them, toenails clicking on the wood floor.

"Nate's room?" Emily asked groggily. "I'm going to sleep with Nate?"

"No, honey, you can't sleep with Nate in this house," Natalie said gently. "His father would have heart failure. But you can sleep in Nate's room." She waited until they were out of hearing before saying, “Of course, you can sleep with him in his apartment over the garage and we won’t say a thing. That’s part of the deal we made with Nate when we gave it to him.”

“Rats,” Emily said as they started up the stairs. “I wanted to sleep with Nate.” She lowered her voice. “I’m still a virgin. I want Nate to be, you know, I want him to be the one.”

Natalie nodded. “I see.” She maneuvered Emily up the stairs and down the hall. “I think he’s a good choice, honey.”

“Can you give me some advice?”

“I’m sure your mother gave you advice.” Natalie pushed Emily gently to the side of the bed and unbuttoned her blouse. Busby watched this exercise with curiosity then he went to the rug near the bed to settle down.

“Mommy died when I was little.” Emily obediently raised and lowered her arms. “Daddy tries, but you know how embarrassed men get whenever you want to talk about sex.”

Natalie sighed. “Yes, I do. All right, honey, what kind of advice do you need?” She nudged Emily and Emily lifted up so Natalie could tug down her shorts. Natalie pulled out one of Nate’s old T-shirts from a dresser and got it on Emily.

“What do I do, Mrs. Boltz?” Emily asked, her fears tumbling out. “I don’t want Nate to be disappointed in me.”

Natalie smoothed back Emily’s hair. “Honey, you just do what feels right. Have you and Nate tried anything yet?” Emily blushed and nodded. “How did it feel?”

"Fabulous," Emily breathed.

"You just tell him what you want. If you want it hard, you tell him. If you want it tender, you tell him. If you want to be on top, you—" She must have seen the startled look on Emily's face. "Oh, yeah, honey, sometimes it's fun to ride the stallion."

Emily reddened but leaned forward to catch every word. Natalie continued. "I'll tell you, sugar, the first time you climb up and ride him he's going to shoot around the moon."

"What do I do when I have my period?" Emily asked as Natalie gently nudged her into the sheets of the twin bed.

"You snuggle. You touch each other. You can keep him occupied."

"Really?" Emily suddenly remembered Peggy. "It looked nasty when they were doing it with Peggy." She swallowed hard. "One of the boys made her suck his—you know, his thing—and the other boy was touching her. I saw it while Greg was touching me." Emily swallowed hard again, her stomach lurching.

Natalie grabbed Emily's head between her hands and peered deep into her eyes. "It wasn't love. It was just screwing. Do you understand?"

Emily nodded mutely.

"Screwing is okay in its place, but don't you ever confuse it with love." Natalie kissed Emily gently on the cheek, rubbing her back softly. "You rest now, honey." She left the room, leaving the door open slightly.

Natalie went downstairs and found Nate and Sam in the kitchen, each holding a beer. "Pop me one of those, would you, honey?" she asked Sam.

He got into the fridge and pulled her out a Schlitz. She took a long swig and belched. "'Suck big hose' indeed," she snorted.

Sam caught Nate's eye and laughed. Nate finally joined in. "She's so damn innocent," he said, running a hand through his curly hair. "I just want to grab her and hold on and not let her find out how nasty the world can be."

Natalie raised an eyebrow. "She has her eye on you. For...you know."

Nate blushed red. "Man, why'd she talk to you about it?"

Natalie shrugged. "She doesn't have a mama. She wanted advice."

Nate regarded his mother suspiciously. "What'd you tell her?"

"I told her to tell you what she wants and you'd provide." Natalie smiled at Sam.

He winked at her. "Works for us. For almost twenty-five years."

"And it'll work for fifty or more." Natalie looked at Nate. "You go say good night, but keep your hands outside the sheet and no deep kissing."

"Aw, Ma," he protested as he pushed away from the table.

"I'm serious, Nathaniel," she called after him as he dashed out of the room. "She's a sweet girl, Sam. There's no doubt about it?"

Sam shook his head. "Nope. I believe Nate. Greg Hoffman was going to rape her and have his friends do it too."

Natalie shivered. "There's a special hell reserved for people like him. I hope she'll be okay for the rest of the summer."

"I plan to make sure of it," Sam said grimly. "Nobody messes with girls on my watch and gets away with it. If I can, I'll see to it that charges are brought." He took a long sip of beer. "And if not, Greg Hoffman is a marked man for the rest of the summer."

Chapter 11

Present Day

"I don't mean to be grumpy, Nate, but I didn't sleep well last night." Emily slogged through the deep sand at the end of the boardwalk. "That phone call bugged me and when I finally fell asleep, I kept waking up, expecting you to be there."

"What phone call?" I led the way to Max's concession stand at the entrance to the pier. "Want a cup of coffee?"

"Sure. I can use a rest."

"You set a mean pace," I said.

"Your legs are too damn long." She shot me a sidelong glare.

"They work for me. You got a good workout this morning."

We went to the concession stand and I ordered while Emily peered at the beach. "Two coffees, Max. One with one cream and one with one cream and one sugar."

"Sure, Chief." Max busied himself with the coffee urn while staring at Emily. He was lucky he didn't end up with third-degree burns. "Is that your girlfriend who's come back to town?"

I sighed and dug money out of my jeans pocket. "She's an old friend."

"Not what I heard," Max said. "From what I hear, you two were deep in love years ago. I hear it was tragedy you've been separated all this time."

"Just rumors, Max," I muttered.

Emily pressed against me. "Got my coffee?" she asked in a pretty little voice. "Oh, Nate. You remember how I like my coffee. How sweet." She beamed a big smile at Max. "Hi. I'm Emily." She looked significantly at me. "I'm with Nate. I mean—the Chief."

Max glowed right back at her. "Hi there, Emily. I'm Max." He stuck a hand over the counter and she shook it. "Heard you might be moving to town here."

Emily sighed, giving me a soulful look. "I'm not sure. We'll see."

I thrust the paper cup of coffee at her. "See you later, Max." I nodded toward Lake Michigan. "Let's walk out on the pier."

"See you, Chief. And you too, Emily," Max called after us.

"See you, Max," Emily called back.

"Cute," I grumbled. "It'll be all over town in an hour."

"Hell, Nate, it already is all over town." Emily chuckled. "I just added some fuel to the rumor."

"Damn it, I have to live here after you go back to Jonas Hawthorne and your city life."

Emily sniffed. "I told you there's nothing between me and Jonas."

"Oh, so he's like me? Just some guy hanging around who you're not sure what to do with? Just a spare guy?"

Emily didn't answer as we walked to a bench near the end of the pier. She handed me her coffee to hold while she tugged on her sweatshirt before sitting.

"Well?" I demanded.

She ran her fingers through her hair and sipped the strong coffee, regarding the waves on the lake. "I told you last night. I don't know what I feel about all of this." She paused then added, "No, that's bullshit. I'm worried. That's one thing I feel. I'm only supposed to stay here for a week. I don't want to get re-involved with you and then go away. I couldn't stand—"

The heartbreak, I thought. *I can't stand to lose you again.* I nodded. "Yeah, I know how you feel. I've thought of that."

Emily regarded the waves thoughtfully then turned her head slowly to look at me. "I don't need to return in a week, though."

I was paralyzed with surprise. She hurried on with talking. "I have an open-ended plane ticket out of Chicago. I can go back any time."

"Oh." I blew out a long breath. "I mean, great. You don't have to make any big commitments here, Emily. You can just give it a try and see what happens."

She nodded, looking down at the beige coffee in her cup. "Remember I told you I didn't feel like I connected with Jonas?"

I nodded.

"I still feel a connection to you."

She met my gaze and I knew I was lying to myself and to her. There was no way to back out of this. This was going to be all or nothing. And damn it, I wanted it all. "What are you saying, Emily?" I asked hoarsely.

"I'm saying I want to see what happens, Nate."

I raised my cup and it trembled a bit. "I know what I want to have happen." I was feeling more self-assured now we were actually talking about it instead of dancing around the topic.

"It's been a long time since I've been interested in a man. And a long time since a man has shown interest in me. Let me take it slow, okay?"

I almost groaned. "Not too slow, okay? I am getting older by the minute."

She laughed softly. "That makes two of us."

I gently cupped her cheek in my palm. "Hell, Max is probably watching and Porter's watching and Mrs. Andronetti is putting out her laundry on the porch of her apartment up above Morton's Tavern so she can watch us."

Emily blinked. "Quite an audience."

"And I don't give a damn. You're so beautiful." I kissed her and she returned it, gently and sweetly, a kiss full of promises and dreams.

When we finished, she said breathlessly, "What did I do to deserve a guy like you?"

"I guess we both just got lucky." I put my arm around her and she snuggled against me, nestled against my warmth. We sipped our coffee and looked at the waves, both of us lost in thought.

I suddenly remembered her earlier words. "What phone call?"

"Hmm?" Her voice was dreamy. I wondered what she was thinking about. If it was anything like my daydreams...

"You said you got a phone call that bugged you?"

"Last night. I was so surprised. The Princess phone on the end table rang." She grinned. "I wonder how many of them are still in operation."

"You know Mom, she's the original recycler. If it

works, she won't replace it."

Emily nodded. "Anyway, I picked it up and somebody said something like, 'Let sleeping whores lie. Otherwise you and your old boyfriend might find trouble.'"

I shifted to look down at her in amazement. "What?"

"Yeah. It was a man's voice, sort of low. Before I said anything, he hung up." Her eyes met mine. "Remember? It was like the note I got years ago." She shook her head in bemusement. "Why would someone try to threaten us, Nate? You're a cop. And besides, who knew I was here?"

I considered it. The phone was a landline, which meant somebody knew the phone number at the apartment. Who knew Emily was here? More to the point, why would anyone care?

"I figured it was probably kids, doing some kind of prank," she said with a shrug.

I didn't disagree, but it bothered me. Although it was great to have Emily back again, this was still a murder investigation. Even though I hadn't found anything concrete yet, it didn't mean we wouldn't find something when all the Summer Kids started arriving. "Yeah. Probably a prank."

We stayed like that until the cold air drove us back, walking through town hand in hand. When we got to the apartment Emily went inside to shower while I went to see my folks. As soon as I entered the back door and came into the kitchen, Mom said, "Looks like you and Emily are getting along fine."

I poured myself a cup of coffee from the pot under the Mr. Coffee on the counter. "I suppose Max called you and told you we were out walking."

Dad rustled his newspaper and snorted. "Pastor called and mentioned it." He peered at me around the sports section. "Seems to me you and Emily always did get along fine. Question is whether she'll stick around long enough for you to work up the courage to propose marriage."

Mom laughed. I took a scalding sip of coffee. "Let's not jump the gun," I said when I could finally speak around the pain. "She's only been in town a day." I set down the mug and regarded my father. "She got a phone call last night at the apartment."

Mom put down the dish she was drying. "How did anyone know she was there?"

I told them what the caller said. My father and I exchanged a look. "Interesting wording," Dad said.

"Yep. Just like before." I knew the unfinished business from thirty-four years ago still bothered him. "Maybe we'll have a chance to tie up some loose ends."

"All kinds of loose ends you might be able to tie up," Mom said with a knowing look. Before I could reply, she went on. "I like Emily's new hairstyle. Her hair used to be so long and she always had it in a braid or a ponytail." Mom shook her own curly head of white hair. She used to have long hair, finally getting it cut when she was in her fifties. "Why bother having all the hair if you always shove it away from your face? I like her new style." Then she grinned. "Probably not new, really, just new to us."

"She hasn't changed much." Dad folded his paper and set it aside to regard me with his dark gray eyes, so like my own. "Should be an interesting week."

I looked out the kitchen window. "Looks like my

date is ready. Talk to you later." I put the coffee mug in the sink and gave my mom a tickle before escaping out the back door. My parents might be in their seventies, but they were both too sharp for comfort.

"You ready?" I called out as Emily walked out to the drive from the apartment stairway.

"Yeah. But I'm going to need a ladder to get into this monster," Emily said, looking at my dark blue pickup.

I went to the passenger door and opened it for her then I lifted her to the running board, both hands around her waist. "You'd better not gain any more weight," I said with exaggerated pain. "I don't think I can lift you if you do."

"If you'd get a civilized set of wheels, it wouldn't be an issue," she snapped.

I swung up behind the steering wheel and grinned at her. "Just teasing." I leaned over for a quick kiss.

"You'd better be." Emily waved to Natalie, who waved in return then turned her attention to my truck. "I thought cops drove Crown Vics?"

"I can if I want to. I like my truck, though. Besides, if I drove a squad, you'd have to sit in the back."

"Fat chance. So who's coming to this shindig? When are they coming?"

"Most folks are coming this afternoon. We'll meet them at the bar downtown." I pulled a list out of my shirt pocket and handed it to her.

"Oh, Pauline is coming. And Esther. And Harv. I wonder if Harv and Pauline have stayed in touch."

"I suspect they have," I said. "They're married."

"Wow. A summer romance that lasted."

Like us, Harv and Pauline met at the resort. They

both attended Michigan State so it was easy for them to stay connected. I wondered briefly if I was making excuses for my failure to stay in touch with Emily but I pushed the thought away.

"And David and Greg. Looks like a good number of the group. What about the cooks? Herves, Emilio and Sergio and the crew?"

I shook my head. "Nobody had addresses for them. Don't know where they are."

"They might not have noticed anyway. They didn't hang out with us."

When we were nearly outside of town, I mentioned casually, "There's my place." Emily swiveled on the seat to look as we drove by my house with the small porch in front and smaller one in back. "Maybe you can come by sometime this week while you're in town."

"I'd like that." Emily looked back at the house. "It's got a nice yard. How long have you lived there?"

"Ten years or so. It's small but it suits me."

"My condo is small. I envy you your yard. I wish I had a garden."

"Not in the summer when it's hot and you've got to mow and weed."

"Maybe." She resumed examining the list. "It's a good turnout. I'm surprised so many folks want to come."

I drove up to the resort gates. "Bobby said he'd meet us here." I pulled into the open front gate and came to a halt in the turnaround in front of the main building. Emily opened her door and flailed around for the running board with one foot before I plucked her out and put her on the ground.

"Thanks. Wow. It's hardly changed."

The main building was as I remembered it, a white rectangular six-storied structure with wide front steps and big picture windows looking out on the long front porch. In the distance Lake Michigan glimmered in the morning light. "Just a few more coats of paint. And new steps."

"Those old ones were so rickety." She paused on the bottom step and looked up at the front door. "You always waited for me on this step after work at night. Then we got dinner and walked home."

Home. The word seemed to vibrate in the air between us. She looked at me over her shoulder and our eyes met and held. *That's what it was*, I thought. *It was home*.

The front door opened and Bobby Goldman came onto the porch. He was still small, slender, and dapper, with pale brown hair and eyes. "Emily Sutherland," he said warmly. "I never thought I'd see you again. Our summer kids so seldom come back."

"I'm surprised you remember me, Bobby." Emily moved up the steps to stand with him on the porch.

He gently hugged her, pressing his cheek to hers. I was surprised. The old Bobby wasn't given to affectionate demonstrations. Of course, with the father he had, it was no wonder. Old Mr. Goldman was mean and probably didn't tolerate affection.

"Of course I remember you." Bobby regarded Emily, his hands still on her shoulders as he looked into her eyes. "You were the prettiest desk clerk we ever had."

"That's hard to believe," Emily said lightly. She looked away from Bobby and took in the facade of the building. "It hasn't changed, has it?"

Bobby released her and followed her gaze. “No, not really. Except for upgrades on the inside.” He glanced at me. “Some you recommended years ago.”

I nodded. “Mostly common sense kind of things, as I recall.”

“Did you guys want to come in or just walk around the grounds?” Bobby asked.

Emily looked inquiringly at me. “I was thinking just the grounds,” I said. “The rest of the group is coming into town tonight and tomorrow.”

Bobby said, “Sure. I’m not slated to leave town until next week anyway.” He looked at Emily as we all walked down the steps. “I go to South Carolina in the winter.”

“I thought your family lived in Chicago in the off-season.”

Bobby made a face as we walked slowly along the front drive. “I decided to buy a house somewhere warmer. Well, you two know your way around here. You don’t need me.” His pale brown eyes seemed to twinkle at us. “Stay as long as you want and close up the gate when you’re done. Just be careful of the construction guys out on the north side, they’re working today. We need to get as much done as we can before the weather turns.”

“Thanks, Bobby,” I said, holding out a hand. After a brief hesitation, he gave it a shake then turned to Emily, who also held out her hand.

“I meant what I said. You were the nicest desk clerk we ever had.” He squeezed her hand and released it.

“Thanks.” We watched as Bobby got into the Porsche sports car parked near our truck. I glanced down at Emily. “Want to take a walk down memory lane?”

She smiled. “Sure, I’m game.”

We spent an hour, meandering around the ground and getting caught up on our pasts. Emily had been running her employment agency since her divorce fifteen years earlier. I told her about my years in football, my job with the Miami-Dade police department then my move back to Little Bay.

“I put in five years in Miami and then four years in Chicago before an opening came available in Little Bay. I worked in the department for eight years before getting the police chief’s job three years ago.” I paused as we approached the truck. “I like it here. I feel like I can make a difference here. I never felt that in Miami.”

“It’s your home, Nate.” She looked around the old resort. “I had a great summer here. Because of you. Despite everything that happened—and almost happened to me—it was a summer of love and happiness. I’ve never felt anything like it, before or since.”

I knew what she meant. “I know. It was almost magic, wasn’t it?”

Our eyes met and held. I knew what she was thinking. It *had* been magic, a very special kind. The magic of love. Then she took my arm. “Let’s go to town and give the gossips something to talk about.”

I left my truck at the station and we walked to Cora’s Cove, the one restaurant in town. Cora made sure we were seated front and center. I spent most of lunch fielding greetings, nods, and raised eyebrows. Emily finally leaned over to whisper, “I think everyone is watching us, Chief.”

I frowned. “Yeah. This might not have been such a good idea.”

“I think it was an excellent idea.”

“You do?”

“Sure. It adds to the whole ‘love lost’ image. You’ll have girls falling out of the woodwork after I’m gone, anxious to mend your broken heart.”

I touched her hand. “I’d rather you stay in town and mend my broken heart.”

She looked into my eyes. “I think I might like that. We’ll have to see.”

When we left the restaurant, I said regretfully, “I really need to go to the office and see to a couple of things.”

“What time did the others say they were arriving?”

“Mid-afternoon.” I glanced at my watch. “About now. I told folks to gather over at Tommy’s, the bar downtown. Remember?”

“Sure do. I think I’ll take a walk then I’ll head over to Tommy’s.”

We paused at the intersection where I would walk west to the police station and Emily would go east, to the beach. “I’ll see you later, then.” I felt suddenly awkward. She squeezed my hand. I think she wanted to hug me but we both felt the impact of watching eyes. I whispered, “It’s tough under a magnifying glass like this.”

She nodded. “Yeah.”

“I’ll see you later.” I squeezed her hand then released it. I started walking toward the police station, two blocks away. I wondered how she was feeling about all the scrutiny we were getting. I wondered if she would consider making a life in Little Bay,

Michigan. Her family was all gone from the Twin Cities and scattered around the country. She was selling her business. I'm sure she had a lot of friends there, but it wasn't so far away. They could visit her or she could visit them.

I paused at the end of the block and looked back. Emily was leaning on the boardwalk and staring at Lake Michigan's gray depths, hands jammed into her jacket pockets. As I watched, Porter Graves came running across the beach and darted onto the boardwalk, running forward to pluck anxiously at Emily's sleeve.

She jerked and pulled away. I hesitated, not sure if she would be bothered by him. Porter was harmless but he got excited now and again. I looked to the right, where the boardwalk joined with the sidewalk behind the business backing onto the lake. A man and woman were just coming on to the boardwalk. Emily wouldn't see them because she had her back to them, dealing with Porter who was dancing with impatience and gesturing urgently.

I recognized the man coming up behind Emily. I started to hurry back to her when I saw him grip her arm and whisper something in her ear.

Chapter 12

Thirty-Four Years Earlier

Nate drove Emily to work the next day after his mom gave her a good breakfast "to get her going." Nate's dad told them he made sure Emily got a day off, so at least she had a day to try to put the nightmare behind her.

As they came onto the grounds, Nate spied Greg near the boy's dorm with a black eye, moving slowly. *Some consolation,* he thought. *The bastard should have trouble*. Greg shot him a murderous look and continued toward the beach with his Summer Kid friends.

Esther came out to greet them when they got to the girl's dorm. "Heard that preppy boy got his butt kicked," she drawled as Emily came into the common room the girls all shared.

"Not as bad as I'd like." Nate grinned. "Tom Judson's a good man to know."

Esther laughed. "He's a good man, for sure. And I know why they call him 'big,' too." She winked and disappeared into her room in the dorm.

Emily looked from Nate to the now empty doorway. "Was that Tom Judson last night?"

Nate nodded. "I'm glad he's on our side. Tom doesn't always operate on the legal side of the law."

Emily's eyes got huge. "Wow. A gangster?"

"Sort of. He might be a good guy to know in case we need some backup again."

"I'm glad Greg got what he deserved. I'm not going to let him ruin my summer." She turned to Nate and put her arms around his neck. "Especially now I've found you."

Nate hugged her. "You should rest. And I have to go to work."

Emily pouted. "What good's a day off if I can't spend it with my guy?"

Nate leaned down to kiss her and she pulled back hesitantly, then she raised her face to his. "Try to forget about it, Emily," he whispered, pulling her to him.

"I trust you, Nate. I know it's not like that."

Nate heard the tears in her voice. "I'll make sure it's right for you if it's what you want."

She pulled away and looked up at him. Her green eyes glistened with tears. "I do want it. But maybe not right now."

"No problem. I told you, it's all up to you." He gently disentangled himself from her arms. "Gotta go. Meet me at the porch tonight?"

She nodded. "See you there."

Nate caught a glimpse of Emily twice during the day, once with Esther going to the beach and once in the gazebo, curled up and reading a book. She looked like she was relaxing, which was probably the best thing for her. His stomach knotted every time he thought about what might have happened if things had worked out differently.

As soon as he knocked off work for the day he went to the porch to meet her. Nate was just going into the main lobby when Greg passed in front of the porch, heading for the kitchen.

"Hey, Townie."

"Yeah?" Nate asked warily.

"Did you fuck her yet?" Greg asked.

Nate took two long strides to the edge of the porch and would have jumped down the stairs, but Bobby Goldman stepped out onto the porch. Nate restrained himself with difficulty. "That's really not your concern, is it, Greg?"

Greg looked first at Nate then at Bobby. "Just thought I'd let you know," Greg said. "If she's used, I don't care."

"If that's what it takes to keep you away from her, you go right on thinking it," Bobby said. "Emily's a good kid. She doesn't need you around her."

Nate looked at Bobby gratefully. It didn't hurt to have the son of the owner on your side. Greg glared at Nate then left. "Thanks, Bobby," Nate said.

"I don't get to do much around this damn place, but I can tell off the help now and then." Bobby's lips twisted in a parody of a smile. "I got into it with Dad again. You'd think I'd learn, wouldn't you? The old bastard will never change."

Nate nodded sympathetically. Old Man Goldman's rages were legendary and his fights with Bobby were common knowledge. Bobby wanted to modernize the resort and sink some money into it. Old Man Goldman wouldn't hear of it, insisting on maintaining the resort's so-called old-world charm. Nate had firsthand knowledge of that "charm" because he had to keep most of it running.

Emily came out the front door and Nate went to her. Bobby watched them, smiling. "There's my guy,"

Emily said, taking Nate's arm.

Bobby winked at Nate. "You've got the prettiest girl now, Nate." There was a sad look in his eyes as he regarded them.

"Bobby, you're such a flatterer." Emily tugged on Nate's arm. "Ready for dinner?"

"You bet." They waved over their shoulder to Bobby and headed toward the kitchen.

"Are you okay? Did you have a good day?" Nate asked as they went into the employee entrance at the kitchen and stood in line to get their food.

"I'm better." She looked nervously at the door the waiters used. "I still can't believe he tried to do that. Greg must be crazy."

Old Man Goldman stomped into the kitchen and bore down on them. "You two! You're the ones causing the problems. Because of you, I have to go to town on Monday and talk to the damn sheriff. Your father," he accused Nate. He rounded on Emily. "And because this is your fault, we have to have the stupid meeting at nine in the morning so you can't miss work. Like you do any work anyway," he grumbled.

"I do more work than your other desk clerks combined and you know it." Emily put her hands on her hips and glared at the old man.

"Don't you lip me, girl," he said, glowering at her.

Emily's eyes narrowed. "You and who else will stop me? You don't scare me, I have four brothers and they can dish it out worse than you can."

He stared at her then nodded. "Truce. Be in the sheriff's office at nine. You, too, Boltz." He shot Nate a frown. "Why they want me there is beyond me."

"Will Bobby come, too?" Nate asked, hoping for

an ally.

"Why? What's he got to do with this?" A look of panic twisted the old man's face then the mask of incivility fell back into place. "Yeah, I suppose he'll be there," Goldman grumbled. "Don't be late."

"Yeah, yeah, yeah." Emily waved her hand. "No problem."

The old man muttered something in Yiddish and gestured to the line cooks who were watching the whole show with great interest. They applauded Emily when the old man had left the room and she took a bow.

"Since when do you talk back to the old man?" Nate asked as they got their food and headed for a table.

"Since I decided I was tired of taking his bullshit," Emily said. "I figured I'll fight fire with fire. Esther dishes it out all the time and he just takes it. Pauline ignores him."

"Good policy," Nate agreed.

Emily finished her dinner in record time, shooting anxious look at the waiters' doorway the whole time. Nate followed suit and soon they were leaving.

Herves left his place behind the cook's counter and came to stand next to Emily, gesturing to Emilio, another cook, to come over. They started talking in Spanish while Emily nodded, listening carefully. Then they shook Nate's hand and the other two cooks came over and shook his hand, all in a very serious, ritual-like fashion. When it was done, they gave a polite round of applause then went back to work.

"What was that all about?" Nate asked Emily as they left the building.

"Herves heard about what Greg tried to do. There are no secrets at this resort." Emily's voice trembled then she cleared her throat. “I told them how you and Tom Judson rescued me. They don’t have much respect for a man who tries to rape a woman.”

Nate put a consoling arm around her shoulders. “Nobody has respect for that kind of man. Mainly because it’s not a man, it’s a monster.”

“Emilio said the same thing. Anyway, they wanted to thank you.” She grinned. “Herves said it was too bad you didn’t get the chance to kill him cleanly, but perhaps such an opportunity will arise in the future.”

Nate blinked in surprise. “Uh, okay I guess.” They paused at the top of the steps and looked out at Lake Michigan, shimmering in the sunset.

“Nate?”

“Hmm?” He draped an arm over Emily’s shoulder and she leaned against him.

“I’m not going to let the memory of it bother me.” She spoke with bravado and Nate wondered just how much of it she meant.

He kissed her quickly. “I’ll do everything I can to erase it.”

“Good.”

****

On Monday morning Emily and Nate went into town. Emily waited with Dorothy in the outer office while Nate and his father talked.

“I got some information about Greg Hoffman I thought Mr. Goldman should have,” Sheriff Boltz said to Nate who was seated across his desk. “I wanted you to know about it ahead of time so you don’t lose your cool when we’re in the meeting.”

Nate drew in a steadying break. “Okay. I’m ready for it.”

Sam Boltz touched a paper on his desk. “He was detained for rape once before. He was let go because the girl refused to go through with the charges.”

“Jesus!” Nate sprang to his feet.

“It’s important we put this in the right perspective. He was detained but not held. So, technically, he’s innocent.” Sam held up a hand when Nate would have spoken. “You know and I know there’s a world of difference between true innocence and technical innocence.”

Nate sat down, his hands clenched into fists. “So now what?”

“Emily is still at risk,” Sam said quietly. “I believe so, at least.”

Nate nodded and told him what Greg said on the steps of the main building. Sam shook his head. “A guy like that, he doesn’t let anything get in his way if he wants a woman. And he thinks she belongs to him. You keep an eye on her this summer. I’m going to write to her father, too. Her family deserves to know she might be in danger.”

Nate’s gut clenched. Her father might insist she come home. *But if it keeps her safe, she should do it.* He nodded mutely.

“Okay.” Sam looked satisfied at Nate’s response. “Let’s have this unpleasant little meeting and get it over with.” He raised his voice. “Dorothy?”

His door opened immediately and Dorothy ushered in Emily, Bobby Goldman, and old Mr. Goldman. The old man grabbed one of the chairs and sat down, grumbling. Bobby gestured Emily to the other chair and she sat nervously, looking from Sam to Nate, who leaned against the wall and stared stonily into space.

Bobby took the remaining chair.

Sam summarized the police report he had on Greg. Bobby looked astonished and the old man sputtered and made noises about firing Greg. "The charges were never filed," Sam said, his voice neutral. "I felt it was my duty, in light of what happened the other night, to tell you that Greg has a history."

Mr. Goldman glared at Emily. She glared back. "It's not my fault."

Bobby held up a conciliatory hand. "Of course it isn't. I hope you don't feel you have to leave us, Emily. We'll do everything we can to keep you safe. And I think we can let Greg know we're aware of his past and we'll be keeping an eye on him. It will make him think twice about harming anyone at our resort." He looked at the sheriff.

Nate's father nodded. "I think it's a wise course of action. You don't have grounds to fire him because he doesn't have a criminal history. The charges were dropped." Sam looked at his son. "Nate will do what he can to ensure Emily's safety and it's reassuring that you're aware of the situation and will do what you can, too."

"Not just me," Emily said. "He's a danger to any girl there."

"Good point. But we'll stay vigilant, just in case."

The meeting broke up a few minutes later and Sam walked with Nate and Emily to the door under the watchful eye of Dorothy. "Nate, we need to talk. Emily, why don't you wait over there?" Sam gestured to the reception area.

Emily went reluctantly to stand next to Dorothy. "You kids be careful," Sam said in a low voice to Nate.

"Greg Hoffman is a mean son of a bitch and his family is rich enough to buy him out of trouble."

"I know." Nate looked at Emily. "I'm not going to let him hurt her."

Sam nodded in understanding. "Call me first if you can, but if you have to, do whatever it takes. I'll back you up all the way." He looked at Emily, who regarded them with sharp-eyed concern. "Now go enjoy your summer."

He watched them as they hurried down the hall, Nate with his arm around Emily's shoulder. "Sweet couple," Dorothy said behind him.

Sam nodded. "I'm going to keep it that way."

Chapter 13

Present Day

I knew the man who was accosting Emily. Even from this distance I saw that Greg Hoffman was still tall, blond, and handsome with an athlete's body and tailored Summer Kid clothes. He looked down the boardwalk at the retreating Porter then said something to Emily. She stiffened, her face going pale.

By the time I got to them, Greg was introducing Emily to the woman with him, a leggy brunette who looked bored. The woman shook Emily's hand then turned away, as though uninterested. I saw Greg slip an arm around Emily's waist. She twisted away, her back to me as I approached. Greg whispered something in her ear then his gaze flickered to me.

"My little Townie and I are having dinner," Emily said frostily.

"All night?" Greg asked with a suggestive leer.

"All night," she said firmly. "I'm cooking."

This was an interesting bit of news. I filed it away for later consideration.

"Hello, Nate," Greg said to me.

Emily turned. "I got done with my business faster than I thought." I put a hand on Emily's shoulder and she leaned slightly backward, against me. "How's it going, Greg?" I held out my hand.

Greg shook my hand briskly then looked at the logo on my sweatshirt. "So you're a cop now?"

"He's Chief of Police, Greg," Emily said, using her *gee, what a moron voice.*

His lips tightened but he ignored her. "Do you really think we'll find out what happened to some whore thirty years ago, Nate?"

"Whore?" I looked at Emily, who regarded Greg as though he was a bit of junk washed up on the beach. "Do you speak from personal experience?"

He started to snap back an answer but the woman turned, putting an arm through Greg's. "Shall we do some shopping before the event this evening?" she asked, sparing a glance for Emily and me.

Greg stared at me for a long moment, his blue eyes as cold as the lake behind him. "If you'd like. See you folks at Tommy's." He and the woman walked back the way they'd come. He shot one long assessing gaze at me over his shoulder then he let the woman pull him toward town.

Emily made a rude noise. " '*My wife is going back tomorrow night. Maybe you and I can get together.*' Kiss my ass, Greg."

"I'd love to have dinner with you. But you don't have to cook. I can buy dinner for us someplace." I took a chance. "And if you don't want dinner all night, it's okay."

She groaned. "I'm sorry. I didn't mean to put you on the spot."

"I don't mind. Believe me. And I would love to have dinner all night with you."

She shot me a suspicious glance but I looked out at the lake so she didn't see my face. "I was sort of hoping to see your house." She scuffed her shoe against the boardwalk planking. "Maybe cook dinner. You know how I enjoy cooking."

"I don't have a lot of fancy cooking stuff at my house," I warned.

"Do you have a stockpot, fry pan, and saucepan?"

I nodded, relieved. "Yeah, I have the basics."

"Then I'll swing by the grocery store and get a few things. It'll be fun, Nate." She beamed up at me, the thousand-watt smile I loved.

My cell phone rang, startling us both. "Damn. I'm supposed to be off-duty." I pulled it off my belt and looked at the message on the display.

"Trouble?" she asked worriedly.

"I doubt it." I clicked the Answer button. "Yeah, Dorothy? What's up?" I listened to her summary then said, "Call Bobby, okay? Tell him we're going out there." I ended the call and looked regretfully at Emily. "Porter's acting up again and I'm usually able to calm him down. But I'm supposed to meet the folks coming in for the weekend."

"I can do it, Nate," she volunteered. "What's wrong with Mr. Graves?"

"Porter goes off on these tears sometimes. I end up talking to him for an hour then he calms down and goes home." I didn't mention that Porter sometimes got his hands on a knife and waved it around when he went on a "tear." It happened sometimes. No need to worry her. I started walking back to town.

"The poor man. I just talked to him a while ago. He seemed agitated, but I wasn't sure if it wasn't his normal state."

"What do you mean, agitated?"

"He seemed upset that I..." Emily paused. I thought she might be trying to figure out what to say. "He was upset I was sitting out on the beach alone," she finished. "He thought you should be with me. He kept talking about 'true love' and 'lovers who are betrayed.' " Emily was concentrating so hard on keeping up with me she almost ran me down when I stopped at the top of the steps leading to the sidewalk.

"Sometimes he just gets these ideas." I hoped she would buy my dismissive tone. I was pretty sure that Porter seeing Emily was what set him off, but I wasn't going to make her feel guilty about it.

"I'm sorry he's upset. What do you want me to do with the folks coming in? Do you want me to just talk with people and see what they remember?"

I considered it. "I want each person to write down what they were doing that night and anything else they remember."

"It's a long time ago, Nate," Emily said softly.

"I remember what I was doing." I looked down at her. I remembered every intimate detail.

"Our situation was a different than for some," she said, her cheeks pink.

"Maybe. But the more folks can remember, the better. I'll join you later."

"Okay. I'll see what I can do, Sherlock."

"Thanks, Watson. I knew I could count on you." I grinned. "And remind them we'll go out to the resort tomorrow at ten. Bobby's letting us walk around out there. It might help jog some memories. I have a lunch scheduled for us in the back room over at Cora's Cove, so we can go there after the resort and talk some more."

"You've got it organized, Chief. Now you'd better

go. Poor Porter might really be in trouble this time. He was awfully upset."

"Thanks, Emily. For everything. For coming here and helping and everything."

She stood up on her tiptoes to brush a light kiss across my lips. "Thanks for calling me. You be careful, okay?" Then she walked away down the sidewalk leading to Tommy's. I watched her for a minute to make sure Greg wasn't lurking around then headed to the police station and Porter's latest crisis.

When I got to the station I climbed into the squad car next to Rob Sloan. "Who called it in?" I asked as I buckled my seat belt.

Rob put the car into gear and started toward the highway. "Mrs. Abernathy saw him going by on his bicycle, swearing up a storm." Rob glanced quickly around the intersection then pulled out onto Highway 8 north, using his lights but not the siren. I silently approved. There was no reason to upset Porter any more than necessary. "She saw him head for the resort and called Bobby. He went out, saw Porter going to the beach then called us."

"I wish I knew what sets Porter off," I muttered. "We can go for months at a time and not have any problems then this kind of stuff happens."

"I know. Mrs. Abernathy said he was shouting about summer kids when he went by. You know how hard it is to understand him sometimes."

I looked at the fall foliage as it went by, the golds and reds blending into a kaleidoscope. "Who knows what goes on in Porter's brain?"

Bobby was waiting for us at the front gate of the resort. When I got out I heard the drone of heavy equipment in the distance. “Sorry about this, Bobby.”

Bobby shrugged, his thin shoulders pulling up his expensive sweater. “It’s just Porter.” He led the way across the grounds. “I think he’s at the steps. That’s what it sounds like.”

“At Mitchell’s Cove?”

“Not so far.” Bobby led the way between the swimming pool and the single-unit hotel building and out to the north steps.

I heard Porter now. He was probably in a cleft in the cliffs because his voice flowed up, over the edge of the bluff. I caught snatches of what sounded like conversation.

“They come in and they take our jobs. The old man should make sure we have jobs first then open it up to kids from the area instead of bringing in outsiders.”

Bobby grimaced. “That old complaint.”

Rob looked puzzled and I explained. “There was a time when folks in town thought Bobby’s dad shouldn’t hire summer kids to come in. Folks thought he should make sure all the kids in town had the jobs first instead of hiring out-of-staters.”

“Why did he hire outsiders?” Rob asked as we started down the north steps.

“Cheap labor,” Bobby said. “College kids are willing to take jobs that don’t pay very good just to get out of the house for the summer. Dad always said they were his best asset when it came to running a resort.” Bobby paused at the bottom of the steps. “They still are. I deduct room and board from their wages but I can’t do that for town kids, so I have more expenses with Townies.” He glanced apologetically at me. “Sorry.”

“I don’t mind.” We started down the beach but

Bobby lagged behind. I noticed and said, "You don't have to come with us."

Bobby looked relieved. "I always feel so uncomfortable around Porter. You know, 'there but for the grace of God' and all."

"No problem. We'll check in with you when we're done."

"Thanks, Nate." Bobby turned and headed back to the steps, saying over his shoulders, "See you tomorrow?"

"Yep," I said. "The folks are already starting to arrive."

"What did he mean—'there but for the grace of God,' " Rob asked as we walked down the beach, staying on the hard-packed shingle.

"Bobby was at the country club the day Porter was hurt. I think he feels guilty."

"Why? Was it his fault?"

"No. Porter was just in the wrong place at the wrong time."

"I heard it was a golf club to the head?" Rob slowed his pace as we neared the shouting ahead.

"He stepped into old man Puckett's back swing. I never could figure it. Porter was a caddy. He knew better than that." I looked at Lake Michigan, gray and restless in the afternoon's fading light. "I heard a rumor he was doing drugs and they screwed him up enough to make him forget basic safety." We rounded a pile of rocks and saw Porter, standing on top of a huge mound of boulders, emoting to the lake.

Porter whirled. "It's about fucking time you got here, Nate." He jutted out his chin at me. "I've been talking to Emily for an hour and she won't answer."

I raised an eyebrow and looked out at the lake. "She's sometimes hard of hearing, Porter." I started forward and Rob followed.

Porter glared at the officer. "Keep him back unless you want your business known all over town."

I resisted the urge to laugh. What business? I had lived a monk's life for the past decade. I glanced at Rob. "Wait here. I'll see what bee's in his bonnet today."

Rob nodded. "He looks harmless enough."

"No weapon this time. That's something." I almost missed Rob's startled look as I walked forward. "Hey, Porter," I said, climbing up on the rock pile.

"Don't come closer, Nate," Porter said softly. I saw the big knife in Porter's right hand, out of sight from Rob. It looked like a butcher's knife, with a blade at least six inches long and sharp on both sides.

"Well, shit, Porter," I said, still in my mildest voice. "What's this about?"

"It's about your love life," Porter said in exasperation. The wind off the lake ruffled his thinning blond hair and he looked like a Mr. Potato Head, all round and lumpy in his saggy brown sweater, baggy denims, and battered sneakers. "You have to talk to Emily and make sure she stays in town this time. If she does, we'll all be saved."

I sat on the rock just beneath Porter. "Why do you care if she stays in town?"

Porter's pale, desperate eyes turned on me imploringly. "Because someone has to be happy!" His voice was like a shriek of despair. "My God, don't you realize the people from that summer are all wounded? All of them! If you and she can find some happiness, then maybe we're not all cursed."

I blew out a breath, not quite sure where to start with this. "Porter, why do you think folks are cursed?"

"Oh, Nate." Porter's voice dripped sympathy. "We all lost so much. I lost my brains. Peggy lost her love and her life. You lost Emily. Bobby lost the fights with his daddy." Porter's mournful, sad eyes raked me. "Who's to say whose loss was more tragic?"

Well, I guess Peggy's would be, I thought but didn't say out loud. "Did you know Peggy?" I asked conversationally, flicking bits of rocks toward the lake.

Porter swayed on his perch, the knife wiggling in his grip. "Sure," he said with a wicked grin. "I knew Peggy good."

Trust Porter to remember having sex with Peggy. It verified what I remembered. Peggy had indeed been promiscuous. "Did she tell you who her boyfriend was? Who her steady was?"

"Oh, it was the summer kid, the blond one. He and Peggy were always going at it." He started making little slashes motions with the knife.

I tensed. It was a wicked looking knife. Somebody might get hurt if Porter decided to get crazy. I glanced at Rob, who had inched closer to the pile of rocks. "Porter, why don't you put down the knife?" I stretched out my legs to get a good grip on the rocks below in case I had to jump quickly.

"I need the knife," Porter said, his face serious. "I need to fight evil with it."

Damn. I had heard Porter go into his fight-evil-and-be-a-crime-buster mode twice before. Each time ended badly. "Come on," I said, shifting balance. "Put down the knife and we'll talk about the evil and how we can all fight it."

Porter swung to look at me. For one eerie moment I saw a sane man in those pale eyes. "Don't you understand, Nate?" His voice had none of the usual wavering, frightened quality. "We all died that summer. Peggy wasn't the only one. Maybe it's time to just kill the dead bodies walking around."

What happened next had the feeling of a bad movie in slow motion. Rob had worked his way around behind Porter to climb. I stood, slowly and carefully. Porter lifted the knife and made a series of slashing, strangely formal gestures, which brought the knife perilously close to my arm.

Then Rob tugged on Porter's pants leg. Porter flailed out and started to fall. I lunged forward to grab him and the knife clattered to the rocks. Somehow I was slammed against a big boulder. My leg took the most of the contact but my grip on Porter didn't lessen.

Porter was dead weight in my grip. It took both Rob and me to manhandle him to the beach.

"You okay?" Rob asked, panting slightly from exertion.

I knelt next to Porter. "Yeah, just bruised. What happened with him?"

Rob pulled out his radio. "Looks like he fainted." He spoke quickly into the radio, directing an ambulance to meet us on the resort grounds.

Porter started to stir, hands scrambling weakly in the cold sand of the beach. "Nate?" Porter murmured, his eyes slowly focusing.

"Hey, Porter," I said gently.

"I'm sorry, Nate. I tried to save Emily. I'm sorry he killed her."

My breath stopped. "What?"

"I tried." Porter turned his head away and concentrated on the lake. He was back in his never-never land and I knew he wouldn't come out until he was ready.

We heard the wail of a siren on the bluff above. "What the hell was he talking about this time?" Rob asked.

"I don't know." What I *did* know was I was suddenly anxious to make sure Emily was safe.

We took Porter to the hospital where they would keep him overnight. The doctor looked at my dirty pants and shirt. "How about you?"

"I got banged up some," I admitted.

That was all it took. I was hustled into an examining room and the doctor started tut-tutting over the swelling on my hip. "Nothing to be done for it," he said. "I'll give you a shot to dull the pain. If you're not feeling better by tomorrow come in and we'll x-ray it." He reached into a drawer and pulled out some pills in small packets. "Take two of these and call me in the morning." He grinned. "I've wanted to say that for years."

I went to the station, leaving Rob to deal with Porter's sister, who was called by the hospital to come and formally admit her brother. When I got to the office, I was relieved to see it was quiet except for Bill Pitts, who did four ten-hour shifts a week from six at night to four in the morning. "Porter again?" Bill asked sympathetically, taking in my dirty clothes.

"Yeah. Figured I'd write it up."

I sat down heavily in my office chair. Poor old Porter was really out of it this time. I remembered

Porter's words about "saving Emily." I picked up the phone and dialed the bar, finally talking to Tommy, the owner.

"Oh, yeah, they're here and they're having a great time. Emily, she's got 'em dancing and talking. You should've seen the dance line those ladies got going when Aretha came on the jukebox singing 'Respect.' " Tommy laughed loudly. "We're deep in the psychedelic Sixties." As he said it, "Purple Haze" started to play in the background.

I grinned, remembering how Esther and Emily used to lip synch "Respect," Esther belting it out with Emily singing background. Emily hated disco and loved rock 'n' roll, so I wasn't surprised the oldies were playing on the jukebox. "Good thing you got a jukebox with old songs on it, Tommy. No telling what Emily would do if you didn't."

Tommy laughed again. "You coming down here to join the crowd?"

"I'm going to give it a try. Tell Emily I called, okay?"

"Will do, Chief."

I turned to my computer and started typing up the night's events. Tonight's episode was bizarre and violent, totally unlike Porter. I pulled over the phone and called Porter's doctor.

"Blood tests?" the doctor asked, surprised. "Sure, we do them routinely before we give any patients sedatives. Let me check."

I waited, watching the second hand chug by on the clock on the wall. "Chief? You're right. There is something odd here. It looks like something's out of whack."

"In what way?"

"His numbers don't quite add up." The doctor sounded confused.

"Check for LSD," I suggested.

There was a long pause on the other end of the phone. "Do you know something I don't?"

"How old are you, Doc?" I asked.

"Thirty."

"I know LSD," I said. "Check for it."

I felt his skepticism flow over the phone line. There was another long pause. "Okay, Chief. Will do. I'll call you back with the results."

I turned back to the computer and within twenty minutes my report was done. I pulled over the folder marked *McBride* and opened it, trying to sort through the facts. I didn't look up until my office door opened and Cynthia Barrett walked in.

"Hi, Chief." She held up a Subway sandwich bag. "Care for some supper?"

On cue, my stomach rumbled. "Sure. I wouldn't mind." I touched the report. "I have the coroner's report here if you want to look at it."

"Great." She sat down in the guest chair and put the Subway bag on a cleared-off corner of my desk. I regarded her, remembering Emily's "perky" comment. *She hit the nail on the head with that one.* Cynthia was pretty in a wholesome, hometown, cheerleader way. She wasn't necessarily cheery but she moved with an athletic, bouncy walk. An attractive girl.

Girl. I'm old enough to be her father. If Emily and I had gotten pregnant, our child would be Cynthia's age. It was an amazing thought.

"I thought you'd be with your friends tonight,

Chief," Cynthia said, nibbling on her half of the sandwich.

"Oh, I was busy with Porter Graves. He went onto the resort grounds and made a fuss. Rob and I went out. Then I decided to look at this report and before I knew it—" I looked at the clock on the wall. "It was 7:15."

"That's too bad." Cynthia came around the desk. "Can I look at it?"

I was suddenly aware we were alone in the office except for Bill, who manned the front desk. I picked up the folder and started to hand it to Cynthia, but instead she leaned over my shoulder and put her arm along the back of my chair. "This is fine, Chief," she said softly, leaning on me.

Her breasts were pushing against my shoulder and her breath was warm on my cheek. "Cynthia, why don't you sit down and I'll hand over the report."

I heard a noise from the doorway. Emily stood there, a smile plastered on her face.

Chapter 14

Thirty-Four Years Earlier

A few days after Greg's attempted assault, Nate and Emily went out for burgers then to the movie to see the latest James Bond. "It won't be as good now that Sean's not playing Bond. Let's go upstairs." Emily tugged Nate's arm and steered him toward the balcony section.

"That's where people go to make out," he hissed. "We shouldn't."

She pouted. "Come on. Just a little?"

He couldn't resist her when she pouted. "Okay."

Nate knew it was a mistake as soon as the lights dimmed. Everyone around them started groping. Emily watched the couple in front of them for a minute then gave him an assessing glance. "Is it really so good?"

"What?"

She whispered, "You know. Having a girl do—*that*." She gestured to the busy couple. No one's hands were visible and there was a lot of moaning going on.

"Yes, it's really that good." Nate tried to wiggle away from Emily, but she was leaning on his shoulder. "Now be quiet. We shouldn't talk." He glanced around them. The lights had barely dimmed and he already saw one naked breast two rows over. "We're leaving, Emily," he said, grabbing her wrist.

"Why?" She dug her feet in as he tugged.

"I'll tell you outside."

She frowned but allowed herself to be pulled out of the theater. "Now tell me," she said when they stood on the pavement outside the movie.

"Because I don't want to sit in a movie theater and watch everybody around me have sex," Nate snapped, striding down the street.

Emily hurried to keep up with him. "Are they?" she asked breathlessly.

Nate shot her a look of disbelief and kept walking. He soon realized she wasn't with him. He turned. Emily was staring at him with a woebegone expression. "Oh, for cryin' out loud, Emily, now what?" He strode back to her.

"Why don't you want to have sex with me?" she asked in a hurt, small voice.

Nate's jaw dropped. "What?"

"I was hoping we could make out." Her voice was as soft as a whisper. "I thought maybe tonight..." She sniffled and Nate realized she was crying, tears rolling down her cheeks.

"Aw, come on, don't cry!" He looked around desperately. An older man walking by gave him a sympathetic look but kept going. "I can't make out with you there, Emily," Nate said, leaning near her.

"Why not?"

How could he explain it to her when he couldn't explain it to himself? She wanted to have sex, but she just had a traumatic experience. He shouldn't force himself on her. She didn't know what she was asking.

"I don't understand it," she said around a hiccupping sob. "The other night you wanted to but now you don't. Do you think Greg did something to me? Aren't I good enough for you now?" She whirled away from him.

Nate grabbed her before she could flee. "Damn it, Emily, I know Greg didn't do anything except scare the hell out of you." Nate pulled her to him.

She looked up at him. "Why?"

His lips came down on hers and they kissed for one long, electric minute then he pulled away. "Don't you know how special you are?" he murmured. "You're not just a Summer Girl." He kissed her jaw and moved his lips onto her throat, inhaling that faint scent that was her own personal fragrance.

She dug her fingers into his thick, curly hair, tugging his head away. "Make me special, Nate. Please. Show me."

"Do you know what you're saying?"

She nodded emphatically but her eyes were wide and a bit afraid.

Nate saw the determination in her eyes. "Okay. Let's go." He headed toward his motorcycle parked across the street.

"Where?" She followed him, skipping to catch up.

"You'll see." He waited until she was securely behind him on the bike then he kicked it into gear and drove away, heading for the resort. He'd been thinking about this moment since he met Emily. He didn't want to use his apartment with his parents so near, they couldn't go to the dorms where there wasn't any privacy, and he didn't want to use the beach.

A few minutes later Nate drove into the back access road at the resort and pulled the cycle onto a rutted path, parking behind a shed. "Where are we?"

Emily asked.

"I know a place. Come on." He took her hand and led the way. Nate had an advantage the other Summer Kids and Townies didn't have. He had master keys to just about everything in the hotel. And he knew the hotel like the back of his hand.

Emily looked up at him shyly. "Nate, have you had sex before?"

Nate tried to look blasé. "Yeah." Sharon Martin, a twenty-five year old waitress, took a liking to him and initiated Nate when Nate was sixteen. Sharon and he had a torrid romance for about three months then she vanished with a truck driver. Since Sharon he had occasional girlfriends, but nobody steady. Nobody special like Emily.

"So is it as good as they say it is?" Emily asked.

Nate considered the question and finally said, "I'll tell you. I never had sex with somebody I really loved. I think if I did, my head might explode because sex with somebody I just liked was so great I thought I was going to die."

"I'm on the pill."

Nate stopped. "What?"

"Yeah. I had bad cramps and stuff." Emily blushed. "So they put me on the pill." She glanced sideways at him and saw his grin. "Well, they did."

"I believe you." He started to whistle.

"What are you so happy about?"

He leaned over and whispered, "I don't have to wear a condom." He put an arm around her shoulder and pulled her to him.

"Oh." They walked for a few more steps. "Is it, like, uncomfortable?"

He looked down at her and started to laugh. "You ask the funniest questions."

"I want to be well-informed but my father and brothers refuse to let me in on their secrets. I found the condoms, of course, but I couldn't figure out how they worked." She blushed again. "Is it really that big?"

"Haven't you ever seen a man who was, well, hard?" How could she live in a house with five men and not see a hard-on?

"Maybe," Emily said doubtfully. "In the shower. I interrupted Ben once in the shower before a date with his girlfriend. It sure looked hard."

"The harder it is, the easier it is to put the condom on." Nate led her through the trees to two isolated cottages on the far northeast side of the grounds.

Emily pulled back when she saw them. "This looks like where Greg brought me."

"No. Those cottages are closer to the hotel. These are some of the first ones built, back in the Twenties. They're not used anymore." He pulled out his key chain, leading her to the one he'd chosen. When the resort was first built, the cottage was tucked into the woods far away from the main building. But now, a hundred years later, it faced the maintenance road running around the hotel on one side and a landfill on the other. Private, secluded, and ignored.

Nate glanced around then opened the door, gesturing Emily inside. He followed, closing the door behind them. He had looked over the cottages when he started seeing Emily on a full-time basis. All of the older ones had small living rooms, a kitchenette, and two bedrooms in the back. This one was far off the beaten path and used for storage.

Nate had marked it *unusable* on the planning charts then he came out and cleaned it when he and Emily started dating. "Are you sure about this, Emily?" he asked, looking down at her intently. "I'd understand, after what happened last night, if you didn't want to."

"It's because of that, I think. Your mom said, she said what they had Peggy do was just screwing and it had nothing to do with love. And she told me not to mistake the two." Emily looked up at him, her eyes thoughtful. "I want love, Nate. I want to know what it's like. Then I won't have those thoughts of the other kind."

Nate ran a finger down her cheek, marveling at the softness and the courage in her. She was right. The only way to counteract ugliness was with loveliness. He'd give her that tonight, if he could. "Are you sure?"

She nodded.

Chapter 15

Present Day

"I see you had supper after all," Emily said, her voice frosty with disapproval. "I saw your truck and just thought I'd check to see how poor Porter is doing."

I cleared my throat and glanced at Cynthia, who was draped over me. "Officer Bartlett?" I kept my voice cool even though the way we were standing, it probably looked pretty warm.

Cynthia straightened and moved away, giving Emily an assessing look.

"Porter's fine," I said. "Rob and I went to the resort and talked to him. We had to take him to the hospital. He's there tonight."

Emily's rigid posture relaxed. "The poor man. I hope I didn't agitate him." Then she stiffened again, her eyes on Cynthia. "I spoke with the summer folks and asked them to write up their memories. I'll see you at the resort tomorrow." She turned to go.

"Emily—"

She looked back. "See you tomorrow." Then she vanished.

I knew her moods. If I tried to talk to her now, she'd tear a strip of skin off of me. I put that worry aside to deal with another one. I turned to Cynthia, who was staring at the doorway. "Your behavior is inappropriate," I said quietly. She started to speak but I overrode her. "I won't put anything in your file about this but consider yourself on notice. I won't have a sexual harassment scandal in my office, do you understand?"

She moved away from me, her hazel eyes as frosty as Emily's voice had been. "Yes, I understand." She stalked out of the room.

Son of a bitch. My life just got more complicated.

I pulled over the computer keyboard and recorded every moment of Cynthia's actions and my reactions. Then I put it in a private electronic folder and made sure it had today's date and time on it. I wasn't kidding. I wasn't having any sexual harassment beefs, especially when they weren't warranted.

I pushed away from the desk and stared out the window. I had hoped to join Emily at the bar and walk her home and maybe talk myself into her arms tonight. That wasn't going to happen today and maybe not tomorrow either. I looked at the coroner's report. I was still a cop, though, and I needed answers. If Emily didn't want to see me, she had to get over it. I had Summer Kids to interview.

I called the hospital and talked to Porter's doctor and he confirmed what I suspected. Porter was on LSD. The question in my mind was did he take it voluntarily or did somebody slip it to him? That raised a new set of questions. Why would somebody do it? And if he did take it voluntarily, where did he get it?

I wasn't stupid enough to believe we didn't have a drug problem in our little town. Whenever you have bored teenagers or bored older people for that matter, you'll have drugs, alcohol, or a mixture of both. But

LSD wasn't on the usual list of Saturday night party drugs. I made a note to check with Rob Sloan, who was probably more current than I was on what drugs were being pedaled around town.

Half an hour after Emily left in a snit, I checked in with Bill at the station's front desk, making sure he knew he could call me on my pager. Then I headed out into the crisp October night.

The police station was three blocks from downtown. It sat high on a hill overlooking the business district and Lake Michigan. I considered walking but force of habit—police habit—made me go to the parking lot and get in my truck for the brief drive. You never know when you might need wheels.

I pulled into the parking lot behind Tommy's bar, checking for Emily's rental Volkswagen Bug. Then I remembered I drove earlier so her car wouldn't be there. I entered the back door, not sure what or who I'd find.

"Nate, there you are!"

Tommy's Lakeside Bar was really a series of "rooms," or alcoves, each separated by a high arched doorway. The Pine Place Inn summer contingent had taken over the alcove to the left of the back door. I scanned the long table full of people but didn't see Emily.

Harv Michaels stood and held out his hand as soon as I entered. He was big-boned and gray-haired, still a handsome man with a wicked gleam in his amber eyes. Pauline, his wife, sat next to him. Her once-blonde hair was faded now and she didn't look like the solid, muscular swimmer she once was, but she still had that same slow smile when she looked at Harv. I was glad to see they were together. It reaffirmed some notion I had about romance.

"It's about time you got here," David Masters said from his spot across from Harv.

"I got tied up at the office." I took the chair Pauline shoved toward me.

"I can't believe you're Chief of Police," she said, leaning over Harv to talk.

"I can," Esther called out. She sat next to Pauline, down the table. I took the beer Harv handed me and saluted her with it. Esther Barton was a tall, statuesque black woman with short-cropped hair and shrewd dark eyes. She, Emily, and Pauline had shared a dorm together back in the old days. There wasn't much that happened that Esther didn't know about. "Like father like son," she said. "How is your dad?"

"He's fine. He retired twenty years ago or so." I sipped the beer and wondered how to ask about Emily. Pauline saved me from my embarrassment.

"Emily said she was having dinner with your folks tonight. Too bad you had to work and missed joining them." She sipped the cup of coffee in front of her. "I'm the designated driver," she explained when I looked from the cup to her.

I silently blessed Emily for her little lie, even though I was pretty sure she did it to save herself from having to tell an even bigger lie to her old friends. "Yeah, I know." I pulled out my cell phone. "That reminds me, I need to check in." I smiled weakly. "Maybe I can still get dessert."

Pauline and Esther both grinned. "Maybe," Pauline said suggestively.

I speed-dialed my parents' phone number. Mom

must have checked the caller ID because she answered with a low-voiced caution. "She's here, Nate. She walked to the house and she's loaded for bear. If I were you I'd come over tomorrow morning with a peace offering."

"Okay," I said blandly, conscious that several people were watching me. "Sounds good." I heard my father call out, "Make it a really good peace offering," then I hung up and took another sip of beer. "So has anybody been able to remember anything about our last weekend at the resort? I know it was a long time ago, but I was hoping between all of us we could figure out what went on."

"I remember it well," David said. He'd been the children's camp counselor at the resort, responsible for day care activities. "Probably because it was the last summer of innocence."

"I thought you left earlier than that," I said, struggling to remember events from so long ago.

He nodded. "I left for a few weeks but I came back. You remember Rachel took over for a while then she left in August so I came back for the final two weeks."

I remembered now. There was some kind of problem. David was gay and he got a threat or something. I vaguely remembered Rachel. She was a wild girl, given to rough sex. She and I had one or two brief nights together, before I met Emily. "What do you mean, summer of innocence?"

"Well, there was Watergate and the fall of Saigon then disco then AIDS." David shrugged eloquently. He'd matured into a handsome man, with brooding dark eyes. "Our summer was a like a cocoon that kept out the bad stuff."

"There was a big fight that night," Pauline said, leaning across the table. "Remember?"

"What fight?"

"You and Emily left the party early," Harv said with a wink. "Greg and John got into it with some Townies."

I glanced at Greg, who sat at the far end of the table, his wife next to him. "Really? Who won?"

Harv sputtered with laughter. "It was a toss-up, as I recall. The sheriff was called out to break it up. Good thing you weren't there, Greg was drunk and acting like a real slob, not that it was much of an act for him." Harv shook his head and glanced down the table at Greg. "I heard the sheriff and his men threw 'em in the lake to sober up."

"Pity they didn't drown," David snapped. "I always suspected they were behind those threatening letters I got."

"Did you know if Greg and Peggy were together that night?" I tried to jerk the conversation back to the topic at hand.

Everyone looked confused. "She was a party girl," Esther said apologetically. "I think she was at the dance, but I don't know who she was with." She frowned. "Peggy was sort of into, well..." She looked at the others and shrugged. "Oh, hell, we're grown-ups. She was into S&M stuff."

I looked blankly at Esther. "S&M?"

Pauline laughed. "Sadism? Masochism?"

"I know what it is." I thrashed over this information. "How did you know?"

"Remember Big Tom? The guy I dated?" Esther asked.

I nodded.

"He knew a man who got her some things she wanted." Esther paused then said, "Sex things and sex toys."

"Whoa." I glanced covertly at Greg. "Was he into that, do you know?"

Esther reared back dramatically and put a hand to her chest. "I have no idea. But it wouldn't surprise me."

"Who was into it?" I pressed. "I know Peggy and Greg had sex now and then." I remembered, too, the time Greg almost raped Emily but I kept the memory to myself. From the look on her face earlier today when Greg startled her, Emily had vivid memories of it, too. "I heard he had odd tastes. He and his friends used to swap girlfriends."

Esther poured herself another beer from the pitcher on the table. "Hell, everybody swapped girlfriends back then. David was right. It was the last summer of innocence. A few of us were steadies." She nodded to Harv and Pauline. "You two. Me and Tom. And Nate and Emily, of course." She shot me a curious look. "Always thought you two might get married."

I decided not to take *that* path down memory lane. "I remember Peggy told me her honey was going to marry her and take her away from Little Bay. She used that term specifically: 'her honey.' Any idea who he was?"

"Sounds like a pipe dream to me," Harv said sadly. "She just wasn't the marrying kind, if you know what I mean."

"Harv's right," David said. "Peggy was a party girl, not the kind of girl a guy would want to marry and take away."

"I wonder who her honey was?" Pauline mused. "It wouldn't have been Greg. No way would he get serious about somebody like Peggy." She took a handful of popcorn from the basket on the table and munched. "Maybe her diary would say."

"Diary?" I looked from Pauline to Esther, who was nodding. "She kept a diary?"

"Everybody back then kept a diary," Esther said. "Emily and I talked about it earlier."

"Really?" I leaned back in my chair. "You did?"

"She said she was going to mention it to you." Pauline shoveled in some more popcorn, her eyes never leaving my face. "She said she was going to the station then she showed back up here, grabbed her coat, and took off for dinner with your folks."

I took a swallow of beer to give myself time to think. "Must have missed her. I had to go deal with Porter Graves."

"Oh, God, that poor guy, is he still walking around?" Harv drained his beer glass and set it back on the table with a *clunk*. "I remember when he got hurt. There he was, a regular guy just like us and the next thing you know, he's like a vegetable." He shuddered dramatically then put an arm around Pauline. "We'd better get going, girlfriend. It's a long drive to the motel."

"Are you ready?" Pauline asked Esther. "We all drove down together," she explained as Esther took one last swallow of beer. "We got rooms at the Holiday Inn over at Kalamazoo."

"I appreciate you guys coming."

"It's not often I get the chance to help solve a cold case," Harv said, standing up and pulling on a leather jacket. He waved expansively to the others still seated at the table. "We'll see you kids in the morning."

Other people started to stand and stretch. The party was breaking up. I wondered if Emily took notes like I asked. Hell, I wondered if she'd even talk to me in the morning. I walked out of the bar, Esther by my side as we followed after Harv and Pauline. "I meant what I said, Esther. I appreciate you coming all this way to help."

She tucked her arm through mine as we walked to Harv's SUV, parked three cars away from my truck. Esther was a tall woman, so different than Emily who barely came up to my chin. It was odd to turn my head and almost look Esther in the eye. "I was happy to see Emily again. I owe that girl a big debt. She saved my life, remember?"

The memory suddenly came crashing back. "You're right. You almost drowned, didn't you?"

Esther nodded. "Some kids were teaching me to swim and I got into trouble. Emily dove in and dragged me up from the bottom of the swimming pool. I'll never forget it." She laughed. "That's one reason Tom Judson stepped forward to help, later on. It was one time the Townies and the Summer Kids all worked together."

"Emily brought a lot of people together," Pauline said as she clicked the car keys and the lights came on in the SUV. "We were so lucky nothing happened to her."

Harv opened the back door of the SUV. Esther paused before sliding in. "I remember one time Emily and I were walking on the beach and we saw Peggy, hiding something in the rocks."

"Where? Do you remember?"

"I'm not sure. Emily and I talked about it earlier tonight. She thought it was just down the beach from Mitchell's Cove, where we used to have those bonfires. It was one of those odd things, we saw Peggy fumbling around in the rocks at the base of the bluff. She made some kind of lame excuse for what she was doing." Esther smiled wryly. "At the time, we figured it was drugs. Everybody was into drugs back then." She got into the SUV and buckled the seat belt. "Even if she did hide something, would it still be there after all these years?"

"Probably not," I admitted. "And even if it was still there, could anybody find it?"

Pauline got behind the wheel. "If anybody can find it, Emily can. We'll see you tomorrow, Nate, bright and early."

Harv groaned from the passenger seat. "Early maybe, but not bright. See you later, Nate." I closed Esther's door and watched as they drove away. Other Summer Kids straggled out of the bar, waving to me. I waved back and got into the truck.

Esther was right. I knew Emily. She wasn't going to rest if she thought she could solve a mystery like this. I drove past my parents' house on the way to my place. The lights were still on in the apartment over the garage and I almost stopped, wanting to clear up the misunderstanding right then.

Nope. When Emily got into a snit, she wasn't easily convinced of anything. Better to wait until morning. I kept driving to my house, parking in the garage and going in to almost stumble over J. Edgar, who meandered in front of me to remind me I was late dishing out his evening meal. I opened a can of food and dumped the contents into a dish then went into the living room, not bothering to turn on a light.

Why did Emily jump to such a conclusion tonight? Good Lord, it was an innocent enough scene. It wasn't like Cynthia and I were entwined in some romantic embrace.

I put my gear in the gun safe then got a beer out of the fridge. I was about half done with the bottle when my mother called. "You sure have Emily upset."

"She's upset?" I drained the beer and considered getting another one, but inertia kept me pinned to the couch. Inertia and ten pounds of tabby cat. "She's jumping to conclusions. I don't know why she's so bent out of shape over something harmless."

"She's fifty years old and feeling insecure. She saw you with a young attractive woman."

My mother's common-sense, pragmatic voice did what it always did. It made me stop, think, and reconsider.

"Honestly, Nate. Look at it from Emily's point of view. She's in the middle of an important business deal, she comes here and you put the moves on her. Then she finds you almost in bed with someone from your office."

"I was not in bed with anyone," I interrupted. "Cynthia was standing a bit too close to me, that's all. Emily is blowing this totally out of proportion."

"She's in love."

I pulled the phone away from my ear and stared at it. I had to be hearing things.

"She's in love. She's afraid she might be in love with the past. She's afraid you might be in love with the past. Do you know what I mean?"

I did know. I'd been wrestling with the idea myself.

"And she's afraid to admit it because it means changing everything in her life. You can't leave here. So if she wants to be with you, she has to come here. It's a big step for a person to take. Add to it that all the other things going on in her life and, well, maybe she did over-react, but it's understandable, don't you think?"

"I don't know if she's in love with me or—"

"I have the feeling she's going to go out early, so why don't you be ready to come by when I call?"

"What do you mean, she's going out early?"

"She was talking about looking for a diary or something. If I know Emily, she'll head out at first light to find it."

I thought about the resort, empty now except for construction workers. Would she really try to go out there and look for a damn diary?

I knew the answer. "Call me in the morning, Mom."

"Will do, Nate. Sleep well."

I didn't.

Chapter 16

Thirty-Four Years Earlier

Nate switched on the small lamp in the living room and led the way into the back bedroom. He had already made up the bed and some towels on the chair near the bed. *Just in case*, he'd told himself. *Just in case I get lucky with Emily.*

He looked at her. Emily looked around the room then she finally turned to look at him. Taking a deep breath, she unbuttoned her blouse and let it fall off her arms to the floor. Then she reached behind her, unhooking the clasp of her bra and pushed it off.

Nate was mesmerized, watching as she unhooked her shorts and slid shorts and panties to the floor. "I want to do this, Nate," she said softly. "And I want you to show me." She crossed the short space to him. Her hands went to his shirt buttons. "I want to."

When she started to fumble with his belt buckle Nate thought his legs would give way. He yanked the belt open and unsnapped his jeans, tugging them and his sneakers off in one move. He stood before her, hard and pulsing.

Her eyes were huge. "Are you sure it will fit?" she asked in a small voice. She reached out then looked at him. "Can I touch it? Will I hurt it if I touch it?"

Nate almost cried with relief. He wasn't huge by

any means but he was bigger than most of the guys and he didn't want her scared. Curiosity was better than fright.

"It's okay to touch it." He cleared his throat, having a hard time getting the words out. He led her to the bed and gently pushed her back, clambering up next to her with his head propped up on one bent elbow.

She's a goddess. Everything about her was perfect. Her breasts were big and firm, her waist so small, her hips, her flat stomach her skin like warm silk under his callused hands.

Emily gently took his erection in her hand. "It's so hard," she breathed softly. "And so smooth." She felt him with little tugs and pulls. Nate willed himself to stillness. "Does it hurt to be so hard?"

"Sometimes," he said through clenched teeth. "Like now, when all I want is to be in you. Don't you ever hurt? Get a throbbing?" His hand strayed down her thighs and cupped her mound. She stiffened as he played gently with one nipple, flicking a finger over it.

"Yes," she said softly. "I do."

"When?" he asked as he gently massaged her. "When do you throb?"

"My breasts," she breathed softly. "What you did the other night."

"With my finger?" he asked softly, his hand moving into her warmth. "Like this?" He lifted one heavy breast and took the nipple in his mouth.

For answer she stiffened even more then suddenly relaxed completely, her legs opening.

"Like this?" he asked as his fingers gently probed her warm, moist depths. He inserted a finger. Emily gasped and tried to pull away then almost immediately she surged to him. "Is that what you like?"

"Please," she breathed, pushing her pelvis against his hand. He pushed a second finger into her, pulsing in and out of her until he saw her tension building. Her hips pressed against his hand, moving with him rhythmically until her breath came in gasps.

It was time. Nate moved, positioning himself over her. "I'm sorry, honey. I'm going to hurt you." He removed his fingers, rubbing his cock at her entrance. Emily tensed as Nate moved his fingers in her folds and found her clitoris, beginning a slow, gentle massage that soon had her gasping again.

"What are you doing?" she asked, her hips pushed up against his hand. "What's happening?"

"You're getting ready to come, honey." Nate put his penis against her entrance again and this time she strained to encompass him.

She tensed at first. Nate reached between them and massaged her and soon she relaxed. He pushed forward a bit more. She was so tight around him. He paused, praying he wasn't hurting her.

Emily shifted under him and he slid deeper. Moving slowly and carefully, he finally felt the barrier. "Put your legs around me," he whispered to her. "Right now. Let me in."

Emily looked up at him, eyes full of trust and love. She raised her legs and Nate surged into her, sinking deeply. He held very still, praying for control as she looked at him, her eyes large and startled.

She moved her hips experimentally. "Nate?" she murmured, rotating her hips so she took him deeper.

"Hang on, honey," he said, his voice raw and hoarse. "Trust me." He pulled away from her, sliding almost out of her. Then he surged into her again and she raised her hips to meet him. Again and again, they met, her blood and dampness lubricating them. His shoulders and neck tightened as he strained and he felt a similar straining in her, a *need* making her urge him deeper.

Nate knew when it started to happen for her. She tensed then urged him even deeper, her body grasping him and warmth enfolding him. With a moan Nate sank into her, his body—his soul—merging with her.

They lay together in a tangle of arms and legs then Nate rolled over slightly and with a feeling of delicious sensuality, his cock slid slowly out of her and lay quiescent on her thigh.

Nate wasn't sure what to say. What did you say to a girl after her first time? "Did you have a good time?" "Did you enjoy it?" How would she know?

Emily sighed. "This is great. Why don't people just screw all the time? It feels so great."

Nate laughed, his breath hot on her throat. "Good question," he murmured as he kissed her chin.

She smoothed her hands down his shoulders then down his back. "Mine," she whispered. "All mine."

Nate stared into the green depths of her eyes. "You're so beautiful."

"You make me feel beautiful. I feel so fabulous. So happy and relaxed."

"I know. It's how I feel, too."

She sighed. "It's lots better than what Susie Barstow told me about. She said it was bloody and it hurt."

"I think there was some blood. And it has to hurt a bit. But I hope it was pleasure, too. If it wasn't, we can try again." He dipped his head to kiss her nipple.

"What?" Emily sat up, almost knocking his head off. She stared down at the bed in dismay.

He gently pushed her back. "Don't worry. I put extra towels down and it's an old bedspread."

"You knew we'd come here?"

"I was hoping we would." Nate drew a finger down her neck to her breast, winding his way down to her stomach. "I had hopes. Emily, you know I care for you. This isn't just some quickie thing for me."

She tangled her fingers in his curly black hair. "You're my guy, Nate. For as long as you want me."

He lay back down, resting his head on the pillow next to her. "I wanted you to know it. You're special, Emily."

"Hmm." Her drowsy response seemed to mesh with his deep breathing. "Nate?" she asked sleepily.

"Hmm?"

"Can we do it again?"

His eyes snapped open. "What?"

She ran a hand down his chest and gently picked up his heavy penis, stroking it with the lightest of touches. "I have a lot to learn. I think we should keep practicing."

To Nate's mortification, his cock was stiffening in her hand and soon was hard enough to pound nails. "Honey, you're going to be sore," he said gently, putting his hand down to her damp pubis. "There's a limit to how much you can do."

"We'll just go slow and easy." She tugged him to get on top of her. "And take some breaks."

Nate smiled. "Whatever you say. I think I'll put you in charge."

"Good. I've read some articles but I need a willing

man to help."

"That's me. I'm willing."

"And you're definitely a man."

"Emily? What are you doing?"

"Does it feel good?"

"You know it does."

"Hmm. I guess those articles were right."

Chapter 17

Present Day

I was already moving by the time my mom called me at 7:15 the next morning. I answered the cell phone in my truck. "She just left, Nate," Mom said. "Going north."

"I figured that." I took a right at the next corner then another right. I stopped well back from the intersection and let the truck idle under an elm tree in Widow Johnson's yard. "How'd she look? Still mad?"

"It was hard to tell with the fog and drizzle. I know she didn't dress for a morning outing, though." My mother's voice sounded exasperated. "She was wearing denim shorts and a green sweatshirt and some red sneakers. She's going to be cold before long."

A red VW Bug shot past me on the highway. "I got her, Mom. Talk to you later." I tucked the phone in my front shirt pocket as I eased the truck out onto the road. At this time on a Sunday morning there wasn't any traffic except me and the Bug, now far in the distance. Emily was setting a mean pace. I'd need to talk to her about it. If she wasn't careful, I might arrest her for speeding.

Emily drove past the main gates of the resort. I slowed until I saw her take a left onto the access road the construction crew used for equipment. I followed cautiously but the Bug was far ahead, inching along the rutted temporary road cut through the grass to accommodate the bulldozers and backhoes.

I turned off my truck lights and waited, peering through the misty window to watch her finally park next to a construction trailer. I saw the light go on then off in the Bug and I knew she was out and going.

I considered my next move. If I confronted her I might scare the piss out of her and justifiably so. It was a ghostly morning, chill and damp with fog coming off the Lake and hanging in threads in the air. I didn't want to leave her out there alone, though. The footing was treacherous on the beach.

I put the boom box I brought as a peace offering on the floor of the passenger side then set off after her. Emily was making a beeline for Mitchell's Cove, which was across the soccer field and a bit north. I wondered if she could traverse the gully leading to the beach. There were access steps down to the beach from the park, just north of the resort but she probably didn't know about it.

Emily was barely in sight, her droopy white socks and red sneakers catching light from the overhead lights, misty in the fog. I followed, keeping well back. When I saw her pause at the top of the bluff and stare down, I knew she'd come to the gully. I silently willed her to go right, go north to the park, but she didn't.

She moved indecisively left then right, peering down and I realized she wasn't quite where she wanted to be. I sent her a mental message to go left and maybe she heard me because she walked about twenty feet to the south, stared downward then took a cautious step forward.

I counted to five then moved again. I didn't want to scare her if she was traversing the boulder-strewn ravine that led down about thirty steep yards to the beach below. If I startled her she was liable to fall. I inched forward slowly until I was close to the bluff then I peered over. The area was in darkness because it faced west toward the lake and the sun was coming up behind me in the east. But there was enough daylight for me to see Emily picking her way carefully down the rocky, steep slope.

As I watched she mis-stepped and I almost had heart failure when she slid along a boulder before coming to a stop and teetering carefully on top of another rock. She looked shaken, moving her arms and legs cautiously. I breathed a sigh of relief when I saw everything seemed to be functioning. Everything, that is, except my pulse, which was beating pretty damn erratically.

Emily dusted herself off and continued more slowly down to the beach and went left, moving out of my direct line of sight. I got down on my stomach and edged forward to peer over the grassy verge to the beach below. Emily was hard against the bluff wall balanced on a piece of driftwood, her hand in what looked like a declivity almost too high for her to reach. She was straining on her tiptoes and her face was screwed up with concentration as she groped inside the cliff. She obviously hadn't considered some lake-side critter might be using the niche for a home. I tensed, getting ready to dash down to the beach and help her if she pulled her hand out and had a bat attached to it.

She stretched even further, reaching as far as she was able. The log started to roll and Emily lunged forward, going hard against the bluff wall before tipping backward and landing on the beach flat on her back.

Something was clutched in her right hand. I stared downward, noting the bloody graze along one leg where a broken-off branch of the log got her. It probably stung like crazy but Emily ignored it, focusing on the object in her hands. It was small and rectangular, covered with what looked like an old vinyl tablecloth.

Then Emily tugged gently on it, and I heard the familiar sound of Velcro. I silently applauded whoever had made it. The cloth on the back was cut significantly larger than the book itself and was used as wrapping. If you're going to store a book at a lake, you want it waterproofed. Good old Velcro. It lasted forever.

Emily stared down at the book for a long minute then seemed to suddenly realize she was sitting on a cold beach at dawn in October in her shorts. She rewrapped the diary in its vinyl cover and tucked it in the waistband of her shorts, near the small of her back before turning to the ravine. I eased away from the edge, peeking over.

Emily stared upward. She wasn't going to be able to climb up. Coming down, she was able to jump down to the next rock. Going up would be impossible given her short legs.

She looked to her right then left then she started walking south, toward the resort to the steps there. Satisfied she was safe and not lying broken on the beach, I stood up and headed back to the truck. I wanted to be in place when she appeared at the apartment.

I had worked myself into a good fit of righteous

indignation by the time the Bug pulled into the drive thirty minutes later. Why didn't she tell me about the diary? If she was going to do some detective work, why not ask a cop—me—to help her? No, Miss Emily had to prove how tough she was, how smart she was. She had to go off and do things her way, just like always. If I didn't do what she wanted, she went ahead and did what she felt like. Damn it, some things never changed.

By the time she appeared, I had worked it around in my head so she was insulting me and my police officers. I tossed in my parents for good measure, imagining how she had them worried because she up and vanished this morning after crying on their shoulders the night before. In short, I was in a good snit myself by the time she pulled into the driveway and was in no frame of mind for Emily's pissy little mood.

When she got out of the Bug, I took in her bedraggled appearance, noting the torn green sweatshirt and the scratches and bruises on her legs. I grabbed my peace offering from the front seat and approached her. "Where have you been?" I shifted the boom box from one hand to the other.

Emily glared at me. "None of your damn business."

"If someone tried to attack you, it's my business," I said coolly. "I *am* the law in town, after all." I followed her up the stairs to the apartment, noting she moved stiffly. Of course, I was stiff, too. My hip was still sore and I had a few scrapes from last night's adventure with Porter. "So are you going to tell me?" I demanded, watching as she opened the door to the apartment. She hadn't locked it and I ground my teeth together.

"No. And I didn't invite you in." She moved

through the small living room and into the bathroom where she kicked off her shoes, dropping the red and white package she held on the end table in passing.

I put my gun and holster into the drawer of the entrance table then set the boom box on the end table near the couch. I followed her down the hallway. "Why are you mad at me?"

"For heaven's sake. After the scene last night in your office?" She rooted around in the medicine chest and emerged with some salve. Then she must have remembered her manners because she asked, "Are you feeling okay? How's Porter?"

"I'm fine and Porter's going home today. His sister will keep an eye on him. What scene in my office are you talking about?"

"Heavens, Nate, it was embarrassing." Emily shot me an exasperated look. "The girl was all over you. I wish I had fair warning I was walking in on something."

I watched as Emily dampened a washcloth and started dabbing at the bloody scratches on her leg. "I told her that her behavior was inappropriate. Unprofessional."

Emily made an incredibly rude noise. "I'm just sure you did. You didn't look too distressed last night when Miss Perky Boobs was leaning on you."

"No reason to get pissy," I said, my temper starting to percolate.

"Oh, excuse me, Chief." She winced when the hot water touched one particularly nasty scratch. "It strikes me as being a bit trashy when you proposition me then turn around and make out with a subordinate a few hours later."

"I did not make out with her. And besides, what's it to you? The last time I checked, you weren't interested in me."

Emily ignored me as she dabbed at her scratches. "If I was entertaining any notions about a romantic attachment to you, I've certainly had them squashed," she said haughtily. "Obviously, you have enough female company and don't need mine."

She was "entertaining notions"? Bullshit. Emily was just pissed off and I was a convenient punching bag. "Give me that." I grabbed for the washcloth. "Sit down."

"No." Her lower lip was trembling. I didn't know whether to kiss her or shake her. I put a hand on her shoulder and pushed. She cried out and sagged down on the side of the tub.

"Emily?" I pulled gently at the neck of her sweatshirt and saw a big bruise on the side of her neck. "What the hell happened? Did somebody hurt you?"

"I fell," she said, gritting her teeth and rotating the shoulder. "It's just a bruise."

"These aren't bruises," I said, touching one bloody scratch.

"I got those at the resort." She reached for the tube of salve. "Climbing down the cliff to the beach. It's where I fell."

"You did what?"

She winced. I suspect it was as much from my tone of voice as from the scratches. "I went to the resort, early this morning."

I recognized this ploy. She had used it many times before. Emily figured if she used a dismissive tone of voice it hid the fact she did something wrong, like trespassing. I glared at the top of her head, which was all I saw when she focused on her cuts.

"I thought I knew where Peggy hid her diary. And this guy chased me down the beach." She frowned at one really bad scratch. "I wonder if he's the one who's called here and threatened me? Whatever." She straightened up and saw me glaring at her.

"You went to the resort, early in the morning, alone? It's a murder scene." Okay, technically the entire resort wasn't a murder scene, but it sounded good. "Someone chased you? You got another call? Did you plan to share any of this?"

Emily knew she screwed up. I saw it in her eyes as she tried to hash out a fresh strategy. "I figured you weren't interested," she said off-handedly. "It looked like you and your policewoman had things well in hand." She paused dramatically. "Well in hand."

That was too much. Her injuries, the whole weekend—it all coalesced to make me lose my wobbly hold on my temper. "Damn it, Emily!" My voice rose, echoing in the tiny bathroom. "I didn't think I'd see you again, did you know that? I thought I would get through life and never have to see you again. But no, there has to be a murder you can help me with. And here you are, back in my life again. Damn it!"

Her eyes welled with tears. "Well, excuse me," she choked. "I guess I should've stayed away." She was crying freely now, swiping at her face and making big snorting noises. "I'll leave. Don't let me get in your way, Mr. Hot Shot Police Guy. I'll move my ugly self out of your life and you can go back messing around with your co-workers."

I threw my head back and almost let out a howl of

rage. "That's not what I meant," I said between clenched teeth.

Emily put her hands on her hips. The bathroom was so small she was chin to chest with me. "Get out of my way. I'm going to pack. I don't need this kind of shit in my life. I'm sure, somewhere, there's a man who might appreciate me." She pushed at me. "Well? Move it!"

I took a long, deep breath. Then I put one arm under her legs and the other under her back and scooped her up. "No."

I paused in the hallway. The bedroom was tempting but I knew I didn't dare. I went to the living room instead and sat down on the couch, keeping a firm hold on her. Emily struggled but I clamped a hand over her legs and kept her pinned on my lap. I held her until she quit wiggling. She was still crying and that did sort of break my heart. "What's going on, Emily?" I asked.

She glanced at me then looked away quickly, wiping at her face with her hand. "I thought of where Peggy might have hid her diary," she said sullenly. "Everybody kept diaries back then. I was sure Peggy must have kept one."

"Why didn't you tell me?" I tried to keep my voice quiet and calm.

"I was going to call you last night, but after seeing you and *her* I realized you probably didn't want to be interrupted."

I sighed, causing her to jiggle in my arms. "I was going over the coroner's report and Cynthia said she wanted to look at it, too. This is the first murder investigation we've had and she was curious." I shot Emily a look when it appeared she was going to speak.

"And that's all. She acted inappropriately and I told her so." Emily struggled in my arms again but I tightened my grip. "Why did you go out there alone?"

She sighed. "I thought if I found the diary you'd think it was cool," she said in a low, small voice. "And I did find it."

"Did you?" I leaned a bit closer.

"It's over there." She tried to sit up but I had my arm over her legs, pushing her down. "On the end table."

"Hmm." My lips were close to hers now.

She looked up. I saw those little gold flecks in her eyes. "Oh."

Then my lips were on hers and I was swept away in a dizzying tide of lust, swamped with heat. I got hard so fast I thought I'd pass out. My body was taking over for my brain. I moved a hand up her leg, under her shorts and once again felt her warm, smooth, silky thigh, those legs that drove me crazy all those years ago. I pulled my lips away from hers long enough to say, "Still smooth."

"I still shave every day." Her eyes took on a hooded look when I moved my hand a bit further and slipped one finger under the elastic of her panties. She was so hot and moist.

Then she shifted slightly and my fingers suddenly had more room. "Oh, God, Emily," I breathed. "You always were so hot."

She leaned back, her sensual smile igniting me. "Just for you, Nate," she said in a low, hoarse voice. "Somehow I've never been as hot as I am with you." We tumbled back on the couch. I moved my hand down to unsnap her shorts.

My phone rang. I bit back a curse. "Oh, man," I moaned.

She laughed softly. "Go ahead. Answer it."

I managed to fumble the phone out of the leather holder on my belt. "Chief Boltz," I said, propping myself up on one elbow and looking down at Emily.

"Nate, what time are the Summer Kids due at the resort?"

It was Dorothy. I willed my dull brain to work. "Ten."

"Okay, a couple of folks have called. Thanks."

I ended the call and turned back to Emily. I was acutely conscious of my rampant erection, which was going to be unused for another day. But I had obligations, not the least of which was to meet the people I asked to come all this distance. "It's almost nine. I told the others we'd meet them at ten."

Emily sat up in my arms. "We need to continue this later. Are we still on for supper tonight?" She gently rolled her bruised shoulder.

I watched, hypnotized, at the sight of her breasts moving under her T-shirt. "If you want to," I said in a suddenly dry throat.

"Oh, yeah." She eyed me. "Oh, yeah, we're still on."

I felt a wave of lust wash over me so strong I almost fainted. "Good," I managed.

"You want some food?" She popped off the couch and walked into the kitchen to pull open the fridge door, bending over and looking in. I almost had heart failure at the sight of her ass in those shorts. She got out a carton of eggs and some other things and started making breakfast.

I picked up the diary and pulled out one of the stools at the kitchen island. I watched Emily as she cooked, humming while she bustled. The nearly-empty wine bottle was sitting on the counter. It looked like Emily had put the Big Hurt on some booze the night before. I grinned at the thought of her sitting there, working herself into a hissy fit while she was drinking.

"Over easy, right?" she asked over her shoulder.

She remembered how I liked my eggs. "Yep." I looked down at the diary and suddenly remembered our conversation. "What did you mean when you said a guy chased you?"

"When I was on the beach. Once I found the diary, I realized I couldn't come back up the gorge." She frowned at her battle-scarred legs. I winced, looking at them. "So I came back to the resort. I was just coming up the steps by the new condo units and I saw a man running down the beach behind me, from the direction I came from." She gestured with the spatula. "He wasn't just jogging. It looked like he was chasing me. I got to the top of the steps and ducked between the buildings, heading for the construction equipment. I forgot it was Sunday. I thought there'd be people there."

Emily set a plate in front of me with two eggs, three strips of bacon and two pieces of toast with raspberry jam. She poured me a cup of coffee then set her own plate next to mine. "So, anyway," she continued, "I was just to the pool and Bobby Goldman showed up. It looked like he came out by the kitchen, behind the main building."

I visualized the scene in my head. Emily came up the south steps, east of the swimming pool. The main building and the kitchen building were southeast of the single units. Bobby was probably in the main building for some reason. I nodded.

"I told Bobby about the guy behind me but he said he didn't see anybody. Then the security guard for the construction company came over and they escorted me to my car." She made a wry face and I imagined the guard giving her a hard time.

"Did you tell Bobby you had the diary?" I asked, savoring breakfast. She was such a great cook. I remembered with fondness the many meals she'd made for me.

"I tucked it into my shorts to carry, you know? I just forgot about it."

I nodded. Back in the old days, if she carried something in her hands, there was a good chance she'd set it down. We often had to backtrack somewhere to retrieve Emily's left-behind something.

I took a sip of coffee. "Probably just as well. No reason to tell anybody." I touched the book. "Did you look through it?"

"No, I didn't have time. Some guy I know came over here and molested me." She grinned at me but I didn't smile back.

"You need to be more careful. You got another call?"

"Just like the first one. I got it last night." She glanced at the clock then collected our plates and put them in the dishwasher. "We need to get to the resort. It's your party. You don't want to be late." She started down the hall to the bathroom. "You look through the diary while I get cleaned up."

"Okay." I went back to the couch to sit. Did someone really chase Emily? I imagined the scene and came to the conclusion it wasn't possible. Bobby would see anyone. It was probably just a jogger. Lots of folks jogged on the shore. The phone calls, though. Those bothered me. This was a small town. It might be some kids playing a prank or someone not anxious to have Peggy's sordid past revealed, or his association with Peggy revealed.

Peggy. I opened her diary, seeing the childish, round handwriting and the little hearts over the *i* letters instead of a dot. This was done back before computers and took a lot of work to maintain.

The first entry was January 1, 1979. It read:

I'm going to keep track of important things because later I may want to look back and see when things happened and who they happened with! I think it's important to keep a record.

Not much exciting is happening with me. I'm just working at the diner and waiting for summer to come along so I can see my Guy again. He's such a Honey (ha, ha). He's my ticket out of town; I know he loves me and I know he cares about me. It's just a matter of time before we can be together.

I heard a shower running and realized Emily was in it, naked and glistening under the stream of water. My erection, which had subsided, was suddenly painful again. I visualized her at my house, lying in bed. Tonight might be great. Maybe we could talk about the future. Maybe there was a future. I sighed and surrendered to daydreams for a few minutes.

The sound of the shower shutting off and Emily belting out "Further On Up The Road" jarred me from my fantasies. I looked down at the book in my hands. Who did Peggy hang out with? It sounded like it wasn't a Summer Boy. It sounded like a Townie or somebody who worked there every summer but went away in the winter.

Like me, I suddenly remembered. I went to college but in the summers I worked at the resort. For one panicked moment I wondered if I was the object of her affection then I calmed down. Peggy and I were warm bodies who occasionally intersected for a good time before I met Emily.

Was it a Townie who killed her? Somebody who was, even today, living and working in Little Bay? I didn't realize until then how badly I wanted the murderer to be a Summer Boy. I knew the people coming back to visit probably had nothing to do with Peggy's death. It would be a stupid killer to come back and visit. I always assumed it was a Summer Boy, one who worked there for a season then left. But what if it was a Townie?

I was still contemplating that possibility when Emily emerged from the bedroom. She was dressed in black jeans (*tight* black jeans, I noticed with satisfaction), a tucked-in flowered blouse in harvest gold colors, a russet brown jacket (a *fitted* jacket) and loafers. "You look very preppy," I commented. I particularly liked the way her blouse emphasized her small waist and large breasts. She looked like a little Venus.

"Thank you, sir. You look pretty good yourself."

I looked down at my dark gray jeans, gray-and-white-striped dress shirt with the sleeves rolled up and boots. Surprisingly I hadn't gotten grass-stained from my climb on the hill. My Little Bay PD jacket took most of the dirt. "Thanks."

She glanced down at the book. "Learn anything?"

"I think we have a lot of reading to do." I frowned down at the diary. "Maybe I'll ask Dad to help. He might pick up on something."

"Good idea. We can leave it with them while we're at the resort."

"My idea exactly. I'd rather not leave it around where anyone can find it."

"Great minds continue to think alike." She gestured toward the door. "Ready to go, Sherlock?"

I rolled my eyes. "Lead on, Watson."

Chapter 18

Thirty-Four Years Earlier

Nate watched Emily the day after her First Time, wondering how she felt. She looked the same. Well, she *sort of* looked the same. He was in the main building after lunch and he watched her for a long moment while he waited for the elevator. She kind of glowed a bit. She was happier than usual. Then Emily caught sight of him and grinned. He waved at her in return before the elevator doors closed.

Yep, he decided. She glowed.

"How are you feeling?" Nate asked that night as they went into the employee entrance at the back of the kitchen building. It was the first time they were alone together since he ran out of the cottage that morning, late for work.

"Great," Emily said. "A bit sleepy but otherwise great."

"Not too sore?" he asked in a low voice.

"For what? I'm not going to go horseback riding any time soon, if that's what you mean." She said something in Spanish to the cooks that had them smiling at her. They filled her plate and Nate's with chicken, Jell-O, baked beans, and bread. Emily and Nate took their seats at an employee table. "But I wouldn't mind a repeat of last night," she whispered.

He nodded to a couple of the evening maintenance crew who were just coming on shift. "Yeah, I'd like it, too. But are you sure? I don't want to hurt you, Emily."

"Damn it, you'd better quit looking at me that way or we won't make it to the cottage."

He looked down at his plate then at her. "How did it feel today?"

"Hmm?"

"I mean, did you feel different? I did. I felt kind of crazy."

"I did, too. It's like somebody changed all the rules or something. I would be talking to somebody and think, 'Wow, I'll bet he has sex with his wife.' Then I'd try to imagine it." Nate laughed out loud. "You know what I mean," Emily hissed. "It's like a whole new world."

He nodded, still chuckling. "I know."

She looked puzzled. "This isn't new for you."

"The way I feel about you is new. I've never cared for a girl the way I care for you, Emily. Remember when I said how sex with somebody you loved must be insane because regular sex is great. I was right. Last night was like having sex for the first time. I felt as though I discovered a whole new world." *Wow*, he thought. *I sort of said I love her in a really roundabout way. Wow.*

Emily must have noticed because she stared at him, her eyes big. Then she nodded. "Yeah. I know."

They finished dinner and went to Emily's dorm where she dashed inside. She emerged quickly, red-faced. "Pauline and Harv are going at it," she whispered as she pushed her little duffle bag at Nate. "Lord, they were loud."

"You were loud last night, sugar," he said, putting an arm around her shoulder.

"Was not."

"We'll see," he said complacently.

She nudged him with an elbow as they walked down the access road, approaching the cottage by a circuitous route. Emily put her things away then they sat in the living room, looking at each other.

Nate wasn't sure what to do. For some reason, he felt awkward around her. Emily still wore her uniform, a Pine Place golf shirt and denim skirt. She wasn't the exciting, sensual stranger he shared the night with.

"Come sit with me," he said, patting one knee.

Emily perched on his knee. "This feels like Santa Claus," she said doubtfully.

His hand started to move under her skirt. "Really?" he asked in a deep, husky voice. "Did Santa do this to you?"

Emily's breathing started to quicken as he found what he was looking for. "No," she admitted. "Santa never did that."

"Good. Now tell me." He tugged at her shirt and pulled it out of the waistband of her skirt. One hand went up to cup her breast. "Have you been a good little girl?"

She smiled dreamily at him. "It depends on your definition of naughty and nice."

****

Their days passed in a warm haze of love. They went to work and at the end of the day they'd have supper together, sometimes joining friends at the beach or going to town to spend the evening with Mike Sawyer and his girlfriend, Donna. Sometimes they would make out in the back of Mike's Chevy or in the balcony of the movie theater with all the other couples.

Often they'd get supper, take a walk then go back to the cottage and make love for hours. Emily had no hang-ups. They tried everything in the book and a few that took Nate totally by surprise. She wanted to try every position, erotic enticement, and outrageous trick she read in *Penthouse* magazine and *Cosmopolitan.* Emily was determined to be a New, Liberated Woman.

There was only one bumpy spot and it occurred early in their relationship. One of the waitresses, Rachel Putnam, pulled Nate aside one night when he and Emily were having dinner. She and Nate talked in low tones. When Nate came back to the table, he looked embarrassed.

"What was that all about?" Emily asked, eyeing Rachel, who was at least twenty, a Townie, and damn pretty. Emily's female radar went on high alert.

Nate looked at his plate and mumbled, "I knew her in high school."

Emily's radar kicked into Def-Con 2. "In what way did you know her?" she asked acidly. "In the Biblical sense?"

Nate flushed a furious red. Emily got so mad she stomped out of the kitchen to the dorm for the night. He didn't follow her and she spent a miserable night, crying and wondering if he was with Rachel. The next day she saw Rachel talk to Nate while he was in one of the resort's trucks. Emily turned away from the sight, not willing to see anything that might hurt.

At night Nate sat waiting for her on the front steps, like usual. As she came down the steps she prepared to walk by him but he reached out a hand and before she knew what was happening, he pulled her to sit next to him. “Emily, I’m sorry,” he said softly.

She tried to look away from him. “Let me go.”

“I love you,” he whispered.

Her heart started to hammer wildly. He said it. He really said it. She stopped tugging and looked at him doubtfully. “What about Rachel? You and she *know* each other.”

“Not the way you and I know each other.”

“It’s not fair. You have these women in your past and I don’t have anything to make you jealous with.”

“Good. Let’s keep it that way.” His voice softened. “I missed you last night. I really did.”

“Oh, Nate. Did you sleep with her?” She turned away, tears in her eyes.

He looked so surprised she knew the answer before he spoke. “Of course not! I told you, I’m your guy and that means I’m not going to be with someone else. Not unless you kick me out of your bed.”

Emily put her arms around him, leaning into his solid warmth. “I’m glad.” They started walking toward the cottage. “So, did she ask you to go out with her?”

“Sort of,” Nate said, looking away from her.

She jabbed him in the ribs. “Tell all. You know I’ll get it out of you one way or another.”

“That might be fun,” Nate said thoughtfully. Emily jabbed him again. “Okay, she wanted to know if I wanted a three-way. She’s into stuff. Remember, we talked about it once? Bondage and stuff.”

Emily stopped in the road and stared at him. “A three-way? What’s that?”

He rolled his eyes. “Two girls and one guy. You know. Her and you and me.”

Emily blinked, trying to imagine it. Nate and Rachel and her and...He was grinning at her. "Have you done that before?" she demanded.

Nate opened his mouth then closed it quickly. "Once. It wasn't all it's cracked up to be."

"I want details. And I mean *details*."

Nate put his arm around her. "If you want to invite another girl we can try it."

"I'm surprised at you." She slanted him a look. "Would you be willing to share me with another man? Would you set up a three-way for me?" She looked thoughtful. "Now, let's see, who can we get? Hmm, Mike Sawyer is awfully cute or maybe Pete. Let's see, there's a lifeguard I noticed." She shot Nate an assessing gaze.

Now it was his turn to stop. "No way. And who's this lifeguard you noticed?"

"Oh, nobody in particular," she said airily. She slipped one hand into Nate's back jeans pocket and cupped his butt. "No sharing while you're my guy. Deal?"

He grinned at her. "Deal."

****

Every Wednesday they went to Nate's parents' house and had supper then excused themselves to go to the apartment "to listen to records."

"We always do listen to records," Nate said as he slowly undressed Emily on the bed in his apartment over the garage. "It's just that we do other things at the same time."

"Speaking of records..." Emily started to unbuckle his belt.

"Hmm?"

"Eric Clapton's new album is coming out soon."

Nate unbuttoned her blouse and pushed it off her shoulders. "Good." His hands moved down to stroke her thighs.

Emily shivered and pressed closer to him. "The Record Mart in Kalamazoo is going to get copies in." She slid his jeans down his legs.

"Good." He put a hand inside her panties.

Emily arched up to meet him. "He's my favorite, you know."

"I know."

"I thought I'd go to Kalamazoo and get a copy."

"Hmm." Nate slowly tugged down her panties then gently pushed down on her shoulders until she was lying on the bed. He knelt in front of her and positioned himself between her legs.

"They're only going to get a couple of hundred copies," she said breathlessly.

"What a drag," he muttered.

"So I'm going to go the night before and camp out with some kids," she said as his tongue flicked out to taste her.

Nate froze and peered up at her. "What?"

She spoke in a rush. "David, Roxie, Margie, and me. We're going to hitchhike up to Kalamazoo and camp out overnight."

Nate propped himself up on his elbows over her thighs and rested his chin on her stomach. "Emily, you're not. It's dangerous. It's dumb." When he saw the outraged look on her face, he realized immediately he said the wrong things. "Okay. Maybe it's not dumb. But it's dangerous. You can't sleep out all night on a city street."

"Why not? Is it against the law?"

"Probably."

She started to get up. "Let's ask your dad, okay?"

He grabbed her around the legs and pushed her back onto the bed, pinning her down with his body. "I'll go with you, okay?"

"No. I don't have to do everything with you."

"Yes, you do. I want to do everything with you."

"Well, I didn't mean *that*," she said, turning to him.

"I did." He pushed her onto her back and poised over her, staring down at her with a devilish grin. "But if we camp out on a city street, we'll miss a night of this." He nudged at her entrance and she obediently opened for him.

"Not necessarily. We'll just take a nice, big sleeping bag."

"Oh, God," he breathed as the erotic possibilities unfolded in his mind.

Ten days later they drove to Kalamazoo on his motorcycle. Mike and Pete, Nate's friends from town, stuffed the other kids into their cars. They all met at the Record Mart on Main Street in downtown.

Natalie had thoroughly approved of the entire adventure and packed them a picnic dinner. Sam made a few phone calls. As long as they behaved themselves and didn't make a nuisance, the owner of the store was amenable to having kids camping out in order to be the first to buy the newest Eric Clapton album. It was great publicity for the store and hey, it was the Seventies, right? Peace, love, and rock and roll, right?

Mike brought lawn chairs in the trunk of his car and Emily made good on her word, bringing along a sleeping bag. She and Nate snuggled on a chaise lounge then tossed the blanket over themselves. They were soon immersed in extremely heavy petting under the blanket, right out in plain sight of everyone. It was one of the most erotic experiences of Nate's life. At about four in the morning, they finally ended up going back to Mike's car and using the back seat.

When the store opened they were first in line to get their copies of the album. Then they had an exhilarating ride back to the resort in the rain, with Emily protecting the albums by stuffing them inside her blouse and covering herself with the blanket. They made it back just in time for Nate to go to work.

Emily was in heaven for days afterward. She played the album so much she had it memorized immediately. Nate would hear her in the shower, singing "Promises." He'd go weak at the knees, remembering their night in Kalamazoo.

Decades later, he still went weak in the knees.

Chapter 19

Present Day

Emily and I stopped at the house to give Dad the diary. He looked intrigued. Both he and Mom promised to look through it. "I think he feels guilty about Peggy," I said as we drove to the resort in my truck. "She was killed while he was sheriff."

"It's not his fault. He didn't even know she was murdered until a week ago." Emily wiggled her feet against the floor of the truck, looking at the town as it passed our windows.

"Doesn't matter. He still feels bad about it."

"Just imagine," Emily said in a thoughtful voice. "Peggy just up and vanished one day. What did her parents imagine? My daddy would have been so upset, not to mention my brothers. Heavens, they'd tear the world apart to find me."

I remembered her brothers, all big guys with a fanatical determination to keep their little sister safe. "They wouldn't have rested." I glanced at her. She looked confused, her eyebrows drawn together in a frown. "What's wrong?"

"Damn. I think I promised Polly McBride we'd speak at a memorial service for Peggy."

"You think you promised? When did you talk to Peggy's mom?" I slowed for the turn leading to the resort.

"I drank some wine last night, when I was upset about you," Emily said. "I called Mrs. McBride to see if she remembered if Peggy had a diary. She asked me—well, you, really—to talk at a service on Monday. Tomorrow," she added helpfully.

"Aw, Emily. I don't like to talk in public."

"Oh, really? How often do you have to talk in public?"

"I have to go to the schools and talk, and city meetings, and ladies' clubs and the Rotary. I have to do it all the time. On Wednesday I'm giving a speech at the pep rally and at the Civics class at the high school. It's a yearly thing for Homecoming. All the city officials come in and talk."

"Then you're good at it," she said complacently. "They wouldn't ask you back if you weren't good. It's just a few words, Nate. I'm going to talk, too."

"You? You hardly knew Peggy."

"Well, if I can do it, you can," she said triumphantly.

"You'll go to the service with me, right? You signed me up for this. The least you can do is go with me."

"Your date?"

"You know what I meant."

"I'll be your date." Then she scooted closer and put one hand on my leg. "You're my date tonight, right? We're having dinner, right?"

I looked down at her hand, which was slowly inching its way up my leg. "Emily, be nice," I warned.

"As I recall, you told me once I was a combination of naughty and nice. Let's see, for now, I'll be nice. But tonight—" She kissed me on the cheek. "Tonight I might decide to be naughty."

My breathing took on a shallow, hollow sound. "How am I supposed to talk to a group of people when I have a hard-on tough enough to drive nails?"

She put her hand on the object under discussion. "It is. I'm flattered."

"You're dangerous." I drove through the gates in the front of the resort. "And if you don't remove your hand, I'll arrest you for public indecency."

She moved away from me and was sitting demurely on her side of the truck when we came to a stop near the front entrance. "I'll get you later," she warned as I came around to her side and opened the passenger door.

"You'd better or I'll die of anticipation." Emily laughed and slid out of the truck. "What did I do to earn such a reaction from you?" I asked softly.

She looked up at me, her cheeks pink with flustered embarrassment. "Like I said on the pier, Nate. I want to see what happens." She looked down, her lashes dark on her cheek. I saw the fine lines around her eyes and the gray in her auburn hair, shining like highlights even though it was a cloudy, miserable day. When she looked up at me, I saw the confusion in her eyes but I also saw determination and honesty. "We deserve to know if what we're feeling is just memories or something real. I don't know why my moods are swinging like a drunk on a chandelier, but I'm going to enjoy myself."

Probably hormones, I thought but kept it to myself. She was that age, after all, and I remembered when my mother went through the Change. My father and I tiptoed around her for most of a year, not sure if she was going to bite our heads off or love us silly. Then I thought of my own swinging moods lately and realized I was probably going through my own Change, too, right alongside Emily.

"You're so much the boy I remember but you're also such a new, interesting stranger."

I waggled my eyebrows. "Nothing like having sex with a stranger," I murmured. "The most exciting sex of all."

"Can't wait." She led the way to where the Summer Kids were assembled, parked in the turnaround near the front of the hotel. They all came forward to greet us.

"I can't tell you how much it means to me that you guys volunteered to help like this." I waved to Bobby Goldman, who was coming toward us from the east side of the property. "It's been so long I'm not sure we can reconstruct what happened, but I'd like to try." I moved toward Bobby and everyone fell into step, forming a small convoy. I heard Emily tell the others about the Memorial Service and a few folks who were staying over said they'd come.

"Let's walk around a bit," Esther said, coming up to me. We linked arms and started to drift toward the swimming pool. "They changed the pool, didn't they?"

"It's bigger," Bobby said. "We added that little bit there," and he pointed out a deeper section, "in 1980. Folks wanted a good diving place."

"They've got Lake Michigan and the diving raft, what more do they want?" Esther turned away from the pool and walked down the back lane leading to the northeast corner of the property, where the individual rental cottages had been located. The other summer people followed, all in small groups and talking.

"I remember the last dance like it was yesterday," Esther said dreamily. "Big Tom Judson got all dressed up. He was a fine-looking man. We had some good times."

I glanced around. Emily was behind us, talking to Harv and some of the others. "I don't remember it. I think we only stayed for an hour or two."

"It was in town," Pauline said, walking up to join us.

Bobby nodded. "It was at the Legion Hall. I remember. There was a DJ from Kalamazoo. He was good."

"I remember how loud it was. You could hear the music all over town." Pauline glanced at Bobby. "I don't remember seeing you there, but there were so many people. It was the first time the Townies and the summer people really got along together." She glanced back at Emily. "Thanks to her and what happened."

Emily moved forward, looking over her shoulder at Lake Michigan in the distance. For an instant her eyes narrowed and I wondered if she was seeing the spot in her memories.

"What happened?" This was from Sabrina, Greg Hoffman's wife, who was walking next to me.

We all exchanged a glance. *Geez*, I thought, *Greg was under suspicion at the time. How do I tell his wife he was considered a suspect in a rape?*

"Emily was abducted," Greg's voice cut through the other voices. "And held captive, at the park." He gestured vaguely toward the city park, north of the resort and just ahead of us, through the trees lining the property.

"Good heavens." Sabrina turned to Emily, obviously startled. "What happened?"

"I honestly don't remember a lot of it," Emily said, kicking at a clump of dirt. "This guy drugged me and tied me up. He had me stuck away at a little cove." She gestured with one hand, overbalancing slightly and I steadied her. She looked up and saw me, smiling down at her. I saw the worry in her eyes. I suppose even after thirty-four years the memories of that day would come back. "Luckily for me, I was able to get away before anything happened."

"Was he—I mean, were you—?" Sabrina stumbled over the words. I didn't miss the look she shot at her husband, Greg the Jerk.

"Oh, I was okay. Nothing really happened."

"Abducted, drugged, stripped naked, tied up, and almost raped. Nothing happens, she says," David said with a shake of his head. "It's enough, girlfriend."

Everyone laughed, breaking the tension. "It was such a weird time, huh?" Pauline said, her hand finding Harv's. "We were so scared but we were also so happy. It was such an odd, mixed-up summer."

I looked down at Emily but as I did I caught a look at Bobby's face. He looked sad and forlorn, like an old memory was bothering him, too. I suppose we reminded him of his father and the family he lost, although the old man was such a bastard, it wasn't much of a loss.

"One good thing came out of it, at least," Emily said. "The Townies and the summer people all worked together to find me. We never had any more trouble afterwards. Maybe that's why the dance was such a success."

Bobby nodded and the forlorn look vanished from his eyes. "You're right, of course. You always did have a way at seeing the bright side of things, Emily." He smiled at her and me but I didn't see any warmth in his brown eyes. We all turned away from the bluff and started walking back toward the hotel. "If anybody would care to come inside and look around, I can let you in," Bobby volunteered.

Several people accepted the invitation, but Emily and I, Pauline, Harv, and Esther continued walking around the grounds, talking about the old days and getting caught up on each other. We ended up at the construction site.

"They tore down the dorms," Esther sighed, looking at the raw earth. "Lord, I had some times in that dorm." She cocked an eyebrow at Harv and Pauline. "You guys did, too, as I recall." Then she looked at me. "Mr. Resort Boy, though, he had someplace private for him and his girl. Is your little house still around?"

I flushed. Emily slipped her hand into mine. "They tore it down," I said regretfully. "It was over this way, though." I led the way through the construction equipment until we stood near the back access road.

Pauline looked around at the lonely spot. "Peggy was found here, right?"

I pointed to the crime scene, marked with yellow tape. "Over there." I gestured to the left. "The old cottages that weren't rented were over here."

"Wouldn't you guys have heard something that night?" Esther asked. I gave her an incredulous look and Esther shook her head. "Okay, stupid question. But surely Peggy didn't just lie down and let somebody bash her head. She must have struggled."

"Unless she was drugged," Emily said thoughtfully. "Like me. Whatever they gave me, it was powerful. I couldn't move at all even when he took my clothes off and started touching me." She shuddered and I put an arm around her shoulders. "It was terrible," she said, her voice breaking. "It was like being all tied up with cotton or something. I wasn't feeling pain but it was so repulsive to know somebody was touching me. I couldn't see them or stop them."

"Hey, hey," Pauline said, moving up to enfold her in a hug. "You're safe now, farm girl. It's okay." Harv and Esther made similar comforting noises and I kept my hand on her shoulder.

Emily sighed. "It's been thirty-four years. You'd think I'd get over it."

"That kind of thing?" Esther shook her head, looking disgusted. "A woman doesn't get over it. You just learn to live with it." She spoke with such authority and conviction that I looked at her, startled. Before I could pursue it, someone called my name and we turned to see Greg and the others approaching us.

"We're going to go on down to the café," Sabrina said. She had her arms crossed across her chest and she looked cold.

I nodded, feeling the autumn dampness in the chilly wind. "We'll meet you there in a few minutes." I glanced at Emily for confirmation. "I wonder if you're right," I said softly. "Maybe Peggy was drugged."

We turned and followed the others back to the cars. "It would explain how the guy got away with it," Emily said. "After all, the resort was full to capacity that weekend. Guests and staff would be all over the place.

If Peggy was drugged and waiting for the killer at the mechanics' shed then it'd be a simple matter to slip away and meet her."

"I remember how out of it you were. It was a powerful drug."

"I recognized you, though. I'll never forget waking up and seeing you there. That's when I knew I was rescued." My hand tightened on her shoulder. "Ow. Bruises, remember?"

"Sorry," I mumbled. I stopped and looked back at the construction site.

"What is it, Nate?"

"I'm just glad you didn't try to find the diary yesterday, when Porter was here." I shook my head. "That coincidence bothers me. Porter was on the beach, almost in the exact spot where you found the diary. Why? Why did he get so upset? Did the sight of these people make him remember all he lost?"

We stopped by the truck. "Come on," Emily urged. "It's raining."

I looked around, surprised at the light mist falling. "Okay. It was probably a stupid idea to come out here anyway."

"I think it was a great idea." She gestured to the truck. "Give me a leg up, cowboy?"

I grinned and helped her into the cab. When I got into the driver's side, she immediately scooted over to sit next to me. She made a small, sinuous little motion on my leg as I put the car into gear.

"You've got your hand on my leg again," I pointed out, putting the truck into gear and driving out of the gates. I nodded to Bobby Goldman, who watched us.

"I sure do." We drove out of the resort and onto the

road for the drive into town. “I heard about Peggy and the S&M thing. Who was into that, do you know?”

I glanced at her. I wonder if she saw a hint of despair in my eyes. “You have no idea what effect you have on me.”

“Oh.” She paused then resumed. “I think I do know the effect I have on you.”

“How would you like it if I did stuff like that to you?” I demanded. “Huh? How would you feel?”

“I might enjoy it. It’s fun sometimes to be teased. But we’ll never know, will we? You’re not really a teaser, are you? Oh, look, there’s Greg and Sabrina. They’re so perfectly matched, aren’t they? She’s snotty and he’s a bore.” Emily smiled prettily at me and moved away on the truck seat. “I know how you want to preserve your reputation. I mean, you are Chief of Police and you have a duty to uphold the moral standards.” She sighed again. “It must really put a crimp in your romantic style.”

I didn’t answer until I parked the truck in front of the café. “I don’t have a romantic style, Emily,” I said, rounding on her. “I don’t have any romance at all in my life.” I sounded a bit frantic but I was feeling desperate.

“You used to. You had a great romantic style. I remember it very well. I especially remember the one time when you were all sweaty and dirty after work and we went to the cottage and you insisted I take off my blouse. Then you—”

“Emily!” It came out as a near howl of frustration. I blew out a long breath. “You’re driving me crazy,” I said, my voice calmer.

She leaned over, just begging for a kiss. “Good. I want you crazy tonight.” Then she slipped out of the door before I could grab her.

Esther appeared at my side of the truck. “Man, she’s got your Jockeys in a jam.”

I banged my head gently on the steering wheel. “She’ll kill me.”

Esther grinned. “So what else is new?”

I got out of the truck. “Some things never change. She can still lead me around by my—”

Esther held up a hand. “Please. We’re in public.”

Emily went ahead to the entrance, tugging open the door. “Come on, you guys!”

Esther took my arm as we entered the restaurant behind Emily. “She’s just begging for a bit of romance, Nate,” Esther said in a low voice.

“She’s begging for something, that’s for sure,” I muttered.

“She told me she really likes it here. She was hoping to move to a small town once she sold her business. Seems to me this place might be tailor-made for her.” Then she said loudly, “Just make sure to invite me to the wedding.”

Emily stopped, stunned. I looked around. Everyone in the restaurant had heard Esther’s words. I looked around, too, at the expectant faces all regarding us.

Emily and I stared at each other across the space.

“Come on, Nate,” Emily called from the door to the private room. “I’m waiting for you.”

I grinned and joined her.

****

“Honestly, that’s all I can remember,” Harv said as he shoved the piece of paper over to me. We’d partaken of Cora’s famous Sunday buffet and were now sitting around, talking. “Sorry it’s so sparse.”

I nodded morosely. “It was worth a try.” I took the papers people prepared, passing them on to Emily. I glanced down at Greg’s before passing it.

Fight with Townies. Screwed Rachel Putnam. Got drunk.

Well, he was at least succinct and to the point. I worked out a rough timeline based on what people had written.

“Okay, here it is.” I pushed over the big piece of butcher paper Cora gave us to write on.

6:30 Esther on duty

7:00 dance starts in town at the Legion Hall

7:30 John, Greg, Paul, Mark at dance; they see Peggy at the dance, don’t talk to her

8:00 Harv and Pauline get to party

9:00 Nate and Emily get to party

9:30 Nate talks to Peggy about running away to get married

10:00 Nate and Emily leave

10:30 fight breaks out

11:00 Greg and others are ejected

11:00 Harv and Pauline leave

11:30 Esther off duty; talks to Peggy at the resort; goes to town

12:00 Greg and others on the beach, have a party with Rachel and other girls

“You need to add Bobby,” Esther said, pointing at the list. “He said he was there.”

“And where did you two disappear?” Greg asked with a sly smile. Sabrina, sitting next to him, nudged him and murmured something. He snorted in derision.

“We had a private party that night,” Emily said haughtily. “As, I believe, Harv and Pauline did and many other people."

"You should add Rachel, too," David said. "I saw her there and not just with Greg. She was at the party and I saw her talking to Peggy."

"Where is Rachel?" Emily asked as she penciled in "Bobby Goldman" and "Rachel" on the timeline.

"She died in a car accident about five years later," I said. "My dad told me about it. He said it was a bad accident, out on the twisty stretch of road beyond the park."

"She was so young." Emily sounded only vaguely regretful and I remembered there was no love lost between the two of them. "So sometime between 9:30 and 11:30, Peggy went back to the resort." Emily tapped the list. "Is the Legion still there?"

"It got torn down when they put up a rec center."

We kept talking, adding details. The party broke up shortly after four in the afternoon. Most people who lived in the area were going home and those who had traveled some distance were staying in Holland or Kalamazoo and had to drive back to stay overnight.

"And don't forget the memorial service tomorrow," Emily reminded everyone as they straggled out of the restaurant.

Pauline made a noise but Esther nodded. "No problem. We're not that busy." She linked an arm through Harv's. "Ready to escort two beautiful women to dinner tonight?"

He grinned. Esther was so tall she could almost look him in the eye. "Sure am, sugar." Harv winked at his wife, who took his other arm then he looked back at me with a gleam in his eye. "Let's go girls. I got my hands full, Chief, and I suspect you do, too."

I caught Emily's eye just as she looked up from the timeline.

"Yep," I said.

Emily gave me a satisfied look. "He surely does."

Chapter 20

Thirty-Four Years Earlier

Emily came out of the resort one evening to see Nate talking with his father and Bobby Goldman in the parking lot in front of the main building. Their grim faces told her that something had happened. She hurried down the stairs in time to hear Sheriff Boltz say, "She'll live. We found her in town. Somebody dumped her out of a car."

Emily stopped in surprise. "What's happened? Is somebody hurt?"

Sam Boltz looked down at her. "One of the girls who works here. She was beaten. And she was raped."

Emily drew in a sharp breath. "My God. Who was it?"

"Janie Sinclair," Sam said. "She lived in town. She was in the cleaning crew."

"Will she be okay?" Emily asked, looking from one man to another.

"It'll take time. He beat her up bad and she was—" Sam stopped, looking at the other men. Something passed between them. "She was hurt badly." He looked at Bobby. "I'm going to need to talk to everybody on your staff. Group meetings."

Bobby nodded. "I'll arrange it. We have three shifts. I'll set up meetings at the first of every shift." He glanced at Emily. “You girls at the front desk come to the morning shift meeting, with Nate. You’re on a different schedule than anybody else.”

“I’ll talk to Pauline and Esther.” Emily turned to Sheriff Boltz. “Can I help somehow? Is Janie in the hospital?”

“I don’t think she wants company,” he said gently.

“I’ll get some flowers for her,” she said, looking at Nate, who nodded.

“We’ll go into town and order them right now,” he promised.

“What else happened, Nate?” Emily asked as they walked to the machinists’ shed to get his motorcycle. She saw the look of disgust in his eyes before he could hide it. “Please tell me. This is scary stuff.”

“She was drugged and sodomized,” he said in a low voice.

“Oh, my God.” Emily stopped, her mind reeling.

“And she was raped, you know, the regular way.” Nate stumbled over the words. “Dad said she must have woken up and tried to get away. That’s when she was beaten.”

“Poor Janie.” Emily drew in a shuddering breath. “I didn’t know her well but that’s awful!”

“Dad wants to set up curfews. He’s afraid it might happen again.”

As they passed the dorm Emily saw Pauline and Harv, standing outside talking. She hurried over to tell them what happened. “Jesus,” Harv said. He was a big, raw-boned boy with light brown hair bleached almost white by the sun and an incredible tan from his time at the beach. He and Pauline were both strong-looking with the highly developed shoulders of swimmers.

"Who the hell would do such a thing?"

Nate shook his head. "Dad said he wants to set up an escort thing, you know? To make sure none of the girls are alone."

Harv nodded. "Makes sense."

"We're having staff meetings," Emily told Pauline. "Can you tell Esther? Bobby said we all should go to the early meeting."

Pauline nodded. "I'll talk to Bobby and to Esther tonight." She looked from Nate to Harv. "I'm glad we've got you guys." She shuddered and Harv put an arm around her shoulders.

Emily and Nate went into town, ordering flowers for Janie at the local florist shop. Emily signed the card "from all the kids at the resort." She couldn't shake the thoughts about what happened that night. Nate just held her as she shivered in his arms until she finally fell asleep. But in the middle of the night, she woke, thrashing from a bad dream.

Nate grabbed her and Emily fought him. "It's okay, it's okay," Nate said. "I won't let anything happen to you. I promise."

She finally subsided in his arms, crying.

****

The next morning Esther, Pauline, and Emily all went to the staff meeting, Bobby filling in for Pauline so she could attend.

Sheriff Boltz was authoritative and calm. "It's important not to blow this out of proportion. This might be an isolated incident but just in case, we want to take some precautions." He looked at the Summer Boys and the Townie boys. "I want you guys to step up and help out."

Every male in the room straightened, even the Mexicans cooks and cleaning crew. Sergio, who had the best English, was translating. "I don't want a girl to walk around this resort alone at any time. If somebody needs an escort, one of you boys makes sure she gets to wherever she's going." His gaze swept the room past Nate and Emily, sitting together and holding hands. "No girl should have to be afraid of walking around and I want to make sure you all stay safe."

The meeting broke up and several people huddled in small groups, murmuring. Emily spoke a few words with Herves and the other Mexicans, who nodded and looked worried. Then she rejoined Nate and Esther. "Herves is worried somebody will try to pin it on them," Emily said in a low voice.

Nate bristled. "My dad's not going to pin it on somebody."

Esther shrugged. "Some groups have always been singled out when shit like this happens. It was blacks for a long time, now it's Mexicans. Trust me, if there's a way to pin it on somebody who ain't white, they'll do it."

Nate started to speak but Emily put a restraining hand on his arm. "I hope not, Esther," she said. "I think Sheriff Boltz is a bit fairer."

Esther nodded skeptically. "I hope so, too." She started to stride away then she seemed to remember something. "You might want to tell your father Peggy is into some odd things," she said off-handedly. "I've heard she likes it rough."

Nate and Esther exchanged a long look and Nate nodded. "I'll mention it."

"What did that mean?" Emily asked as Esther

disappeared into the dorm.

Nate ignored her question, brushing a kiss against her cheek. “Gotta go to work. Are you okay? You had some bad dreams last night.”

“I’m just bummed out. It’s so awful.”

“It won’t happen again. Don’t worry. I’ll see you tonight.”

Emily went into the dorm, intending to change for a quick swim. Esther was waiting for her. “I didn’t mean to offend.”

"I know you didn't." Emily brushed past Esther and headed for her room. "But I know the sheriff pretty well. I don’t think he’ll jump to conclusions.”

Esther still looked skeptical, but she said, “I hope so. You going swimming? Can I join you?”

“More swimming lessons?” Emily asked with a grin.

Esther was a terrible swimmer but she had been practicing all summer. “I’m going to figure out swimming if it’s the last thing I do.” Esther looked critically at Emily’s lush figure. “I got flotation devices almost as big as yours. I don’t know why I sink and you don’t.”

“Must be all that clean living I do,” Emily said.

They both laughed.

An hour later, Emily drowsed by the swimming pool in her almost-bikini, purchased after much cajoling to get past her father’s objections. She sat up, peering around sleepily. “Where’s Esther?”

David, the children’s counselor who was lying on the chair next to hers, said, “She was here a minute ago.”

“She’s not supposed to go in the pool unless one of

us goes with her." Emily scrambled off her lounge chair and looked down into the pool. "Oh, my God." Esther was at the bottom of the nine-foot section, her black body standing out in sharp contrast to the pale blue painted surface. She was thrashing around, pushing off the bottom then sinking back.

"Get help!" Emily called then she dove in and was at Esther's side in a few strong strokes. As she neared the other girl, Emily saw Esther was panicked. She had somehow gotten to the bottom of the pool and she didn't know how to get herself back up.

Emily made it to Esther's side and held out a hand then crouched on the bottom of the pool and, clinging to Esther's hand, she pushed off as hard as she could. When Esther popped off the bottom, Emily propelled the other girl ahead of her by putting a hand on Esther's butt and pushing her. Willing hands reached down into the pool and grasped Esther. Emily propelled herself upward in time to see Esther being hauled out of the pool by Harv, the lifeguard coming on duty.

Emily swam to the side and clung to the edge, coughing. Esther sat on the pool apron, Harv bent over her and talking. Then Esther caught Emily's eye. "My God, Farm Girl," Esther said in a choked voice. "You saved my life."

Emily hauled herself out of the pool and crossed quickly to kneel by Esther. "What happened? You're not supposed to go in unless one of us is with you."

Esther choked a bit and Harv pounded her on the back. "I was on the side, holding on, and somehow I just lost my grip," Esther said between sobs. "I floated down there and I didn't know what to do." She suddenly grabbed Emily and hugged her tightly, tears flowing down her face. "Oh, Farm Girl, you rescued me."

"Just don't ever do that again." Emily gave Esther a little shake. It was almost time for the pool to open for guests, so everyone gathered up their gear and started walking to the dorms, Emily with her arm linked with Esther's, each giving the other badly needed comfort. Word spread ahead of them and they were greeted along the way with looks, pats on the shoulders, and congratulations. Bobby came out of the main hotel then Nate came running from the kitchen, followed by Sergio.

"We're fine, we're fine," Esther kept saying even as tears rolled down her face. "Emily just saved my dumb ass, that's all."

Emily laughed shakily and Nate looked so scared Emily put her arms around him and got him wet. "I'm fine. Esther just got to the bottom of the pool and didn't know what to do." She grinned at Sergio, who was agog at the sight of both Esther and Emily in their bikinis. "We're fine."

Esther repeated the whole story. "I was down there and my life flashed in front of my eyes," she said with a sigh. "I knew I was going to die because I couldn't figure out what to do. What a stupid way to die."

Emily transferred her hug from Nate to Esther. "You're my friend, you silly goose. I wasn't going to let you die."

Esther laughed shakily. "You got some special mojo, Farm Girl, that's for sure."

Later that night, Emily and Nate were in town at the Ice Cream Piggery with Mike Sawyer and his girlfriend, Donna. The sundaes and splits at the Piggery were so big they came in little pig troughs. The four of them had been splitting troughs all summer and tonight was Emily's turn to keep the trough.

Emily dug her spoon into the little trough and emerged with a big dollop of chocolate ice cream. "Yum. My favorite." Just as the spoon neared her mouth, a huge black man approached them. Emily hadn't gotten a good look at Tom Judson when he rescued her before, but now she saw he was easily as big as her brother, Silas. He looked like either a professional football player or a hit man. Emily wasn't sure which.

He extended his hand and Emily put hers in it. "I'm Tom. Esther's summer boy." The man gave Emily's hand such a brisk shake her head wobbled. "Wanted to thank you for what you did for Esther. She's a good girl."

Emily gulped in surprise. "Esther's my friend. I'm glad I was able to help. And I'm glad I was able to pay you back for helping me."

Judson's gaze swept over Nate and Mike. "You let me know if you need help with this rape thing. Nobody does that to a woman and gets away with it. It's not right."

"Thanks," Nate said. "Thanks a lot. We'll keep it in mind. I'll tell my dad."

"I'll tell my boys to keep an eye out," Judson said as he moved away from their table. He suddenly smiled at Emily and she beamed back at him. "Thanks, Farm Girl."

Emily made a little dismissive gesture. "You just take care of Esther, you hear me?" She gave him a serious look. "She was very upset. She needs some extra special care, you know?" She winked.

He grinned. "I hear you, ma'am." They heard him chuckling as he left.

Saul Rubinstein, the proprietor, came hurrying over. "That was Big Tom Judson," he said, his hands mangling a small towel.

Emily nodded gravely. "It was. He's a friend of a friend."

"Wow." Saul hurried away and had a whispered conversation with several other patrons, all of whom regarded Emily and her friends with respect mingled with apprehension.

Emily smiled at Mike and Nate and Donna. "He seemed like a nice man. I'm sure he and Esther get along well together."

Nate made an indecipherable noise and focused on the banana split. Mike just grinned at Emily and winked. "You got that right, Farm Girl."

Chapter 21

Present Day

"I meant to get groceries last night," Emily said as we left Cora's and went to the truck. She was still looking at the timeline we prepared, frowning. "But then I got distracted."

"That's okay," I said hastily, not willing to revisit the Cynthia Scandal. "We can go out to eat someplace."

"Don't you want me to come to your house?" Emily's attention shifted from the timeline. "What are you hiding? Nudie pictures? X-rated movies in the DVD player?"

"None of the above. I just thought you'd like to go out."

"Nate, I love to cook. I thought you'd remember that about me."

"I do remember," I said as we drove into the meager traffic of Little Bay on a Sunday night. "I'm surprised you even thought about groceries." I gave her a sideways look. "You were pretty pissed off at me."

"Yeah, I was. I thought about getting rat poison but I figured since you were both cops they might investigate a suspicious death closely."

It was hard to tell if she was joking or not. "Glad you forgave me."

She gave me a sly look. "You need to keep

convincing me of your sincerity then I *might* forgive you."

"Good. I'll work on it."

"So let's just go to your place. I'm sure you have something in your fridge I can use."

I mentally inventoried the contents of my larder. "We need to stop by the apartment and get the diary. Dad said he'd leave it inside."

"Good. I want to look through it."

My visions of a romantic night with her at my place started to fade.

"Before we..." she said.

"Before we what?" I asked.

"What's going on? Where's my car?" She looked at the cars parked in the driveway at my parents' house.

"On the street, right there." I nodded toward her rental Volkswagen parked at the curb near the shrubs bordering my parents' house. "It's card club night. Dad probably moved it so their company would have easier access to the house. With luck, we'll get in and out and no one will see us."

I pulled up to the curb and Emily scampered up the stairs to the apartment, dashing back with the diary and a grocery bag in hand. We were out of there in five minutes, no one the wiser.

"I remembered your mom stocked the fridge," she said, setting the bag on the seat between us. "I think I can come up with a nice meal."

I was nervous about her seeing my place. I had cleaned it up, hoping she might come over, but I couldn't disguise the fact it wasn't much, just a little place with a bedroom, den, a bathroom, living room, and a kitchen. When she walked in, J. Edgar immediately flopped down at her feet and she obliged him with a brisk belly rub, sending him into kitty paradise.

"It's nice," she murmured, straightening and looking at the white-painted cupboards in the kitchen, the small stove and sink, the little dishwasher tucked into one corner. She turned to me with a grin. "It's cozy. So old-fashioned and nice."

I blew out a sigh of relief. "It's old-fashioned, that's for sure." I watched as she started unpacking the bag. Some pasta came out, as well as hamburger, some onions, a bunch of green stuff I think were herbs, and various other things.

Emily looked around the kitchen, taking in the kitchen table and chairs. "You. Sit there," she commanded. "I like to have an audience." She reached in the sack and pulled out a bottle of wine. "Be useful. Open this and pour me a glass."

I got out the wine opener and took care of that little chore then settled at the table to watch her cook. She moved quickly and efficiently, dicing, chopping, sautéing, digging around in the drawers for the right knife or pan or implement. Soon a fantastic odor started to waft out from the saucepan on the stove. She put a bit of browned hamburger on a plate for J. Edgar and the old guy purred so loud while he ate I was afraid he'd hurt himself.

"What's your favorite meal?" she asked, stirring briskly at a pot. "I love a good macaroni and cheese, I have to admit. That's comfort food for me."

"Egg salad sandwich. I love those. Or chicken salad. I like a good chicken salad with a lot of mustard. Ham is good, too. Remember how Herves used to make his ham and cheese casserole, with the potatoes?" I watched as the cat ambled out of the room, still purring. I was feeling like him right about now, full of love and happiness. I didn't dare think beyond the moment. The anticipation might kill me.

Emily turned around and leaned against the stove. "I forgot about it. I have a recipe like it. I should make it sometime. Wow, yeah, it was good." She grinned and turned back to her mixing. "I may have to make that soon."

"Make it for me?" I asked.

She glanced at me over her shoulder. "Sure."

"What's cooking tonight?" I eyed the various pots, all different sizes.

Emily looked at me again over her shoulder. "On the stove or otherwise?"

My breath hitched. "Oh, however you care to answer."

"Hmm." She carefully turned down the heat on all of the pots and turned. "Well, I was thinking," she said slowly, crossing the room to where I sat. "I thought we'd have something to eat," she murmured, sliding onto my lap and putting a small kiss along the side of my neck, just inside my collar.

My arms went around her waist. "Really?" I moved my head a bit so she could kiss me some more.

"Yeah." Her lips moved up toward the angle of my head and neck. "And then I thought we might listen to some music and relax." A few more nibbles went onto my neck while her hands went around me, rubbing at my shoulders.

"Really?" I asked, moving a hand over her denim-clad leg.

She moved her lips up toward my ear and whispered, “Then you drive me home.”

I pulled away from her and stared at her in astonishment. “Tell me you’re kidding.” My hand tightened on her thigh. “Please.”

Her golden eyes were laughing. “Can’t you tell when I’m teasing, Nate?” Then her lips met mine and I thought I was going to shoot right off the chair. My hands went to her waist then moved up to cup her breasts. She made a small moaning noise deep in her throat as I thumbed her nipples until they were erect. Then she moved off my lap and was suddenly straddling me on the chair, her knees tightening on my hips and her body pressed against me.

“Damn it, Emily,” I managed to gasp. “Don’t tease me like that.”

She laughed softly, a low, throaty sound. “I plan to tease you all night long, Nate Boltz. Just not like that.” She bent her head to mine again and this time the kiss was sweet and so sensual my bones went to water. I was hardly aware of her as she slid off and went back to the stove. “I need to feed you to keep up your strength. As well as keep up certain other parts.”

“Honey, I have the feeling that around you, it’s not going to be a problem.”

Dinner was like some magic feast. She may have made “just spaghetti and meatballs,” but she added something extra to the sauce so it was better than anything I ever tasted. The whole night was turning out like magic.

“I made enough so you’ll have some leftovers,” she said when we finished. “Just nuke it in the microwave and you’ll have a nice little meal.” Unspoken but hanging between us was the knowledge that when I did that, she'd be gone.

I looked down at my plate and tried hard to think of the positives. She was here. For however long she stayed, I'd enjoy it. "Nice to know you're thinking about me."

"I sure am." Something flickered in her eyes and I thought for a moment it was regret. Then the golden highlights flared again and I saw the mischief. "Why don't you go in the living room and I'll get the coffee going?"

"I'll clean up," I said, standing up. "Only fair, since you cooked."

"Not a chance. I'm putting your dishwasher to use." She scooped up several dirty dishes and rinsed them, then stacked them in the dishwasher. I helped and soon the kitchen was clean, the coffee made, and the dishwasher humming as we moved to the living room. I loaded up the CD changer with Clapton, CSNY, and Neil Young.

Emily sat on the couch and picked up the diary. I sat on the other end and watched her. J. Edgar took his recliner and watched us both through sleepy green eyes. "She seemed to have one steady guy," Emily mused, opening the book.

I sipped my coffee and considered it. "From the little I read, it sounds like a town kid or somebody who went away then came back in the summer. But I can't remember her being with one of us for any length of time." I shrugged. "Peggy didn't seem to like any one guy in particular."

I watched Emily as she kicked off her shoes and tucked her legs up under her on the couch. It felt like a dream. Emily was here, in my house. How many times had I imagined this? She was sitting here, drinking coffee, laughing with me, looking at me. Oh. She was looking at me. I struggled for something to say. "There's a mention in the diary of that girl, Janie. Remember?"

Emily quickly skimmed through the pages. "July, wasn't it?" Without waiting for an answer she kept skimming then stopped. "Oh. Here it is." She read intently and I watched her. She tugged on her lower lip as she read, her eyes getting bigger at the graphic detail. "Wow. That was worse than even I thought it was and I thought it was awful." She looked up at me, eyes wide. "Those poor girls."

"Girls?"

"Peggy and Janie. I mean, yeah, Janie was raped but Peggy thought her boyfriend did it." She tapped the diary. "What a feeling." Emily shuddered and kept skimming through the book, shaking her head.

Now that she was sitting here, it felt like this was a scene from a movie. In a way it was, I guess. I played this out in my head a hundred times. Played it out, thinking about what I'd do if she were here. And now she was here. "Emily?" I said softly.

She looked up. "What?"

Words stuck in my throat. Emily was sitting here with me, on my couch, in my house. She must have seen some of it in my eyes. Emily gently closed the cover on Peggy's diary and set it on the floor at her feet. "Is it time for me to start teasing you?" she asked, her gaze direct.

"I don't know if my heart can take it," I said hoarsely. "It's been a long time since I was with a woman." *And you're not just another woman*, I thought.

She lounged back. "There are some things you just don't forget."

I slid along the couch until I was next to her. "You may need to teach me. I may have forgotten."

Emily pulled me down to her, opening her legs so I settled between her denim-clad thighs. "My pleasure. I'll return the favor you did for me so many years ago."

"Favor?"

She ran a hand down my back. "When you initiated me into the mysteries of love." She raised her hips slightly and I pressed solidly against her crotch. "I'll be glad to repay the favor," she whispered as our lips met.

The passion flared immediately. I stroked her body, feeling, touching, molding the shape of her. She was changed. She was a bit heavier than before and her breasts weren't so high and firm. But God, she was still beautiful. Emily was so small, and petite, and voluptuous, like some kind of miniature woman made just for me.

Her fingers worked at my shirt. I had a sudden panicked moment. What if she thought I was too old? She was so beautiful, but what about me? I wasn't the same. I didn't have all the muscles I used to have.

"Oh, Nate," she murmured, as she pushed off my shirt. "You're still so good-looking." She slid her hand over my chest. I twitched when I felt her light touch. "You look good enough to eat." She pulled away from me, her green eyes laughing. "I may just do that later."

I thought my heart would stop. I'd never forget the feeling of her lips on me. To think I might feel it again.

"But first I want you on top of me," she said, her voice husky. "I love looking up and seeing you. I love to see your face and feel you in me so hard and deep. Let's get comfortable." She pushed gently at my shoulders.

I moved away from her and before I could blink, she shed her blouse, her bra, and she was working on her pants. She shot me a mischievous grin. "Come on, lazy. I'll race you."

I stared in amazement at the charm dangling around her neck. I touched it gently, lifting it off her skin. It was the necklace I gave her years ago, the gold and silver hands entwined together. "Is that the same one?

"Yep. I've replaced the chain a few times but I still wear it." She unzipped her jeans. "I'm ahead of you. Get going."

I frantically obeyed, kicking off my boots and tugging at my pants. By the time I turned back to her, she was naked and stretched out on the couch, watching me with anticipation. When I turned to her and she saw me erect, she immediately reached out her hands.

"Oh, Nate, you look beautiful."

I sank down on top of her, covering her and pressing her into the cushions. "Emily," I managed to say before all the breath left me. I put a trembling kiss along her neck and she arched up to me, her hands stroking and running over my body. I couldn't remember when I was this excited. For all I knew it had been thirty-some years. I was in shock, my system on overload.

She shifted one leg and suddenly I pressed hard against her, my cock pushing at her entrance. "Please."

I reached down and touched her, feeling her incredible heat and moisture. I rubbed myself with it, getting lubrication then with a groan I positioned myself. She lifted, nudging me. I closed my eyes and prayed for self-control. Then I sank into her, deeply and fully, with one long, hard stroke.

"Deeper. Please, Nate, please." She lifted her hips. "More," she commanded in a soft, silky voice.

I withdrew then slid into her again, this time all the way. I felt myself touch the one special spot that made her back arch in a spasm of pleasure. My back and shoulders were sweaty in her hands. My entire body was on fire and only Emily could put it out. Every nerve ending was alight with anticipation and energy. I quickly found the rhythm we knew years before. When I pulled out and stroked into her again I felt her climax start. It began to build in me, too. I hadn't felt anything this strong, this all-encompassing for years. In fact, I started to wonder if I wasn't past such stirrings and maybe heading into some kind of sexual retirement.

Until I touched her. The minute my hands roamed over her, the minute I felt those smooth, soft breasts and her cushioning thighs, I felt my sex awakening with a vengeance. Only Emily could satisfy me now.

She arched up to me, silently pleading...Then she moved her hips...and I put my hand there...and her lips...

Sorry. My mother raised me right.

A gentleman doesn't tell.

****

I awoke the next morning in my bed like I was hit by electricity. Emily had been here. I sank back on the pillows. The feeling of her in my hands, her moans and, oh, God, the feeling of entering her. It was like coming home.

I looked around. The alarm clock read six a.m. I had to go to work in a few hours. Why didn't I just take vacation while she here? I wanted to lie in bed with Emily all day and make love and doze and make love. How many times did we? I was sore but I didn't care. It felt great to have a woman again, and not just any woman. This was The Woman.

Emily walked into the room wearing one of my Western Michigan T-shirts and holding a coffee mug. "Hey, cutie. How do you feel today?" she asked with a grin.

"I feel pretty good for a man who's just had the greatest sex possible." I reached for her as she sat on the side of the bed.

"Careful, hot coffee." She grinned. "Greatest sex possible, huh? You sure know how to compliment a girl."

"Set the damn coffee down and come back to bed. I have a morning hunger that's got nothing to do with food. And only you can satisfy it."

"Only me?" She set the coffee on the bedside table and leaned over me.

I tugged her, giggling, into bed. "Yes, only you. How do you feel today?"

"I'm a bit sore," she admitted. "It's been a while since I had such a stud for a lover."

"Lucky for us this old stud wasn't put out to pasture yet."

We managed to shower with just a bit of hanky-panky. I dressed in my gray uniform shirt and dark pants, wondering how I was going to get through an entire day, waiting to see her again. When I came out, Emily was waiting in the kitchen, a small brown paper bag in one hand and a mug of coffee in the other. "I made you a present."

"What?" She wore one of my dress shirts and a pair of socks and nothing else. I considered calling in sick. "A present?"

She handed me the sack. "Lunch."

"What?" I opened up the sack. Two sandwiches in wax paper were inside, with an orange and a small container of some kind. "Is this some of your pasta?"

Emily smiled. "Cold pasta salad. I think you'll like it. And egg salad sandwiches."

"Egg salad?" I started salivating just thinking about it. "When did you do this?"

"Oh, while you were getting your beauty sleep," she said, sipping her coffee.

Wow. She made me lunch. I could get used to this.

"I'll get dressed and you can drop me off," she said, brushing by me.

I grabbed her in a hug, careful of her coffee. "Thanks."

She twitched her butt under my hand. "Payment for services rendered, sir."

I dropped Emily off at the apartment on my way to work. "Memorial service at ten," she reminded me. "I told your dad and mom I'd go with them. And your dad wants to talk with me about the diary."

I groaned. "I forgot about the service. I'll be there."

"You bet you'll be there. I coerced some of the others into attending, too. I'll go through the diary again, too. I *know* there's something there I'm not getting."

"I know. I feel like there's a clue just out of reach." I put a hand on her arm when she started to open the door. "Can we get together later on today?"

"Get together?" She waggled her eyebrows.

"Have dinner tonight?"

"Sure. My place this time."

"Okay. I'll drop by at five, okay?"

"That sounds like a plan. I'll see you then."

I pulled her to me, giving her a long, deep kiss. "Thanks, Emily."

"For what?"

"For being here."

She snuggled in my arms. "I like being here. See you tonight."

A man could survive a day apart on words like those.

Chapter 22

Thirty-Four Years Earlier

To celebrate their two-month anniversary, Nate and Emily went to nearby Benton Harbor to a fancy French restaurant. Emily wore a miniscule black dress that clung to her like second skin and two-inch heels with black nylons. Nate wore a summer weight gray suit with a black shirt. He took his old Chevy out of storage for the event. He usually just used the car at college and used his cycle in the summer. But this was a special day. They made quite an entrance when they pulled up to the entrance in a 1959 silver-and-gray Impala.

The restaurant was near the Yacht Club. Emily created a stir in her tiny dress with her hair upswept off her neck. They watched the big boats moving in and out of the bay. Nate's menu had prices on it but Emily's didn't. "So you can order for me and you can order what you can afford," she whispered across the table.

Nate studied the menu with what he hoped was a nonchalant air. At Emily's insistence, they pooled their money. "It's time women started paying their way more. There's no reason men have to always pay our way." Nate tallied the prices in his head and breathed a sigh of relief. They could manage it with some to spare. Then he remembered the tip and drinks and revised his previous estimate.

They had white wine, fish in cream sauce, and huge salads with fresh grated cheese and croutons the size of Nate's thumb. For dessert they split a big piece of apple pie with cheese then they had coffee and watched the boats moving under the night sky. Their waiter was an older man and he made suggestions, pointing out the right wine and suggesting they split the dessert. "Our portions are too large," he said with a small shake of his head. Nate suspected the guy knew to a penny how much Nate could afford to spend and still leave a tip.

Only one thing marred the beauty of the night. The restaurant had piped-in music and the Muzak was grating, especially to two people who loved rock and roll. "I swear to God, I didn't think anybody could ruin "Sgt. Pepper's" but those guys did it," Emily hissed.

Nate rolled his eyes. "I can't believe they can get away with it."

When Bobby Goldsboro's "Honey" started to play, Emily was ready to shoot somebody. Luckily they were almost done with dinner and didn't mind beating a hasty retreat. As they left, Emily mentioned to the waiter "you guys might want to update your musical selections a bit." The waiter just nodded and pocketed his tip.

"Could have been worse," Nate said as he tucked her back into the car. "It could be Lawrence Welk."

Emily laughed then gave him a coquettish glance. "Do you like my dress?"

His eyes swept over her. "Sure. It's cute." She lifted the hem of her skirt slightly and his eyes almost bugged out of his head when he saw the tops of her elastic-top nylons. "I thought you were wearing those panty-hose things," he said in a hoarse voice.

"Nope." She looked at the gentle rain. "Good thing you brought the car."

He put a hand on her thigh and moved it slowly upward. He almost crashed the car when he realized she wasn't wearing any underwear. "Emily!" he said in shocked outrage.

"Now how do you like my dress? You still think it's cute?"

Nate made a quick decision and turned the car onto one of the many back highways that would take them to Little Bay. "We'll talk about it. Just as soon as I find a good place to pull over." He looked at her in the darkness. "I love you, Emily."

"I love you, too, Nate."

They had another month together. He intended to savor every moment.

****

A week after Janie Sinclair was attacked, Esther and Emily went for a morning walk. "I heard Janie is just now able to talk to the sheriff about what happened," Esther said quietly as they went to the beach steps.

Emily nodded. She saw the sheriff every Wednesday when she went to Nate's house for dinner. "She talked to a female policewoman from Kalamazoo right after it happened. The sheriff is waiting until she feels better to question her. I get the feeling he's not sure there's much they can do."

They negotiated the wooden steps down to the beach, each silent with their own thoughts. It was a cool, overcast day, with dark scudding clouds dipping low over the lake. Both girls wore jeans, sneakers, and

T-shirts with the Pine Place logo. Emily had on a windbreaker and Esther wore one of Tom Judson's flannel shirts over her T-shirt.

"I heard you're staying in town for a few days," Esther asked.

"Yeah, in a few weeks," Emily said. "In Nate's apartment. The sheriff wanted us to keep an eye on things when he and Mrs. Boltz go to a police convention in Chicago. Keep an eye on the house and on Busby, their dog."

Esther kicked at a rock on the beach. "It's been a good summer." She slanted a look at Emily. "You've grown up a lot."

Emily paused. "Really?"

Esther grinned. "A good man will do that to a girl." Emily blushed and Esther laughed. "Nothing to be embarrassed about, Farm Girl. Nate's a good teacher, I think." She shook her head in regret. "Not like what Janie had or probably Peggy." She made a *tsk* noise. "I don't think they've known much love."

Emily's eyes widened in surprise. "You think?"

Esther nodded, confident with the meager seniority of two years she had over Emily. "Oh, yeah. From the little they've told me, they have some odd tastes. But that don't mean it's okay for what happened to Janie."

"It's so awful. I just can't imagine it."

"Hey, look there." Esther gestured down the beach. Emily saw Peggy McBride edging her way around some boulders at the base of the beach. "I wonder what she's doing down here? Maids don't go on duty until noon."

Peggy didn't see them. She scrambled up on some rocks and it looked like she was peering at the rock wall of the bluff. "She's probably just hanging out," Emily said.

"I wonder what she's up to," Esther muttered.

Peggy glanced up and saw Emily and Esther, watching her. She looked surprised then she walked away from the bluff toward them, moving in a casual way that didn't fool Emily for a minute. "What are you guys doing out here?" Peggy called out.

Esther and Emily approached, skirting the smaller boulders. Peggy had moved away from the bluff base and stood near the water's edge. "Just out for a stroll," Esther said, glancing at the cliff wall then to Peggy.

Remembering what Esther said, Emily eyed Peggy. The other girl always looked tired and haggard as though she didn't sleep well. She had very blonde shoulder-length hair that was stiff and unyielding in the breeze off the lake. As always she wore obvious make-up: heavy eyeliner, lots of mascara, and a heavy foundation.

"What's up, Peggy?" Emily always felt awkward around Peggy since she saw the other girl having sex with Greg and his friends. *I should have gone for help. I should have stopped them.*

Peggy put her hands on her hips and stared at the lake, a small smile on her overly pink lips. "Just taking care of the future."

"Good," Esther said, shrugging to Emily. "Wanna walk back with us?"

Peggy turned from her contemplation of the lake and stared at Emily. "How's Nate?"

"Fine. Let's go, Esther." Emily turned to head back to the resort.

"He's a nice boy," Peggy said. "Really nice." The

implication in her voice was obvious. Emily flushed angrily. She knew Nate and Peggy had sex the previous summer and she tried not to let it bother her, but she usually failed miserably.

Esther laughed. “And he got the really nice girl, too.” She looped her arm through Emily’s. “Let’s walk, Farm Girl.”

Fuming, Emily allowed herself to be tugged back to the resort. Esther started to chuckle. “Don’t let her bother you, honey. She’s just jealous.”

“I know. It’s just that Nate’s so experienced and I’m just a little hick with no experience.”

Esther laughed out loud. “Honey, there’s experienced and then there’s experienced. Nate may have sampled a girl or two, but trust me, you’re the Big Experience of his life.”

“You think so?”

Esther nodded solemnly. “Oh, yeah.” She gave Emily a little hug. “I sure wish summer wouldn’t end.”

I know, Emily thought. *I know.*

Chapter 23

Present Day

When I walked into the police station after my night with Emily, I went to the little kitchenette to stow my lunch.

Dorothy regarded me with suspicion. "What's that? Evidence?" She still hadn't forgiven me for the time I stored a severed finger in the refrigerator. It was found in a fish caught off of Wilson's Point and I kept it to run fingerprints. Dorothy almost had a conniption fit when she saw the bloody thing.

"It's my lunch."

Sada looked up from the other desk. "You don't bring lunch."

"I did today." I slammed the fridge door and went down the hall to my office.

I heard a scuffling noise and glanced back to see Dorothy and Sada going into the kitchenette and pulling open the fridge door. Dorothy nudged Sada and nodded toward the lunch. "I'll bet *she* made him lunch," Dorothy said in a loud whisper. "But when did she have time?"

Their eyes swung to me. "None of your business," I said.

"I've heard she's a good cook," Sada said as she and Dorothy ambled back to their desks.

Two sets of female eyes regarded me. "No comment." I fled into my office.

At 9:45 Dorothy knocked on the door. "You ready to go to the memorial service, Chief?"

I looked up. "You going?"

She nodded. "I knew Polly back in the old days. It's a hard thing for a woman to lose a child. Won't hurt me to go to a service."

"That's nice of you." We went out to the Crown Vic in the back parking lot. "Mrs. McBride asked Emily to ask me if I'd say a word." I made a face as we pulled into the street. "Don't know what to say."

Dorothy hummed softly to herself. "Just say you remember Peggy in high school," she suggested. "Find some nice thing she did and talk about it."

I snorted. "You know how Peggy was. I don't think her mama wants to hear about the nice things she did for boys."

Dorothy gave me an assessing glance. "I suspect some people got sex on the brain today. Now they've gotten themselves some."

"Dorothy!" I slowly grinned at her. "Maybe."

She chuckled. "You got that look, Chief. I can't wait to see what Miss Emily looks like."

"Don't you dare," I warned as we pulled up to the Presbyterian Church. Then I saw Emily, standing on the steps with my parents. She was wearing dark brown slacks and a sweater set of dark amber. Yep. She had *that* look.

Dorothy chuckled as we walked forward to join my family. "You're especially pretty today, Emily. You sort of glow with color."

"Why, thank you, Dorothy." Emily beamed at me

and took my arm.

Dorothy raised one eyebrow. "Some folks just got that look, Chief." Then she walked ahead of us to greet some friends going into the church.

"What's she mean?" Emily asked as we went into the church behind my parents.

"Dorothy's an expert on my love life today," I said softly, pausing inside the door to examine the nave. There was a small turnout, as I expected. The McBrides sat up front with some younger people, probably grandkids. If I remembered right, Peggy had an older sister, Janice. Those were probably her kids. I was glad there was some family there. After all this time, there weren't a lot of tears. People gave up on Peggy a long time ago and this service had the air of formality, not grief. But it was still nice her family had turned out.

Mom, Dad, Emily, and I took a pew behind some Summer Kids just as the service got underway. Pastor Roberts came in and read some words from the Bible and gave a mercifully short sermon. One of the church ladies sang "Amazing Grace" then the minister asked if anyone wanted to say a few words. Mrs. McBride turned in her pew to look at Emily and me.

To my surprise, Greg stood up and walked to the front of the church. "My name is Greg Hoffman and I knew Peggy years ago when I worked here in the summer. Peggy was a great girl. She and I dated a few times. It was nice for me to come here, as a stranger, and be able to meet someone as friendly and kind as Peggy. I had a bit of homesickness before I met her, but she made me feel right at home." He smiled very sincerely at Polly McBride. If I hadn't known what a rat he was, I'd believe him.

"For an asshole, he's a good actor," Emily whispered as we watched Greg walk back to the pew where he sat with the other Summer Kids.

"Hope I do as good," I murmured. Emily squeezed my hand in reassurance.

I went to the front. "I knew Peggy almost all of my life." I leaned on the podium, talking conversationally to the McBrides, seated in front. "She was in Civics class with me in high school. I remember her being on the pep squad when I was on the football team."

The McBrides nodded, obviously pleased someone had remembered this little known fact about their daughter.

"Peggy and I lost touch with each other when I went to college, but I saw her in the summers when I worked at the resort and she was working there, too."

I hoped my voice didn't convey that I occasionally saw quite a bit of Peggy, sometimes naked. "She was an outgoing and trusting girl. I'm sorry for what happened to her. If it's any consolation, I'll make sure we find out what did happen." I tried to put reassurance into my voice. I think I succeeded because Polly McBride smiled sadly and nodded in acknowledgement.

Emily started to edge out of the pew to go to the front but Bobby Goldman beat her to it, passing me in the aisle. I slid in next to Emily and she pressed her leg against mine. "Good work," she whispered.

I put an arm around her. "Thanks."

Bobby nodded to the McBrides then said, "Peggy worked for us at the resort for about four or five summers. A more loyal, hard-working girl couldn't be found. She was always ready when we needed her, always willing to do whatever was asked of her." His smile seemed to take on a beatific quality as he reminisced, emphasized by his thin, pale face and wispy hair. He looked like one of the angels, smiling down at us from the mural on the ceiling. "She was missed in the following years. You have my deepest sympathy and condolences for your loss." He bowed his head briefly then resumed his seat.

"Nicely done," Emily whispered. "I'm surprised."

"Me, too. Are you going to talk?"

"Why don't we have a final prayer and a moment of meditative quiet while we all revisit our individual memories of Peggy?" the minister suggested.

Emily breathed a sigh of relief, exchanging a wry glance with Esther. *Saved by the pastor*.

As we emerged into the cool October sunlight, my mother stopped to talk to Polly McBride, hugging her in consolation as my father talked to Jack McBride, Peggy's father. Emily and I waited on the sidewalk for them, Emily's arm through mine. It felt so good to have her beside me. It felt *right*. "What are you going to do this afternoon?" I asked her.

"Your mom and I were going to make cookies for tomorrow."

I stared at her blankly. "Tomorrow?"

"Tuesday Treats? The all-town bake sale?"

I completely forgot about Homecoming and the week's festivities. "Save a couple of cookies for me."

She grinned. "I have something special saved for you."

I shivered. I recognized that mischievous look in her devilish green eyes.

"I may do a bit of shopping downtown today, too. It's Monday Merchant Madness Day, you know." She leaned closer to me. “I saw the cutest pair of high heels at Simon’s Shoe Shop. I may have to stop and try them on. They’d look great with my little black dress.”

Emily wearing high heels? I had memories of Emily in high heels, stockings, and very little else. I started to feel a bit warm.

“Nate, Polly McBride said she found something she thought you should have.”

I jerked my thoughts away from hopeful daydreams and stared numbly at my mother. “She what?”

“She said she found a ledger,” my father said. “Emily’s call last night made her remember it. I thought I’d drive over there and get it.”

“A ledger? What kind?”

Dad shrugged. “She said it belonged to Peggy and was in a box up in the attic along with a bunch of other junk.” His dark gray eyes looked sympathetic. “Apparently when you found Peggy they got her stuff out and started going through it.”

“It’s a hard thing to lose a child,” my mother said softly.

Emily put an arm around her shoulders. They were about the same height and seeing them together brought back so many memories of the times we spent together years before. I knew Emily was remembering that my mother had two miscarriages before they finally had me, their only child.

Bobby Goldman was hovering nearby, glancing at us and listening to Harv, Pauline, and Greg. I edged away from my parents and Emily. “If you can get the ledger from Polly, Dad, I’d appreciate it. Bring it and the diary to the station later on.” I nodded to Greg, who was almost back-to-back with Emily. "That was a nice talk you gave. I'm sure the McBrides appreciated it." I looked at Bobby. "Yours was nice, too, Bobby. I didn't expect you to talk."

He looked up at me, squinting in the sunlight before pulling out a pair of expensive-looking sunglasses from his suit pocket. "I was glad to do it. I meant what I said, too."

"I did, too," Greg said with a sneer. "She made me feel right at home."

I rolled my eyes with exasperation. Trust him to cheapen even a memorial service.

Greg leaned over and said something to Emily. She whirled and glared at him. I moved to her side. "I need to get back to work," I said.

She turned her back on Greg and I saw the dislike in her eyes. "What did he say?" I asked as we walked slowly toward the parking lot next to the church.

"Looks like you and Nate have gone back to old times," she mimicked. "Getting ready for small-town life as a small-town wife?"

I glanced back at Greg, who was watching us, his lips pursed. "Asshole."

"Lord, I never liked him thirty years ago," Esther said in her slow, liquid voice. "And I still don't like him."

"Amen to that," Pauline said.

"Are you guys heading out?" I asked.

"Yep," Harv said, leading the way to his SUV. "Time for us to go back to work."

"I appreciate you coming." I watched as Emily and the women all hugged then it was my turn, getting enthusiastic hugs and kisses from Pauline and Esther, who whispered, "Go ahead and pop the question, damn it. I want to attend your wedding before I die." I shook hands with Harv and watched as they bundled into the SUV with promises to write.

I glimpsed Dorothy standing nearby, waiting patiently. "We're going back to the office now. I'll see you later today." I looked down at Emily, wanting nothing more than to put my arms around her and sink into a long, exploratory kiss. I saw my desire reflected in her eyes.

"Let's go, Chief," Dorothy said briskly. "We got criminals to catch."

I tore my eyes from Emily's, bending down to give her a quick kiss on the cheek. "I'll see you later."

I spent the rest of the morning trying to focus on budget allocations for the police department but I had a hell of a time. Images of Emily kept popping into my brain. I kept getting mental pictures of her lying in bed, lying under me, on top of me, laughing. I'd jerk my attention back to the figures then drift off in another daydream.

The lunch she packed for me helped reinforce those images. I imagined her humming in my kitchen, boiling the eggs and making the sandwiches for me, packing them up in a little sack. A man could get used to such treatment.

My father came by early in the afternoon. "I got the ledger and the diary." He entered and took a guest chair across from me. His shrewd eyes saw the spreadsheets on my computer screen and he grimaced. "Budgets. I hated them, too."

I came around the desk and took the oilcloth-covered diary from him. "Did you have a chance to look through the diary? I didn't have much time last night."

Dad laughed. "I'll bet." I rolled my eyes and he chuckled some more. "I made some notes." He pulled out the small lined notebook he always carried. "Okay, here we are. Look at November fifth."

I flipped through the diary to the correct page and read aloud:

" 'I was surprised Honey wasn't upset but he understood. It's too late to take care of it, so I'll go away. But he's going away, too, so that's fine. We can't be together anyway. And in the spring we'll be together again. Like before. I wish we could spend Christmas together but he told me he had to spend it with his family. I understand. Soon we'll be a family of our own.' "

"She was pregnant," Dad said. "Rumors went around town about it. She went away at Thanksgiving. Polly said her other girl, Janice, was sick and they were sending Peggy to her to help out at home. Janice had a toddler and one on the way, as I recall."

"But why would 'he,' whoever he is, be going away as late as November?" I asked. "If it was a town kid, he'd go back to college in September."

"Unless it was a town kid and she saw him on weekends," Dad pointed out. "Then maybe he transferred to a different college or something."

"If the school was on a quarter system instead of a semester it might fit." I pulled over a legal pad. "I need to get a list of town kids who transferred schools that year."

"I thought maybe she was having it off with some married guy and he was going on vacation. The note about spending the holidays with his family made me wonder." Dad flipped through his notes. "Here's another one. January fifth."

I found the spot in the book and read:

" 'I'm so mad! He could've called on New Year's Eve. Here I am, all big and blimpy, sitting around with Janice and her scumbag husband, drinking beer and watching Dick Clark. It's not like anyone is monitoring his calls. His father is such a jerk. He doesn't notice anything unless it costs money. Maybe that's why? Maybe he's afraid of the phone bills? He can afford it. He could have found a way!' "

"Sounds like he's living with his parents," I said. "Maybe he didn't go back to college. Maybe he moved back home." I jotted another note. "I need to add drop-outs to my list."

"There's a baby one." Dad looked at his notebook and I smiled at the sight. It brought back memories of him as sheriff. Once a cop always a cop, I guess. "March twentieth."

I did some quick calculations in my head. "She must have been four months along in November. That means she got pregnant in July or August." Dad and I exchanged a look. "Summertime." I found the March twentieth entry:

" 'A perfect baby boy! So pretty and he looks like his daddy. I wish my Honey would come to visit me, but the flowers were beautiful. And the bracelet he sent is fabulous! I wonder if they're real diamonds? I can't wait until we can be together again. I'll go back to him in May, just like the other times. And we'll have the whole summer together.' "

"It's just about the only mention she makes of the

baby," Dad said with a bewildered shake of his head. "The only times she mentions him is when she says she named him after his daddy and when she complains about how noisy he is. Then, in May, the diary starts again with her at the resort and there's no mention of the baby."

I rifled through the pages. "What happened? Did she put the baby up for adoption?"

"No mention. Look at the entry for the fourth of July."

I remembered that Fourth of July. Silas, Emily's brother, visited the resort and got pissed off she and I were sleeping together. We'd almost come to blows. I read the entry for the Fourth, my mouth sagging open in surprise:

" *'We had so much fun tonight. We did* It *on the balcony of the resort and no one noticed! We were right out there in public; he was behind me and did* It *while the fireworks were going off! It hurt but it was so exciting. I know he loves me so much, he tells me while we're doing* It. *He's so mature and exciting!'* "

"Okay," I muttered. "The balcony?" Dad nodded. "If it's the one I'm thinking of, it was on the southeast side of the main building. Nobody used it. It was run-down."

"Sounds like somebody used it for their own private parties."

"But who? It opened off a big suite, but they cut the suite up into rooms and stuck the door to the porch in a storage room so nobody would get out there. Mr. Goldman was always worried about guests getting hurt and suing him."

I worked to dredge up the memory. On Fourth of

July we went down to the beach to have a bonfire with some of the other kids. Rachel flirted with Emily's brother, Silas, and I think they slept together. "That narrows it down. Only a few people knew the exact location of the door. It was kept locked and none of the master keys to the resort would work." I smiled wryly. "I know. I tried."

Dad grinned. "Sounds like a good place to take a girl." He looked at the diary in my hands. "Peggy says he's 'mature.' It implies he's older."

"Or just more sophisticated." I thought of Greg and his prep school attitude. "Let's face it, it wouldn't have taken much to impress Peggy."

"She wasn't the brightest bulb on the Christmas tree," Dad agreed. "She might be taken in by somebody's airs."

"I seem to remember Peggy got hurt and missed some work. I remember because Rachel had to fill in. It was when that poor girl, Janie, got raped."

Dad nodded grimly and consulted his notebook. "That still bugs me. I never believed it was the cook. But when he disappeared, there wasn't anything I could do. Here it is. August fourteenth she was hurt."

I opened the diary and looked for a corresponding date, but there wasn't one. The nearest entry was August nineteenth:

" 'He hurt me bad this time. The other times, when he hurt me, I knew he loved me. But this time I wasn't sure. And what he did to Janie—he told me he wouldn't touch her if she didn't want to, and she screamed and cried. Why did he do it? He said he was paying me back for Greg but he told me to go with Greg! It doesn't make any sense!' "

"Esther said she was into S&M," I said, thinking out loud.

"Really? How did Esther know?"

"She knew someone who sold Peggy some kind of sex toy." I heard a sound and looked up to see Rob Sloan in the doorway, his plain face curious.

"I wondered if you wanted any help with your old case, Chief." Dad started to get up but Rob gestured to him to keep sitting. "I'm interested in the girl who was killed so many years ago." He seemed honestly sympathetic.

Dad shot him a curious look and Rob noticed. "Well, she was so young. Just in her twenties. And a young mother."

"Mother?" I hoped my voice didn't reveal anything. Where did Rob get that tidbit of information?

"Dorothy mentioned it, said this McBride girl went away and had a baby the winter before she was killed."

"Oh, that old rumor. Stuff like that was kept quiet." I shook my head. "Not like today, with celebrities having babies without benefit of husbands."

"Things have changed quite a bit since then." Rob looked hopefully at me. "I was wondering if I can look at the diary. Maybe another set of eyes might see something."

Dad and I exchanged a look. Rob was right. Maybe someone with no knowledge of the past might be able to see something we were skimming over. "Sure." I held up the diary and Rob came forward to take it. I had another thought. "I have another bit of work for you to do. Emily received a couple of calls to the apartment."

Dad nodded. "I almost forgot about it. Who's got the phone number? The last tenant just moved out a few weeks ago and we haven't switched the line yet."

Rob looked thoughtful. "Interesting."

"I thought so, too." The calendar on my computer screen pinged and I sighed. "Budget meetings. Get a list of calls to the number in the last few days." I stood.

My father got to his feet, holding up a plain green book, spiral bound. "This is the other book Polly McBride had. I'll look through it and see if anything pops out."

"Thanks, Dad. I'll check in with you later on this afternoon." I grabbed my jacket from the rack near the door and walked out with him and Rob. We parted at the front desk where Dad paused to chat with Dorothy. Rob and I went toward the back door and the parking lot.

Rob glanced back and smiled when we heard Dad and Dorothy laugh about something—probably about me and the moony way I was acting. "You're lucky to have parents. All I had was my dad and he passed on years ago." He opened the back door and gestured me to precede him out. "I'll work on those phone calls."

"Thanks, Rob. I appreciate it." I paused in mid-stride when I saw Cynthia Bartlett coming toward us then I took the coward's way out and nodded to her before angling off and cutting through the parking lot to the City Hall across the street.

It wasn't until I was sitting in a budget meeting that I realized I had gone from being womanless to having two women with their eye on me in a little less than twenty-four hours. And in just a few days, I'd go back to being womanless when Emily left.

The thought made my tedious meeting drag on even longer.

Chapter 24

Thirty-Four Years Earlier

Nate was in the machine shed, working on an air conditioning unit late one afternoon in early July. His supervisor, an overweight man named Harry, pulled him aside. "There's a guest out there and he wants to talk to you." He glanced nervously at the door. "He looks mad as hell."

Nate looked up, surprised. Guests seldom noticed the maintenance workers, much less tracked them down to talk to them. He walked outside, wiping his hands on a rag. The biggest man he'd ever seen in his life was waiting for him. The guy was at least six-six and must have weighed two-fifty. He looked all muscle, too, from his huge shoulders down to his huge feet. He had a brown buzz cut, like a Marine, and his face was so fixed it looked like granite. He scowled at Nate when he emerged and Nate instinctively took a step back.

"I'm Nate Boltz," he said, eyeing the man warily.

The man raked Nate with a scathing look from the top of his head to his feet. Then he growled, "I'm Silas Sutherland. And if what I hear is right, you're the guy who's screwing my baby sister."

Oh, shit Emily's older brother. He looks really pissed. Nate wasn't sure what to do. He decided to tell the truth and hope for the best. "Yes, I am sleeping with her. I'm not screwing her. I love Emily a lot and I care about what happens to her."

The man hesitated, obviously caught off guard by the truth. "I heard you saved her from that bastard, Greg Hoffman."

Nate shrugged with what he hoped was nonchalance. "I just wish I had a chance to pound on Greg a bit more. The asshole almost got away with it."

Sutherland raked Nate with a long, assessing gaze. "I talked to your dad."

"And?"

"He told me about this Hoffman guy's background. He also told me you and your friends are keeping an eye on Emily." He glared at Nate. "I think you're keeping an eye on her too closely, maybe."

"She's an adult. She can make up her own mind."

"Yeah, and I trust her," Silas said grudgingly. He looked around. "I heard you're a mechanic." Then his eyes lit on Nate's cycle, parked behind the shop. "That yours?"

"Yeah."

"Looks modified."

Nate shrugged. "Some."

That's where Emily found them, an hour and a half later. "Silas!" she yelled as she came running down the path.

Her brother looked up and grinned. "Oh, man, we're in trouble now," he told Nate. "She'll chew me out for making you miss supper or something."

Emily flung herself at the big man and Silas scooped her up in a hug. "How's it going, Baby Sister?" he asked, nuzzling her neck.

Emily screamed with laughter and pounded him on

the shoulders. "You rat! You made Nate miss supper." She looked at Nate while Silas twirled her around. "Bobby told me you sneaked in while my back was turned."

Nate and Silas both laughed as Emily was deposited back on the ground, staggering slightly. "I wanted to see for myself what was happening out here," he told Emily, his expression suddenly serious.

She slapped him on the arm. "I told Nate's dad you'd come out here," she said triumphantly. "I told him you'd come out here and pound on Greg." She looked up at Nate. "Nate saved me. He really did."

"Why don't we all go to dinner and talk about it?" Silas looked at his watch. "I'm scheduled to eat in the second seating, at 7:30. Why don't you guys join me?"

Emily and Nate looked at each other. "Can we?" Emily asked.

"Why not?" Silas asked.

"We work here," Nate said. "We'll ask Bobby, see what he says."

"Hell, you're my guests. And I'm a guest here. You can eat with me." Silas looked at Emily's front desk outfit of pale green golf shirt and miniskirt. "Emily, how many times have I told you to wear more clothes? You're a walking advertisement for—" He stopped abruptly and clamped his jaws shut. Nate hid a grin.

"For what?" Emily demanded, thrusting her face up into his. "Sex?"

Silas looked away from her to Nate, who carefully smoothed his expression. "I'm just not used to seeing you this way."

"I know, Silas. It's okay." Emily looped one arm

through his and through Nate's as they started to stroll toward the main hotel. "I'll check with Bobby about dinner, okay?" Emily looked pointedly at Nate's dirty shirt. "You'll want to shower?"

"Yes, ma'am." Nate kissed her quickly on the cheek. "I'll meet you on the porch."

****

Emily sighed as he walked away. She was so focused on Nate it took a minute to notice Silas watching her. "I like him a lot."

Silas laughed, a big, booming sound. "No shit. And I think he likes you." He put an arm around Emily's shoulders and let her steer him toward the front porch of the main hotel building. "He seems like a good kid. And his dad's okay, too."

"You talked to the sheriff?" Emily asked.

"Yep. First thing. That reminds me, we're all invited for supper tomorrow night." Silas grinned at her. "The sheriff said his wife would never forgive us if we didn't."

"Mrs. B is a force of nature. You don't mess with her."

Silas dropped into one of the Adirondack chairs on the porch and Emily gestured staff members over for introductions. Silas soon met David, Esther, Pauline, Mark, Harv, and an assortment of others.

Then Bobby came out on the porch. "Silas wants Nate and me to eat dinner with him in the dining room? Is it okay?" She looked up anxiously at Bobby who smiled down at her upturned face.

"Of course." Bobby put a friendly hand on her shoulder and glanced at Silas and winked. "Anything for our favorite desk clerk." He added, "And her boyfriend."

Emily peered past him and saw Nate walking toward them, dressed in clean jeans and a pale yellow dress shirt. "Oh, he's so handsome," she said dreamily. "Bobby said it was okay," she called, waving.

Nate waved in return. Emily frowned when she saw Rachel stop Nate and chat briefly. Nate nodded once and glanced at Silas then he grinned at Emily and winked. Emily sat up straighter in her chair, her gaze going from her brother to Rachel. Nate came up the stairs two at a time and leaned over to kiss Emily. "Your brother caught her eye," he murmured.

Emily scowled. "Hussy," she muttered.

Rachel glanced back once over her shoulder and Silas raised an eyebrow. Then Emily slapped him on the arm. "Dinner time," she said sweetly.

Silas grinned at her. "Lead on."

Emily popped to her feet and shot Rachel a narrow-eyed look. "Come on." She led them into the dining room, head held high. Their arrival caused a sensation. Marcia the hostess, a college senior from Alabama, was flustered until Bobby came in and murmured something in her ear. Then she nodded to Silas and winked at Emily and Nate.

"This way, Mr. Sutherland," she said, making a notation on her seating charts. Emily followed Marcia to a secluded table in the back, set for four.

"I hope Greg isn't our waiter," Emily muttered as Marcia set menus in front of them.

She grinned at Emily. "No way, sugar. I wouldn't do that to you. You guys have Chuck. He's fun."

"Good." Emily snapped open the menu and looked over it at Silas. "You behave yourself. I know how you get." She glanced nervously around the dining room.

Silas smiled innocently. "*Moi*? Would I do anything to embarrass you?"

She returned to studying her menu. "If you could get away with it you would."

Nate snorted and studiously looked at the menu. "I've never eaten here. I've worked here almost four years and never eaten here."

Emily smiled at the tall young man with long dark brown hair who approached them. She'd seen him around at staff picnics but had never talked to him. He grinned at her and Nate. "Hey, guys. I'm Chuck." He looked at Silas. "I'm your waiter for your stay here."

Silas nodded, and turned back to study the menu and Emily did the same, only glancing up when Chuck described the chef specials available that night.

"Make sure to tell Herves and the crew we're here," Emily said, closing her menu. "We're friends," she confided.

"I don't doubt it." Chuck turned his attention to Silas. "Care for an appetizer?"

They ordered their meals and Silas also ordered a bottle of wine. He and Chuck debated the merits of a French versus a California chardonnay and Silas allowed himself to be persuaded to accept Chuck's suggestion. Chuck shot Emily a skeptical look but Silas shook his head. "I'll handle it," he said. Chuck shrugged and left.

"Okay, which one is he?" Silas demanded, looking around the dining room.

Nate glanced to the left. "Blond guy, blue shirt and white denims, at the table of six." Nate sipped his water as Silas eyed Greg Hoffman.

"Asshole." Silas turned his gaze on Emily. "He didn't touch you?"

Emily sniffed. "Nope." Her hand trembled as she lifted her water glass. "He just scared me."

"For that alone I should pound the shit out of him," Silas said as Chuck came back to the table with rolls and butter.

"I'll help hold him down," Chuck said pleasantly. Silas shot him a questioning look and Chuck shrugged. "He's a poacher." He disappeared again, waiting on one of his other tables.

"Poacher?" Emily asked, looking from Nate to Silas.

Silas took a roll and butter and pushed the basket to Nate. "He's probably schmoozing some of Chuck's guests," Silas said, looking around the dining room. "Getting the tips."

Emily wrinkled her nose. "Rude."

Nate grinned at her. "That's one word for it."

The dinner was fabulous. As Chuck said, "Once Herves and Emilio knew you were here, they pulled out all the stops." He grinned as he set down their plates with a flourish and Emily saw what he meant.

"Wow. This is, like, art or something." Emily regarded her beautifully orchestrated fish with dilled potatoes, all tastefully decorated with a drizzle of wine sauce and carefully placed dill leaves. "I have to thank those guys when we're done." She smiled at Chuck, who beamed back at her. "They're the best."

Silas half-filled her wine glass then filled his glass and Nate's. Emily scowled at him but he shrugged. "I don't want to contribute to the delinquency of a minor."

"Why can a person have sex at any age but they

can't drink until a certain age? Or vote at a certain age? The people who make the rules have a really skewed idea of delinquency," she muttered.

Nate laughed and Silas shook his head. "Emily, quit trying to overthrow the government. I work for them. If you overthrow the government, I'm out a paycheck." He saw Nate's surprise and nodded. "Yeah, instead of going to Viet Nam, Dan and I got sucked into intelligence. Although why it's called 'intelligence,' I don't know." Silas shrugged. "But at least it kept us off the battlefield. I'd rather work with computers than guns any day."

Nate nodded. "You bet. I was glad they stopped the draft when they did."

Greg paused by their table. "Hey, Emily. Slumming?" He glanced at Nate and his gaze slid over Silas, who stared back impassively.

"Not until you stopped by." Emily nodded to Silas. "This is my brother Silas Sutherland. Silas, this is Greg Hoffman. The asshole."

Silas stood up and Greg's jaw sagged as Silas towered over him. "Not pleased to meet you," Silas rumbled. Their corner of the dining room quieted and people turned to stare. Nate watched, his face impassive.

"Silas?"

Her brother turned to regard Emily. "Yes, honey?"

"Don't beat him up here. It might reflect badly on Chuck and everybody knows he's the best waiter here." Her voice was just loud enough to carry to the other nearby tables. Silas pursed his lips and looked thoughtful.

"Good point. You're right." He sat down. "Good-bye," he said, snapping his napkin and replacing it on his lap.

Greg stared at him then at Emily. Then with a smirk he turned and left. Chuck materialized at Silas' side. "Care for some more wine, sir?" Chuck asked.

Silas nodded. "I believe we'll have another bottle. And pour a glass for yourself, if you can. Your recommendation was excellent."

"Thank you, sir." Chuck glided away, smiling at the nearby diners who were watching.

They lingered over coffee and wine and Chuck sat down and joined them once his other tables left. He soon had them laughing over stories of kitchen mishaps, which reminded Emily she had to go and thank the cooks. She and Nate and Silas went to the employee entrance of the kitchen and Emily poked her head in.

Herves spotted her and a shout went up. She entered and started chatting immediately in Spanish. Then Silas was introduced and all of the cooks came out to shake his hand and talk to him. Silas responded in fluent Spanish and everyone talked and gestured and pointed to Nate and pointed to the dining room entrance. Emily blushed when the guys told Silas that if Nate fell down on the job of protecting Emily, they would fill in for him. Silas pulled Herves, Sergio, and Emilio aside and they all had an intense, low-voiced conversation.

"Some macho thing," Emily whispered to Nate. "Silas lived in Mexico for a year and they're into the whole male thing."

"So am I," Nate whispered back. He looked at her, his gray eyes smoky and intense. "With you, at least."

She met his gaze. “Excellent.”

When Silas finished his conversation, they meandered back outside. “Bonfire on the beach,” David called out to Emily, who waved.

“Want to join us?” Emily invited Silas. “It’s just the staff.”

“Maybe for a while.” He watched Nate drape an arm over Emily’s shoulders. The two kids looked good together. The guys in the kitchen told him Nate was a solid worker and dependable. They also told him he treated Emily like a lady. Silas was starting to like him.

When they got to the bonfire, Silas saw many of the people he’d been introduced to earlier around the fire, drinking beer and listening to music on a portable radio. He accepted a beer and watched as Emily got into a spirited discussion with a tall, thin man (“the tennis pro,” someone told him) about Watergate. Silas noticed that although Nate didn’t stay by Emily’s side, his eyes seldom left her and he always knew where she was. Silas nodded with approval. The kid was all right.

“Your sister’s very pretty,” a soft voice said next to him.

Silas turned. A slender girl stood next to him looking at Emily, who gestured with passion as she and the tennis pro argued. “Yeah, she got the looks in the family.”

“I wouldn’t say that. I’m Rachel. I just graduated from Michigan State.”

“Really?” Silas took another sip of beer. “What major?”

“Math.”

He almost choked on his beer. “Math?”

She nodded. “Nate said you live out East. I’m

trying to decide between M.I.T. and Stanford for graduate work. What do you think of M.I.T.?"

"Let's sit down and talk," he suggested, gesturing to a nearby log.

The next time Silas looked around, Nate and Emily had vanished. Rachel noticed. "Emily and Nate are sort of involved."

"Yeah, I guess they are." He regarded her. "Are you involved with someone?"

"There's a guy. He and I get together now and then." She regarded Silas with a frank, sensual gaze. "But we're not together now."

"Ah." Silas glanced around. "Maybe we can go somewhere and talk."

She grinned. "I thought you'd never ask."

Chapter 25

Present Day

Rob Sloan poked his head in my office late in the afternoon. "Hey, Chief? I went over to see your—" He stopped and flushed. "Miss Sutherland. I wanted to ask her a couple of questions about the diary."

I appreciated his discretion. "Tell me about it." I waved him in.

He took the guest chair in front of my desk. I was once again reminded of why I liked Rob. He was small and compact with a reassuring air of quiet competency. So many people went into police work as a way to intimate or control others. Rob seemed to honestly enjoy helping other people.

"I skimmed through the diary. It's like there's a code in there or something. She uses special names for people and I just wondered who they were." He pulled out a small notebook from his uniform pocket. "She mentioned her Honey, and her sister and her brother-in-law." Rob glanced at me. "I got the feeling something might be going on there. She mentioned about Greg Hoffman, Emily—Miss Sutherland—once, and someone named Esther. Your dad was there when I looked at the diary and he told me your idea about the college kids being on quarters. I'm going to work on it. It's the kind of research I like to do."

I hadn't seen this facet of Rob's personality. "You like doing computer stuff?"

"Kind of. But mostly it's going to the library and calling the colleges, and talking to people." He looked a bit embarrassed. "I'm good at it. A lot of what a cop does is take all these pieces of information, line them up and look at them. Sometimes the pieces fall in place." He shook his head. "The diary is a big piece I can't quite figure."

Something in his tone told me he was intrigued by this puzzle. "Run with it," I said. "We can use all the help we can get."

"While I was there, she got a phone call."

I tensed. "I was hoping we were done with that."

"Not that kind. It was Peggy McBride's mother, Polly. She was wondering if you had a chance to look at the other diary they found."

I sighed. "I've been too busy to look at it."

He nodded. "I said you had delegated it to me. She seemed okay with that."

I once again thanked providence Rob Sloan had landed on my doorstep. "Thanks, Rob. I don't want it to seem like we're not taking this seriously."

He looked pleased but hid it by examining his notebook. "The old lady wanted to thank your—" He cleared his throat. "She wanted to thank Miss Sutherland. Mrs. McBride was pleased that Miss Sutherland got folks to come to the service."

"Did you have a chance to look through the other diary?" I asked, bouncing a pencil on the pile of budget figures awaiting my study.

"It's like a bookkeeper's journal or something. I just glanced through it but your dad and Miss

Sutherland were going at it hammer and tongs when I left." He suddenly smiled, his plain face briefly handsome. "Your parents are something, Chief."

I grinned. "Yeah, they are." I glanced at the clock.

Rob saw my look and immediately stood. "I'll get busy on my research," he said, tucking his notebook back in his pocket.

"Thanks, Rob. I appreciate the update." I stood and held out my hand. "And I'm glad we have you on board here. Detroit's loss is our gain."

After a momentary hesitation, he took my hand. "Thanks, Chief. I like it here. It feels like home."

As I drove to Mom and Dad's house, I thought about the new journal. I was at a dead end investigating Peggy McBride's death, but, to be honest, I hadn't expected much. All we had to go on were thirty-year-old memories and guesswork. And let's face it, memories fade with time.

Of course, mine hadn't. I pulled into the driveway and sat for a minute, thinking. What was I going to do about Emily? I needed to start facing reality. She wasn't going to move here. Even if she were selling her business and would consider moving here, she'd be bored in Little Bay, Michigan, population 4,500. This was just a fun diversion for her, a weekend away.

I took a long breath and tried to shake away the depressing thought. If this was temporary then I had to store up enough memories to last me. I wouldn't let another minute slip away.

I ran up the stairs and found Emily and my parents in the living room. For a minute I was struck by how familiar and yet how changed the scene was. I often saw them together when we dated, sitting and talking at the house. Now my dad looked so old and frail and Mom looked like a strong wind could blow her away.

Then they turned at my arrival and I saw the shrewd intelligence in Dad's gray eyes. Not much had really changed, I decided.

I held out the sack of CDs. "I thought you might like some music."

She opened it, looked inside and started laughing. "You've got a helluva memory." She pulled out Eric Clapton, Neil Young, and Pink Floyd. "From your private collection?"

I undid my tie and put it, my gun, and my jacket in the hall closet then moved over to sit next to her on the couch. "Yep, my private collection."

Emily rooted around in the bag and pulled out CDs. "Ooh, look at this. *Greatest Hits of the 60s* and *Greatest Hits of the 70s.*" She pointed to one of the songs on the CD. "I remember this one. I was so disappointed the first time I went to San Francisco," she confided to Mom. "I had visions of this Scott MacKenzie song. All those gentle people." She made a face. "It's just another big old dirty city."

I laughed. "Did you go to the Haight?"

"Of course. And the Fillmore. But it just wasn't the same."

"When did you go?"

"1990."

"Well, that explains it," I said. "Time doesn't stand still."

"There should be some shrines left standing," she mumbled.

"Yep. They paved paradise and put up a parking lot," Mom said regretfully.

"Did you guys figure out anything from the diary?" I propped my feet up on the old coffee table.

"We've been trying to figure out who Peggy's Secret Sweetie was."

"Secret Sweetie?" Dad asked. He exchanged a look with Mom, who hid a grin.

"Yeah, that's what we called it when girls had boyfriends but they wouldn't tell who they were," Emily explained. "She said when they used the balcony it hurt."

"The balcony hurt?" I asked.

"No, sex. When they had sex on the balcony she said it hurt."

"What?" I tried to remember the diary entry but I had focused on the location, not the act.

With an exasperated sigh, Emily pulled the diary over to her. She quickly found the appropriate entry and read it out loud.

"Oh." I looked at Dad. He nodded.

"What?" Emily demanded. "Come on, tell!"

"Maybe it was sodomy," Dad said.

She stared at him in shocked surprise. "Gross," she finally said. "I mean, yuck!"

I laughed shakily. Trust Emily to get right to the heart of the matter. "If Peggy was into S&M that might be it."

"She might not have known any better." Mom shook her head. "We can't know what people are thinking or feeling sometimes."

"Not known any better?" Emily asked. "Oh. You mean she thought it was love?"

Mom nodded. "The bastard she was seeing might have told her some story about how true lovers do things like that or how special she was. We'll never know. And anyway, we have a new mystery to solve." She pointed to the small green book my father was examining.

"Rob told me about it. What've you got?"

"It looks like a bookkeeper's ledger or something. We've been staring at it for an hour but it doesn't make sense." Dad handed me the book.

I leafed through it, looking at the various columns. Each page was much the same, filled with initials and numbers, like this:

5/19	MC	MJ	2K	PG	1-4/5-5
6/3	R	H	1B	BG	4-23/8-12
6/13	P	Hs	5K	EM	19-25/29-3
6/30	T	MJ	2K	BG	3-23/5-19

"The first one must be a date," Emily said, leaning against me to look around my arm at the book. "The last column can't be a date. It doesn't make sense."

"How many different initials are there?" Mom asked, pencil poised over a pad of paper.

"Good question," Dad said. "Let's see if there's a pattern."

I gave the book to Emily and went to the kitchen to get a beer, listening as they analyzed the small journal. We soon discovered the only discernible pattern was that the dates progressed in a regular fashion. In the second column, there were only four values: *MC, R, P, T*, usually in that order.

In the third column, four values appeared on a regular basis: *C, H, Hs, MJ*. In the fifth column, only four values appeared: *PG, BG, RP, EM, PB*. Of those, the one occurring most often was *BG*.

One other odd fact appeared after we stared at the

initials for a while. "Do you notice when the EM initials stopped, the RP initials started?" Mom said. "Once the RP initials start there're no more EM initials."

Emily sat back and stared at the notes she and Mom made. "There's another thing." She tapped her notepaper thoughtfully. "There're no entries in the wintertime."

I leafed through the book. "You're right. The last entry is in late October and the earliest entry is in March, if the first column really is a date."

We all looked at each other. "So what's it about?" Dad asked. "Why did Peggy have it?"

Emily pulled out the diary she found at the beach. "I think it's different handwriting. In fact, it has to be. Look at the way the numbers are formed. They're different."

I took the two books and looked at them. "You're right. So if Peggy didn't keep this journal, why did she have it?"

Dad leafed through it to the end. "It looks like it covers three years. But there's no year designation in it. So who knows when it really started?" He glanced at his watch. "Damn. We need to get going."

Mom nodded. "Monday night we rent a movie and have dinner at a friend's house." She stood and gave Dad a hand up.

Emily got up and stretched. "I better get supper started." She headed toward the kitchen, pausing to pop a CD into the boom box.

I walked with Mom and Dad to the door. Mom glanced at the gym bag I put next to the entrance. "I take it you're planning on staying here tonight."

I grinned. “I hope to.”

She gave me a brisk hug. “It’s nice to see you so happy, honey.”

I glanced at Emily, who was humming along with Eric Clapton. “I’d like it to stay that way.”

Mom looked past me. “Won’t hurt to ask.” She nudged Dad. “Move along there, Sheriff.”

Dad led the way down the stairs, calling back over his shoulder, “See you later. I’ll talk to you in the morning. Don’t work too hard, Emily.”

“Thanks, Sam,” Emily called back.

I joined her in the kitchen. “I remember this Eric Clapton album.” I touched the CD cover. “Remember when we camped out to buy it?”

“How could I forget? Listen, thanks for sending over Rob Sloan. He’s a nice guy.”

I sipped my beer. “I was surprised he stopped by.”

Emily giggled.

“What?” I asked, glass raised halfway to my mouth.

“Your mom and I did some shopping. We went to the liquor store and as I was checking out, the clerk said, ‘Remind the Chief he’s got a nine o’clock meeting with me tomorrow. You make sure he’s not late.’ So I’m reminding you.” She raised her wine glass to me.

“What?” I almost choked on my beer.

“And then this nice lady at the FlowerRama came out and gave me some flowers. Your mom stayed in the car. Natalie said Mrs. Petrosky was in her book club.” Emily grinned. “I get the feeling we’re town property, Nate.”

I opened my mouth but no words came out.

Emily laughed. “I think everybody knows where

you're sleeping tonight." She grinned impishly at me. "Wait a minute." She slipped past me into the bedroom.

"What?" I asked, following her.

"You stay out there," she warned. "I'm sure I brought it."

"Brought what?"

"You'll see. Stay out there."

I heard her moving something around. "What are you doing?"

Emily emerged wearing an *Eric Clapton World Tour 2000* T-shirt. "Ta da!" she said triumphantly.

"You didn't." The shirt fit her *very* well.

"It's the fourth time I saw him in concert."

I put one hand on the guitar logo, which just happened to be positioned over her right breast. "Nice shirt. Why don't you take it off?"

"You're right. I might get it dirty when I cook." Emily opened a kitchen drawer and pulled out an apron. "This should do it."

"Is that your little French maid's outfit?"

"It is when I take off my jeans." She gestured threateningly with her wooden spoon. "Later. Now I cook."

I took a seat at the kitchen island. She expertly diced some cabbage and started making coleslaw. The delicious aroma of chicken in the oven and potatoes bubbling in a pot on the stove drifted to me. She moved with a grace and an effortless efficiency, humming to Eric as she mixed, poured, and diced. "I found apples at the store, so I thought we'd have pie."

It took a minute for the words to soak in. "Homemade apple pie?"

She nodded, her hand in a mixing bowl, fiddling

with some flour. "Yep. I'm making the crust now. If you'd like to help, you can cut up the apples."

"Homemade apple pie?" I repeated.

She laughed. "Yes. It's not hard to do."

"Wow. I didn't think anybody made apple pie anymore."

"I do." She nodded to the bowl of apples on the counter in front of me. "Just do a rough peel and a rough cut. I like a nice, chunky apple pie."

"Yes, ma'am." I pulled the bowl over and took the knife Emily offered and started to whack at the apples, filled with warm contentment. The smells in the kitchen were fabulous, a beautiful woman was cooking me dinner, and after we ate, we'd lie around and talk and then we'd make love. Damn. Life just couldn't get any better than this.

The cell in the charging cradle on the counter rang. Emily's hands were covered with flour. "Get it, okay?"

I put down my apple. "Emily's phone."

"Why do you always answer her phone?" Jonas Hawthorne demanded after a pause.

I grinned. "Because I'm always with her. She's busy. Can she call you back?"

"Busy doing what? She's on vacation. For heaven's sake, she's probably in the kitchen cooking instead of resting."

I pulled the phone aside. "It's Jonas Hawthorne. He's said I'm forcing you to cook."

Emily rolled her eyes and grabbed a kitchen towel to wipe her hands. She held out one flour-covered hand for the phone. "Hello, Jonas," she said sweetly. She turned her back and stared at the fridge but didn't attempt to move away, so I eavesdropped shamelessly.

"You know how cooking relaxes me, Jonas."

I felt a stab of jealousy. This guy knew her good enough to know how she loved to cook. I hadn't thought they were close. I scowled at the apples.

Emily's shoulders tensed as she listened to what the moron was saying. "Is everything still good to go?" She dragged over a napkin and scrawled *lawyer, 10.*

I glanced at the scrap of paper then away, not wanting to pry.

"I'm busy now. I'll talk to you later." She listened some more, her eyes narrowing. "I'll see you soon." She folded up the phone and put it in the charging cradle. "Business."

"Hmm." I wasn't buying it for a minute. She was pink-faced, and a pink-faced Emily meant she was hiding something.

I struggled with curiosity while enjoying one of the best meals of my life. I tried to get information out of her while we ate. "How long have you known this Hawthorne guy?" I asked as I poured us both another glass of the crisp white wine she bought.

"A few months. He started courting me in June."

I almost spit out the wine. "Courting?"

"Hmm. He started shopping for a branch office then. I wasn't interested but we had a rough summer this year. A couple of our resorts changed management and the kids had trouble, and some kids walked off the job, and suddenly, by August, Jonas's proposal was looking a lot better."

I'll bet it was. He was probably looking better, too. Hawthorne was a handsome guy and he was richer than sin. I did some discreet research on the guy when Dorothy mentioned him. Hawthorne owned a big boat and raced in Chicago races, and he had a house in California as well as a penthouse in Chicago.

"What will you do if you sell? Retire?"

"Jonas wants me to stay on as executive manager. I can keep my hand in the business but I wouldn't have all the responsibility. And Jonas wants me to go to some of his other branch offices and work there and see how they operate." She swirled the wine in her glass. "It might be interesting."

"Sounds like it." It sounded like she had a nice future mapped out. There was no room in there for a small-town cop. She'd be traveling and doing interesting things. The thought made my gloom deepen.

We took the warm apple pie and coffee into the living room and sat down, stretching out on the battered old furniture. "This is such a great apartment," Emily said with a sigh. "I'm surprised it hasn't been rented."

"The last tenant left in August and I guess Dad just hadn't gotten around to renting it again." I spoke with only half a mind, the majority of my mind in a whirl. Why did Emily go to bed with me the other night? Heck, she had this Jonas guy and a great future waiting for her. What was this, some quickie vacation then back to her exciting life in the Cities?

The more I thought about it, the more my jaw tightened and my simmering anger built. Why did she come back here? Okay, I asked for her help, but she could leave if she wanted to. There was no reason to stay.

I drank the last of my coffee and set down my pie plate. I wish I hadn't seen her again. I wish she hadn't come back into my life like this. I was managing to get along without her. Now she was going to go away again and it would probably take me another thirty years to forget her.

I stood up, so tense I couldn't bear sitting still any longer. "I think I'd better leave." I took my plate and coffee mug to the kitchen.

She straightened, surprised. "It's early yet. Don't you want to stay?"

"Emily, I can't stay. How would it look? The chief of police sleeping over with a woman?" I tried to sound civic-minded but I suspected I just sounded pissed off.

She crossed her arms. "I'm just 'a woman' to you?" I opened my mouth to argue, but didn't get the chance. "I stayed at your place last night."

"But I picked you up. Your car wasn't there. I need to think how it looks."

"You're worried about how it will look?" She advanced on me, five-foot-two of quivering fury. "Mrs. Patchel at the grocery store asked me what I was fixing you for breakfast the other day." She stared up at me. "There are no secrets in this town, mister."

"Just because a few busybodies are being nosy, doesn't mean..." I said weakly. Who was I kidding? An invading army would have to pry me away from her. I didn't care why she was sleeping with me or how long she stayed. I'd take what she gave me.

She poked me in the chest with a finger. "You're staying, bub. And that's that."

"What about Jonas?" I asked, putting my arms around her.

She wiggled in my arms and suddenly one of my thighs was between her legs. "Jonas who?" she asked, putting her arms around my neck.

"Good answer," I said.

Chapter 26

Thirty-Four Years Earlier

The morning after the bonfire, Silas meandered past the desk when Emily was working. She eyed him. "Have a good time last night?" she asked as she sorted keys.

"I had a very interesting time last night," he said, hands stuck into the pockets of his shorts. *That's the understatement of the year,* Silas thought. *Rachel is beyond belief. I can't remember the last time I was so thoroughly screwed, blown, and used.* He felt great. "What time are we going out for supper tonight?"

Emily looked at him blankly.

"Your boyfriend's house?" he prompted.

"Oh, yeah. I get off at six, so I'll run back and change and we can leave then."

Silas nodded. "Where do you stay?" he asked, looking around the lobby.

Emily lowered her voice. "Nate and I have this place. Officially I live in the dorm with the other girls, but he and I have a special place."

Mr. Goldman came around the counter and Silas leaned back. "I should check out your dorm sometime," he said in a conversational voice. "Just to tell Dad everything's okay."

Emily nodded. "Tonight. You can see it then."

"Deal." Silas nodded to Mr. Goldman, who scowled back. "I think I'll just lounge around a bit and enjoy your great resort."

Goldman smiled and chomped down on his cigar. "Good. I like to see guests relaxing." He looked from Silas to Emily. "Not much family resemblance."

"I take after Mommy," Emily said breezily.

"Thank God." Silas gave her a kiss on the cheek then went outside. He and Rachel had been busy until almost dawn and a day lying in the sun seemed like a good plan. He was going to leave tomorrow afternoon, so maybe he and Rachel might have another "talk" tonight, after Silas and Emily had dinner with the Boltz family. Silas grinned and headed for the beach.

****

After a day of drowsing and swimming Silas saw Nate on the front steps of the resort so he went over to join him.

Nate looked up as Silas approached. "Have fun last night?"

Silas sat down next to Nate and they exchanged a long look. "Helluva girl," Silas said with a small shake of the head.

Nate grinned and nodded. Silas raised an eyebrow and Nate said, "For about two weeks, last year. She was too much for me." They both looked up as Emily came out of the front door and grinned at them. "There's *my* girl," Nate said, standing up.

Emily beamed at him and Silas thought it had been a long time since he'd seen two people so happy with each other. *Like Dad and Mommy,* Silas thought suddenly. *They used to look like that.*

"Look at this, two escorts," Emily said. She put an

arm around Nate's waist and started steering them toward the dorm where she shared a space with Pauline and Esther. "I wanted to show Silas where I bunk," Emily explained with a perfectly straight face.

"Ah." Nate glanced over her head at Silas, who shrugged and nodded.

They all inspected the dorm then Nate and Emily took Silas to the small cottage they were sharing. Nate gave him the dime tour while Emily changed then she and Silas sat outside and waited for Nate to change. "He's a nice guy," Silas commented.

"Yep," Emily agreed. She wore jeans and a gingham blouse and looked very young and pretty as she stretched out her legs to prop them on the porch rail.

"You guys getting serious?" Silas asked casually.

"I'm eighteen, Silas," Emily said with something like despair. "I'm serious but how serious can we be?" She looked at him and sighed. "I love him so much."

He put an arm around her shoulders. "Just see what happens, honey. Don't worry about it."

She nodded and Silas saw the tears in her eyes. "I'm trying not to worry. It's just that summer is so short."

Silas nodded as Nate came out the door. "No kidding," he agreed.

They drove in Silas's rental car to the Boltz house, where Sam was outside manning a grill. "Beer's in the cooler," he said, waving a spatula at a bright purple cooler near the back porch. "Natalie, company's here," he called out.

Natalie came out onto the back stoop, looking like a bright bird of paradise in her tie-dyed sheer dress draped over a crimson thin-strapped camisole and shorts. “Emily, there you are,” she said, dashing down the steps, her crimson Dr. Scholl sandals clattering on the wooden stairs.

“Wow. Great shoes,” Emily said after Natalie gave her a big hug. Natalie loved to paint her shoes and she went to town on the wooden sandals with psychedelic colors and catchphrases like *far out*, *groovy* and *hip*, as well as flowers and peace symbols. “They’re cool.”

Natalie held out one foot for inspection. “I thought so.” She looked at Silas, who was regarding her with interest. “I’m Natalie, Nate’s mom.” She stuck out a hand. “Lord, you must have gotten all the muscle in the family.”

Silas grinned and shook her hand. “You should see Dan. And Ben.” He looked at Emily. “He’s getting huge.”

“Poor Daddy. His food bills must be astronomical. I know Jason will out-grow all of you. He’s only a teenager.”

“It’s a pleasure to meet you, ma’am,” Silas said. “Emily speaks highly of you.”

“And I speak highly of her,” Natalie said. “She’s a marvelous girl.”

“Well, heavens,” Emily said, blushing. “Just embarrass me.”

Natalie and Silas laughed and Natalie pushed back a handful of long, curly black hair. “Did my husband offer you a beer, Silas?” She tucked a hand under his arm and they wandered over to the grill.

“I want to thank you, ma’am, for taking such an interest in Emily,” Silas said. “Our mother died when Emily was young and I’m afraid there hasn’t been much maternal influence around her."

Natalie sipped her beer. "She's a sweet child. She and my son make a pretty couple."

Silas nodded, eyeing Nate and Emily sitting on the red metal glider, their heads touching as they talked. "They are, aren't they?" He glanced at Sam Boltz, who was idly tapping the hamburgers on the grill. "I met Greg Hoffman last night at the resort."

Sam snorted. "Asshole," he muttered.

Silas laughed. "That seems to be the consensus. Do you think he's still a problem?"

Sam looked at Emily then at Nate. "He really has it in for Nate," Sam said softly. "And he'd probably hurt Emily just to get back at Nate." Sam shrugged and glanced at Natalie. "I suspect now Emily's with Nate, Hoffman won't be a problem." He looked at Silas and the two men exchanged a look. "I'll keep an eye on her this summer."

Silas took a long swallow of beer. "I'd appreciate it, Sheriff."

"We both will, Silas," Natalie said. "Tell your Daddy not to worry about his girl."

Silas shook his head. "Could I tell you not to worry about your boy?"

Natalie sighed ruefully. "No, you couldn't. But I hope you'll be comforted knowing we're doing all we can to keep her safe."

Silas nodded and drained his beer. "Yes, ma'am, I know." He looked at Emily, who was letting Nate win at horseshoes. "She's so sweet and naïve and gentle. I don't want to see her hurt."

Natalie patted his arm. "We'll do our best."

They had a pleasant evening. Natalie filled them in

on gossip from town then they all talked about the national situation. Silas found it interesting that Emily, a notorious critic of all authority figures, listened with respect when Sheriff Boltz talked about the problems facing law officers. It was one of the more intelligent conversations Silas had in a long time and he was ashamed it surprised him to have found such intelligence in a small town.

They drove back to the resort, Emily in the middle of the Impala's car seat between the two men. Silas noticed Nate's hand on Emily's leg but he didn't say anything. He liked the kid and he liked the kid's family. Good, solid people, Silas decided.

"Do you have plans tonight?" Emily asked as they pulled into the parking lot outside the main resort building.

"As a matter of fact, I do."

Emily kissed him on the cheek then gave him a little shove. "You go off and have fun."

"Right back at you," Silas said, watching as Nate looked at Emily with an adoring look.

"We will," Emily promised. She slid out of the car after Nate.

Silas watched them walk off, arms around each other. Cute kids, he thought. Then he considered his own plans for the night and grinned. He saw Rachel earlier and she mentioned that she and a girlfriend might be available.

Should be interesting.

Chapter 27

Present Day

At some point during the night I awoke and she was gone. "Emily?" I raised my head groggily. "Everything okay?"

"Just fine," she called back. "I'll be there in a minute."

I settled into the warm spot she left, inhaling her fragrance. Soon she returned, snuggling into my arms. "Where'd you go?" I asked sleepily.

"Just fixing your lunch," she whispered, kissing me on the cheek.

"Huh?"

"Go to sleep, honey."

I obeyed.

At six o'clock the alarm woke us. "I don't have to be at work until eight-thirty," I complained as Emily shut off the alarm.

She rolled over and fit herself to me. "We should have enough time," she said with a wicked little grin.

I pulled her close. "You know me too well."

"Not nearly as well as I'm going to," she promised.

By eight o'clock, I was shaved, showered and ready to go. She handed me a small brown paper bag. "Lunch."

I opened it and peeked inside. Once again, I saw

two sandwiches in wax paper, a container with what looked like her coleslaw and another container with what looked like a slice of her apple pie. "Aw, Emily. You shouldn't have."

"Chicken salad," she said, leaning in the doorway and smiling. She wore her Eric Clapton T-shirt again and she looked so beddable I was hard pressed to leave the apartment.

"Wow. You're something." I bent down and kissed her, one hand going to her bare bottom and caressing it. "Can I see you tonight?"

She laughed softly. "I suspect you will. I don't have any other plans." Then she shook her head. "No, I take that back. I'm going to be busy today."

"Busy? Doing what? The bake sale?"

She looked momentarily surprised. "Oh, yeah, the sale. I should be back later in the afternoon, though." She smiled smugly, like she had a special secret. I figured she had shopping to do or something. Maybe those high heels were in my future after all.

I grinned at her. "Your place or mine tonight?"

"Let's wait and see how the mood takes us," she said, leaning into my caress. "Maybe we'll want a motel room."

"You're too much."

"No, baby, I'm just enough." She twined herself around me and gave me a deep, passionate kiss. Then she unwrapped herself and gave me a little nudge. "Go to work now. Think good thoughts all day about how you'll please me tonight."

"If I do, I'll lift my desk off the floor with my hard-on." I looked down into her laughing green eyes. "I love you, Emily." Then I turned and left so I didn't have to see the confusion in her eyes.

When I got to the station, I put the brown paper bag in the fridge, Dorothy watching. "What's that?" she demanded.

"Lunch."

"Again?"

"Again." I started down the hall to my office.

Dorothy smiled. "Twice in one week. My, my, my. You must be doing something special to get lunch twice in one week." She gave me a sly look.

"What did he say?" Sada's white-haired head peeked up over a file cabinet.

"He said she made him lunch again," Dorothy answered.

"I didn't say that," I called back over my shoulder. "I did *not* say that."

The morning passed quickly even though I thought about Emily constantly, wondering what she was doing, where she was, what she was wearing, who she was talking to, what she was thinking. At one o'clock I had a break and got out my lunch. Dorothy watched as I unpacked the feast on the little dinette table in the kitchen area.

"Good looking lunch," she commented.

I looked into the bottom of the sack and saw a folded-up piece of paper. I stuck it in my pocket. "She's just concerned I'm not eating right." I bit into the first sandwich and almost groaned with pleasure at the taste of homemade chicken salad.

"Uh-huh. More likely she wants you to keep up your strength." Dorothy grinned and sashayed out of the room.

I finished the sandwich and took the other

sandwich and the coleslaw back to my desk, saving the pie for later. I closed the door to the office then pulled out the note.

First of all, I want you to know this has been one of the happiest weeks of my life. You've made me feel so loved and wanted.

I wish I knew how I feel. I think I am in love with you but I'm so afraid of being wrong and hurting us all over again. I'm so afraid of making wrong choices.

But I'm not going to worry about the future now. My plane ticket is open-ended, so I don't have to leave on Saturday unless I want to. Right now I don't want to.

Nate, please give me a little time. It's been a long time since I've loved and been loved. I'm out of practice.

Emily

I touched the handwritten words. She thought she loved me but she wasn't sure. I could work with that. I hesitated briefly then decided to tell her so. I dialed her cell phone number.

Jonas Hawthorne answered. "Emily's phone."

It was like a bad dream come true. The food in my stomach congealed. "This is Police Chief Boltz. I'd like to speak with Emily, please," I managed to say civilly enough.

"She's busy." His voice was smugly self-satisfied. I knew he loved throwing my own words back at me.

I heard Emily laughing in the background. "Jonas, get out here and finish what you started," she called.

My hand was sweating so bad the phone slipped. "You sound busy." I had to talk around the sour taste in my mouth.

"A friend brought her boat up from Chicago for

winter storage at Holland, just north of here so I invited Emily along for a day away from her Michigan Mystery." *And from the boring man she was spending time with*, his voice implied. "Hold on a second." His voice faded a bit but I heard him clearly say, "Emily, cover up or you'll get sunburn."

I didn't hear her reply. He must have had his hand over the phone. A few seconds later, he came back on the line. "My pleasure, Emily. Impatient little creature, isn't she?" he asked, his voice amused. "It's tough to keep her happy, but I'm enjoying the attempt."

I had a stabbing memory of Emily this morning, her green eyes warm and sensual. Was she looking at Hawthorne the same way? "Sorry to interrupt," I snapped.

"I'll tell her you called," he said. "Boltz, was it?"

"Don't bother." It took two attempts for me to hang up the phone. I stared down at the note on my desk, my head so full of pain I fleetingly wondered if I might be having a stroke. Emily and Jonas Hawthorne were out together for the day. They were out on his yacht or boat or whatever it was, lounging around in the sun and...

I didn't finish the thought. The food was turning to lumps of lead in my stomach. I felt like I was suffocating. Movement. I had to move. I stood so fast my chair flew back and knocked into the credenza under the window. Snatching my jacket from the coat rack, I started to leave. Then I turned back to my desk and swept up the remaining sandwich and the small container of coleslaw. I dropped them in the wastebasket in the kitchen as I headed for the back door.

"Going out," I called to Dorothy.

"You got the pager?" I saw the top of her dark head behind the high counter around the reception area, her eyes curious at my abrupt departure.

"Yep."

"Don't forget the budget meetings at three o'clock."

"Got it." I fled out the back door, so anxious to be gone I almost ran to my truck. As I strode across the lot I finally noticed the blue sky, warm temperatures and balmy breezes. *Perfect day for a boat outing*, I thought bitterly.

A police car pulled into the parking lot. Cynthia got out and started walking toward me. "I was hoping for a chance to talk with you." Her eyes flickered to the back door of the station. "In private if you have time."

I leaned against my truck. "How's this?"

"I'd prefer to talk to you in your office."

"I'd prefer to talk here. What's your concern, Officer Bartlett?"

Resentment and anger flashed in her eyes. What did I do to deserve this? I was polite and professional and treated her with the respect she deserved. What was her beef? "I wanted to inform you I've been in contact with Jonas Hawthorne. He asked me to keep an eye on Miss Sutherland while she was here."

Small, disjointed facts suddenly made sense. I made a mental note to tell Rob. "And how did he know he could contact you?" I asked, keeping my voice even.

"His lawyer contacted me," Cynthia said. "It's not a conflict of interest. I checked with the city attorney."

"Really?" I hid the anger starting to boil. "What did the attorney say?"

"He said as long as I didn't do anything to

jeopardize ongoing investigations or shirk my duties, then I was free to work for an outside party in a consulting capacity."

"Really?" I had a hard time being civil, but I managed. "I appreciate you telling me. It was very professional of you."

She stiffened but her smirky expression didn't waver. "I spoke with Mr. Hawthorne about an hour ago. He said he was planning on staying on the boat for a while longer then he and Miss Sutherland would be coming back to her apartment."

I shrugged but it was an effort. "I expect him to give her a ride."

Cynthia's eyes were cool and calculating. "It sounds like they were having a little party. Maybe that's what got Porter so upset. You know how he thinks you and she need to be together. Maybe Porter's just realized she might have other ideas."

"Porter?"

"His sister called. He was upset. She wondered if you can stop by."

I pushed away from the truck, the rage of jealousy hot in my gut. "I'm busy right now. Please tell Nancy I'll stop by later on today?"

Cynthia seemed disappointed at my reaction. I suppose she was hoping I'd be pissed off. Well, I was, but I'd be damned if I'd show it. "She wanted you to talk to him. She said he always calms down when you talk with him."

"I'll wrap up a few things then stop."

"Good," Cynthia said with a bright smile. "I'll tell her."

I got into the truck and fumbled the key into the

ignition. My guilty conscience nagged at me but I knew I was in no condition to calm Porter Graves at the moment. I would go for a drive and try to get my life into perspective then stop at his sister's house. If I went there now, it would only make things worse.

Satisfied with my reasoning, I was soon driving north, along the lakeshore road. Then I remembered. Emily was out there on Lake Michigan somewhere. What if I saw their boat offshore? What if I saw her?

I turned right at the next county road and headed inland, toward Kalamazoo on one of the many blacktop highways crisscrossing the countryside. I drove aimlessly for almost forty-five minutes, taking right and left turns trying to get lost.

It didn't work, of course. I knew where I was: in love with a woman who didn't love me and who would be leaving soon. My hurt and disappointment coalesced into anger so intense I was burning with it. By the time I turned around and headed back to the office, I had relegated Emily Sutherland to a memory I would never visit again. I would call her later and tell her I appreciated her visit but it would be best if she left.

I pulled into the parking lot at 2:45, ran into the office and got the folders I needed then went over to City Hall for another round of haggling and dickering for money. I was happy for the distraction and although my anger with Emily simmered over into the discussions, I'd rehearsed my arguments beforehand so none of my temper leaked out in my voice. I presented statistics about crime, other towns our size, federal and state guidelines, and architectural recommendations for the current station.

"We can't keep up," I said bluntly in summary. If I

hadn't been so angry, I probably would have modulated my tone, but I let my disgust with Emily color my voice and my words, adding weight to what I was saying. "We are understaffed and poorly equipped. I can't keep criminals here for any length of time because of safety and health concerns, both for my staff and the incarcerated. So if we don't build a new facility, we need to add a substantial amount of money to our operating budget so we can transport detainees to the nearest facility in Benton Harbor and pay a surcharge to use their services. Your choice." I held up the report I painstakingly put together over the last six months. "I'm happy to answer any questions."

They dithered and talked and questioned, then did what I knew they'd do. They postponed making a decision. I agreed to come back the next day and answer any remaining questions but I knew I almost convinced them. I had to swing enough votes from them to get a referendum on November's ballot then I would have to do some campaigning in town to get the new facility built. But I'd face it in a week or two once I knew we'd be going to a vote.

A new police facility would be a good legacy to leave the town once I retired, I considered as I walked across the lot to the office. I would stay around long enough to see it built. I wasn't in any hurry to retire. There was nothing to retire to and nobody to retire with.

I let the thought fester as I came back into the police station. "Did you get me a new office?" Dorothy asked as I stomped past the reception desk to the hall leading to my office.

"I'm working on it," I snapped.

"Before you get comfortable, Nancy Thompson

called. Porter's gone missing."

"Damn it!" The words slipped out before I could stop myself. "Porter Graves is not my responsibility."

Dorothy raised one eyebrow and regarded me impassively. "And Emily called. Asked you to call her back."

I dropped my files on the receptionist's counter and wheeled around. "File those in my desk, would you? I'm going out to the resort. Maybe Porter went there again."

"What should I tell Emily if she calls?"

I almost said, *Tell her to go to hell*, but I restrained myself. "I'll talk to her later." I slammed the back door for good measure and went back to the parking lot. I started to get in my truck then realized a police sedan might be a better bet in case I had to transport Porter. I slid behind the wheel of the Crown Vic I used and headed north, toward the resort.

Some perverse imp made me drive by my parents' house. A black sedan was parked in the driveway outside the detached garage.

I drove slowly by, noting the license plate number. I hated myself for doing it, but I entered it on the computer tucked under the dashboard.

The information that came back confirmed what I suspected. The Jaguar parked outside the apartment belonged to Jonas Hawthorne. The son of a bitch was with her.

Anger warred with disappointment and hurt. It was hard to tell which emotion was the strongest. I guess in the end it didn't matter. All three signified the end of my brief dreams about a happily ever after with Emily Sutherland. By the time I drove through the resort gates, I was detached and removed from any emotion. I was a robot, going through the motions of being human.

The construction crew was wrapping up for the day. They'd been working on east side of the resort, well away from the spot where we found Peggy's body.

I waved to the foreman and parked the sedan. "Mr. Goldman is out there," the foreman called, gesturing toward the six-story building of hotel units facing Lake Michigan. I waved my thanks and walked across the grounds, skirting the empty swimming pool and closed concession stand and coming around the building on the west, or lake, side.

Bobby stood on the large wooden patio that jutted over the beach below, staring at the waves with his hands jammed deeply in his windbreaker's pockets. He turned when he heard me call his name.

"What's up, Nate? I haven't seen this much of you since you used to work here." He smiled when he said it, but I knew he wasn't pleased to have me interrupting him.

"Nancy called and said Porter had gone missing," I said apologetically. "I thought I'd check and see if he showed up here." I looked to my left, at the big lake that was such a part of my life and the lives of everyone in town. We depended on the tourist industry Lake Michigan brought in as well as the fishing and boating trade.

But now it reminded me of disappointment. I wondered if I would ever be able to see the lake's beauty again or would it always be tainted by my thoughts of Emily? I shook the idea aside and peered down at the beach. "Did you see Porter today?"

Bobby shook his head. "I've been holed up in the

main building, closing the books for the season. I just stepped out for a breath of air." He looked at the building behind us, peering up at the walls of windows reflecting the setting sun. "I had the beach fence taken down a week or so ago. He may have come onto the property from town or from the park."

The beach fences were low fences, like a snow fence, marking the north and south end of the resort property. I used to set them up in March and take them down in October, long before or after Mr. Goldman and his family arrived for the season. The fences didn't keep out trespassers. They just marked the property line.

"You're welcome to check the beach, but I doubt he's here. Porter doesn't like being out here when I'm here." Bobby frowned. "We've had words in the past."

"If he's off his medication, he might not be thinking straight." I nodded my thanks and started for the wooden steps leading to the beach below.

"Nate."

I looked back at Bobby. He was at the patio railing, the wind ruffling his fine hair. "How are things with you and Emily? Is she going to be moving here permanently?"

Anger pulsed through me, making me dizzy. I grabbed the railing for support. "I don't think so, Bobby." I kept my voice neutral. "I don't think a small town has much appeal for her."

His face tightened and for just a minute he looked as angry as I felt. Then he seemed to relax. "Sorry to hear that. I always liked Emily. She was the sweetest girl." His eyes looked a bit misty, like he was deep in a memory. "She was special."

"Yeah." I didn't trust myself to say more. I started down the steps but movement out of the corner of my eye made me stop. Porter was peeking around the side of the north end of the building, one hand to his mouth in a *shh* gesture and the other arm waving wildly. He wore a black T-shirt and denims, the dark fabric helping him fade into the bushes that framed the side of the building.

I paused and stared out at the lake. "I think you're right. I doubt he came out here. It's getting dark, anyway. He'll probably show up at home for dinner." I walked back the way I came. Bobby turned to follow my movement, his back now to Porter. "Thanks for everything, Bobby. I appreciate you letting us visit the other day."

He hunched his shoulders in his jacket even though it wasn't very cold. "It's tough taking a walk down memory lane." His voice was bitter and low. "Sometimes you don't know what might turn up."

"Amen to that. See you later." I went around the south end of the building but instead of going directly east, I went a bit north to pick up the path through the landscaped tree-lined walk and the arbor that hid the cottages from the view of the main resort.

As I suspected, Porter was lying in wait for me in the gazebo near the front gate. "Your sister's worried about you," I said as I neared.

He had his back to me and when he turned I stopped. Instead of a vague, unfocused look, a lucid man stared at me. "I had to talk to you, Nate." His voice was low and intense.

I stepped up into the gazebo and approached him slowly. "About what, Porter?"

He leaned against a doorway support. The gazebo was situated on the compass points and Porter was now blocking the east side. I had a fleeting memory of Emily and me, lying on the bench in the gazebo and necking one night until Bob Dwight, the night watchman, chased us away. I ruthlessly banished the thought and focused on Porter.

"I can't just come out and say what I know. If I did, he'd hurt me even more than he did. He's tried to kill me before, but he failed and now he doesn't dare try again because I wrote it all down and he knows I'll hurt him if he tries to hurt me."

I blinked at the onslaught of words. "Where did you write it?"

"In the bank, of course." He sounded disappointed, as though he expected better of me.

"Who is he?"

"I can't tell you," Porter said. "Don't trust him, Nate." Porter straightened and I winced when I saw the bright red rash on his left forearm.

I started to ask him what happened then he began a slow, steady scratching, his right fingers methodically raking over the crimson skin on his left arm. He spoke in time to the rhythm of his fingers. It was mesmerizing. "Look what happened to Peggy's baby."

"What? How did you know about Peggy's baby?"

He gave a short, abrupt laugh. "Everybody knew about the baby." He looked over my shoulder. "Be careful, Nate. Nothing's the way it seems. Nothing, not even Emily."

I looked behind me but only shadows filled the space between the trees. I turned around again but Porter was running down the path around the front of the grounds. I considered following him but decided I'd done enough for one afternoon. I cut across the empty grounds and got into my sedan, Porter's words echoing in my brain.

Chapter 28

Thirty-Four Years Earlier

Janie Sinclair couldn't identify her attacker. Sam borrowed a policewoman from the Kalamazoo PD and it was the first thing the policewoman asked Janie immediately after the attack. Sam asked her again when she emerged from surgery for her broken ribs but the poor kid said she didn't see the guy.

She was at a party on the beach ("Emily and Nate were there," she told Sam with a wistful smile. He nodded in return and thanked God those two hadn't been hurt). Someone pressed a drink into her hand. She started to feel woozy and she went off to sit down. The next thing she knew, someone was helping her walk down the beach. She must have passed out because when she came to she was lying on her stomach.

The next thing Janie remembered was the pain.

Sam nodded. He read the medical report. The poor girl had been brutalized. She'd heal but it would take time. "Did he say anything?" Sam asked gently.

Janie shook her head and the tears rolled down her cheeks. "He was grunting and swearing. I started to struggle and he got mad. That's when he hit me." She took a deep shuddering breath. "Then he turned me over and did it the regular way." She glanced at Sam then away, as though ashamed. "It's hard to explain.

It's like I knew what was happening but I wasn't really there."

"It was the drugs," Sam said. "According to the doctor, it was powerful. They've never seen it before. The doctor thinks it's like a sedative. You'd be awake but not alert."

Janie nodded. "I knew what was happening but I couldn't move. But when they turned me over, I should have been able to get away," she whispered angrily.

"They?" Sam asked casually. "Was there more than one?"

Janie looked startled. "Oh." She thought about it, eyes narrowing again in concentration. She had been a pretty girl, with somewhat plain features enlivened by her blue eyes and a wide, engaging smile. Sam hoped her smile would come back once the pain of this started to wear away. "Yes, there were two. I felt two sets of hands on me." She made a "yuck" face. "God, were there two men there?"

"Maybe it was the woman? The one who helped you walk down the beach?"

"Oh, yeah. Maybe. But why would a woman help someone like that? Wouldn't a woman want to help me?"

"Most men would want to help you," Sam said. "Not all men are mean."

She took a deep, wavering sigh and nodded. "I know," she said but Sam heard the doubt in her voice. He made a note to have a counselor help her. It was bad enough she was physically abused. He didn't want her carrying emotional scars, too.

Sam asked her a few more questions but she remembered very little. The man wore cologne she couldn't identify. And he wasn't big. She blushed. "It felt like his shoulders and legs weren't big."

"Good." Sam made a note and wondered if he could get a female nurse to talk to the girl. Or maybe Dorothy, from down at the station. Janie might open up more to a woman. Sam closed his little notebook and tucked it back in the breast pocket of his uniform. "If you remember anything else, you make sure to tell me.

Janie nodded. "Please thank Emily for the flowers." She looked at the big bouquet of roses and greenery on the sideboard. "I figured she sent them."

Sam nodded and admired the bouquet. It must have set Emily and Nate back some cash. He made a mental note to slip Nate some money. "I'll tell her. If there's anything she can do to help, you just have to tell her."

Sam knew Janie would never ask for help. A crime like this was something people didn't want to advertise, he thought sadly as he left the hospital room.

When he got back to the sheriff's office, Dorothy was waiting for him. She followed him into his office and shut the door behind her. "This came," she said shortly, thrusting something at Sam.

He took the piece of paper gingerly. She'd put it between two plastic sheets and he looked a question at her.

She just gestured to the paper. "Read it."

Sam looked down at the note. The letters were in block capitals, as though someone wrote them either with a cast on his or her hand, or with the wrong hand. The words seemed to wobble and go all over the page.

Emily Sutherland is a whore and your son is as dirty as she is.

"Well, shit," Sam said softly.

Dorothy nodded. "It came in today's mail. As soon as I saw what it was, I got it in plastic. In case you wanted to look for fingerprints."

"Good thinking, Dorothy." He stared at the note. "Where does this fit in?" He looked up as he heard the sound of voices at his door. Emily and Nate came bursting in. Sam slid a piece of paper over the ugly note.

Then he saw he didn't have to bother. Nate was carrying a file folder and he put it on his father's desk. When Nate opened the folder, Sam saw a similar note:

Be careful. What happened to Janie could happen to you, you whore.

Nate's face looked like it was set in granite and Sam suddenly saw the man his son would become. *Correction*, Sam thought. *The man my son is becoming.* He wanted to curse at the frightened, stricken look he saw on Emily's face. "Damn. I'm sorry you saw that. Where did you get it?"

"It was waiting at the dorm at the resort," Emily said in a small voice.

Sam nodded briskly. "Don't you worry about it. I promised your brother nothing would happen to you, and I keep my promise." Her look of relief made him hope that he could keep that promise.

He took down the information Emily gave him and made a note to talk to the other girls in the dorm. Then he shooed the kids out and sat down to compare the two notes. Who had it in for Emily? And why? There wasn't a sweeter kid on the planet.

Sam got up and went out to the main office, where Dorothy was glaring at her new electric typewriter. "I suppose you're thinking about canceling your speech at the convention," she said. "After I learned how to use this machine just to get it typed."

Sam frowned. "I should. I shouldn't leave down with an unsolved rape and threats against my son and his girlfriend."

"Chicago is just a three hour drive away. It's a convention of police officers." Dorothy shot him a wry look. "I suspect I can get in touch with you if I need to."

"I suppose," he said doubtfully.

"Plus, how long has it been since you and Mrs. B had a nice little trip out of town?" She tugged a piece of paper out of the machine, muttering under her breath. In her opinion, a good manual typewriter, carbon paper, and a stencil copier were all a well-equipped office needed. That and a good file system would get them through this century and well into the next as far as she was concerned. "Don't you think it's time you took your wife out now and again?"

Sam opened his mouth to protest then closed it again. Dorothy was right. Chicago was just a short drive away, his deputies would take care of things while he was gone, and Sam could talk to officers from bigger cities and see if they had experience with similar rape crimes. Little Bay and the surrounding towns normally didn't have such crimes. Sam was feeling out of his depth.

That decision made, the next day Sam went to the resort to fill Bobby in on the investigation into the rape. "Seems like the Townies and the summer kids are sort of pulling together," Bobby commented.

Sam was relieved old man Goldman wasn't in the office. The old man smoked the foulest-smelling cigars

Sam had ever experienced and the odor of the cigars always wafted around him like a stale cloud. Bobby, on the other hand, was small, tidy, and dapper, and he always smelled faintly of mint or cologne.

"Pulling together?" Sam asked. They were in the office behind the front desk and Sam saw Emily, chatting with some guests. She looked fresh and pretty in her denim shorts and golf shirt.

"The boys are making sure no girl is left unescorted. And they've come up with an escort schedule. Even the cooks are in on it." Bobby frowned.

Sam's attention snapped back to him. "Problem?"

Bobby's glance slid away from Sam. "It's one of the cooks. I'm not sure if it's a problem or not." He tapped the desk and Sam waited patiently. He had discovered people tended to talk a lot when there was an empty silence around them.

"We might not have done such a good background check." Bobby flushed an unpleasant shade of red and Sam thought of Greg Hoffman. He didn't comment. "There are some things on his job application that don't hang together. I pulled out all the applications and looked them over after the business with Greg," Bobby explained. He ran a hand over his thin brown hair. "I may have you look into something for me."

"You let me know," Sam said. "I have to go to a convention next week, but Dorothy knows how to get in touch with me."

"I forgot you were a speaker there." The local newspaper had run a piece on Sam's upcoming debut as a national public speaker.

Sam stood. "It's just an hour-long speech out of four days of speeches."

"Yes, but you're still the local boy who made good," Bobby said and Sam thought he detected a note of envy or maybe jealousy. Sam shrugged it off. There was nothing for Bobby to be jealous about. He was a Chicagoan and had no real ties to Little Bay the way Sam did. Then Sam did a little mental shake. Bobby and old man Goldman had been coming up here for summers for almost forty years. If that didn't make them Little Bay citizens, what did? Sam tucked the thought away for reflection later and went out to chat with Emily.

That night Sam and Natalie discussed the upcoming trip. "Well, it's up to you, Sam," Natalie said as they sat in the back yard on the glider rocker and watched the fireflies while drinking their after-dinner brandy. "You're the one supposed to deliver the speech. You could drive there on Tuesday, give your speech, and come back home."

She tilted her head to one side and Sam thought he'd never seen a prettier woman than his own wife. Her hair was long and curly with just a hint of gray and she let it fall naturally, held in place by two barrettes shaped like butterflies. Her face was small and oval-shaped and she had a flawless complexion. After twenty-five years of marriage Sam was still in love with her and she still excited him in bed like no other woman ever had.

"Don't you want to go?" She was tucked under his arm, just where he liked her, so he didn't see her expression.

Natalie swung one bare foot, her legs in the pedal-pushers looking smooth and tanned. "Sure." She looked up at him with a grin. "It's a chance for me to infiltrate into the heart of the Beast." Natalie was always referring to the government as the Beast and it didn't seem to faze her that her husband worked for the Beast. "Maybe I can convert a few folks over to non-violence and pacifism."

Sam snorted and hugged her. "I doubt it."

"Worth a try. Seriously, Sam, I think it's safe to leave the kids. They'll be okay. Nate's responsible and you know he won't have any wild parties. Parties, yes. Wild parties, no."

Sam laughed. "They always have the wild parties out on the beach," he noted.

Natalie laughed, too. "It's useful living near a big lake. But you know he and Emily will just play house for a week." She craned her neck to look up at him. "Does it bother you?"

"Not really. There's no way to keep a secret in a town this small. And it's not like it's a secret he and Emily have been steady all summer." He looked down at Natalie affectionately. "What do you think will happen to them?"

She put her hand on his thigh and began a slow, gentle massage that soon had his blood racing. "I don't know, Sam. They're probably too young to know any better, but I think they're meant to be together." Natalie sighed sadly. "I don't think it'll happen."

Sam bent his head and nuzzled at her neck, his breath warm on her skin. "We've got to let them work it out." He looked at her with a gleam in his gray eyes. "Care to go in the house and chat about it?"

Natalie looked around the secluded back yard then she glanced at Nate's apartment that was, as usual, dark. "Why go inside?" she asked softly.

Chapter 29

Present Day

I sat at my desk in my office, staring at my computer screen as Porter's words echoed in my brain. Rachel Putnam died in a car accident in 1977. The car she was driving had mechanical failure and it drove off one of the winding roads that hugged the shoreline of Lake Michigan. Peggy presumably died in 1974. Did anyone else from those summer years die?

I pulled over the list of names Emily put together, comparing it to the timeline we compiled on Sunday afternoon with the Summer Kids. Then I started the laborious process of running computer checks on everyone, searching for anything unusual. I was two names into the list when my cell phone rang. It was Emily.

"Nate? Where are you? Are you coming over tonight?"

Curiosity warred with anger warred with pride. Pride won. "Are you back from your outing with Hawthorne?"

There was long silence on the other end of the line. "I beg your pardon?"

"I called you today."

"I was busy."

"I know. I thought you were going to the bake

sale."

"I didn't say I was going to the bake sale."

"You did, too."

"No, I didn't." She sounded patient and calm, which pissed me off even more. "I told you I was going to a sale. I didn't say what kind."

"You're splitting hairs."

"I'm telling the truth." There was another simmering silence. "You're mad about something. Why don't you just tell me?"

"I called you today and Jonas Hawthorne answered." I spat out the words like they were a bad taste in my mouth. Hell, who was I kidding? I had a bad taste.

"He didn't mention it." Now she sounded mad. Good. See how it felt. "Jonas and I had business to discuss. About a *sale*." She emphasized the word like it had some kind of special meaning.

"Right. Business on a yacht in the middle of Lake Michigan."

"Yacht?"

"Whatever it was."

"Jonas called last night and said he'd be in the area and wanted to see me. He wanted to have lunch."

"How long does it take to have lunch?"

There was a long pause. "What are you implying?"

"I'm not implying anything. It's just that you've been gone a long time. I thought we were going to be together tonight."

"I thought we would, too. It's only seven. You can come over if you'd like."

I was so pissed off I didn't know if I wanted to see her. "I don't think so," I snapped, but almost immediately regretted it.

There was another long pause. "Are you sure you and Office Bartlett are only in a professional relationship?"

Now where the hell did that come from? "Why are you asking?"

"I'm just curious."

"There is nothing going on between me and Cynthia Bartlett. How many ways do I have to tell you?"

"Has there ever been anything between you two?" Emily asked.

I counted to five, slowly. "Why are you asking this? Did Hawthorne imply something?" She hesitated and I jumped on it. "He did, didn't he? Damn it, Emily, when are you going to believe me? When will you trust me?"

"Why do you believe there's something going on with me and Jonas?" she shot back, thoroughly angry now. "This works both ways, Nate."

She was right. I was a fool to think there might ever be anything between us again. I was a fifty-five-year-old fool. I was too old for this crap.

"You're right," I said. "A relationship should work both ways. And I guess ours doesn't. If you'd rather not wait around in town for the party on Thursday, I understand. Just let me know if you still want to go." I closed the phone with a snap and jumped to my feet, putting yet another dent into the credenza behind me.

I looked down at the list on my desk. It was in Emily's handwriting. Damn. I opened a new file on my computer and typed in the names then I jammed the handwritten list into my bottom desk drawer. I did a few searches but my heart wasn't in it. I had to get out and move.

I stopped by the front desk and checked the logs then escaped out the back door. It was a crisp October night with a nearly full moon already shimmering in the sky. If the weather held, we'd have a beautiful evening for the big Homecoming events, starting on Thursday with the JV game and the dance then Friday with the Varsity game and dinner.

I considered it as I drove through town, force of habit making me do a pass through the downtown area before driving by my parents' house to make sure things were quiet. Hawthorne's car was still in the driveway and it threw me for a loop. What was she doing calling me while Hawthorne was still there? My brain was so addled with anger I wasn't thinking straight.

When I got home I stomped into the kitchen and almost jerked the fridge over as I rummaged in it for a beer. Damn it, how did things get so screwed up? What did they do all day on that damn boat? I stowed my gear then dropped onto the couch, the same couch Emily and I made love on just a couple of nights ago. Everything would remind me of her from now on. The couch where we made love, the bed where she slept, the shower, the kitchen. Shit. I'd have to sell the damn house to get away from the memories.

J. Edgar wandered in, gave me a haughty stare then wandered back out as though to comment on my foul manners. I took a long gulp of beer and stared at the wall, thoughts all jumbling up in my brain. Images of Emily, Porter, Bobby, and the Summer Kids all flittered through my mind. Why did I ever think I could solve a thirty-four year old murder? Why did I call Emily and ask her to come here?

I knew the answer and I finally had to face it.

I had to know if the love I felt was real. Was it just first love? Was it young love? Or was it something real and lasting?

I laughed bitterly. J. Edgar paused before jumping up into his recliner and regarded me with cool curiosity. "I guess I have the answer." I felt a sorrow so big it threatened to suffocate me. *This is depression*, I thought.

I never understood it before. Once in Miami I was with the team who tried to talk a man out of killing himself. We didn't succeed. The man jumped and I'd never forget the look of despair in the man's eyes as he launched himself from the roof.

This was what it felt like. This crushing heaviness, this lack of motivation, this lack of *caring*. Someone could come through the door with a gun right now and aim it at me and I wouldn't care. They could go ahead and shoot. I wouldn't give a shit. I closed my eyes and tried to push away the memories.

The pager on my hip thumped, reminding me I was still bruised and sore—and still a cop. I considered ignoring it briefly but I was always on call. I looked at the phone number on the small LED screen.

Something was wrong at my parents' house.

I was out of the house, in the truck and pulling up to the driveway in ten minutes. A squad car was in the drive, blocking the dark colored sedan still sitting there like some kind of malignant monster.

My father waited for me at the bottom of the steps to the apartment. "I told Emily we should call you, but she said you had a fight," Dad said. "So I called the station. I knew they'd call you. Emily's in the house with Natalie."

"What happened?" I looked up the enclosed staircase.

"She's okay. She was just shaken up in the accident. But when she saw this—"

"Accident?" I paused, one foot on the staircase.

"She was run off the road today on her way to meet Hawthorne for her business meeting." Dad looked surprised. "Didn't she tell you?"

"Run off the road?" I looked at the top of the stairs. Cynthia Bartlett looked down at me, her hand on her gun. Her face was in shadow but she was listening to our conversation, which echoed slightly in the enclosed space.

"In Holland. She drove there for a meeting and somebody ran her off the road. Her rental car had to be towed so she borrowed Hawthorne's car." Dad gestured to the Jaguar in the drive. "Then when she got back and found it upstairs, she was upset."

"Chief? You need to see this." Cynthia's voice was cool and professional but I thought I heard a note of satisfaction that grated on my already jangled nerves.

"Wait for me in the house, Dad. I'll be right there." I raced up the steps two at a time, careful not to touch the handrail. "What's happening?" I asked Cynthia.

For answer she led the way through the apartment, down the hallway and into the bedroom. Rob Sloan looked up, the department's digital camera in his hand.

The bedspread was slashed and a bloody knife was impaled in the middle of Emily's pillow. A shriveled-up rose lay next to the knife, looking like an amputated body part left for her to find.

"She found it about twenty minutes ago," Rob said. "She ran to your folks' house and your dad called it in."

I stared at the eerily familiar scene. "It's a repeat." I walked carefully around the bed.

"What do you mean?" Cynthia had her notebook out and was jotting down something.

"Thirty-four years ago the same thing happened." I peered down at the bed. "It was handled very discreetly, though. As far as I know, only a handful of people even knew about it."

"The same thing?" Rob asked, taking another picture. My eyes went to the camera in his hand and he lifted it slightly. "I thought I should take photos right away. When your dad called, I put in a call to Benton Harbor and asked them to send down their crime scene unit."

"Thanks, Rob. Good thinking." I saw Cynthia's thin-lipped frown but ignored it. Some little fact was clamoring for attention. "It was my pillow before," I muttered. "The knife back then was in my pillow, on my side of the bed. And this time it's on Emily's side of the bed."

"Really?" Cynthia injected a wealth of innuendo into one word.

I flushed but nodded. I wasn't going to tell her Emily always slept on the right side of the bed, even when she slept alone. I remembered coming on her when she napped and she always curled up on that side of the bed. This time the knife was embedded in that pillow. "I wonder if the placement of the knife has any significance."

"I took her statement," Rob said. "I caught the call

when it came in." He glanced at Cynthia then away and I knew what he was thinking: Why was she here?

"Let me know if the crime scene techs come up with anything," I said, moving to the door. "Officer Bartlett?" I stepped into the hallway, waiting for her to join me.

Cynthia reluctantly edged away from the grisly bed. "Yes?"

"Officer Sloan is in charge of this crime scene," I said in a low voice. "If he hasn't specifically requested your help, I suggest you return to your regular duties."

Two bright spots of color flared on her cheeks. Unlike Emily's pale, porcelain skin, Cynthia's face was tanned and somewhat roughened from outdoor activities. The color on her cheeks only darkened her tan. "Regular duties? Chasing drunks and catching speeders?"

I considered and discarded several responses, finally settling for, "We're lucky that's all the crime we get here."

She started to say something but appeared to think better of it. Closing her mouth with a snap she strode down the hall, almost running over a man with BHCSU emblazoned on his jacket. "Rob? Crime scene unit is here." I directed the man to the hallway where Rob was waiting then I hurried down the steps in time to see Cynthia getting into the squad car at the curb and pulling away like a bat out of hell.

I stared after her for a long minute then went to the back door of my parents' house and went into the kitchen. Dad stood at the counter, peering out the window at the garage and the people going in and out. I wondered if he missed the job. He'd been in law enforcement most of his life until his retirement.

"Emily's in the living room with your mother," he said, opening the fridge and pulling out a bottle of beer. He opened it with a church key hanging on the fridge and took a sip before speaking. "From the way Emily talked, it sounded like she was pushed into traffic. Her car was tapped on the rear right bumper. It slid her into traffic on a busy six-laner. Lucky for her she was slowed to make the turn and the car pushing her had to fight inertia. Plus she turned into the curb."

I went cold. Emily might have been killed. If Emily died, what would I do? The thought suddenly consumed me. In such a brief time, she had become essential in my life. Why was I so tied to this woman? Was it the past? Was it my memories of the past that haunted me?

Almost as soon as I thought it, I knew it was wrong. The memories of the Emily-then were almost completely replaced by the Emily-now. I remembered the other Emily, the bouncing, pretty, innocent girl. But she was a completely different person from the Emily now. It was the Emily now I loved so completely, as well as the memory of the girl from my past.

This is how my Dad feels, I thought. It wasn't until Emily came back in my life I understood such love. Dad would be lost without Mom. Oh, he'd limp along, but an essential part of him would die when Mom died. I shook my head, amazed by the power of such a thing.

These thoughts coalesced and vanished in the time it took my father to take a sip of his beer. He looked at me now. "You guys had a fight?"

I nodded.

Sam sighed. "You kids. You're making this way more complicated than it is."

Emily walked into the room with my mom. "Why does this keep happening to me?" She glanced at me then away before sitting at the table.

I longed to put my arms around her but our argument seemed to hang in the air between us. Mom must have sensed it because she answered Emily's question.

"I don't know, honey. Somehow, somebody thinks you know something about what happened."

Emily rubbed her eyes. "I'd better get a hotel room. I won't be able to sleep in the apartment anymore." Then she groaned. "I have to call the rental car company. I don't even have a car to drive to a hotel. This is such a mess."

"You can sleep here tonight, of course."

"Thanks, Natalie." She finally looked at me. "I suppose that will be okay."

I looked down at her. Her face was ashen and her eyes were red. "Are you okay?"

She tried for nonchalance and almost made it. "Sure."

"What happened?" I pulled out a chair, sitting across from her. My eyes settled on the Holland Yacht Club logo on her sweatshirt.

Emily blushed. "Well, as you know, I was out of town. And when I came back, I found that." She jerked her head toward the garage-apartment.

"When did you find it? How long ago?"

"Oh." Emily looked down at her hands. "I was going to pack to leave. After I talked to you. That's when I found it."

Mom cleared her throat. "Sam, let's leave Emily and Nate to talk." She patted Emily's hand. "Like I said, honey, you can always sleep upstairs in the spare room, so don't fret."

Emily nodded. "As Nate pointed out, there's no reason for me to stay, so I'll probably leave tomorrow." She looked as surprised as I was at her words.

"We'll talk about it later," Mom said calmly. Then Dad and she left the room with one last significant glance at me.

I propped my elbows on the table and put my head in my hands. "Emily, I didn't say there was no reason for you to stay."

She looked all teary. "You did so."

I shook my head and decided to be honest. She knew how I felt. I had nothing to lose. "I can't handle this uncertainty with you. There are times when I think you care for me. There are times when I think you might love me. And then you vanish for hours with Jonas Hawthorne or you say something about Cynthia Bartlett. I don't know what to do. I don't know how you feel."

Emily reached for my hand and I took it, holding it firmly in mine. "I don't know how I feel most of the time, Nate. I'm sorry, but like I told you, it's been so long since I was involved with anyone." She rubbed her other hand over her face. I saw the worry and the strain etched there. "I had the car accident and I have to review some papers from my business meeting. There's a lot riding on this deal, Nate. An awful lot."

I nodded, not quite sure why it was so important. How much was involved in selling a business? Maybe it was important, but it didn't stack up against what was happening here, did it? She must have seen my thoughts in my face because she looked disappointed. I wished I understood.

"I can't tell you about it yet. It's confidential because of stock and the details aren't worked out." She sighed. "You have to trust me, Nate."

Trust. The word hung in the air between us. "That goes both ways, Emily."

Her gaze went to the back door and I wondered if she saw Cynthia Bartlett earlier. "I know. But Nate, you have to understand, I feel as though everyone in this town is conspiring to keep me here. I walk down the street and people watch me, and your mom is right there, being so sweet and nice. And all these memories!" She pulled away and stood up abruptly, pacing around the small kitchen. "The way I feel is all confused with the way I felt years ago. I can't make sense of it."

I was exhausted with emotions I couldn't reveal. "You don't make sense of it," I said softly. "You just feel it." I stood up and put a hand on her cheek, cupping her face. "If you want to leave, then please do. I don't want to hold you here against your will. And God knows it might be safer for you to be gone. Someone sure thinks you're worth scaring." I gently caressed her cheek. "I want you to stay. But if you leave, I'll understand."

Emily gave a small cry and put her arms around me. I hugged her tightly, feeling as though my heart was breaking all over again. "Oh, Nate, I care about you. I really do. I'm just too confused about it all right now."

I set my chin on her head and nodded. "You get some rest tonight, honey. And we'll talk tomorrow, okay?" Then I remembered. Tomorrow was

Wednesday. I was busy. "I have a bunch of meetings, but I'll see you in the afternoon, okay?"

"Okay." Her voice sounded small. She was scared, probably not just of physical injury but emotional injury as well. I knew exactly how she felt. "What about tomorrow? Can I sleep in the apartment tomorrow?" Unspoken between us was, *Will you sleep with me tomorrow?* "In case I do decide to stay for the dance on Thursday," she added.

"We'll be done processing it by morning. The lab boys are there now and it'll need some cleaning, but you'll be able to use it again tomorrow."

"Okay." She snuggled a bit closer.

I hugged her and closed my eyes against the pain. I had her for two more days.

Two more days.

Chapter 30

Thirty-Four Years Earlier

Sam's speech was well received by the other officers at the national convention. It helped that Natalie made a big hit by buttonholing several sheriffs and their wives the night before at the hotel and talking up a storm with them. But Sam's remarks were also calm, considered, and spoke to the heart of what concerned a lot of people at the convention: the changing moral climate in the country and how peace officers should respond.

At the end of his talk, he said, "I want to take this chance to ask for some help from my fellow officers. We had a vicious rape last week in my town. We don't get crime like that in a small town like ours." He paused and said regretfully, "At least, we never used to." Sam briefly described what happened to Janie. "If you're aware of crimes like this in your areas, I want to talk with you. I need to catch the person who did this and I'd like to pick your brains on how best to do it."

There was more than polite applause when he ended his speech. He went into the next room at the convention center for the question and answer period. It was almost five o'clock before he got back to the hotel where he and Natalie were staying.

When Sam entered the lobby he saw Natalie,

brightly dressed in red bell-bottom pants, a tie-dyed shirt, and white platform sandals, her glorious black hair a curly, tumbled mass cascading around her shoulders. He grinned when he saw her, sitting and talking merrily with two men who had "cop" written all over their big burly bodies and their solid, impassive faces.

"Hello, honey," he murmured as he joined them.

"Sam, there you are. Sam, this is Nathan Samuelson and Neil Harris. They're with the Chicago police." She looked apologetically at the two men. "I'm sorry, I know it's not Chicago PD but I don't remember the suburb."

"Downer's Grove," one of the men said. "I'm Samuelson," he said, extending a hand, which Sam shook.

"Harris," the other man said, extending a hand as Sam sat down with them.

Natalie beamed at Sam, so excited she barely sat still. "They've had experience with rapes like what happened to Janie," she said. "Maybe they can help."

"Really?"

Harris nodded, his big round head bobbing once. "Yeah. Two years ago. In the fall, it was. The bastard almost beat her to death." He shook his head in disgust. "Sodomized her and left her lying in the middle of Naples Park, on the south edge of town."

Sam sat back and pulled out his notebook. "Can we talk about it?"

The two men exchanged a look and as one, said, "Sure."

Natalie smiled brightly. "I'm so glad." She stood up, settling her enormous belt on her hip-huggers. The three men scrambled to their feet. "I'll just go talk to the maître d' and see if he can't get us a nice, quiet table in the back where we can talk undisturbed." She looked at the two surprised lawmen. "You *will* join us for dinner?"

"Glad to," Harris said. "If you don't mind us talking shop."

Natalie made a graceful, dismissive gesture. "I may talk shop, too, so it'll be fair and square. I'll be right back." The three men sat down and watched her go across the lobby, stopping to chat with a bellboy, a desk clerk, and several conference attendees and their wives.

"She's going to talk shop?" Samuelson asked curiously.

"She's into the anti-war movement," Sam said, looking at his notes. "She'll probably try to talk you into using a Zen approach when handling demonstrators." He looked up, catching the confused look on the two men's faces. "She means well." He tapped his notebook and Harris nodded. "About this case of yours."

They talked about their respective cases over dinner, joined later by two policemen from the Dade County Sheriff's Department in Florida. They had three similar cases, all within the last five years and all occurring in January or early February.

Sam looked around the crowded dining room and decided to take the conversation to the bar, where they could talk without being overheard. Natalie was lured away by some of the other wives, who were going to listen to a jazz band at another hotel. She solemnly promised Sam she wouldn't get arrested for anything requiring bail money. Sam thanked her equally solemnly as the other officers grinned.

"She's a handful," one of the men said. His tone of voice suggested that Natalie's handful would be a good thing.

Sam shook his head. "You have no idea. But I have to agree with her on some of the things she protests against. Some of our laws are just so stupid." He sighed. "But it's still my job to uphold them, no matter what she says."

"And let's not even talk about politics," Harris said glumly.

All the men around the table nodded and sipped their respective drinks.

"I don't understand these rapes," Johnson, one of the Dade County men said. He was a light-skinned Hispanic, which surprised Sam. Not many minorities had made it into the sheriff's departments. Sam sometimes wished they had a Hispanic officer in Little Bay because the resort and the fishing cannery brought in migrants to work. "Where's he getting the drugs?"

Sam looked surprised. "I don't know. I didn't even consider it."

Johnson sipped his beer. "This is a sophisticated drug. It's not just MJ or LSD or stuff you can get on any college campus. Our forensic guys said the drug was still in development at a big drug companies. It means the guy has access to good drugs." Johnson glanced at his compatriot, a dour, thin man named Burnett. "It might mean the mob."

Burnett nodded. "Or just an inside source at a company."

"But if he's got a source, chances are he's selling drugs." Johnson's eyes swung to Sam. "You guys have a drug problem?"

Sam sat back and considered it. "Not that I know of. But we're only two hours from Lansing and three hours to Chicago. Six hours to Detroit. Maybe this guy is bringing in drugs to take to a bigger town." He sipped his bourbon and water. "If it is the same guy."

All the men around the table looked thoughtful. "How can it be the same guy? Rapes in Michigan, Florida, and Illinois?" Harris shook his head skeptically. "What have we got, a world traveler?"

"Lots of Chicago folks go up to the resorts on the shore," Samuelson said. "And lots of Chicago folks winter in Florida."

"You're right. Snowbirds, we call 'em," Burnett said.

"There's a thought. Maybe it's a guest at the resort." Sam made a note to call Dorothy and have her get Charlie working on the resort records. If it was a guest, he was probably long gone, but it wouldn't hurt to try.

They talked some more, their voices quiet. "I don't understand what makes a man do it," Johnson finally said, speaking out loud what they were all thinking. "Why would a man want to do that to a woman?"

"Power thing," Samuelson said. "Control. Fear."

"That's what rape is. It's not about sex. It's about fear and control."

The other men nodded glumly. "And now with all these miniskirts and things, it makes it all harder to prosecute," Burnett said. He saw the surprised look on the other faces. "It's true. I agree, it's no excuse for a man to attack a woman, but some of these judges look at the girls in court and start to talk all moralistic."

Sam thought of Emily in her miniskirt and golf shirt. "I know." He remembered Silas Sutherland's exasperation at the way Emily dressed. "Unless they're indecent, they've got a right to dress how they want to," Sam said. "But I know what you mean."

Natalie and several other women chose that moment to breeze into the bar, bringing the smell of cigarette smoke with them. "Lord, the bar was like an opium den," Natalie declared, dragging a chair over to sit near Sam.

"You've been in an opium den before?" Burnett asked.

"A figure of speech," Natalie said. She smiled at the table of men. "Make any progress on poor Janie's case?"

Sam ordered his wife a drink from the hovering waiter. "Got some leads. Some ideas."

"Good." Natalie looked around the table. "Then maybe we can move on to something else. Anybody care to talk about the Watergate cover-up and the opinion that the CIA was behind it?"

Chapter 31

Present Day

The next day was Wednesday of Homecoming week. I was a minor celebrity in town because of my pro football status and my Big City cop days, so I was always required to do my civic duty. I spent the morning at the high school talking to the government classes then I had lunch with the football team and gave them my "go out and win one for the Gipper" speech. I also had to make time to attend the city council meeting in the afternoon and beg for the chance to beg for money from the citizens. The council granted my wish and the request for funding would go on the ballot in November.

I managed to track down Rob Sloan and had a brief meeting with him. "I checked into her car accident," Rob said as he sat in my office on Wednesday afternoon. "I thought the accident and the knife thing might be related."

I leaned forward anxiously. I called the Holland PD the night before, but there weren't any results yet from their investigation. Rob handed me a copy of the police report. The paint scrapings from the car were from a Ford SUV.

I thought of the Volkswagen Bug versus an SUV and winced. Emily was lucky she came out of it only bruised. There were no reports of an SUV with that paint color coming into a shop anywhere within a fifty-mile radius for work. But Chicago, Lansing, and Detroit were relatively close. The SUV could be long gone within a few minutes of the accident.

"Not much to go on," Rob said, watching me as I read the report.

I set it down. "The thing with the pillow in the apartment bothers me more than the car accident. Only a few people knew about what happened years ago." I met Rob's eyes across my desk. "Who's still in town from that summer?"

"I checked on it." He pulled out his notebook. "Greg Hoffman, Mark Reston, Emily Sutherland. Hoffman's wife went back to Chicago on Sunday and he's supposed to go back tomorrow. He said he was visiting relatives near here." Rob looked up. "I checked and he does have an aunt in Benton Harbor. He said he was going there today and would stay overnight to play golf with his cousins then leave. Reston is going back to Chicago today." Rob closed his notebook. "Miss Sutherland said her plans were unclear."

"Good work, Rob, I appreciate it." He looked pleased. I stared at the list of Summer Kids on my computer. "I was wondering if you can do one other thing for me. I meant to get to this last night but I got sidetracked by the knife." I printed the list and related what Porter had said. "I need to know if anyone has died under unusual circumstances."

His pale brown eyebrows rose. "I'll check. Oh, by the way, I did look into the college kid angle in regards to the ledger."

I struggled to remember what we discussed. Had it

only been the day before yesterday? It felt like a lifetime had passed since then.

"There weren't any kids from town who dropped out. And the only kids who went to schools on a quarter system never worked at the resort."

"It was a long shot." I looked at the doorway. Cynthia stood there, listening. "Can I help you?"

"I was hoping for a chance to talk with you." She glanced at Rob. "In private."

Rob stood immediately. "I'll get to work on the list," he said, holding up the paper I handed him.

"Call me if you find anything." I watched as he passed Cynthia in the doorway. She turned to close the door behind him.

"I'd rather you left it open."

"This is private."

"We won't be disturbed." I gestured to the guest chair. "Please leave it open."

Cynthia came into the office, anger briefly making her face look harsh. She settled into the chair, sitting carefully so as not to ruin the crease in her uniform pants. "As you probably know, Mr. Hawthorne and Miss Sutherland spent the day together yesterday."

I felt a bubble of rage forming. "That's none of my concern."

She gave me a cool, assessing look. "Maybe not. But he is an employer of mine. I was wondering if you and Miss Sutherland were going to be together today. Because if you are, then I'll know when Mr. Hawthorne will be free so I can talk to him."

My hold on my temper was starting to fray. "I don't know, Officer Bartlett. I suggest you talk to Mr. Hawthorne directly. And now, if you'll excuse me, I have work to do."

She stood. "Perhaps I'll do that," she said thoughtfully. "Maybe I'll call Miss Sutherland and check on his location."

"You do that." I pulled papers from a file and stared fixedly at them. I lifted my head when I heard her footsteps leaving. Emily didn't mention anything about being with Hawthorne today. Were they together again? I told her I'd call her. I looked at the clock. It was almost three in the afternoon. The beach bonfire would be starting at dusk and I planned to see her then. Would she be available or would she be with Hawthorne?

I replayed my conversation with Emily over and over in my mind. I understood her uncertainty and her confusion. It was disappointing she didn't put that all aside and decide to just love me. But she was afraid of being hurt and she was afraid of hurting me. Plus she had all this business stuff on her mind.

A chirping, beeping noise came from my hip. I looked down at my cell phone, which reminded me I forgot to charge it. I put it into the charger on my desk and turned back to thinking while pretending to work.

"Chief?"

I looked up at Dorothy who was in my office doorway.

"Mrs. Struebel called—you know her, she lives on Fourth and Walnut? She said Porter's out there, talking to your mother and Emily."

"Talking?" I stood up and headed toward the door.

"Waving his arms and talking."

I shook my head. "What the hell has gotten into Porter lately?" I grabbed my jacket and was out the door in a minute.

I drove down Walnut but didn't see Porter. I did see Emily and Mom a block away, standing on the sidewalk and staring suspiciously at a big car parked at the curb. Greg Hoffman got out as I watched.

My relief at seeing Emily here in town and not with Hawthorne lifted my earlier worries away as though they were just so much foolishness. At this rate, I'd go through a couple of dozen mood swings in a day. I felt a brief moment of sympathy for women with PMS and menopause. Looking at Emily, I decided all the crap might be worth it.

I also decided it might be nice to chat with my mom and my girlfriend. I parked the squad car in the next block and walked down the street.

Greg leaned against the open door of the car, his gaze to the right. I checked what he was watching and saw Porter, who reached the corner and turned south, glancing over his shoulder as though the wrath of God was after him.

I joined them. "Hey, Greg."

He looked surprised to see me. "Nate. How's it going?"

I looked down at Emily. Her face was flushed and her eyes were narrowed, a sure sign she was getting ready to have a temper fit. She flicked at glance at me but her gaze snapped right back to Greg. "Your mom and I were out for a walk and we ran into Porter," she explained.

It was Mom who worried me. Her face was pale and she looked upset. My mother never looked upset unless she was angry, but this wasn't anger I saw. Porter paused at the end of the block to watch us then he scurried away. “It’s just Porter Graves,” I said. “He lives in town.”

Greg frowned. “He was at the boardwalk the other day, right?” Emily nodded and Greg nodded, too, slowly. “I knew him. He was a caddy at the course.”

“Yes,” Mom said. “Years ago. He was hurt, poor boy, and hasn’t been right since.”

Greg’s eyes took on the unfocused look people get when they’re trying to dredge up a memory. “I remember. He got hit in the head with a golf club, didn’t he?”

“You were there?”

Greg nodded. “The club manager gave the resort kids a deal on Tuesdays and Thursdays. Those were slow days at the club so we got to play for cheap. He was one of the caddies. We didn’t use caddies, of course, but the old guys who golfed out there did. I remember John and me and—” Greg paused, searching his memory. “I don’t know, maybe Mark were golfing. We heard the ambulance and police car pull up.” He shrugged. “Mike Sawyer’s girlfriend was there. She had blood on her uniform. I’ve never seen so much blood.”

I must have looked surprised because Greg nodded. “She worked in the coffee shop in the clubhouse. We were coming in after playing nine and they’d just driven the guy away. She was sitting outside and she had blood on her apron.”

“Donna Preston,” Natalie said. “Mike dated Donna. I’ll bet it was her.”

“I remember her,” Emily said. She looked at me. “We used to double-date.”

Greg glanced down the street but Porter had long since vanished. “I was just coming to your apartment,” he said to Emily. "I'm going back to Chicago today. I wanted to say good-bye." He moved away from the car and joined us on the sidewalk. "It was good to see you, Emily."

I moved a bit closer to Emily and Mom. Emily eyed Greg suspiciously. "It was interesting," she admitted grudgingly.

Greg glanced at me. He looked mad and, I don't know, he looked sad, too. "It was thirty-four years ago. I was a stupid kid. Can't you forgive me?"

Emily was startled and it showed. "Why would you care?"

Something softened in his face and his cynical mask seemed to slip. I saw a haunted, frightened look in his eyes. "I don't know. Maybe because I'm getting older." He looked away then seemed to make a decision. "Maybe I realize it's important to make things right if I can."

Emily continued to look suspicious but Mom said, "That's the first step to wisdom, you know. We need to understand our own mortality."

Greg looked at her and some understanding passed between them. "Right." Before Emily could stop him, he kissed her quickly on the cheek. "I am sorry, Emily." He glanced at me. "I hope you and Nate will be happy." Then with a nod to Mom he got back into the car, waving once then driving away.

"What was that all about?" Emily asked.

"He's ill, dear," Mom said with calm assurance. "Very ill. He's trying to set things right before he dies."

Emily stared at Mom. "What? How do you know?"

Mom nodded. "His aura. It's very muddy. Probably a cancer of some kind."

I didn't want to delve into any of Mom's philosophical certainties at the moment. "Where were you ladies headed?" I asked.

"We were just out for a walk when Porter decided to stop and chat," Mom said.

"We should write this stuff down," Emily said. "All the stuff Porter said and Greg said."

"What stuff?" I asked.

"Porter said some things that sounded, I don't know, like they meant something."

"What happened to Porter years ago has nothing to do with Peggy," Mom said.

"It might," Emily said. She looked at me. "We should write it down."

We were only a couple of blocks from town. "Let's go talk to Mike Sawyer. He can take down what we say and probably help add to it. He used to hang out at the golf course a lot back then, because of Donna."

Mom nodded. "He's just the person to see." She looked at me then at the squad car. "I'd rather not be seen pulling up to the courthouse in a police car, if you don't mind. Why don't you just meet us there?"

"Why, Natalie, are you worried about how it might look? Seems to me you got tossed in jail a few times for protesting the war. Are you getting discreet in your old age?" Emily laughed, her head back and the sun glinting on her shiny auburn hair.

There was something about her green eyes, her hair, the way she put her arm around Mom's shoulders and gave her a hug—it all just combined to make me lose my breath. Emily grinned at me. "We'll meet you there, Nate."

By the time I drove around the block and found

parking, they were walking up the steps to the courthouse. I joined them as they went into Mike's office. He was at a secretary's desk, holding a sheaf of papers. He looked up when we entered.

"The Boltz ladies out for a stroll?" He winked at Emily. "I haven't had a chance to see much of you since you came back." His gaze went to me. "Nate's keeping you busy."

Emily grinned at him. Mike had accepted Emily into our circle of friends immediately and since he was my best friend back then, it was important to her. I thought he'd aged well. He was a bit overweight but his dark brown hair had just a touch of gray and he still had a big, bushy mustache.

"Natalie and I were out, taking some fresh air and we ran into Porter Graves," she said.

Mike looked worriedly at me. "It's fine," I said. "But Porter said some things we wanted to check with you about." I looked at his secretary, who was listening without even trying to pretend not to. "Not in a legal capacity. I know how legal fees can add up."

Mike laughed. "This way. We can talk off the clock if you like." He handed the papers to his secretary. "It'll be good to go with those corrections, Paula. Thanks." He led the way down a short hallway into a large office with windows looking out over the parking lot and the lake in the distance.

"I'm glad Porter didn't give you any real problems." Mike settled himself behind the big desk and regarded us with curiosity. "Now and then somebody complains and wants him put in a home. We talk them out of it and make sure he can stay with his sister. But if he ever did anything really harmful, we'd have to reconsider how we handle him."

"He said some things and we thought we should write them down," Emily said, shooting Mom a quick glance.

Mom nodded. "Porter made it sound like he knew who the murderer was."

I leaned forward in my chair, remembering Porter's agitation on the previous night. "In all these years, he's never said anything. Why would he start to do it now?"

Emily cleared her throat. "I think it's me." She blushed and I felt my own face get a bit hot, too. "There's the whole 'separated lovers reunited' thing. Porter was around the summer Nate and I were—"

She bit her lip as she sought an appropriate word. "Together," I finished. "Porter's brain is goofy from the hit on the head he took."

Emily shook her head. "It was more than that, though. He said something like 'he's still around. He's still here. He's here all the time. You know him. You know how he is.'" Emily looked at my mother. "As though you know who it is."

Natalie nodded. "He said something like, 'Mrs. Sheriff, you know he's a mean man. He'll hurt me." Then she shook her head, looking puzzled. "I wish I could figure out what goes on in Porter's head."

There was no way of figuring out Porter's train of thought, so I decided to focus on something more factual. "Greg Hoffman said Donna was out there the day Porter was hurt."

"Greg Hoffman?" Mike asked. "That bastard? Why were you two talking to him?"

The anger and disgust in Mike's voice startled the women. It didn't surprise me, though. Mike and I shared similar memories.

"Why shouldn't we talk to Greg?" Emily asked.

"After what he did to you?" Mike asked.

She took a deep breath. "Mike, it was years ago. Years."

"I'll never forget the night he threatened you, when Nate and I were in the bar. Never." Mike looked at me. "A man shouldn't be allowed to say things like that. And then when he attacked you I thought he should have been locked up."

Emily sat back, surprised. "What did he say?" She looked at Mom. "Sheriff Boltz—Sam, he said Greg threatened me. He never told me what he said."

I shook my head. "Let's not dig it up."

"Aw, come on," Emily wheedled. "I'm a grown-up now. I can handle it."

Mike and I exchanged a long look. I shrugged and Mike said, "He described you, very loudly and in very graphic terms, then he said you were a virgin and you belonged to him. He said he was going to have you, your—" Mike hurried on, "He said he'd screw your brains out by the end of the summer whether you wanted it or not."

There was a long outraged pause. "He said what?" Emily asked, looking at me.

I nodded.

"That's when I had the bartender call the sheriff, because I knew Nate was going to pound the son of a bitch into the ground." Mike almost spat the words. "The other guys in the bar heard it, too. Hoffman was a marked man for the rest of the summer. I always wondered if—"

I shook my head slightly. Mike shut up. Greg had

an alibi for the night Emily was abducted. There was no use raking it up again. I hurried to fill in the angry silence simmering around Emily. "Write down what Porter said. And Mike, add your memories, too. I think maybe what happened to Porter had something to do with what happened to Peggy later on." I took Emily's hand.

The gold flecks in her green eyes were snapping with fire. "Greg said that?"

I nodded. "Back then, a man could get away with it. Now he'd be slapped with a restraining order."

My mother murmured, "We've come a long way, baby."

"No shit." Mike turned to his computer and pressed a few keys then he looked expectantly at us. "Recollect away," he said. "I'll transcribe. Just talk slow, okay?"

Emily and Mom helped each other remember the bits and pieces of the conversation Porter threw at them. "And he said Emily had to be especially careful because he thinks she's so nice," Mom finished.

"No, not nice," Emily corrected. "Porter said 'pretty.' Whoever this is, he thinks I'm so pretty." She frowned.

"What?" I asked.

"I heard something like that recently. I can't remember exactly what, though."

Mike tapped some more keys. "What does this have to do with Donna?"

"Greg said Donna was there the day Porter was hurt," Mom said. "I thought you might remember her talking about it. Donna's moved to California," Mom said in an aside to Emily. "Mike broke her heart and she had to leave."

Mike rolled his eyes. "Once I met Jamie I knew she was the one for me. I hadn't even talked to Donna for ten years before she moved."

"Oh, she pined for you," Mom said complacently.

"Not much. She got married twice."

"Hmm." Mom gave up on the teasing. "What happened that day?"

Mike stared thoughtfully at his keyboard, fingers tapping a rhythm on the desk. "It happened on number five, I think," he said slowly. "It's the hole farthest from the clubhouse. Porter was acting odd. Donna thought he did drugs. Let's see, Porter and Johnny Donovan were caddying for a foursome: Puckett, and Schultz, and Donovan and—" Mike stopped and looked at me. "Bobby Goldman? Was he the fourth?"

I nodded. "I think so. I know he was there. He mentioned it to me."

"They were on number five. Johnny came running into the clubhouse, yelling at Donna to call an ambulance. They were afraid to move Porter. Donna called the emergency number then she went back out in another cart because she had some first aid training and she thought she could help." Mike shook his head, pity in his eyes. "Nothing would help, of course. Donna got down on the ground next to Porter and tried to hold his hand. Somehow when they lifted him up, once the ambulance folks got there, he ended up bleeding all over poor Donna. She was upset. She called me at the hardware store and I went out to sit with her." He looked at me. "She didn't know Porter very well, he was my age and she was like, five years younger."

Mom nodded sympathetically. "Everyone was upset about it. He was so young. I think Sam said they ran blood tests and Porter did have some kind of mind-altering thing, like LSD, in him. Something that made him feel euphoric."

I remembered the test results we got back. Was Porter still doing drugs? Where was he getting them?

"That explains why he walked into someone's back-swing," Emily said. "He was a trained caddy. It had to be drugs."

Mike printed out the document he'd typed and gave us a copy. As we walked to the door, he said, "It's good seeing you again, Emily. I hope you'll think about staying in town. It's a nice place to live."

I held my breath, waiting to hear what she'd say.

She laughed softly. "I know it is. Thanks, Mike."

I can work with that, I decided. "What are you ladies going to do now?"

Emily pulled me to one side. Mom smiled at her encouragingly. "I have to talk to Jonas," Emily said in a low voice. "Some last minute things to work out on our business deal." She looked up at me imploringly, as though begging me to understand.

I took a deep breath. "I'm sure it's complicated." I put an arm around her and gave her a squeeze. "Make sure you're not too worn out to go out to dinner with me tonight." I tried to make my voice light and casual. The relief in her eyes was so evident I felt like a heel. Was I really such a jerk she worried so much what I thought?

Yeah, I was. I tried to force my insecurity away. "I have work to catch up on, too. I'll see you at the bonfire tonight." I leaned over and whispered, "If not there, then later. I'll call."

"Thanks, Nate." She held out her arm to my mom

and they went down the stairs together, Mom throwing me a grateful look over her shoulder.

I went back to my office and stared at the papers on my desk for a half hour then decided it wasn't getting me anywhere. I decided to go to Holland and see if there was any progress on the accident. At least it would give me something to do while I went crazy.

Chapter 32

Thirty-Four Years Earlier

Emily and Nate stayed at the apartment and "watched the house" while his parents were at the convention. They had one mild party for the resort kids that resulted in puking in the bushes in the backyard from too much beer and heavy petting in the living room. Other than the puking, it was a rousing success.

The next day was their day off. They put Busby in his outdoor kennel with his water bowl and squeeze toys then took the cycle to Kalamazoo for a day of window-shopping. Emily had been agonizing over the purchase of a denim jacket embroidered with the Rolling Stones tongue logo. Today Nate finally talked her into buying it. To celebrate, he bought her a necklace with two hands entwined around each other, one gold and one silver. It hung on a thin gold chain. Emily was entranced by it.

When they got back to Little Bay, they went to the resort to show off their purchases. Consequently, it was almost eight at night before they pulled into the driveway on Piney Ridge Road. Almost as soon as Nate shut off the cycle, a police car pulled into the drive behind him. Surprised, Emily stood outlined in the headlights.

"Problem, Charlie?" Nate asked, taking Emily's

hand. Busby, alerted to the presence of his two favorite people, was barking.

Charlie Madison, one of the deputies in the sheriff's office, got out of the car. He was a small, thin man with protruding eyes. Charlie glanced at Busby, who was pacing around the kennel on the far side of the yard.

"Got a complaint about Busby earlier. Came out and didn't see any problem. Neighbor said he was barking like crazy." Charlie glanced at Emily, his bland face unworried. "I was thinking I might check the house, just to be sure." He and Nate exchanged a long look.

"Oh." Emily suddenly understood. "You think somebody broke in while we were gone?"

"Damn," Nate muttered. She could tell Nate was more angry than worried. His parents had left him in charge and how would it look if a damn burglar broke into the house? "Sure, Charlie. Come on. We'll check." He led the way to the back stoop, Charlie close behind him, trailed by Emily.

At the back door, Nate turned to Emily. "Why don't you get Busby out of his kennel? Stay outside until we're sure everything's okay."

Emily started to protest but the words died on her lips at the calm, impassive look on Charlie Madison's face. "Sure." She watched worriedly as the two men disappeared into the house, then she turned to the kennel.

Busby bounded out joyfully, running circles around Emily and dashing into the different corners of the fenced backyard, piddling gleefully on shrubs and flowers. She waited anxiously by the back door and didn't relax until she heard Charlie and Nate in the kitchen, talking.

"Come on, Buzz," she said, heading toward the apartment. Everything was obviously okay. It would have been awful if somebody broke in while Nate was supposed to be watching the house. He'd never forgive himself if something happened.

Busby thundered ahead of her on the stairs to the apartment above the garage. She opened the apartment door and stepped inside. Busby ranged ahead of her, snuffling along the floor in big patterns, nails clicking on the hardwood floors and silent on the rag rug. Emily watched him disappear into the bedroom and she followed, anxious to admire her new necklace in the mirror on the vanity table.

She stopped in the threshold, astonishment turning to icy fear.

The bed she and Nate shared was doused in blood. There was a heavy, thick smell in the air. And on the left side of the bed, where Nate always slept, a huge butcher knife was jammed into his pillow. Emily's eyes lifted to the wall behind the bed. On the pale beige and blue flowered wallpaper was a single word, written in blood: WHORE.

"NATE!!" she screamed, backing slowly away. Busby came back from his examination of the bed and snuffled at her knees. She continued to back out of the room and down the small hallway, staring with wide eyes at the bedroom. Busby, torn between investigating the smells in the bedroom and Emily's strange behavior, sat in the hallway, confused.

Nate came pounding up the stairs two at a time. He burst into the living room where Emily was staring at the bedroom door. She pointed down the hall. Nate raced to the bedroom. Charlie, older and less fit, came laboring into the room, took one look at her face, and followed Nate down the hallway.

Emily heard their low voices but she stood rooted to the spot, unable to move. Nate soon emerged and came to her. "Sit down." He steered her to the couch and she obediently sat down like a robot. Busby waddled over and sat on her feet, craning his neck to look up at her. "It'll be okay."

Emily wiped her eyes. "No, it won't, Nate."

****

Five hours later, Sheriff Boltz and Natalie sat in their living room, Emily and Nate on the couch across from them. For the tenth time Natalie reassured Emily she hadn't interrupted their trip. "We were coming home tomorrow anyway," Natalie said. "It's more important we be home to help you deal with this."

Emily took a deep, shuddering breath and absently rubbed Busby's ears. The dog rumbled with pleasure and opened one eye, in bliss because all four of his people were together again. "It just startled me," she said, trying to sound mature. "I wasn't scared or anything."

"I hope you were scared," Sam said. "I wouldn't blame you if you were."

"I can't figure it, Dad," Nate said. "Who'd break in here in the middle of the day? That was taking a risk."

"Someone who knew you two were gone for the day and someone who knew we were gone out of town at the convention."

Natalie snorted. "Well, that's the whole town, isn't it?"

"I'm sorry about your apartment," Emily said. "I'll help clean it up. I'm sorry."

"We can fix it. And it's not your fault."

"I feel like it is my fault. It's all directed at me."

"I talked with this with some folks over at Chicago, at the conference," Sam said. "This kind of thing is about power and control. It's not about your morals." He spoke with such firm conviction Emily felt reassured. "Be careful. Don't be alone with strangers and make sure you stay with other kids when you're at the resort." His gaze slid to Nate. "You, too. Whoever this is, he's got it in for you, too."

Nate nodded. "I figured that."

Emily looked with despair at Natalie. "We've only got a few weeks left," she murmured.

Natalie nodded sadly. "I know, honey. I know."

****

The knife was one of a set from the resort. Sam discovered that the next morning when he went to talk to old man Goldman and they discovered one of the Mexican cooks was missing.

"Damn it," Goldman complained. "We shouldn't hire those damn Mexicans."

Sam refrained from mentioning the low wages and poor working conditions. The job was like heaven compared to jobs in Mexico but it was hell compared to jobs in the States.

"He raped that girl and now he's caught red-fingered, threatening Emily and her boyfriend." The old man blew out a moist, cigar-laden breath, filling the air in the cramped office.

Sam hid his distaste with difficulty. "Maybe. We need to check the fingerprints and make sure there's a match."

"Must be a match," the old man muttered. "Why else would he run?"

Sam had no ready answer. He went to the kitchen to talk with Emilio and the other cooks, wishing again he had a Spanish-speaking officer on the force. He saw the fear and the worry on all the faces and he couldn't blame them. He tried to sound calm and fair, but wasn't sure if he succeeded.

He was hitting a wall on Janie's case, too. No one at the beach party recalled who handed Janie the drink. And they had no luck tracing the drug, either. Sam had requested FBI assistance on the blood tests and the remnants in Janie's system were tentatively identified, but the FBI forensics scientist told Sam bluntly the odds of getting a complete ID were impossible. "We don't have the technology," the man said. "I wish we did, but we don't." Sam hadn't expected much but it was still a disappointment.

Nate helped Natalie pull off the wallpaper and re-do the apartment bedroom with a fresh coat of pale yellow paint. Emily volunteered to help but she was obviously afraid to set foot in the place again. Sam didn't blame her. It may have been chicken blood and the word done in red paint, but the effect was chilling.

Labor Day was fast approaching. Soon it would be the last weekend of the summer season. The Summer Kids would all go home. Nate would go back to college and Sam had the gut feeling things would settle down and get back to normal.

He just hoped nothing happened between now and then to disturb the fragile peace.

Chapter 33

Present Day

"The brakes were jimmied," the detective told me.

I looked down at the report he printed for me. I was sitting in the Holland PD's Motor Vehicle Division, talking to the detective assigned to Emily's car accident. I had wondered at first why a detective was assigned to it. Now I knew.

"They were rigged," I said slowly.

"Yep." He leaned back and regarded me curiously. "Any ideas on when or why?"

"Today's Wednesday." I thought back to the previous days. "She drove the car on Sunday morning out to the resort. Then I picked her up. We had the memorial service on Monday, she drove with my parents." I shook my head, the days blending together. "Monday night I was there. Tuesday she had the accident. It had to be Sunday night. She wasn't there and her car sat out on the street because of card club."

"It takes some guts to tamper with a car belonging to the, um, friend of the police chief. What kind of case are you involved in?"

I folded the report carefully, keeping my anger at bay. "I'm starting to wonder myself. Thanks for this."

"Glad to help. If you find out anything, let us know."

I drove back to Little Bay deep in thought. Somebody tampered with Emily's car. Did they plan on her having an accident on Monday? Did the day when it happen matter? What if she was on the lakeshore road and the brakes failed? The thought made me break out in a cold sweat. I sped up, suddenly anxious to be with her. I was late for the bonfire lighting on the beach but if I hurried, I'd get there in time for most of the Homecoming activities.

I got back to the office around seven o'clock that night and Dorothy met me inside the back door. I knew right away something was wrong. "It's Emily," she said. "There was an accident at the bonfire in town. They just took her to the hospital."

"Why didn't you call me?" I was moving before Dorothy finished speaking. "What's her condition?"

"Light burns, maybe a concussion, possible cracked ribs. Your parents are with her. I tried calling but you didn't have your phone and—"

I pulled open the back door as Rob Sloan and Cynthia Bartlett came in. I hurried past them. "Chief, can I talk to you?" Cynthia asked sweetly.

"I'm busy right now."

"Oh." Her tone frosted up. "Of course." She moved aside and I almost tore the door off its hinges trying to get out.

Dorothy said, "Nate. Slow down. She's okay."

I took a deep breath. "Thanks, Dorothy."

I heard Rob ask, "What happened?" then I was out the door and running to the squad car. I turned on the siren and drove on autopilot for the four miles to the hospital, clinging to the steering wheel with a death grip.

First Emily took a tumble down the cliff at the resort, then the car accident, and now this. She was going to kill me with fear if the lust didn't drop me first. I jammed the car into a handicapped slot near the emergency room entrance and tossed the Police Emergency placard into the front window. I must have looked like I meant business because the front desk receptionist took one look at me and almost saluted.

"Emily Sutherland. Where is she?" I demanded.

"Nate!"

I whirled. My parents were coming toward me down a branching hallway, the carpet muffling their footsteps. "She's okay, Nate." My mother put her arms around me and I was briefly comforted. "Just minor burns and a nasty gash on one leg. She'll be fine."

I pulled away from her and looked at my father. "What happened? The last time I saw her, she was going to meet with Hawthorne." I kept my arm around my mom and she started to walk back the way they'd come.

"Hawthorne stopped by the house and picked her up. They were going to the courthouse to sign some papers. I think they needed a notary public. She said she'd meet us at the pep rally bonfire on the beach at six." My mother tensed under my arm. "He's a smarmy bastard, I have to admit. He's too handsome for his own good."

"I was at the bonfire, looking for Emily," Dad said. "You know, the Homecoming bonfire, down on the beach." He looked exhausted and I wondered what toll this was taking on him. "Your mom and I have gone to every Harvest Day bonfire in the last thirty years," he continued. "I didn't want Emily there alone, either, after what happened with the car and all."

"How did it happen?" I didn't mean to sound so abrupt but I know I did.

"The football coach was saying something at the microphone but I couldn't make out the words. I saw her ahead of me in the crowd. The bonfire got lit when I was about four people behind Emily. Everybody took a big step back. I stumbled against the people behind me and by the time I turned to face front again, I lost track of her."

Mom put a calming hand on his arm. He patted her hand and continued. "I finally caught sight of Emily just when somebody tossed a firecracker into the flames and all hell broke loose."

"I thought the whole bonfire pile was coming down," Mom said. "I was at the back of the crowd and people started shouting and running."

Dad nodded. "Emily got shoved in the crowd. I saw her start to go down and one football player make a grab for her. Then another firecracker went off, this time in the crowd. It started a stampede. Emily was spun around and I pushed my way to her. The next time I saw her, she stumbled toward the bonfire. I called out to her."

"I saw it," Mom said. "It was so scary."

I held back my urge to shake the story out of Dad. He must have been the impatience on my face. "I knew she was going to fall past the snow-fence barrier and go into the bonfire unless I got to her. She sort of staggered then she fell backwards, toward the fire." We all paused outside a door. I was itching to go inside where I knew Emily lay, but I restrained myself.

"I reached her just as Porter Graves was

scrambling in the flames at the edge of the fire, tugging on Emily's sweatshirt. He was screaming at her to get up. Emily was lying against a log that had just caught fire. She looked dazed so I grabbed one leg while Porter grabbed one arm. We heaved her away from the flames. It wasn't until we got her out onto the sand near the bonfire I saw the right arm of her sweatshirt had caught fire. I dumped a bunch of sand on her arm. Porter was doing the same thing then I saw he was burned."

Dad's hand trembled on Mom's arm. "That's when I sort of passed out, too. I kind of collapsed and Emily got one of the football boys to come and help us."

My mom picked up the story. "Emily got Paul Johnson, the quarterback's attention. He and some of his buddies bulldozed a path through the crowd and got to Sam, Porter, and Emily. When Paul picked her up, though, she passed out. From the pain, I guess."

I closed my eyes, fear making me sick. Dad and Emily had almost been killed. Dear God.

"Porter's hands were lightly burned. He was lucky. At the ambulance Emily kept saying what a hero he'd been. You should have seen the pleasure on his face. It almost broke my heart." Mom sniffled, dabbing at her nose with a hanky. "Emily kept saying, 'He deserves the Medal of Honor. He jumped in the bonfire to rescue me.' " She gave a shaky laugh. "The paramedics told her they'd see to it he'd get a citation. Porter was so excited he didn't talk. He just held Emily's hand while the doctors worked on her and refused to let go until I got here and told him I'd make sure Emily was safe now. That seemed to reassure Porter, but he still wouldn't let Emily out of his sight until the doctor told him it was okay."

For the first time I noticed how pale my father was and how his hand on my mom's arm was shaky. "Are you okay?"

He nodded. "She's inside there. Go on and see her. We can talk more later."

"Was it an accident?" I asked, thinking out loud.

"She wasn't sure," Dad said. "She said it felt like somebody deliberately pushed her, but there were so many people bumping around out there. It's hard to say."

I ran a hand through my hair. "What the hell is going on? Why would somebody be after her? There were those calls, the car accident, the knife—what does she know? What does somebody think she knows? This is a thirty-four-year-old murder. If it wasn't for what is happening to Emily, I wouldn't have a clue where to start. But it has to have something to do with the last night we were at the resort. But what?"

"Nate?"

Emily's wavering voice came to me from the room. I was just taking a step inside when Doctor Christian, one of Little Bay's four doctors, came down the hall holding a clipboard. "I'll be right there, Emily," I called into the room. "I need to talk to your doctor."

"She'll be fine, Nate," the doctor said. "Porter moved her before serious damage was done. Her hair is singed and she got a bang on her head when your father and Porter pulled her away. Mild concussion plus a ton of scratches and bruises on her legs. I want to keep her overnight, the concussion might cause problems."

"The scratches and bruises are from Sunday," I said. "She fell at the beach." I ignored the startled look from my mother. "Can I see her?"

"Sure."

"I'll be staying with her."

Doc Christian nodded. "We can arrange it. Any other security needed?" I gave her a questioning look. "The accident sounded a bit iffy to me."

"You know more than I do right now. I'll talk to security as soon as I've seen Emily."

"I'll have them meet you here." She went into the room.

Mom patted my arm. "Go on, honey."

I didn't need any more encouragement. I walked into the room, peering around the curtain until I saw Emily. My heart lurched at the sight of her. She had a bandage on her forehead, her arm was bandaged, and the bruise on her neck stood out in stark relief against her whiteness. She moved her head when she heard the doctor. "I've got a bitch of a headache."

Dr. Christian moved to Emily's side. "And you'll continue to have one. I'm not giving you anything for the pain until I'm sure you kept all your marbles."

"Damn. What's the use of being in a hospital if you can't get good drugs?" Emily looked beyond the doctor and saw me. "Oh, Nate!" she cried, holding up her arms. I gently hugged her. "I'm so sorry. We were supposed to be together tonight, but the doctor says I have to stay here."

"It's okay. We'll have supper together anyway. I'm going to stay here with you."

She looked at me with such obvious relief I hugged her again. "I'm glad you're staying." Her eyes were unfocused and she squinted, as though in pain. "Porter was such a hero, Nate. He jumped into the fire to save me."

I glanced at the doctor, who nodded. "I heard," I said, keeping my voice even. "I have a lot to thank him for."

"No kidding." She yawned. "Now you're here, I can relax."

I smoothed the hair back on her forehead. "You sure can. I'm going to chat with the doctor then I'll be right back."

Emily nodded sleepily. "I'm just going to nap a bit."

"The best thing for you," the doctor said. She moved to the doorway and I followed her.

"What did you hear about the accident?" I asked.

"I treated Porter and your father. Porter had some burns but he's okay. Miss Sutherland took the worst of it."

"My father? You treated him?" I looked down the hall but my parents weren't in sight.

"It wasn't a heart attack but it was close." The doctor shook her head. "The strain of pulling her out of the fire and the adrenaline took its toll."

I nodded my understanding. "I'm going to get to the bottom of this. Hopefully his stress-filled days are behind him."

"Good." She walked over to a nurse's desk and gestured to the nurse there for a phone. "I'll call security and have them meet you here."

I headed for Emily's door. "Thanks, Doc."

"Remember me if I ever come through town and I'm speeding," she said with a grin.

"You got it." I stepped to the public phone on the desk. I had calls to make.

Two hours later I had talked to the paramedics, the

witnesses, and my father once again. I went to the apartment and got the ledger and the diary then to the station where I got my cell phone out of the charger. Then I went back into Emily's hospital room where my mother was sitting by her bed. "How's she doing?" I asked.

"She's bored," Emily said grumpily from the bed.

Mom stood up. "I'll go home and make sure your father is resting like he's supposed to. I'll be back tomorrow." She waggled an admonishing finger at me. "No hanky-panky."

"Would I try? She's defenseless."

"She's not that weak," Emily protested from the bed. "A little hanky-panky might be just what the doctor ordered."

"If you need anything, you call," Mom said as she left.

I nodded and moved to Emily's bedside, sitting carefully on the edge. "How's the headache?"

"It sucks." She lay back and stared at the dark TV screen. "Was it deliberate, Nate?"

My hand tightened on hers. "I think so."

She closed her eyes tiredly. "Why would someone do that? None of this makes sense."

"I'm not sure." I kissed her gently on the forehead. "Why don't you rest now? I'm going to just sit here for a while."

"Okay." Her voice was very small and faint. "Nate?"

"Hmm?"

"Thanks for coming here and being with me."

I looked down at her. She was already drifting off to sleep. I wanted to pick her up and hold her. Instead, I smoothed back her hair. “There’s no place I’d rather be. You sleep now. I’ll just watch TV.”

She nodded drowsily. By the time I took the chair in the corner of the room, she was dozing. I sat there, watching her for a half an hour or more, my thoughts in turmoil.

Emily was right. None of this made sense. If she knew something about the murder long ago, she’d either forgotten or didn’t realize she held a clue. Why would someone target her today?

I shifted in the chair, seeking comfort for sore muscles. Muscles not only sore from tussling with Porter but from loving Emily. I felt as though my very breathing was tied to her safety. If anything happened to her, I honestly didn’t know how I’d go on.

A noise interrupted my thoughts. Emily’s cell phone, the ringing coming from the tiny closet near the doorway. I opened the closet door and saw her clothing hanging inside. I delved into the pocket of her jeans. “Emily’s phone,” I said quietly, moving toward the doorway.

“This is Jonas Hawthorne. I heard Emily was hurt. What’s going on there?”

Once again I was reminded why I didn’t like this guy. “Emily’s had an accident. She’s resting.”

“My God. Is she all right? Where is she? Who is this?”

“This is Chief of Police Boltz.” I moved out into the hallway. A passing nurse glared at me until she saw my badge. Then she just sniffed and moved on. “She’s fine, but the doctor wants her to remain in the hospital for observation.”

“My God. I’m driving there tonight. Emily needs

someone to take care of her."

I reined in my temper. "I'm taking care of Emily."

"And obviously doing a terrible job of it."

I considered pitching the phone in the nearest trashcan, but restrained myself. It was, after all, Emily's phone. "The accident is under investigation. Now if you'll excuse me, I'd like to return to Emily. I'm sure if you call her tomorrow, she can talk with you."

"When is she getting released from the hospital? I want to be there for her."

I looked at the phone and reconsidered the trashcan. Instead I clicked the Power button. That's all I needed, some rich guy coming here and taking Emily away. I went to the room and slipped the phone back into the pocket of her jeans. I stood by the bed for a long minute, looking at Emily then I sat again in the corner. It was going to be a long night.

"I was supposed to cook you a nice romantic dinner," Emily murmured from the bed. "It's not every day a girl gets a million dollars."

I leaned over the bed. Her eyes were closed and I think she was half-asleep. "What?"

"I signed the contract today. I'm getting half a million for signing and another half in three years. I was going to cook us a nice celebration dinner."

A million dollars? She had to be kidding, right? "What are you going to do with all the cash?" I asked softly, touching her hair where it lay on the pillow.

"I'm not sure. I'm pretty sure I'm going to retire, though." She yawned. "Did I get bruised really bad? Do I have a black eye?" She sounded anxious.

"You look beautiful." I kissed her gently. "Just one bruise on your forehead and a bit of a burn on your arm.

You're bruised on your shoulder and your leg and your brains got scrambled a bit." I was lying, of course. She did look banged up, but I still thought she looked beautiful.

"Okay." She seemed satisfied. "You should go home. What time is it?"

I glanced at my watch. "Almost nine at night. You need to get your sleep."

"I wanted to be sleeping in your arms tonight," she complained weakly. "This accident has put a big crimp in my plans to make you putty in my hands."

"I already am putty. Don't make me any weaker, okay? I'll fall apart."

She exhaled sleepily. "Nate?"

"Yes, Emily?"

"I love you, Nate," she murmured.

I held very still then said, "I love you, too, Emily." I watched as her eyes fluttered closed. I put a hand on her delicate shoulder, marveling at the fragility of life.

"Chief?"

I looked up. Rob Sloan was in the doorway to the room, his plain face anxious but calm. "I got the info you asked me to compile."

I reluctantly left Emily and went to the door. Rob and I went outside in the hall. "What's it look like, Rob?"

"You got the report on her car accident, right?" I nodded. "I ran the names you gave me from the Summer Kids. Nothing popped out. You knew about Rachel Putnam. One other person died of cancer and another one killed himself, but other than that, there's nothing unusual."

"What about the bonfire tonight?"

“We’re still working it as a crime scene,” Rob said. “Cynthia is out there now, working with the crime scene people from Benton Harbor. It’s the same team who processed the knife in the apartment.”

“The car, the knife, the bonfire—what is going on?” I suddenly remembered Hawthorne’s phone call. “I meant to tell you, Cynthia is working for Jonas Hawthorne. You might want to be careful how much you tell her.”

Rob’s eyes widened. “Is that legal?”

“I haven’t had a chance to talk to the city attorney about it yet. For now, just be careful what you say.”

He nodded thoughtfully. “Cynthia told me she was thinking about filing a sex discrimination lawsuit. She said I get all the choice assignments.”

I leaned tiredly against the wall. “That’s all I need.”

“I told her to go ahead and try,” Rob said with a wry smile. “I’ll testify she was putting the moves on you and got turned down.”

I straightened in surprise. “You knew?”

He snorted. “Everybody knew. She wasn’t exactly discreet. Don’t worry about it.”

I pushed that anxiety away. I had other priorities. “I’ll think about it when it happens.” I glanced over my shoulder. “I’m going to stay here tonight, make sure she stays safe.”

“Makes sense.” He moved toward the exit. “I think I’ll go chat with the crime scene techs, see what they’ve got.”

“Thanks, Rob.” I watched him leave, stopping to chat with the security guard on his way to the elevator. I went back into the room. The other bed in the twin room wasn't made up and the nurse had told me I could lie down. I was tempted. I didn't sleep much the night before, worrying about Emily and the damn knife.

Emily's eyes opened and she held out her arms. I sat down on the edge of her bed, putting my arms around her. *I almost lost her*, I thought. *Dear God, I almost lost her.* I hugged her as tightly as I dared. She finally started wiggling and I loosened my grip.

"Lie down with me?" she asked, patting the bed next to her.

"I'd better not. You've been in an accident, you need your sleep."

"I'll sleep better with you here. Come on, just sit up here and hold me for a bit."

I looked at the bed then at the chair. Oh, the hell with it. I kicked off my shoes and got on Emily's bed, careful not to shake it too much. I adjusted the bed so it was propped up. She snuggled up against my side, her head on my chest.

"Much better," she breathed into my shirt. "I like having you here with me."

I put an arm around her and soon heard her heavier breathing.

"Nate?"

"Hmm?"

"I meant it."

I looked down at her in amazement. How did she know what I was thinking? She snuffled a bit and blew a breath into my shirt before relaxing completely. I reached out a hand and snatched the diary and ledger from the table near the bed. Maybe a little nighttime reading would help calm my nerves.

I picked up the ledger and thumbed through it,

staring at the columns of initials. Something was nagging me, some little remembered fact, some anecdote or piece of gossip. RP, EM, BG, PG. I put the book down and fell asleep, the initials and numbers rattling around in my head.

Chapter 34

Thirty-Four Years Earlier

It was on a Friday night, three weeks before the end of summer, when Porter Graves was critically injured. Sam heard the call come over the radio in his squad car as he drove home from work. He'd been in Kalamazoo for most of the day, meeting with the police chief there. The country club was on Sam's way into town, so he stopped as the ambulance medics were putting a gurney into the truck. He saw the pale face of Porter Graves, looking terribly young.

Sam went around the corner of the clubhouse and stopped when he saw Donna Preston, her waitress uniform covered in blood. Mike Sawyer was next to her, an arm around her shoulders. Donna looked ashen and ill. Given the amount of blood on her, Sam didn't blame her. He asked, "Is she okay?"

Mike nodded. "Just shock." He jerked his head toward the golf course. "It happened out there. She tried to help."

Sam moved aside to talk to Martin O'Keefe, one of the local police. "Looks like an accident," Martin said. "Bobby Goldman and the others say Porter was acting a bit odd today. Apparently he stepped right into the backswing."

Sam looked at the golf course then to Donna

Preston, still crying quietly in Mike's arms. "It's your case, of course. But you might check for drugs."

O'Keefe looked surprised. "Drugs? Why?"

"I don't know. Just seems odd. Porter's caddied for what, five, six years? Why would he step into somebody's backswing?"

O'Keefe nodded. "And with what happened to Janie Madison..." His voice trailed off. "You're right."

"I'm afraid so." Sam watched Mike help Donna to her feet. "Poor kid," he said, and he wasn't sure if he meant Donna or Porter.

Sam thought about Porter on the drive home. Porter had been in class with Nate in high school. Sam knew the family. They couldn't afford high-priced medical care. Jake Graves worked at the canning factory and Mavis, his wife, did cleaning. Sam made a mental note to check with Natalie and see if she could get a fund-raiser going for Porter's care. Sam had the feeling the family would need the money.

All thoughts of Porter fled from his mind, though, because later that night his son almost died and Emily disappeared.

****

Nate woke up and wished he hadn't. His head was pounding and he was freezing. He kept his eyes closed and tried to analyze the smells, sounds, and feelings all around him.

"Relax," someone said, putting a heavy hand on Nate's shoulder.

He closed his eyes and tried to swallow back the nausea. He and Emily were at a party on the beach. They walked away from the others, going to a group of rocks to sit down. He sat up suddenly and almost passed out from the pain. "Emily."

"We're looking for her."

Nate looked up. The only light came from flashlights held in the hands of the people grouped around Nate. Sam's face looked ghostly in the wavering light. "What happened?" Nate asked. His brain felt sluggish, like it was stuffed with cotton.

"You were at a party," Sam said. "On the beach. Remember?"

"Yeah. Emily and I walked a bit away from the others." He shook his head gingerly, trying to remember.

"You passed out. Somebody dragged you into the lake. Luckily Mike noticed you were missing and came looking for you."

Nate looked around and saw Mike Sawyer, standing with a group of other kids. Nate recognized Pauline, Harv, Paul, Herves, and David from the resort.

Mike saw Nate's look and hurried over. "You okay?" He kneeled next to Nate on the cold beach.

"Where's Emily?" Nate demanded, trying to struggle to his feet. He grabbed for the blankets draped over him, shivering, his clammy jeans clinging to his legs. He looked from his father to Mike. "Where is she?" Mike put a hand under Nate's arm and helped him stand.

"We're looking for her," Sam said. When Nate would have spoken Sam raised a hand. "Nate, let me get this organized. We'll talk in a few minutes."

Nate looked at his father, mutely begging for a word of hope. When none came, Nate nodded. Mike gestured to the other kids. They all came to stand in a semi-circle around Sam.

"I want search parties of four people each," Sam said to the assembled group. Nate saw now there were about forty people on the beach, a mixture of Townies and Summer Kids, police and state troopers. They were on the beach below the north steps of the resort. Nate wondered groggily how he got there. The party was several hundred yards further south.

"I want two Townies, one lawman, and one other in each group. Townies, you know the beach the best. Don't walk the beach, walk the bluffs." Several people in the crowd nodded knowledgeably. "I want three groups north of here, starting in the park and three groups south. Find a good spot on the beach and build a bonfire. If she's on a boat, she might see it. Two of you stay and man all the bonfires. Take one-hour shifts."

He stared at the group of people, all watching him silently. "No one goes off alone, do you hear me? If somebody has to pee, somebody else goes with them. No one is alone." Sam watched as the implications of this sank in. People started to sort themselves out. When he was satisfied the beach was covered, he turned to the remainder of the people.

"I want every inch of this resort searched. Emily was carried away from here." Sam glanced at Nate. "If what happened to Nate is any indication, she's unconscious. I want guests interviewed. I want cars accounted for." He glanced at the troopers and the remaining Townies and Summer Kids. "The troopers will organize it. Split up the buildings between you." He looked around the crowd. "If somebody can find Bobby Goldman, send him down here. Or somebody find Mr. Goldman. We'll need keys to some of the buildings." Pauline and Harv raced away immediately.

There was a stirring in the crowd. Big Tom Judson, Esther, and ten large black men came forward. "Need some help, Sheriff?" Judson asked quietly.

Sam eyed Esther, who looked scared and defiant at the same time. "Yes, sir, we do," Sam said, making a quick decision. "I need somebody to check in town. See if anybody saw anything suspicious. See if there were strangers around. See if anybody was buying unusual drugs or—" Sam looked at Esther and cleared his throat, "things."

Judson shot Sam a look and nodded abruptly. Both men knew what Sam was talking about: drugs, ropes, guns. Tom could check any rumors on the street or hints about somebody's odd sexual tastes. "We'll handle it. You need us to help out here?"

Sam exchanged a look with Charlie Madison, who shook his head slightly. "I think you can help us best in town, Mr. Judson," Sam said.

Big Tom nodded once then looked at Esther. "You stay here, honey," he said in a surprisingly gentle voice. "You help the folks here."

Esther looked like she would protest but Sam said quickly, "I need somebody to help Nate. He's still wobbly on his feet." He saw Natalie working her way through the crowd. "You and Mrs. Boltz can help him."

Esther looked with despair at Tom then at Sam. "Okay," she said in a little voice. She pulled Tom aside, saying something in a low fierce voice. Then she kissed him hard on the mouth and watched as he and his friends walked away, blending into the darkness of the beach steps. She went to Nate and put an arm around his shoulders. "Come on, sugar. Let's get you patched up so you can go out and look for our Farm Girl."

Natalie came up on Nate's other side. "Mom," Nate said thickly, still struggling with the drugs in his system and the near drowning. "I have to find Emily."

"We will," Natalie said. "I've read her Tarot cards. You and she have a long life together. Don't worry. Just let your father handle it for now." She and Esther each put an arm around Nate, steering him away from the crowd to the bonfire on the beach. "Let's sit down. The doctor's on his way." Natalie got her son settled and made sure Esther would stay with him then she went to stand by Sam, who was dispatching the last of the searchers.

"How long a head start does he have?" Natalie asked in a low voice.

"At least a half hour," Sam said. "It took a while to notice Nate and Emily were gone from the party."

Natalie took a deep breath. "We're lucky Nate didn't die."

Sam nodded abruptly. "I know." He looked at Nate then at the night sky. It was almost midnight. It was a new moon. There wouldn't be any light. "You'd better call Silas Sutherland. I don't want to call her father yet."

Natalie started to cry, a soft tear rolling down her cheek. "I'll call him," she promised in a wavering voice. "But I meant what I said, Sam. I read Emily's cards. She'll be okay."

Sam struggled to put confidence in his voice. "I hope you're right."

But he knew, as well as she did, his hopes were hollow.

He didn't think they'd find Emily untouched or alive.

Chapter 35

Present Day

"Hey! Where's my bed partner?"

I poked my head out of the bathroom door, having just finished my morning business. "I'm in here."

"Come here and help me," Emily commanded, swinging her legs over the edge of the hospital bed.

"Wait until the doctor comes and says it's okay."

She flailed with one foot, searching for the floor. "I'm not using a bed pan. Come on, help me to the bathroom."

I helped her down from the bed then held her arm as she toddled to the bathroom. "Go away," she said, making little shooing motions. "I can do this by myself." Her gown fluttered open and I smiled at her bare butt, bouncing in the breeze.

"You're sure?" I asked.

"Quit looking at my butt. I've been doing it for forty-some years." She made a beeline for the toilet. "Damn. This bathrobe thing is all open."

"I noticed." I closed the door and leaned against the wall.

A few minutes later she called out, "Well, that's better," then I heard a flush.

Doctor Christian walked into the room. "How's she doing?"

“She’s doing fine,” Emily called from the bathroom. “She’s brushing her teeth and washing her face.”

The doctor and I exchanged a look as the door was dramatically flung open and Emily paused on the threshold. “I look like shit but I feel like a million.” She saw our skeptical looks. “Okay, I feel like ten bucks and change, but it’s better than how I felt yesterday.” She shuffled across the floor in her hospital socks, grabbing futilely at the hospital gown. “Lots of cold air in here, isn’t there? Where’re my clothes?”

The doctor followed, helping her crawl back up on the bed. “Why don’t you eat some breakfast, let me examine you, then we’ll talk about letting you go home. I might want to get another x-ray and run a few simple tests.”

“I’m fine. Let’s get this show on the road so I can get on with my life.”

The doctor looked at me where I was leaned against the wall near the bathroom. “Is she always this bossy?”

“She always is,” Emily said.

I nodded agreement.

The doctor checked Emily’s blood pressure, temperature, and asked her a bunch of questions about the date, her name and her birthday, obviously checking to see if her brains were intact. By the time the doctor finished, breakfast arrived not only for Emily but for me, too. “Oh, oops, must be a mistake,” the nurse said with a deadpan expression. “You may as well eat it. I hate to see it go to waste.”

I nodded gratefully. We ate watery eggs, crisp bacon, and soggy toast while the doctor conferred with the nurse on duty. When she returned, she held some forms. “You get time off for bad behavior. Sign away your life and you leave.”

Emily snatched the forms eagerly. “Good. I have stuff to do.”

“Like what?” I asked curiously.

“We’ve got to figure out who’s trying to get me, of course. It’s got to have something to do with the murder, but I can’t figure it out. I need to look at the diary again and maybe bounce some ideas off your dad.” She looked at the surprised doctor. “His dad used to be sheriff and he’s a good guy to bounce ideas off of.”

“I’m sure.” The doctor turned to me. “Murder?”

“Thirty-year-old murder,” I said as she started signing papers at the marked spots. “Somehow Emily got involved in it.”

“I can’t figure it.” Emily flipped through all the pages. “Well, that takes care of that. Let’s go, Sherlock.” I looked pointedly at her bare legs. “Oh. Yeah.”

“She’s good to go,” the doctor said, sweeping up the papers. “And I hope I don’t see you again soon.”

Emily grinned at her. “Feeling’s mutual. Thanks.” She staggered to her feet and aimed for the closet.

I pulled out the bag containing her clothes. “Need help?”

“Nope.” She disappeared into the bathroom again and soon emerged dressed in jeans and the Holland Yacht Club sweatshirt. “Nothing like a good night’s sleep.”

I put an arm around her shoulders. “Right.” I gestured to a wheelchair the nurse had brought in. “Hop on." She started to protest but I said, "Hospital rules. I get to drive you out, though."

I wheeled her to the front door and helped her walk the few steps to the squad car, still parked in the emergency slot. I considered making her sit in the back but decided this once to dispense with protocol. She looked with interest at the radio, small computer, and video camera on the dash. "Wow. A police car." She relaxed back on the seat but almost immediately jerked forward. "My God. You're wearing a gun."

I looked at her, amused. "I always wear a gun."

"No, you don't. I've never seen you wear a gun."

"I've always worn a coat," I pointed out. "And when I'm not wearing a coat, I take the gun off and put it away."

She looked thoughtful. "You always wear a gun?"

"Yep. It's sort of a rule."

"Oh."

"Does it bother you?"

"I guess not. It's just part of what you do. It's not who you are." She looked at me quizzically. "Is it?"

"No. And in case you're wondering, I've never used my gun since I moved to Little Bay. That's one reason I moved here. It's not like Miami. I used it too much there." I glanced at her as we pulled out onto the highway and headed back to Little Bay.

"What?" she asked suspiciously. "I didn't have any makeup with me. I probably look like the far side of a Saturday night."

I couldn't quit looking at her. I was so relieved to see her like her old self again. "You look great."

"A police car sort of cramps my style. Oh, shit. My rental car." She slapped a hand to her head and pulled out her phone. "I need to call my insurance company." She opened the cell phone and looked at it blankly. "It's off."

"Jonas Hawthorne called last night and wouldn't shut up. So I turned it off."

"Jonas called?"

"Yeah. Said he heard you had an accident and he wanted to know when you were getting released so he can come here and take care of you." I tried to keep the anger out of my voice, but I suspect she heard it.

Emily snorted. "Arrogant son of a bitch. Like I need somebody to take care of me." I think she saw the relieved look on my face because she smiled as she paged through her cell phonebook. "Okay, here it is, insurance." She looked at her watch. "They should be open."

"Different time zone," I said.

"Oh, poop, you're right." She closed the cell phone and looked at the scenery rolling by. The amazing fall colors were just starting. Right now the land was rich in shades of green, gold, and brown. The reds and oranges wouldn't start for another two weeks or so. "I wonder how Jonas knew I was hurt," she mused. "He and I separated late in the afternoon."

"Yeah," I said softly. "I wonder about it, too."

Mom and Dad were watching for us. When I pulled into the drive, they were out the back door before I even shut off the engine. "Oh, honey, we were so worried," Mom said, enfolding Emily in a gentle hug. She looked searchingly at her. "How are you? Are you okay?"

"I'm fine. Just a bit tired. Nothing bad."

"Do you want to stay at the apartment or come into the house and lie down?"

"The apartment. I don't want to be in the way." Emily looked at me and winked.

"Let's get you settled," Sam said, putting out an arm. They helped each other up the stairs and he went immediately to the fridge. "Milk. That's what you need. Build up your strength."

Emily sank down on the couch. "I'm fine. Really."

I handed her the diary and ledger, which I brought with me from the hospital. "Maybe while you're recuperating you can look through these again." I looked at my watch. "Will you guys keep an eye on Emily today? I've asked Rob to drop by and Mike Sawyer said he'd visit, too."

Dad made a shooing motion. "We'll be here. You coming by tonight?"

I gave him a *duh* look. "Of course."

"What time tonight?" Emily asked.

"The dance starts after the game," Mom said. "Usually around eight o'clock."

Emily looked as doubtful as I felt. "I don't want you to overdo it," I said. "Why don't we skip the game and I'll come by at eight and get you."

"Good." Emily put her arms around me and I kissed her gently, conscious of her bruises. "See you tonight."

"Rest up," I whispered in her ear.

Her laughter followed me out the door. I stopped by my house to change clothes and was at my office by nine o'clock. "What the hell is happening, Nate?" Sada demanded as I paused in our kitchenette for coffee. "Car accidents, break-ins, firecrackers. We haven't had this much excitement since Donny Haskell got drunk and shot up the canning factory."

"We've never had a murder," Dorothy commented, coming in behind me and adding a dollop of cream to her *It's Good to be Queen* mug. "Officer Bartlett and Officer Sloan each compiled a report for you, Chief. They're on your desk."

I raised an eyebrow at her use of formal titles. Whenever Dorothy got picky about names it usually meant somebody was on her Shit List. "I'll look it over, thank you." I beat a retreat, not anxious to get embroiled in any potential office politics.

I read through the reports. As I suspected, there was little usable evidence from the bonfire scene. It was trampled by a hundred pairs of feet and charred by a pile of burning driftwood and scrap wood gathered by the juniors from the high school, a tradition extending well into the past. Every year's class vied to build the most elaborate bonfire and this year had been no exception.

I dragged over a legal pad, turned to a fresh page, and started jotting questions.

- Did Rob find out anything about the phone calls to the apartment?
- Did a man chase Emily at the resort on Sunday, like she thought?
- What did the abbreviations in the ledger mean?
- Who was Peggy's "Honey"?
- Who knew about the knife incident, thirty-four years ago?
- When was Emily's car tampered with?

I stared at the questions and added some more:

- Who tried to rape Emily thirty-four years ago?
- Who raped Janie Sinclair?
- Is the old crime tied to what's happening now?

I stared out my window at the sunny October day. The weather was perfect for a parade, a football game, and a dance. It couldn't be any better if I ordered it special. I tapped the blotter, my thoughts whirling.

If she wasn't hallucinating, Emily sold her business for a million dollars. What would she do with all that money? It was sort of breathtaking, really, to think about. I had a damn good salary when I was in pro football and I banked a big chunk of it, but I never saw a million dollars.

How would it affect her? I almost picked up the phone to call her then restrained myself. She was committed to staying in town for one more day. I wouldn't push my luck. Maybe tonight we could talk about the future.

I called Mom at lunchtime and she said Emily was sleeping. "We'll go with her to the parade this afternoon."

"I'm not sure she should go out. I'm worried something else might happen."

"Then I guess you should join us," Mom said. "If she needs a bodyguard, who better than you, Nate?"

I didn't argue with her logic. "I'll try." I knew damn well I'd be there unless a full-scale war broke out.

I forced myself to focus on the upcoming PR campaign for the vote in November, looking at the clock every fifteen minutes or so until it was finally four o'clock. I heard Dorothy and Sada in the outer office laughing and knew it was time for the parade. I grabbed my jacket and came out as Dorothy was modeling her outfit.

"Okay," I said slowly. "What's this year's theme?" Dorothy always rode on the law enforcement float in the Homecoming parade and this year she persuaded Dave Nielsen, a night shift officer, and Cynthia Bartlett to join her. Dorothy was wearing what looked like an old-time prison outfit with black-and-white-striped pants and shirt, a faux ball and chain, and a prison cap which was red, of course, in keeping with her personal theme.

"Ditch the dogs," Dorothy said, flinging her plastic chain over one arm. "It's the Little Bay Warriors versus the Hamilton Park Bulldogs. We're digging a ditch on the float."

I shook my head, once again amazed at the ingenuity of the sophomore class who was in charge of the floats and the theme. "Where's the rest of the police contingent?"

"I'm meeting them at the high school." She waved good-bye as she headed out the back door. "See you there."

I grabbed the department pager then left, too, taking the squad car and parking on the east side of town, well away from the parade route. I heard the band in the distance. I walked down the tree-lined street, soaking up the autumn sunlight, content with the world. Emily was here and she said she loved me. I didn't need anything more.

I approached the corner where I knew my parents

had front row seats. They always sat in their lawn chairs on that corner whenever a parade went by. People were lined up for the parade, which started at the pier and wended its way through town out to the high school, ending at the pep rally for the game tonight.

"Hey, Nate."

Bobby Goldman was approaching, coming across the street from the direction of the hardware store. "Hi, Bobby. How's it going out at the resort?"

"I'm wrapping it up for the year. I wanted to ask a favor."

I peered over the heads of the people in front of me, looking for Emily. I paused to look at him.

"I heard your folks talking about a diary Peggy had."

I nodded. The diary wasn't a secret, really. "Yeah, it's a high school kind of thing, just gossipy stuff."

He stuck his hands in his pockets, his face taut. "I wondered if there was anything in it about my father." He hurried on when I started to speak. "My old man was hard on some kids. I was curious if it mentioned him."

I shook my head. "I read through it last night but didn't see any mention of him by name, either there or in the ledger." I finally spied Emily through the crowd, just a glimpse of her face turned as she talked to someone near her. "I can check with Emily, though. She was going through them today."

"Would you? I'd appreciate it."

"Sure, no problem." I moved off, working my way through the crowd that was two and three people deep in spots, with little kids sitting on the curb in front in order to catch the candy tossed out. The Shriners were going by in their funky little cars when I glimpsed Emily again, talking to Mrs. Williams from the library. She was in jeans and a dark green sweater, looking so preppy and perfect I had to smile.

Then I saw Jonas Hawthorne, standing at her right side. He wore pressed jeans, a golf shirt, and had a sweater tied around his shoulders. He looked as preppy, if not more so, than Emily. I looked down at my police uniform, the gray shirt, dark pants, and black jacket I always wore. No Yacht Club guys here.

I checked the parade. The Future Farmers of America were marching past, a dozen red-cheeked boys and girls wearing matching blue jackets and denims. They looked so fresh and young. Was I ever that young once? I felt a million years old.

Emily laughed, raising her arms to catch candy. *Trust*, I reminded myself. *I have to trust her*. She turned to Hawthorne, smiling. *Trust. I have to trust.* Hawthorne looked down at her, his eyes warm and proprietary. He put an arm around her and held her to him, brushing a quick kiss against her forehead. She looked up at him, surprised and he bent his head and kissed her.

Trust only goes so far, I guess. I turned and beat a hasty retreat, not wanting to see any more. If there was something between her and Hawthorne, I didn't want to know. And if there wasn't, then I'd pretend ignorance.

That's what I told myself, at least, as I drove back to the station. The truth was I didn't want to know. I wanted to hold on to my memories of this weekend when she left tomorrow. And if that meant turning a blind eye to Jonas Hawthorne, then I would do it.

Sada was at the parade and Tom Bellinger was manning the front desk in her place. I waved hello then went into my office and closed the door. I sat down, swiveled my chair, and stared out the window, my brain numb. Images flittered through my brain, images of Emily, Hawthorne, my parents, my life. It was like everything in my past was racing past my mind, coalescing into this moment.

I don't know how long I sat but I know it was full dark when someone knocked on my door. "Come in."

Mike Sawyer poked his head in. "Hey, there you are. I wondered what happened to you. Did you get to the parade?"

I turned to face him and shook my head. "Got stuck in meetings and things."

He grinned as he came into the room and flopped down in the guest chair. He was dressed in a suit and tie, which surprised me until I looked at the clock and realized it was seven-thirty. He and his wife Jamie would be going to the dance tonight, too. I needed to leave soon to get dressed. "You missed all the fun," he said with a chuckle.

"Fun?"

Mike laughed. "Emily decked some guy in town and Cynthia jumped off her float and was going to arrest her. I thought those two would have an all-out cat fight on Main Street." He grinned broadly. "Emily got some punches in."

"What?" I started to stand then sat back down with a thump.

"You should have seen it. I was standing right behind her and saw the whole thing. That Hawthorne guy leans over and kisses her and Emily pushed him away. He said something like, 'Now our business is over so we can pursue our personal relationship.' "

I almost choked. "He said it in public? At the parade?"

Mike nodded. "Emily mentioned something about it to me this afternoon when I dropped by to visit. She was putting him off, using the old 'we shouldn't get involved while we're negotiating' ploy." Mike crossed his right ankle on his left knees and jiggled his leg. "Emily must be one hell of a negotiator. I heard Hawthorne's lawyer, Sylvia Swanson, was there during the negotiations on Monday and she's a tough contract lawyer."

"Monday? Monday they were out on a boat all day."

"Yeah, Swanson brought her boat up the coast to dry dock. Emily said she had her own lawyer on the phone and between the two of them they managed to get the contracts modified. Swanson has a reputation as a mean negotiator." He winked at me. "From what I heard, she swings both ways. Emily was lucky to get out of there intact, if you catch my drift."

"What?"

"Yeah. You know how word gets around about crap like that. I wonder if Swanson and Hawthorne celebrated when they finished the deal." Mike shook his head in bemusement. "How long were they gone? I've heard Swanson's negotiations can go for hours."

"Most of the day," I mumbled. "I think they were finalizing things today."

"That explains Hawthorne's comment, then. Emily probably signed the contracts today and he took it to mean she was fair game."

"What did she do?" I was starting to grin, imagining Emily's anger.

"She pushed him away after he kissed her but he leaned over again. She slapped him. Then he grabbed her by the arm and I know it was the one hurt yesterday. Your Dad got in the mix and tried to pull her away, and Emily was crying. Then the float came around the corner as Emily hauls off and kicks Hawthorne. Cynthia saw Emily and your dad and Hawthorne, all shoving around, and she tore off the float and got tangled up in it, too." Mike laughed again. "It was a real brawl."

I looked past him at the quiet hallway. "Where are the combatants? Nobody got tossed in jail that I know about."

"Rob Sloan was there and he broke it up. He sent Cynthia to one corner and Emily to another and made Dorothy get back on the float."

"Dorothy?" Now I *did* choke, on laughter. "She got involved?"

"She was swinging that ball and chain of hers. Lucky it was just made out of plastic. Otherwise Cynthia Bartlett would have a concussion." Mike grimaced. "She's not well liked in town, Nate. You should talk to her. Tell her to be a bit more, I don't know, friendly." Mike stood. "I thought I'd stop by and see if any legal counsel was needed, but I guess nobody filed any charges. Will I see you at the dance?"

The dance. Damn. I almost forgot about it. I stood, too.

"I saw your parents going out to the Country Club. Is your mom still on the committee? It wouldn't be a JV dance without her decorations."

"Yeah, you know how she is—" I suddenly realized Emily would be alone. "I need to get over there. I don't want Emily left alone."

"Not to worry. Rob Sloan said he'd wait with her until you showed up once he heard your parents wouldn't be around." Mike moved to the door. "See you later."

I joined him, snatching my jacket from the rack at the door. "I've got to get changed. I have a date tonight." I started to laugh, imagining the look on Jonas Hawthorne's face.

Chapter 36

Thirty-Four Years Earlier

Emily's face pressed hard against something and her arms were pulled up over her head. She tried to struggle but she couldn't move. She felt buoyant and yet weighted down. Movement required more effort than she possessed.

She wiggled her jaw then realized it was sand pressing against her. That meant she was on her stomach. She heard the surf. There was a crackling sound and a smoky, damp smell. Was it a bonfire? There was a bonfire near. She tried to blink but her eyes wouldn't move. That's when she felt the blindfold, tight across her eyes and covering most of her nose.

Emily wiggled her body slightly. There was a blanket under her but not under all of her. She felt coarse sand on her neck and her breasts. It rubbed when she breathed.

Breasts? Am I naked? What's going on?

Someone touched her. Emily tried to scream, but she words felt jammed in her mouth. The hand stroked her back, moving slowly down her spine, caressing her lower back then it moved over her butt, sinuously rubbing each cheek, squeezing and feeling her. Then a finger nudged into her female area. Emily exerted every ounce of energy to close her legs but when the ropes pressed against her, she realized she was tied down with her legs apart. She focused on screaming as hard as she could and a moan escaped.

The hand stopped. “Are you awake, honey?”

It was a low voice, husky. A man. Emily choked. A man had her. He had her tied up and he was touching her.

“I’m glad you’re awake.” His hand moved languidly over her again. She felt herself being lifted, her hips positioned so he gently moved a finger into her folds. She felt him probing, moving fingers in and out of her. Another moan escaped.

“You like that, don’t you? You’re hot.” Soft laughter was behind her and she felt someone on her, felt legs on her. Then she felt a hard, insistent thing poking at her, testing her. “I want you on your back.” He touched her again, his hand rubbing her. “That’s it, baby,” he said softly. “We’re going to play tonight.”

He removed his hand and his body. Emily breathed a sigh of relief. Soft voices were nearby, a man and a woman. The woman sounded angry. The man laughed then there were other noises, a sharp cry or moaning. God, were they having sex? Emily tried to struggle but the lethargy was coming back. Was this a dream? A nightmare?

She might have dozed or gone unconscious. When Emily was next aware, she was on her back, cold air on her breasts as something warm dripped over her stomach. She twitched, jerking against the ropes binding her. Warm baby oil was being poured onto her body. Her breasts were slick as he rubbed oil over her, his touch sinuous. He massaged the oil onto her breasts, playing with her nipples until they stood up in painful distension. Then he moved on to her belly.

Emily felt another set of hands rubbing oil onto her legs and up her thighs. Those other hands gently parted her then warm oil was drizzled onto her cleft and the hand (*a smaller hand?* her mind chaotically wondered) inserted fingers and started to play with her. Bile rose in her throat. She was almost glad for the blindfold so she didn't see who was staring at her and playing with her. The initial set of hands was still playing with her nipples and her arms, moving over her body in a long, slow, sensual massage.

"She's ready," a voice said. The hairs rose on the back of Emily's neck. She knew that voice. It was a woman and it was *almost* familiar. It somehow penetrated the fog in her brain. "Are you going to do her this way first?"

"No," the male voice said. "I want her cherry. Nate's already had her this way."

"Oh." It was a small sound but Emily knew the woman was upset.

"Roll her over."

Emily was tugged over onto her stomach. Her arms jerked over her head and her legs pulled apart and staked out. The entire time she struggled to scream or fight, but she couldn't. She was trapped in her own skin.

"Do you know what's happening, honey?" the male voice asked, close to her ear.

The oil drizzled onto her back and he climbed on her. She felt his erection sliding over her as he worked the oil into her shoulders, her arms, and down her sides. Then he poured oil onto her bottom and he began to massage her there, pulling apart her cheeks and drizzling oil onto her. "I taught them to love it and you'll love it, too."

The hands continued their sinuous touching, moving around her buttocks, into her cleft, and then into her *other* place. A scream choked her and Emily knew if she didn't give vent to it, she might die from shock. He was going to sodomize her. He was going to hurt her. She began to gag. If he touched her again, she'd vomit.

Something hard pushed at her and she tried to tense against it. "It'll hurt more if you resist," the voice said. He straddled her now, a hand pushing her head down into the sand, her face painfully grating against the grit.

Emily moaned loudly.

"She needs another dose," the woman said. "She'll fight it too much."

The man hesitated, his grip slackening. "I want her to feel it," he said. Who was that? The accent, or the voice or...who was it?

"She'll feel it," the woman murmured. "But you want her relaxed. Otherwise it's not as much fun, for anyone. I remember how it felt and I was drugged."

There was a long pause. "All right. I left it in my jacket. I'll get it." He got off Emily and she heard footsteps in the distance.

"I'm going to untie you." The voice was a bare whisper in Emily's ear. "When he's distracted run for the lake. Swim south."

Emily was still paralyzed. If she got the chance, could she even move her arms and legs?

"The drug is almost gone now. You'll have a hard time of it, but swim south. Go to the left. Go south. The resort isn't far away."

Emily sensed the woman leave. She jerked her arms and the loose ties gave way. The blindfold knot was too tight, so she tugged it down to hang around her neck. Emily crawled to her hands and knees, her legs numb. She scrabbled through the sand to the shadows of the rocks, away from the light of the fire then she collapsed, trembling.

Sounds came from the nearby, grunting and moaning and then the woman cried out. “You’re hurting me. Oh, God, you’re hurting me.”

Emily leaned over and retched then forced herself upright. She was naked, alone, and lost. But she was free. Feeling was returning to her arms and legs. She said a silent prayer for the poor woman who helped her then she moved out of the rocks and toward the shoreline. She stumbled through the rocky shale, knowing she was cutting her feet but pushing that pain aside.

It was dark, but she’d been blindfolded so her eyes adapted quickly. Emily saw the glint of water and headed for it. When the lake water hit her she bit back a cry of agony. The water was so cold she was sure she’d cramp. She took a deep breath and waded out into the surf and then, with a prayer she could trust her rescuer, she plunged headfirst into the waves and started struggling to swim.

Emily tried to keep the shoreline in sight but at times she was pulled out into the deeper currents. She kicked and struggled, but exhaustion, shock, and drugs soon made her wonder why she was struggling so hard. She let her arms and legs rest then the water swamped her.

Panic hit. Emily kicked out, her feet sometimes

touching the bottom, and other times she sensed the bottomless depths of the lake. It was a nightmare of remembered images, terror, and voices in her head.

Then she saw light on the beach. For one terrifying moment she thought she'd come back to the place she started from. But she saw several people on the bluff over the beach.

She let the current carry her to the shore.

Chapter 37

Present Day

My cell phone rang while I was getting dressed in my Sunday finest. “Hey, where’s my date?” Emily demanded.

I laughed out loud, feeling so light I wondered I didn’t float away. I pulled on my black dress pants. “On his way. Are you all dressed up with no place to go?” I heard music in the background. It sounded like Tina Turner was belting out “Proud Mary.” Emily was listening to the Greatest Hits of the 70s.

“You bet. I’m wearing a little black dress that’ll knock your socks off. I think we should find a quiet spot and go out and neck.”

“I’m Chief of Police. I can’t neck in public,” I pointed out. “I heard you had quite a fight today at the parade.”

“That bitch Cynthia took a swing at me after I took a swing at Jonas. I’m sorry Nate, but I don’t think I can get along with her.”

“You don’t have to.” I buttoned my shirt, the phone wedged against my shoulder.

“The wife of the chief of police has to get along with his officers. And we need to campaign for the new station. I’ll have to work with your officers for that, won’t I?”

The phone dropped on the bed when I straightened up in stunned surprise. I scrambled for the phone, almost closing it in my haste to hear her answer. "What?"

She laughed. "Hell, Nate, I'm tired of waiting for you to ask me to marry you. Will you marry me?"

"What do you mean I never asked you to marry me?" I cursed softly as I realized I buttoned my shirt wrong. I fumbled with the buttons while I tried to talk.

"You've never asked me to marry you. I realized today I'm retired, I'm wealthy, and I can do whatever I want." Her voice lowered. "I'm wearing nylons with elastic tops. Remember? I wore the same thing on our date when we got dressed up and went out for dinner."

I closed my eyes briefly. "You're teasing me."

"It was at a place in Benton Harbor called ParFait's or something that."

I slipped my tie on and checked it in the mirror. "I remember everything about our date including the ride home afterward. So does this mean we're getting married?"

"Your menu had prices on it and mine didn't. It was some kind of male code. It was a beautiful restaurant but they played awful music. I remember asking the waiter to turn down the music because they kept playing that damn—" She stopped.

"Emily?" I pulled on my gray sports coat as I walked into the kitchen. "Did you really mean what you said about marriage?"

"That's it." Her voice was suddenly distant and remote. "It's the key. I stared at her ledger all day. I know what the numbers and letters mean."

"You do?" I wasn't really tracking what she was

saying. I was busy wondering what she was wearing. I was looking forward to finding out.

"The restaurant...they played awful music, remember? Where is that journal, it's...there it is."

"What are you doing?" I looked down at J. Edgar, who eyed my black dress slacks with interest. I had a vision of a dusting of gray cat hair and moved out of the line of fire.

"Here it is. It's the initials. Remember how we always talked about 'EC'? 'EC' stood for Eric Clapton. Think of the initials. Think about it. PG. BG. EM."

I grabbed my car keys from the counter and slipped my gun into the holster at my back. "What are you talking about?"

"Porter Graves. Elizabeth MacBride. Bobby Goldman. Rachel Putnam."

I stopped, nodding slowly. "That might be." I snapped my gun into place. "You're right. But what were they keeping track of?"

"Here it is. Hold on." There was a brief pause then she came back on the line. "There are other initials. Remember? There are three columns of initials. Here, let me read it: 5/19, MC, MJ, 2K, PG, 1-4/5-5. Think about it. What did 'MJ' stand for back then?"

It suddenly hit me. "Mary Jane." It made sense. Little Bay was in a perfect spot for drugs because it had good bays and inlets, and wasn't too far from big cities.

"I'll bet one column is the kind of drug: marijuana. Hash. Heroin. Cocaine. I'll bet somebody was bringing drugs in, over the Lake, probably from Chicago. It's a short run up the coast. Hell, Sylvia drove her boat up the other day."

"MC," I said, struggling to remember the entries in

the ledger. "Mitchell's Cove. What were some of the other ones?"

"MC, R, P, T."

I ran over the possible locations in my mind. "Mitchell's, Resort, Pier, Town?" *It might work. They could bring drugs in by boat, via a guest at the resort, to the pier, or via someone in town.* I pushed the speculation aside for the moment. "The dates were mainly summer dates, weren't they?"

"Hold on...You're right. There aren't any winter dates. Is Mitchell's Cove deep enough for a boat?"

"Sure. I'll be there in a minute. Put Rob on the line, okay?" I wanted him to take possession of the diary. They could meet me at the station.

"Why did Peggy MacBride have this?" Emily mused.

I heard a voice, muffled but distinct. "Because she stole it from me."

"What is—is that a gun? What are you doing?" Emily's voice was suddenly far away and faint.

I grabbed my home phone and dialed 911.

"Why what? Why did she steal it? Or why did I bother with her? Oh, and the last column? It's a cross-reference to another book where I recorded the payment amounts. I didn't like to keep too much information in one place."

The voice was tantalizingly familiar but indistinct. The 911 operator came on the line. I pulled my cell phone away from my ear long enough to talk. "Robbery in progress," I snapped and I gave my parents' address. "This is Little Bay Police Chief Nate Boltz. I'll meet you there." I dropped the phone and started toward the door.

"...drugs came in by boat and I sold them in...or Lansing. Porter and I started it, and Peggy found out. Then Rachel...too. She was into kicks."

"How long did it last?" Emily asked. I realized she must have lowered the phone and had it at her side, probably hidden behind her. Whoever had her didn't know she still held an open line. I blessed her for her quick thinking. I jerked open my truck door and settled on the seat, jamming the key in the ignition before I closed the door.

"Seven years...enough money to be respectable but...nobody knew what..."

I slammed my truck into gear, the phone wedged up on my shoulder.

"Anybody who knew was dead or incapacitated." That was Rob's voice. He must be standing near Emily, who still held the phone. "Rachel Putnam dead in a car accident. Peggy vanished. And Porter injured on the golf course. Everything would have been fine if Peggy's body wasn't found."

"...pregnant once before and when...pregnant again...blackmail me into marrying...Like I'd marry...like her."

Emily's voice was suddenly loud. I realized she was shouting. "It was you on the beach that night, wasn't it? You bastard! You almost raped me, you son of a bitch."

There was a long silence broken only by the muffled voice. I strained to catch words. "...had you...all summer...the first for you..."

Rob's voice was loud and eerily calm. "You wouldn't shoot your own son, would you?"

I thought frantically. Rob? What son? Then it hit

me—Peggy's baby. When she went away during the year she went to help her sister, Janice. I drove wildly through the darkened streets. It was only another mile or two. Just another few blocks.

The gunshot was loud in my ear.

Chapter 38

Thirty-Four Years Earlier

"Good, you're awake. I'm going to tell those men you're awake." A nurse in a starched uniform beamed at Emily.

"Men?" Emily opened her eyes with an effort and looked around groggily.

The woman laughed softly. "The waiting room is chock full of men."

Emily stared around her, bewildered. The last thing she remembered was standing with Peggy, talking and drinking lemonade. A small memory, something unpleasant, niggled at her mind. Then the door to her room opened and Nate, Sheriff Boltz, Bobby Goldman, and, to her astonishment, her brother Dan came in. Natalie pushed her way through the crowd.

"Give her room to breathe." She smiled, but her eyes were concerned and her gaze flickered over Emily's body as though assessing her.

"What's happening? Dan, why are you here? Nate?" Emily looked up at the huge bulk of her older brother. Dan, like Silas, was almost six-six and weighed well over two hundred pounds. Unlike Silas, Dan's hair was long and bleached blonde. He kept it tied back with a small piece of leather.

He strode to the bed and took Emily's hand. "As

soon as we knew you were missing, I called a stewardess friend of mine and she got me on a red-eye to Chicago. I got a car there and came up here."

"Missing?" Emily held out her other hand to Nate.

"I guess that answers that question." Natalie patted Emily's foot from her spot at the foot of the bed. "Today is Sunday. You went missing on Friday night. You've been asleep for almost twenty-four hours."

Sheriff Boltz stepped forward. "I need to talk to her."

"Not without family present," Dan said.

"What is it?" Emily looked from one man to the other. "What happened?"

"I'm staying," Natalie said firmly. "And a nurse will stay." She gave Dan a frosty glance. "We'll watch out for her."

"She's my baby sister."

"And she's like a daughter to me," Natalie said in a softer voice. "Don't worry. We'll take care of her." She looked at her son, who clung to Emily's hand. "Nate? You need to leave, too."

Nate looked beseechingly at his father, but Sam shook his head. "Police business. Since there's no policewoman available, your mom is filling in."

"Police business?" Emily frantically grabbed for Nate's hand as he moved away. "What happened? Did I do something wrong?" She stared at Dan. "I was at a party and I *knew* the lemonade tasted funny. Was it drugs? I didn't mean to take them," she said pleadingly to Sam Boltz.

"You haven't done anything wrong." Sam glanced at Dan, Bobby, and Nate. "As soon as these guys leave, we can get started and get it over with."

Emily took a deep breath then gave her brother's hand a shake. "You heard the man. Scram." Her voice wavered but she met his gaze without flinching.

"Are you sure you'll be okay?" Dan demanded.

"Fine. Mrs. B won't let anything bad happen. Now get out of here."

Dan kissed Emily on the forehead then he edged toward the door behind Bobby Goldman. Nate leaned over and kissed Emily's cheek. "I'll be just outside," he said, gently touching her hair.

She looked at him, surprised by the tender look in his eyes. "Okay."

Nate exchanged a look with his father then he left the room just as the elderly nurse came back in. Natalie took her son's place, sitting on the bed with the nurse standing nearby. Sam stood at the foot of the bed, his small notebook out and a pen poised to take notes.

"Emily, I need to ask you some questions. When we're done, I'm going to have somebody write up what you said. Then you and these ladies, here"—and he nodded to his wife and the nurse—"will sign it, as long as it's an accurate statement."

"Okay," Emily agreed. He smiled at her and she relaxed. *Heavens*, she thought. *This is Nate's dad. Nothing bad is going to happen.*

"Now, you said the last thing you remember is you were at the party and someone handed you some lemonade."

She nodded. "Peggy McBride. She gave me a glass of lemonade." Emily glanced at Natalie. "I was surprised. Peggy's not usually friendly."

"Hmm." Sheriff Boltz noted something in his notepad. "Do you remember anything after that?"

"Not really. I mean, sort of."

"Try, Emily," Natalie encouraged. "It's important."

Emily took a deep breath and closed her eyes. "Nate and I went off to sit." She blushed. "To talk. And to get away from the others."

"What happened then?" Sam asked, busily writing in his notebook.

"I woke up. I was on a beach," she said, confused. "There were two people there." She hesitated and suddenly her face got hot. "Oh!"

"What is it?" the sheriff prodded.

"Oh." Emily's eyes fastened on Natalie's sympathetic eyes. "I was naked," she whispered. "Somebody took off my clothes."

The sheriff nodded as though it was an everyday occurrence. Emily relaxed at his matter-of-fact attitude. "What else do you remember?" Natalie prompted.

"They had me tied down. They touched me." She shuddered, looking from the nurse to Natalie, avoiding looking at Sam. "They touched me *there.*"

Sam cleared his throat. "Let me get this clear. Two people had you on the beach and they tied you up. And they were touching your genitals."

"They touched me all over." Her stomach knotted with remembered fear. "They even touched my—" She looked at the nurse. "All of me. My bottom."

"Anal area?" the nurse prompted.

"Yes." Emily's face reddened at the medical term. "I think he—"

"He?" Sam prompted.

"It was a man and a woman. I think he was going to—you know—" She looked at Natalie, confused. "He was going to do it *there*. He was all hard and excited."

Emily grimaced. “He kept touching me with his—you know—his—”

“Penis,” the nurse supplied matter-of-factly.

“Yes.” Emily sighed, glad someone else said the word.

Natalie tried to nod coolly, but her hand tightened on Emily’s. “Some men are like that, dear. Not many, but some. They enjoy sex that way. Did you know him? Could you see his face? Him or the woman?”

“I was blindfolded, except at the end. They gave me a drug. I heard what was going on, but I couldn’t react. It was awful. I heard them and felt them but I couldn’t do anything. It was like my body didn’t belong to me.” Emily’s voice started to rise. “I felt them touching me and I knew he wanted—you know—in my—but I couldn’t do anything about it!” She looked frantically at Sam.

Natalie kept a gentle hand on Emily’s arm, smoothing it over her skin. “How did you get away? How did you escape?”

“The woman helped me. She untied me when they went to get more of the drug.”

“Did you swim all the way back?” Sam asked.

“When she untied me, she told me to swim south. I had no idea where we were. I didn’t see any lights or steps. I think maybe I was at the park.”

“I’ll be right back,” Sam said quickly, leaving the room.

Natalie patted Emily’s hand. “Now we know where to search. Maybe they’ll find clues.”

“There was a bonfire,” Emily said helpfully. “And I had to run around some big rocks to get to the beach.” Then she frowned. “I guess it describes just about every cove on Lake Michigan, doesn't it?"

Sam came back in the room. "Just a few more questions. Besides touching you, did the people do anything to you?"

Emily shook her head. "They put this baby oil all over me, even into my—" She swallowed hard. "My female places and *there*. But the woman helped me escape before he could do anything." Emily trembled and Natalie increased the pressure on the hand she was holding. "This is like Janie, isn't it?"

Sam closed his notebook. "It looks like it."

"I wish I remembered more. I don't understand, though. He had a woman there with him. Why did he need me?" She looked from Natalie to Sam.

"It may not have been just to hurt you," he said. "It would have hurt Nate, too."

"But I still don't understand."

"For some men, there just aren't enough women in the world," the nurse said, her voice matter-of-fact. "And if you're lucky enough to find him, for one man you're the only woman in the world."

Emily looked at the nurse with the beginning of a smile. "I think you're right."

The nurse patted Emily's hand. "You can take it to the bank, sugar."

Chapter 39

Present Day

The two on-duty Little Bay PD officers and the two off-duty ones arrived at the apartment at the same moment I did. I flung open my truck door and raced up the apartment steps but I knew when I saw the opened door at the top I was too late.

Rob Sloan lay on the floor in the living room. I stooped over him. “Call it in,” I said to Cynthia Bartlett, who followed close behind me. Rob’s chest was bloody but there weren’t any air bubbles out of the wound, so maybe his lung wasn’t punctured. I felt his neck and found an erratic pulse.

“Chief.” His raspy whisper sounded painful. “The resort. Goldman.”

“Hang on, Rob. Ambulance is coming.”

“Goldman taking her to the resort. Porter there.” Rob’s eyes closed and I checked his pulse again, then sat back, relieved. He was still alive, but the pulse was thready.

“Cynthia, you and Dave are with me.” I looked at my other two officers, part-timers and near retirement. “You stay with Rob, get his statement when you can and handle anything else that comes up. Call Dorothy and let her know what’s happening.” I whirled and was racing down the stairs before anyone moved.

At the driveway I said, "I'm taking my truck. You follow in the squads, no lights, no sirens. I don't want to scare him. He's got Emily Sutherland and maybe Porter Graves as hostages. We're going in quiet. Follow me."

Cynthia started to speak then she must have correctly interpreted my look. She got into her squad car without a word. I focused on trying to map out a strategy as I drove north but it was no good. I wouldn't know what to do until we got there. I did know one thing for sure, though.

If anyone prevented Emily from marrying me, I would kill the son of a bitch.

We pulled up to the main entrance. The metal gate was unlocked, the doors slightly ajar. I parked the truck and moved to stand next to Dave's squad car. Cynthia got out of her car and approached us, leaning down to listen as I talked.

"We'll go in on foot. Dave, you circle the property in your car. I'm going down by the old steps, north of here. Cynthia, you come in from the south, on the beach. Don't do anything to upset him."

"Who is it?" Cynthia asked softly. "Is it the murderer?"

"It's Bobby Goldman. I'm not sure if he's the murderer. All I know is what Rob was able to tell me. Be careful. Be quiet. If you're not sure what to do, do nothing."

Cynthia nodded and started moving through the quiet resort. I took a deep, steadying breath. Everything always happened at Mitchell's Cove and I had no doubt it was where they were now. I took my time, though, just in case, pausing and listening as I skirted the dark gazebo and trees. I was about halfway to the bluffs when I heard voices, wafting up from the beach, borne to me on the prevailing west winds that always came over the lake. I nodded with satisfaction. They weren't far away.

One thought kept pounding through my brain. If that son of a bitch hurt Emily, I'd kill him. I pushed my hands through my hair then glanced at my dark suit and shirt. I jerked off my black necktie with the bright white stripe in it and stuffed it in my pocket. Then I pulled out my gun, made sure the safety was on, and started walking along the top of the bluff.

I worked my way north and found the crumbling ruins of the old steps at the state park. I made my way carefully down the rickety stairs, making a mental note to talk to the city council about demolishing them. I finally got to the beach, grateful for the bit of starlight peeking through the clouds. If I calculated it right, I was about a hundred yards north from where I heard the voices. I stuck close to the bluff and its shadows then moved cautiously down the beach, inching my way along.

It took forever. I walked a few paces then paused to listen, straining to hear past the surf and wind whistling over the bluff. I edged forward, step by step, until I came to an outcropping in the bluff. I pressed against the wall and peered past it. What I saw made me stop.

A bonfire was burning, the flames making deeper shadows against the cliff. Emily sat on the beach, her back against the bluffs overlooking the lake and her feet tied in front of her. True to her word, she wore a little black dress—a *very* little black dress. It was hitched up and I saw the top of her stockings, her thighs creamy white in the firelight. Two narrow black straps held the dress up. She was showing a lot of shoulder, breasts, and arms. She was also probably freezing.

"He's coming," Bobby Goldman said, sounding smug. He sat on a log to Emily's left, the gun in his hand. The way he stared at her made my skin crawl. I remembered what she said on the phone. Had Bobby really tried to rape her, years ago?

"Where's Rob?" Emily asked.

"Probably dead now." Bobby's voice was calm. "And soon Nate will be dead and you'll be dead." He paused and seemed to reconsider something. "I'd like to have you first, but I don't think there'll be time."

"You'd like to..." Emily's voice trailed off as she realized what he was saying.

"The only people who know about it will die. Porter will go crazy and kill you and Nate. The police will have to do something about Porter then. And Rob was killed when he surprised an intruder in your apartment."

I peered at Bobby in the dark and realized he wasn't rational any more. Hell, he probably wasn't rational for years, but he got away with it, fooling everyone with his Pleasant Host routine. Something tipped him over the edge and I knew with a sick certainty what tipped him. Finding Peggy's body and raking up all the old memories was what triggered this tonight.

"I can't prove anything," Emily said. "It would be my word against yours."

"And Peggy's word. Her diary." Bobby shook his head, thin hair wisping in the breeze off the lake. "Do you know what it's like to live with a dead body for years?" He drew in a long breath. "She's haunted me for years. Her and that damn baby of hers."

That stupid diary. I cursed softly. *If we hadn't found it or the ledger, none of this would have happened.* A good lawyer could make a lot out of Peggy's diary.

Bobby smiled wistfully at Emily. "You look very pretty. You and Nate always looked good together. But, of course, you always were the prettiest one."

Emily scrunched up and shivered. "Bobby, I'm freezing."

He sprang to his feet and began to pace. I pulled back, hiding in the shadows at the bluff's base. "Who are you looking for?" Emily said loudly, raising her voice to be heard over the surf.

"Porter. He should have been here by now. I told him to meet me here."

"I hate to point this out, but Porter's not playing with a full deck." Emily shifted position, trying to huddle behind one of the larger rocks. She looked almost directly at me but I blended in the shadows with my dark gray shirt and coat and black pants. Bobby stood with his back to the lake, staring at the bluffs then swiveling his gaze north and south.

I glanced at Emily and stood slightly away from the bluff so she could see me. Emily tried to struggle to her feet. I gestured frantically and she stumbled back against the rocks as I melted back into the shadows. "I'm freezing here," she complained.

Bobby's attention riveted on her. "I don't remember you being such a complainer." He shifted his gaze back to the bluff.

Move, move, move, I silently urged her. *There's too*

much open space between Bobby and the bluffs. I couldn't cross the space and disarm him before he shot Emily. And I didn't dare shoot Bobby for fear Bobby would get a shot off before he dropped.

"What are you going to do when Porter gets here?" Emily staggered as she finally got to her feet, grabbing a rock for support and angling more toward the lake, forcing Bobby to turn to face her.

I silently thanked her for using her brains. "Move, move," I whispered under my breath. If she could get something between her and Bobby then I could take the shot and have a reasonable chance for success. I started to draw a bead.

"I won't have to do anything. Porter will do it all."

"I think you're giving him too much credit." Emily's eyes darted toward me then back to Bobby.

"Bobby?"

The voice drifted from the top of the bluffs. Emily whirled, staring upward and almost overbalancing.

"Porter?" Bobby called out, taking a step forward to stare upward.

I looked beyond Emily and saw Cynthia, slipping into place behind a pile of boulders at the base of the bluff. I tore my gaze away and looked at Bobby, who stared at the top of the bluff.

Emily looked behind her then crouched behind a rock, putting its solid bulk between her and Bobby's gun. I moved slightly out of the shadows and made a *get down* gesture with one hand. Emily tucked herself into a tight little ball and lowered her head.

"This isn't going to work," a voice said from the top of the bluffs. "Rob Sloan is hurt but he's going to be okay."

Bobby's face went ashen. I thought he might faint. "How do you know?"

"I saw him," the voice said.

I recognized the voice at the same moment the speaker stepped forward.

My father stood there, looking down at Bobby and Emily.

Chapter 40

Thirty-Four Years Earlier

Emily's brother Dan wanted to take Emily to a motel but Sam put his foot down. "She'll stay at our house." When Emily started to speak he raised a hand. "You and your brother will stay with us." He glanced at Nate. "You stay at the apartment."

Emily looked with despair at Nate. Natalie saw the look and patted Emily's hand. "Just for now," she whispered into Emily's ear. "For a day or so."

Emily squeezed her eyes shut, holding back her tears. "But we have so little time left together."

"I know." Natalie gestured to the men gathered around Emily's hospital bed. "Out. She needs to get dressed and she doesn't need company."

Natalie kept the conversational ball rolling during the drive to the Boltz house, dinner preparations, and the evening meal. Dan made two phone calls, one to Silas and one to his father. Emily participated in each call on the upstairs extension, assuring everyone she was fine and firmly repeating she would not leave Little Bay until Labor Day, when her father and her brother Jason would come to get her.

At one point Natalie and Nate heard shouting upstairs. Nate grinned when he heard Emily shout, "Well, you can just bite me, Dan! I know what I'm doing!"

Dan came into the kitchen from the living room where he had used the phone and leaned against the doorframe, eyeing Nate. "Silas says you're okay."

Nate nodded acknowledgement. "I think Silas is okay, too."

Emily came into the room and glared at Dan. She wore shorts and a Pine Place golf shirt. Nate saw the bruises on her legs and arms. "You don't scare me, Dan," she huffed, pulling out a chair and flopping down next to Nate. "I'll be fine."

Nate read the accusation in Dan's pale blue eyes. "We didn't think we'd be drugged. That's the only way it could've happened." He met and held Dan's gaze.

Finally the other man nodded, once. "I know," he admitted.

Emily threw up her hands in exasperation. "Then be pleasant. When do you have to go back? You can stay tonight, can't you?"

Dan smiled, his face transforming into that of a youthful, impertinent young boy. "I just have to call Cindy. She'll get me a stand-by ticket. I'll go back tomorrow morning." He glanced at Natalie. "Are you sure it's okay if we stay here tonight?" He subtly emphasized the "we."

Natalie nodded serenely. "There's plenty of room. Emily will stay in Nate's room and you can sleep in the den. The couch there is a hide-a-bed." She put an arm out to Emily then glanced at the used dishes on the kitchen table. "Let's go make up the beds while someone cleans up in here."

Nate and Dan cleared the table. "She's the only sister I have," Dan said.

"She's the only girlfriend I have." The two men exchanged a look.

"Jesus, it was a near thing, though." Dan's voice cracked.

Nate took a long, shuddering breath. "I know. If I ever find out who did it... "

"If you ever find out, make sure to share the knowledge."

Nate nodded. "Will do."

Emily and Nate were given the next day off. They ate a leisurely breakfast with Dan then saw him on the road to Chicago and his flight back to Boston. "Stay in touch," he said as he put the car into gear. "If you don't, Ben is liable to show up and give you hell." He winked at Nate. "You don't want to deal with Ben. He's tough."

"You and Silas aren't?" Nate asked incredulously.

Dan laughed and waved to them as he drove down the street.

Emily and Nate turned to each other. It was the first time they'd been alone since Emily's capture. They moved into an embrace and she rested her head on his chest. "I was so scared," Nate whispered.

"So was I." She shivered in Nate's arms and he hugged her tighter.

****

Natalie watched them from the kitchen window. "I wish they weren't so young," she murmured to Sam, seated at the kitchen table.

Sam made an assenting noise. "They're good together."

"I know. But they're too young to make it last." She shook her head, her dark curls dancing. "Maybe it's just not meant to be."

Sam looked up at the wistful tone of her voice. "They've got their whole lives ahead of them. There's no telling what will happen."

He considered the two rape cases now facing the police department, as well as the breaking and entering in Nate's apartment. The line cook, Emilio, remained missing and it was assumed he fled back to Mexico. His fingerprints were on the butcher knife used to desecrate Nate's pillow, but Sam expected that. The man was a cook. Of course his fingerprints would be on a kitchen knife.

There was no luck tracing the handwriting on the threatening notes. They found the cove where Emily was kept and the FBI sent a crime scene team to go over the site but they had a light rain since then. Sam doubted anything useful would come of it.

Big Tom Judson reported no strangers and no guests expressed a need for a "special girl." Judson promised to keep his eyes open and report anything that might help. Sam felt vaguely reassured to know that even in the underworld, there were certain standards and rules.

Sam looked at Natalie as she watched Nate and Emily ride away on Nate's cycle. If Emily were just a bit older, Sam would've told Nate to get married. Sam and Natalie married when they were in their early twenties. Of course, Sam had just finished three years of service in the Army during the Korean War and that tended to age a person. Once again, Sam thanked God Nate didn't have to worry about the draft. War was a fate he wouldn't wish on anyone.

"Nothing we can do about it, Natalie."

She turned away from the window and he saw the sorrow in her eyes. "I know." She went to him and he put an arm around her waist, drawing her to him so he laid his head against her breasts. "I'm so lucky to have you, Sam."

"No luckier than me," he replied.

They held each other, in comfort and love, for a long moment.

Chapter 41

Present Day

I silently cursed, wondering why my father was getting himself in the middle of a potential firefight.

Bobby's gun shifted position and aimed upward, at Dad. "Son of a bitch," I muttered, knowing I didn't dare shoot.

"Bobby," Dad said in his calmest voice. "This has to stop now. Put the gun down."

Bobby's frantic gaze swept from Dad then to the beach. I saw Emily, peeking around a bit of rock. "Where is she?" Bobby screamed. "Nate can't have her!"

"Why not?" I stepped out of the shadows, my gun leveled at Bobby's heart.

Bobby stepped back one pace and kept his own gun aimed at Dad, on the bluff above him. "Shoot me and your father dies."

"I know. Why can't I have her?" I continued to move forward slowly, stepping toward the lake. The footing on the beach was uneven and I moved cautiously, hoping my dark suit and shirt would make me appear like another ghost, another moonlit shadow.

"Because you're a Townie. You're a football player." Bobby's face twisted with disgust. "She's better than you."

"*She* is getting tired of hearing that," Emily called from her hiding place. "*She* has other ideas. *She* knows what's right for her."

Bobby glanced at Emily and I advanced several tiny steps.

"I know how lucky I am." I slowly moved forward. My eyes never wavered from Bobby's face but his eyes darted from me then to Dad then around the beach, looking for Emily. "She and I are going to get married."

"No." Bobby's whisper was more terrifying than a scream. "No, it's not fair. You can't find each other again and still be in love."

"That's how it is, Bobby." Porter's voice rang out and Bobby shifted to look behind me. I glanced back once, wondering where the hell Porter came from.

It was just enough distraction.

Dad drew his gun and shot. It went slightly wide but it startled Bobby into turning again. I took advantage of the moment and took my shot.

Bobby went down with a bullet in his leg.

Emily came bouncing up out of her hiding place and forgot her legs were tied. She went down in a heap but managed to scramble to her feet. I dashed forward and kicked away Bobby's gun as Cynthia ran to help.

"Bobby, you son of a bitch," Emily spat. "You tried to rape me thirty years ago."

I holstered my gun. Emily looked cold, scared, and angry, but okay. "Are you all right?" I took off my suit coat to drape it over her bare shoulders. Then I pulled out my pocketknife and bent to cut the thin rope on her arms and legs.

As soon as her arms were free, she stuck them into the sleeves of my suit coat and huddled into its warmth, swallowed by the jacket. “I’m fine. That son of a bitch shot Rob Sloan. He shot his own son.”

“His son?”

“Peggy’s boy,” Porter said suddenly. “Poor Peggy.”

Emily crossed the beach to where Porter stood, watching us shyly. “Yes. Poor Peggy’s baby.”

Porter nodded. “I’m glad you and Nate are getting married,” he said with a wide, engaging grin. “Can I come to the wedding?”

Emily started to laugh and then, to my surprise, she started to cry. “Porter, you can be my maid of honor,” she said as she threw her arms around him.

He gave a whoop of laughter and hugged her enthusiastically.

I looked up at my father. “Just what the hell are you doing here?”

I saw his grin in the moonlight. “I’ll meet you at the station and explain there. Your mother’s getting cold.”

“Mom?”

Chapter 42

Thirty-Four Years Earlier

Fourteen days left.

Thirteen days left.

Twelve days left.

In a few short days Emily wouldn't wake up and have Nate in her arms. She wouldn't hear his laugh or his snores or the beat of his heart next to her. She dug out her camera and in a frenzy of activity took rolls of pictures of Nate, the cottage, the beach, the resort, Pauline and Harv, David, Esther. She even cajoled Big Tom Judson into posing for a picture one night in town when they were with Mike Sawyer and Donna. And Big Tom insisted on taking a picture of Emily and Nate, sitting on the bumper of Mike's Chevy.

Ten days left.

Nine days left.

Sam still worked the cases, but there were few leads. Fingerprints were examined, crime scene evidence examined, and the drug used on Janie and Emily was being analyzed. Sam knew, deep in his gut, they'd never have answers to what happened to the two girls. Summer was ending and their rapist would leave. Sam knew it with every instinct he possessed. It made him sick. He *wanted* this guy.

Eight days left.

Seven days left.

Nate mentioned he thought he'd come visit her in the fall, and wondered aloud if she'd come out for his Homecoming at college. Emily looked at him like he was crazy.

"Of course I can." He was reassured she was thinking of seeing him beyond the summer. Emily mentioned she had a friend with an apartment they could use if he visited over Christmas. Nate started to calculate the distance between Michigan and Minnesota, for the first time realizing that Wisconsin was a damn fat state.

Six days left.

Five days left.

Four days left.

Three days left.

Two days left.

Sunday was the End of the Season dance, held in town at the American Legion. The big checkout day this week would be Labor Day Monday, but none of the rooms had to be made up for incoming guests, so everyone just had to work the morning. All the Summer Kids would leave in the afternoon and some of the Townies, Nate included, would come back on Tuesday to wrap up the resort for the winter. Then Nate would go home, pack, and head for college.

Emily thought about it as she dressed to go to the dance in town. She was determined not to cry. They'd be separated for five weeks. His Homecoming was in the first part of October and she would go to Michigan for it. In the meantime, she'd write to him every day. They'd get through it. They'd be okay.

Then she turned to look at Nate as he tugged on his

jeans. His back was strong and smooth, tapering to his waist. He was heavily muscled from working and from football. He zipped the jeans then turned to look at her. Emily felt like her heart was splitting in two. She wondered how she'd survive the next five weeks.

When they got to the Legion Hall, everyone from the resort who wasn't on duty was there, as well as most of the Townies who worked at the resort. It was hot and humid in the small building even though all the windows were open. Emily soon had to wedge her way out of the crowd and go outside for fresh air. Nate followed her, his shirt clinging damply to his back.

"I didn't realize so many people worked the resort," Emily said, fanning herself.

Nate handed her his beer. "I think they're all here. Including Greg and the Ugly Bunch."

Emily looked at the parking lot, where Greg and some other Summer Boys were lounging near their cars. "He's such an idiot." Rachel Putnam approached Greg. Emily slanted a glance at Nate, to see his reaction. They both watched as Rachel said something to Greg then she looked at his two friends and shrugged. She said something else that made the guys all look interested and the entire group went back into the Legion Hall.

"Looks like Rachel's got her dates for the night," Nate said dryly.

Emily handed him back his beer. "She's just the tiniest bit..."

"Promiscuous?"

She looped her arm through his. "Slutty," she corrected.

"Indeed. She obviously hasn't heard about the joys

of monogamy."

"There are joys in monogamy?" Emily asked.

Nate leaned his head against hers. "There are."

"Let's go back in and dance a slow dance." Emily pressed against him. "I like the way you dance."

"We've never danced a slow dance before."

"Oh, yes we have. We've just done it horizontally."

He laughed and let her to tug him back to the building. Before they entered, Peggy stepped out. She looked hot and flushed. Her bouffant hair looked askew, flattened on one side. She grinned widely and Emily realized she was drunk.

"The two lovebirds," Peggy slurred. "You guys going to get married?"

Emily and Nate exchanged a look. "Not right now," Emily said.

"I am," Peggy said triumphantly. "Our family is going to be together. All of us."

Emily opened her mouth but wasn't sure what to say. Nate said it for her. "That's great, Peggy. When?"

She looked surprised someone would offer her congratulations. "Soon. Very soon. We're going away."

"Eloping," Emily said with forced gaiety. "How romantic."

Peggy looked at her suspiciously but Emily kept a smile plastered to her face. Peggy's look changed to one of complicity. "Yeah. Romantic."

Emily heard "Unchained Melody" start to play inside. "Come on," she said to Nate. "They're playing our song."

"Good luck, Peggy," Nate said. Emily grabbed his hand and pulled him toward the door.

Peggy's smile turned to a mournful frown. "I'm

glad he didn't hurt you, Emily."

Before Emily could respond, Peggy turned and moved off into the dark parking lot. Nate and Emily stared after her for a moment then they went inside to dance.

****

Emily and Nate left the dance soon and went back to the cottage. They showered and made love and talked into the night. At one point they both cried, already feeling the pain of loss. Then they made love again and dozed.

When Nate awoke Emily was in his arms. He stared down at her, so overcome by grief he didn't know what to do. Her father would come and take her away. Nate knew nothing would ever be the same. Emily had changed him forever. No matter how much he wanted to keep her in his life, he knew he couldn't. He couldn't tie her down to him and he couldn't tie himself down to her.

He remembered Peggy's question last night. He had never thought about marriage before. There was a part of him that wanted to have Emily with him for the rest of his life. And another part nagged him, pointing out there were a lot of women in the world and who knew what's out there?

Then Emily turned over and opened her eyes. "I love you," she whispered. She put her arms around his neck.

Nate felt her silky, smooth body, so soft and pliable under him. "I love you, Emily," he said. "Forever."

****

A few hours later they transferred Emily's things to the dorm so when her father arrived, he would have no idea Emily spent very little time in the dorm. They worked like maniacs in the morning, helping the maids, checking out all the guests, helping other kids load up and get out. The place was chaos all morning. When Emily's father arrived at two in the afternoon, things were just starting to quiet down.

Nate and Emily said good-bye to Harv, Pauline, and Esther, and helped David load his bags into his mother's Buick. Emily got everybody's addresses and she promised to write and send photos.

Nate watched as Sam and Natalie arrived to say good-bye to Emily. Natalie and Emily went aside and hugged for a long time, both crying. Nate heard Natalie promise to write and Emily's promise in return. Sam and Emily's father had a long talk. There were no leads and no resolution on Emily's case. Nate knew it bothered his dad, but there was nothing he could do.

Nate helped Mr. Sutherland and Emily's brother, Jason, load Emily's bags into the back of the car. Then Nate and Emily walked a short distance away.

Emily's eyes were full of tears. "I love you, Nate." Her arms went around him.

Nate put his arms around her and lifted her so she was held tightly against him. "I love you, too, Emily," he murmured as tears rolled down his face.

They kissed one last time and he walked her to the car. Her father said something to Emily's younger brother. The boy got into the front seat, leaving the back to Emily. Nate opened the door for her and she climbed in. Then she looked at him through the rolled-down window. "I'll see you soon," she whispered.

He nodded and watched the car drive away.

Chapter 43

Present Day

"We were at the dance and saw Cynthia Bartlett get paged and leave," Dad said. "So we followed her. We got to the house and saw an ambulance. I sort of eavesdropped, one thing led to another, and your mother and I decided to tag along and see if we could help."

He made it sound so logical. I shook my head. It was an hour and a half after the shooting. Bobby was at the hospital under police guard and I was facing a night of paperwork. We all sat in my office, almost knee-to-knee in the tiny space. Emily still wore my coat and my mom, dad, Dorothy, and Sada were perched on chairs pulled in from the lunchroom, acting as audience.

"Pity all this had to come along and spoil the dance for you," my mother said. "Although I see you dressed for it." Her glance took in Emily's skimpy attire.

"I was prepared to do whatever it took to get him to propose. Then I figured, oh, what the hell, and I asked him to marry me." Emily grinned. "He said yes. And I asked Porter if he'd be my maid of honor." She shrugged. "Why not? He saved Nate's life. And mine, probably."

"You asked Nate to marry you?" Mom asked.

"Okay, I never quite got around to it," I admitted.

"I raised an idiot child," Mom muttered.

I decided to ignore that comment. "How did you figure out the codes in the book? What was the key?" I asked Emily.

"It was the restaurant we went to in Benton Harbor. The food was great but their taste in music sucked. They kept playing that damn Bobby Goldsboro song, "Honey." I hated that song." She saw Mom's blank expression. "BG. Bobby Goldsboro. Peggy called him Honey in her diary. Bobby Goldman."

I was impressed. "And one set of initials led to another?"

"Yep. But I don't understand how Rob fits into all this."

Dorothy sighed. "It all started with that poor child getting pregnant."

Sada nodded. "Peggy got pregnant and left town, to Lansing with her sister."

I took up the story. "Janice Sloan."

"Sloan," Emily said softly.

I had the story from Rob before he went into surgery. "Peggy had a baby and left it with Janice. Janice and her husband adopted Rob. Peggy said she named the baby for the father. While Peggy was busy having the baby, Bobby took up with another girl. Remember in the diary, how the initials EM and RP never overlapped?" I asked. Emily nodded. "That's why. Peggy was gone to have the baby and Rachel stepped in."

"But why didn't Peggy's parents recognize Rob Sloan?" Emily asked.

Mom took up the story. "He was a toddler when Janice divorced James Sloan. Rob went to live with his father. As far as they knew, Peggy's child was placed with a good family and good riddance to bad rubbish." She made a rude noise. "Sorry. It was the attitude was back then."

"So then Rob came back here to try to find out about his mother," Emily said.

"That was part of it," I said. "I think he wanted to find out who his father was. Let's face it, Peggy's disappearance was odd. And Rob wanted to find out what happened. That may be part of why he went into law enforcement."

"Peggy, Rachel, and Porter helped Bobby with the drugs?" Mom asked.

I remembered my rambling conversation with Porter. "Porter said he had something in the bank. I wonder if he wrote down a journal of his own."

"But Bobby made sure he was hurt before he could reveal anything." Mom shook her head in disgust. "Bobby ruined a lot of lives."

"Why did Bobby try to rape me all those years ago?" Emily asked.

"You were the pretty one. You were the sweet one." Dad's voice was full of understanding and pity. "You were the one he fell in love with."

Emily shook her head. "I don't get it."

Mom smiled. "It's all to do with men, so it doesn't have to add up."

"Thanks for that vote of confidence, Mom," I said wryly.

"People talk about how bad PMS and menopause is. It's nothing compared to a man with a hard-on."

"Amen," Dorothy intoned.

"Ready to go home, Sheriff?" Mom stood.

"Yep." Dad grinned at Emily and me. "You kids take care."

Emily beamed at him. "We will. Thanks, Sam."

"No problem. I'm glad to wrap up those old cases."

Mom laughed. "They've been bothering him for lo, these many years."

Dad and Mom left, passing Jonas Hawthorne who strode into the office, making a beeline for Emily. "Emily, are you okay? My God, that man was a maniac. You might have been hurt."

"No shit," Sada muttered, stepping back and crossing her arms to eye Hawthorne in tandem with Dorothy.

"Nothing I'm not accustomed to," Emily said with a wink at me.

"We need to talk." Hawthorne came to stop in front of her.

She looked at me. "No, Nate and I need to talk," she said firmly. "I just want this all cleared up, once and for all. Are you and she—?" Emily looked at Cynthia, who peered around the doorframe. "Jonas said he has a detective who said you two—"

"It wouldn't be professional," I interrupted. "And besides, she's too young."

Cynthia threw up her hands in disgust. "That's the lamest excuse I've ever heard." She shot a withering stare at Emily. "If you hadn't come into town, none of this would've happened."

I shook my head. "No, we wouldn't have, Cynthia."

"Well," Hawthorne said, interjecting himself into the conversation, "it's a moot point, really, since Emily and I are in a relationship."

I looked at Emily and was glad to see she looked surprised. “What do you mean, Jonas?” Her voice was deceptively quiet. I winced. I knew that tone of voice. She was getting ready to take a strip of skin off of somebody. I eased my chair back toward the window, edging away from the impact zone.

“As we discussed, we wanted to wrap up our business dealings before turning to more romantic pursuits.”

Emily made a small noise deep in her throat. “Let me get this straight, Jonas. You figure because we signed the deal, I’ll go to bed with you, right?” Her voice was very quiet and calm. I inched back a bit more. I didn’t want to be in shrapnel range.

Hawthorne smiled. No. He smirked. “That’s a bit crude, dear, to discuss something as gratifying as our relationship.”

“Gratifying?” Emily muttered.

“Gratifying?” Sada echoed softly.

“Gratifying?” Dorothy rumbled.

Emily got slowly out of her chair and looked at Hawthorne, her head tilted to one side. Then she started to advance. His smirk wavered. “I don’t want gratifying sex, Jonas,” Emily said softly. Her green eyes were spitting fire. “I don’t *like* gratifying sex.” She took a deep breath and I had a heart palpitation when I saw the dance her breasts did in her little black dress under my suit coat.

“I like sex that makes me moan so loud it makes the neighbors squirm. I like sex that makes me slide off the sheets because I’ve melted down. I like sex that makes me groan and beg for more.” Her voice suddenly got husky on “more.” A shiver ran down my spine.

"Tell the truth, girl," I muttered. I'd heard Emily beg for more and it was something that would indeed make the neighbors squirm. Dorothy, Cynthia, and Sada shot me a wild look then they all started to grin.

Emily continued to advance on Jonas, her face taut with anger. "I want 'take me on the carpet' sex. I want 'maybe we'll make it to the bed sometime tonight' sex."

"You go, girl," Sada muttered.

"I want kicking, moaning, and thrashing sex," Emily continued, building up a head of steam. Hawthorne stared at her, his eyes wide with amazement. "I want it in the shower and I want it in the bed. I want it in the morning and afternoon and night."

"Testify, sister, testify," someone encouraged loudly behind me. I looked around and saw Dorothy, dark eyes snapping and a wicked grin on her face.

Emily looked like she was just getting warmed up. "I want to be waked up with it, poking at me from behind. I want to go to bed with it, pushing the sheets up and making a tent. I want it in my hands and"—she paused and put her hands on her hips—"I want it in me."

Emily stared down the big man who was now leaned against the wall, trying to get away from the small woman advancing on him. "I want 'tie me up and spank me' sex," she said with a laugh in her voice. She swaggered as she advanced the final foot until she was chin to chest with Hawthorne. "I. Don't. Want. Gratifying. Sex," she enunciated clearly.

I cleared my throat and all eyes in the room swung to me. I raised a hand and waggled it slightly. "I can do all that, Emily," I volunteered in a sincere, eager voice.

She smiled sweetly. "I know *you* can, honey. After all, you're the man who set the standard. I just want this jerk-brain to understand what I expect out of a man."

"Oh." I glanced at the ladies who eyed me with speculative looks. "We haven't actually tried the spanking," I admitted.

"Yet," Emily said over her shoulder. Her green eyes snapped with mischief.

I winked at her. "Yet," I corrected.

"Emily," Hawthorne protested, glancing wildly at the spectators to this humiliation, "this isn't like you. You're not a frivolous person. You don't worry about frivolous things."

I heard the harsh intake of breath from four women. "You think sex with me is frivolous?" Emily shook her head at his obvious stupidity. "I should hit you, just for trying to screw up my life." She paused. "Did you wire the money to my private account?"

Hawthorne nodded frantically.

I grimaced. "Wrong answer."

Emily's fist shot out and landed a solid punch on the edge of his chin. "Good. That means I can hit you and not worry about losing any cash." She stepped back and shook her hand gingerly. "Damn, that hurts."

"Come on, sugar," Dorothy said, bustling forward. "Let's put ice on your hand. Don't want it to swell up so you can't use it for something fun." She waggled her eyebrows at me and swept Emily into a motherly embrace and out of the room, the other women in her wake. I heard someone say "the last time I had it on the floor it was because my husband fell down. He couldn't get up but he did manage to get it up." That elicited merry peals of laughter as they swept into the tiny kitchenette.

I looked at Hawthorne, who was touching the bruise on his jaw. "You got off easy," I commented. "She might have gone for the balls."

He raised an eyebrow. "I thought she did." He pushed away from the wall and we left the office. "Good luck with her. She's too high maintenance for me."

I thought about it. "Yeah. But she's worth it." I glanced into the hallway and saw Emily eyeing us. I looked back at my desk. I had a pile of paperwork to do. Then I looked at Emily again.

Paperwork could wait.

I watched as Hawthorne walked down the short corridor to the front door where a Jaguar sat outside. Then I looked to the right, where Emily, Sada, and Dorothy were emerging from the kitchenette, Emily's hand adorned with a small bag of ice. "Your business partner is leaving, in case you'd like to say goodbye," I commented, leaning in the doorway.

She glanced toward the parking lot and stuck out her tongue. For good measure, she raised her uninjured hand and projected her middle finger in true Townie form. Then she started to chuckle. "Check it out."

I looked out at the front parking lot and saw Cynthia Bartlett and Jonas Hawthorne in conversation, another woman eyeing them from inside the car. "Oh, for heaven's sake," I said, not sure whether to be annoyed or amused.

Emily grinned. "Cynthia is just their type."

"And what type would that be?"

"Athletic, fun-loving, and perky." She scowled at the three out in the parking lot. "They can just bite me."

I shoved away from the doorway. “Nope. That’s my job.”

Dorothy reeled back from Emily’s side, fanning herself with one hand. “Lord, the hormones are flying through the air tonight. You two children better get on out of here.”

I put an arm around Emily’s shoulders and steered her toward the back door and my truck parked there. “You weren’t just teasing me when you said we’d get married, were you?” I asked as we emerged into the cold October air.

“What do you think?” she demanded, putting her hands on her hips and glaring up at me.

“Emily. Come on. Give me a break. Don’t play games with me. I’ve thought about this moment for more than thirty years.”

She sort of flowed into my arms, dropping the ice bag on the ground to clasp her arms around my neck. “I’m crazy about you. I want to marry you. I want to live here with you. I love you.” She kicked her feet and dangled in my arms. “Man, this little black dress sure did the trick, didn’t it?”

“What do you mean?” I fumbled with the handle of the truck and finally got it open. As I maneuvered Emily up onto the seat, my coat slid open and her dress hiked up almost to her waist, revealing the tops of her elastic-topped black stockings. I sucked in a breath at the sight of her creamy white thighs and the tiny little patch of black panty I glimpsed.

“That’s what I mean,” she said smugly, tugging primly at the hemline. I pushed her hand away and clasped one hand around her thigh.

“You were half naked tonight,” I accused.

"You bet. And you know something else?"

"What?" I couldn't drag my eyes away from her smooth thighs. I looked up in time to see her shrug off my suit coat. The straps of her dress slid off. Her breasts popped free from their confinement.

"I was braless, too."

"Damn it, Emily." I raced around the truck and fumbled to get up into the driver's seat. I took a deep, steadying breath. "I think we have a date," I said as I pulled her to me across the expanse of car seat.

"We do?"

My pulling had succeeded in messing her dress even further so now it was, essentially, just wadded around her waist. My eyes almost bugged out of my head. "I believe spanking was mentioned."

She looked at me with green eyes alight with mischief. "It was indeed mentioned as I recall. Do you want to go first or should I?"

My mother raised me right. "Ladies first," I said graciously.

A word about the author...

J L Wilson is a Midwestern author who writes "mysteries with a touch of romance...and romance with a touch of gray." She also writes time travel books and has a paranormal-political thriller series, set on another planet.

She can be found on Twitter, Facebook, and a few blogs here and there. She is also a full-time writer for a large software company and is happy to talk gadgets with anyone...

Find out more at jayellwilson.com

Other J L Wilson titles available from The Wild Rose Press, Inc.

Autographs, Abductions, and A-List Authors

Brownies, Bodies, and Breaking the Code

Candy, Corpses, and Classified Ads

Daisies, Deadly Force, and Disastrous Divorce Disputes

Ex-Wives, Extortion and Erotic First Editions

Foxgloves, Fancy Fungus, and Fatal Family Feuds

Homicide, Hostages, and Hot Rod Restoration

Human Touch

Leap of Faith

Lilacs, Litigation, and Lethal Love Affairs

Living Proof

Mayhem, Marriage, and Murderous Mystery Manuscripts

Phds, Pornography and Premeditated Murder

Sun, Surf and Sandy Strangulation